The

Doctor

Was

Dark

A Triple Threat Novel

KRISTEN CASEY

The Triple Threat Series

About This Book

One

IT COULDN'T BE him. There was no way, not on God's green earth, that Daisy's erstwhile fling—her freak in the sheets, her flame who shall not be named—was here and standing a scant seven yards away from her at this engagement party.

Luca, after all, was only a humble family doctor who practiced medicine in a sleepy part of Florence, Italy. He was the kind of guy who doted on his grandmother in his spare time—when he wasn't setting hapless expats on fire from the inside out, that was.

Luca barely had to lift a finger to do it, either. He was that good.

But Daisy had left that man behind a year ago, and at the time, she'd thought it was the only thing she could do. She and Luca had only worked as a couple during their brief time together because he hadn't known her from a hole in the wall.

He didn't know her people, such as they were. Okay, make that *person*—the plural was totally unnecessary. Daisy had exactly one person that she could sort-of call family, and occasionally she didn't even have that much.

The point was, Luca hadn't known anyone at all who knew Daisy, and that was what had made him so perfect for her. Well, besides his shiny black hair. And his full, seductive mouth. And his long, strong…everything.

Because he didn't know anything about her, Daisy had been able to be herself with him. *Only* herself. She'd been lighter and freer than at any other time in her life. She'd been *fun*, for fuck's sake, without the albatross of her stupid past dragging her down.

She'd planned to carry the golden memory of her affair with the gorgeous Italian throughout the rest of her life. It was going to be a vivid window into what might have been, if she'd only been dealt a better hand. A kinder one.

Instead, he appeared to be here, in Daisy's hometown, in the flesh. Where he should not be.

There was no conceivable reason why Luca, *her* Luca, should be standing in the middle of her boss's engagement party, looking as urbane and polished as a GQ fashion spread. Maybe she was hallucinating.

Daisy scowled down at her drink, a bright-red Shirley Temple with a healthy shot of bourbon in it. The bartender had called it a *Dirty Shirley*, but now she wondered whether he'd added something a little more illicit to it than liquor.

Did she feel like she'd been drugged? Daisy rapidly assessed her motor function and the clarity of her vision. Both seemed fine. She shook out her hair, but the room stayed steady. None of her extremities were remotely numb.

Well, with the possible exception of her toes. But she was almost positive that was because she rarely wore heels and it was about nine degrees outside. The swanky apartment she was in was obviously heated, but it was still old, and a chilly draft was lingering near the floor despite the many people standing around chatting.

And her heels, while hot as sin, were brutal to stand in for long periods of time. Both perfectly reasonable explanations for foot malfunctions.

However, if it turned out that her eyesight hadn't taken a sudden, ill-timed plunge into near-blindness—if that *was*, in fact, Dr. Luca in the flesh over there—then Daisy was happy to be wearing these shoes.

She was happy for her fire-engine red flamenco dress, and thrilled that she'd taken the time to wash her hair yesterday. She'd even worn some shiny, sticky lip gloss in a nod to her surroundings.

Okay, fine—she hadn't started out wearing it. She'd only dug it out from the bottom of her bag and slathered it on five minutes after arrival, once she'd gotten a look at the other high-dollar attendees.

Still, it suddenly felt fortuitous that Daisy was so bad at cleaning out old purses, and terrible at throwing shit away, in general. Especially since she didn't even think that lip gloss belonged to her. The brand sounded more like something you'd scrape off the bottom of your shoe than something you'd want near your piehole.

She'd probably been holding it for Poppy sometime when they'd gone out on the town. Daisy couldn't remember actually doing that, but given her friend's affection for cosmetics, it certainly seemed possible. And, since she'd only moved back to New York from Boston a couple of months ago, that meant the lip gloss couldn't be very old.

Poppy wasn't the type to keep a lip gloss around for years. Daisy, sadly, was. But that was irrelevant.

Watching Maybe-Luca mingle with the other guests like he belonged here, Daisy pressed her coated lips together, and hoped like hell that the glop she'd used on herself looked normal.

She was afraid the odds of getting out of here unseen by her one-time flame were slim to none. Daisy knew she was…noticeable. For one thing, she was taller than a lot of the women there, and hardly blending into the woodwork with her bright red dress.

For another, her distinctive coloring had always garnered her second and third looks from people. It wasn't that there were no other people of color at this WASPy party—it was just that Daisy was hard to categorize.

Was she white? No. Black? Also, no. She was…well, she didn't know exactly what she was, but she had her theories.

Other people didn't seem happy not knowing what box to put her in, however. So, their eyes lingered on Daisy's face, and the gears turned behind their eyes as they tried to figure out where she fit in.

She wished one of them would clue her in, if they figured it out. As it was, the extra attention had always made her uncomfortable. Still, Daisy was no shrinking violet, and she wasn't going to cower in a corner just because some idiots didn't know what to make of her.

She had bigger fish to fry at the moment, anyway.

Daisy edged closer to the man she'd spotted—the man who might be Dr. Luca—as her boss ushered a little couple into his orbit. The pair was short and squat compared to Red's daunting 6'6 build, but the future groom was definitely not in intimidation mode tonight. Instead, he looked positively thrilled to be celebrating his engagement.

Daisy turned her attention to the new arrivals, hoping for some clue that would confirm her suspicions. The small man had full, brushed-back silver hair and chunky black glasses, and the woman on his arm was all smiles, her wrists covered in a startling number of jingling gold bracelets.

"Luca," Red boomed, establishing somewhat that Daisy wasn't seeing things, "May I introduce Dr. Harlan Green, and his wife, Dr. Shari Green?"

Luca, also a tall man at 6'2, leaned down slightly to shake each of their hands in turn, but it came off as a formal, sophisticated bow.

"I'm honored," he said, and Daisy's chest constricted when she picked up a trace of his accent. How could this be happening?

Harlan Green was nearly bouncing in his dress shoes, he was so excited. "Trust me, the honor is all mine. When MacLellan told me Gianluca Delledonna was his college roommate, I just assumed he was…"

Red turned and raised an amused brow at the diminutive man.

"Full of it," Shari Green supplied merrily.

"He often is," Luca chuckled back, sharing a mischievous grin with Daisy's boss that made it obvious the two men were more than passing acquaintances. *Oh, God*—what were the freaking odds? She was so screwed.

"However, I never expected…" Harlan Green tried again.

Red just shook his head, cutting him off. "I promised, didn't I?"

Luca looked like he was at a loss for words, blinking rapidly as he underwent the other doctor's scrutiny. Finally, he turned instead to Harlan's wife, inquiring smoothly, "I'm certain I heard a 'Dr.' attached to your name as well. What kind of medicine do you practice?"

Shari toasted him with her champagne flute. "Psychiatry," she declared with a flourish. "I doubt you want to talk shop with me right now, though. This guy's the one with the goods." She bumped her husband's shoulder fondly with hers.

"Why don't we leave these two to make friends?" Red asked her. "Have you seen that dessert table yet? I can't stop eating the cream puffs. I'm due for another drive-by, for sure."

With that, there was a flurry of handshakes and back-slapping, and then Daisy's boss was steering his charge resolutely away, bound for the far corner of the party.

Daisy felt like the worst sort of lurker as she watched Harlan Green move in. He was clearly determined not to waste his opportunity. She risked shifting another few steps closer, keeping herself out of Luca's peripheral vision as best as she could.

"Dr. Delledonna, I've been following your research, and the chance to meet you in person was too tempting to resist. I hope you'll forgive me for ambushing you here."

Luca made a sound that would translate as "Nonsense!" in any language.

"And I must admit—I had another goal tonight, if MacLellan did end up producing you."

Luca cocked his head, drawing Daisy's attention to the tendons in his tanned neck. The same tendons she'd once licked up and down. "And what was that?" he said.

Green backtracked slightly. "I don't know if you've heard of the research I've done on cancer cells and the body's immune response?"

"Of course. The paper your team published last summer was fascinating. We discussed how it might apply to our theories for weeks."

"That's just it," Green exclaimed, delighted and clapping his hands. "What if we were able to work *together*?"

"I…" Luca's face was alive and focused, homing in on the other man with alert interest now. "That would be…"

Dr. Green interrupted him. "I'll be blunt. I've got an opening at Weill Cornell and I want you. You wouldn't have to pick up more than a class or two for the first couple of years, until your work is really up and running. I can promise you state-of-the-art lab facilities in the same wing as mine, plus a highly-skilled pool of students and residents to assist you."

"That's…"

"Dr. Delledonna, if you know about anything I've done in the last ten years, then you know this is a match made in heaven. Together, you and I could potentially find a cure for gastric cancer."

Daisy held her breath, waiting to see what Luca would say. What Green was offering would require Luca to move to New York, wouldn't it? She felt like the floor had dropped out of the room, only to be replaced with a spinning carnival ride.

At last, Luca's broad chest expanded with a deep breath. "If we're going to do that, you should call me Luca," he rumbled in his smooth baritone.

Immediately, the men launched into making arrangements, pulling out phones and scheduling meetings, and Daisy knew in her bones that Luca intended to take the job.

Red's fiancée Piper popped up at her elbow, nearly making her jump out of her skin. "See something you like?" the woman grinned.

"Cripes, Piper! You scared me!"

"Sorry. But the question still stands."

Daisy sighed. "I…think I might know the guy with the dark hair," she admitted reluctantly.

"Luca?" Piper smiled. "Red suspected you might. They're such good friends, but I just got to meet him for the first time yesterday." And then the bride elbowed her with a conspiratorial wink. "He's something, am I right?"

No way was Daisy going to get into *that* discussion. But as long as Piper was here and feeling chatty, she supposed she could do some digging. "Who's the other guy?"

"Oh, that's Dr. Green. He has it bad for Luca. I'm a little surprised he's keeping his composure and not falling on his knees begging, though."

"Why?"

"We met him for dinner a few weeks ago. When it came up in conversation that Red was friendly with the famous Gianluca Delledonna, Green nearly drooled in his moo goo gai pan."

Daisy felt a little light-headed. Her voice sounded weak when she asked, "Famous?"

"Oh, sure. He's, like, an international badass in cancer research. And so charming, too. If I wasn't getting hitched to my own tall drink of water, I'd totally want to steal him from you."

Daisy didn't even know where to begin with that bit of insanity. "He's not mine. You can't steal something that doesn't even belong to me."

"Save it, sister. I'm not blind. Luca may as well have a big neon sign around his neck, blinking *Taken As All Get Out.*"

"Piper!"

The party's honoree just snorted, supremely unapologetic. "Anyway, I'd better go cut that damn cake. My future mother-in-law is beckoning, and I've already avoided her for as long as I can." With a friendly half-hug, Piper began moving through the crowd, but she called over her shoulder, "Hey, text me next week! The four of us can go out together sometime!"

Daisy stood there, blinking stupidly after her and wondering how her evening had veered so far into absurdity.

DAISY COULDN'T FOOL herself that she'd remain incognito at this party for long, or that she and Luca would never run into each other around town. New York might be a big place with about a bazillion people crammed into it, but the shared association to Red and Piper was too much of a coincidence.

The fix was definitely in, but Daisy was confounded by how her boss—or Luca, for that matter—had managed to figure out the connection.

True, Luca had known she was affiliated with the NYU study abroad program in Florence last year, and she must have mentioned at some point during the semester that she lived in Manhattan.

However, in the intervening twelve months, Daisy's life had undergone a massive upheaval. When she'd come back from Italy, she'd opened her own solo graphic design shop, then had to shutter it months later when the building she leased space in kicked all its tenants out to revamp into luxury lofts.

From there, she'd ended up in Boston, helping her college friend Poppy at a contemporary art museum she worked for.

Daisy had only come back to New York recently, when she'd landed the gig at Trident Publishing. Red's company, PKM Conglomerates, had bought the small, struggling press and managed to turn it around—barely—and in the process he had met and fallen for Piper, a successful romance author there.

Daisy had helped him propose to Piper by putting together a picture book he'd conceived about their relationship. Now, strangely, the couple seemed to have decided she was a friend of theirs.

That wasn't a bad thing, necessarily. They were good people, decent and non-irritating. She just had to wonder why they'd spend a single minute bothering with her.

Regardless, for Luca to have tracked Daisy to her current job after all the recent changes in her life was too far-fetched for words.

It had to have come from MacLellan. Maybe he'd seen the Florence job on her resumé when she was hired at Trident. Maybe he'd overheard something when H.R. called her references. In any case, for Red to have connected the dots all the way, Luca *had* to have talked to him about Daisy.

A panicked sound escaped her throat. Daisy needed to get out of here, quickly, but it felt like her feet were glued to the floor. She was utterly paralyzed from her face to her toes, watching the suave man across the room. The man it had killed her to leave behind. The man who still haunted her dreams.

God, he looked good.

As if Luca could feel her eyes on him, he suddenly raised his chin and looked over Dr. Green's head, searching the room with a small perplexed divot between his dark brows.

He turned slightly to the side, taking in the sight of Red and Piper cutting their cake and joking with their guests.

And then Luca pivoted in Daisy's direction. She shrank back, trying to commune with the potted plant behind her, but it was too late.

He'd seen her. Their gazes clashed, her breath locked up in her throat, and her heart flapped around like a wild, panicked bird in her chest. His lips were moving, but she couldn't process whatever he was trying to say.

Luca's face was pale with shock. His hand shot out, reaching unsteadily toward her. "Daisy?" he croaked.

She swallowed and spun, dodging the banana palm and banging her shoulder into a corner as she fled toward the front door.

Behind her, Luca cried out, *"Daisy, no!"*

Two

Eighteen Months Ago

LEAVE IT TO Daisy to ruin the best thing that had ever happened to her. Here she was, deathly ill when she only had a precious few months to enjoy Italy. Though maybe that wasn't the best choice of words—up until last week, she'd done just fine exploring and discovering everything wonderful about her temporary home. What was more, she'd done it all without the asshole man she was supposed to be doing those things with.

Besides, Daisy was pretty sure whatever bug had laid her out wasn't *actually* deadly. At least…she hoped it wasn't. Still, she'd been barfing like a champion for six days straight with no end in sight, and she didn't seem to be turning a corner at all.

She'd been able to get the other adjunct professors to cover her classes so far, but much more of this and Daisy was likely to find herself out of a job and back in New York, where she would definitely have to address all kinds of irritating things—such as her lack of residence, lack of steady employment, and utter dearth of romantic companionship.

Assuming she made it that far.

Daisy groaned and rolled to her side, curling up against the wave of cramping that hit her midsection right on schedule. She had no idea how she could possibly have anything left in her system to throw up. She hadn't ingested much more than crackers and water for days. Her room was a mess. *She* was a mess.

While she hated to admit it, Daisy knew she needed help. Somehow, she had to make herself reasonably presentable, then struggle down three flights of stairs to get it, though.

Hopefully, the kindly old lady who ran the pensione where Daisy lived would be in her apartment and would know of a doctor that Daisy could call.

With a little more luck, everyone she encountered on the way would hold their noses and forget to wear their glasses.

Look away, I'm hideous, and all that.

Once the pain in her stomach began to subside, Daisy pushed herself upright and grimly waited for the room to stop spinning. From there, she snagged a pair of black jeans on the floor with her foot, dragged them closer, and somehow managed to get into them from a horizontal position.

That small effort was exhausting enough that she had to lay there through another few waves of pain, letting the nausea subside and reevaluating whether she even had the fortitude for this task.

Maybe she'd never get up again. Maybe Daisy would die here in this cramped little room, unknown and unloved for all eternity.

Screw that. She sat upright again, pissed at herself now. All she needed to do was go downstairs and get a damn doctor to check her out. Once she did that, she could crawl back up here and wallow for the rest of the night, if she wanted.

Maybe, with a little more time and some strong medicine, Daisy could someday return to the land of the great showered masses. *Easy.*

IT TOOK AN eternity to make it to her destination. Daisy scooted most of the way on her ass, gripping the handrail over her head and resting her cheek on the warm plaster wall when she got too tired.

Once she made it to the bottom, she ran a shaky hand over her hair to make sure it wasn't sticking out all over the place and mopped off her clammy face with the hem of her t-shirt. She felt gross but hoped the sour smell of her skin wouldn't be as noticeable to other people as it was to her.

Signora Magnani, the friendly woman who ran the pensione, lived in the only apartment on the first floor, and her front door was wide open as usual.

Daisy hauled herself to her feet when she heard the exuberant voices drifting from within. It wasn't quite dinnertime, but if Signora Magnani had guests, maybe she shouldn't interrupt.

On the other hand, Daisy wasn't entirely convinced she'd be able to get back up to her room without serious assistance.

While she stood there trying to decide what to do, a middle-aged woman walked past the doorway, stopped, and came out to greet her.

"*Buon giorno,*" she smiled. "*Posso aiutarla?*"

"I'm sorry," Daisy said, shaking her head. She was thankful that she'd managed to brush her teeth, at least, before dragging ass down here, but her meager Italian was failing her at the moment. "*Parla Inglese?*"

"*Mi dispiace. No.*"

"Is Signora Magnani home, then? I'm sick. I need a doctor."

The woman smiled faintly and shrugged, then turned toward the interior of the apartment. "*Mamma!*" she called. "*Vieni qui!*"

Signora Magnani shuffled out and the instant she caught sight of Daisy, she gasped. Wrapping her solid arm around Daisy, she pulled her into the front room and parked her on the small loveseat under the window.

Daisy tried to pantomime what was wrong with her while the two women efficiently felt her cheeks and forehead, then gripped her clammy hands in theirs.

A flurry of incomprehensible, rapid-fire Italian washed over and around her while she swayed in her seat, but at last Daisy recognized the word she was hoping to hear.

"*Dottore*," she agreed, with relief. "Yes, that's what I need. *Il dottore, per favore.*"

Nodding all around. Then, at the top of her lungs, Signora Magnani called out, "Luca!"

Immediately, Daisy heard a chair scraping across the floor of the kitchen, but her dizziness had brought the nausea back with a vengeance. She had to get out of this nice woman's parlor before she humiliated herself.

Somehow, she managed to push to her feet again. "I have to go back upstairs," she told them. "I'm sorry. Can you…"

"No, no," Signora Magnani's companion instructed sharply. "*Restare. Siediti.*"

"…just…tell me when the doctor's…here…" Daisy mumbled. And then, exactly like a Saturday morning cartoon from her childhood, a deep black abyss pushed in from the corners of her vision, the room went whirling around her head, and she was out.

WHEN DAISY CAME to, she found herself tucked back into her bed upstairs, still in her clothes and blinking up at two of the most handsome faces she'd ever laid eyes on.

Nearly mirror images of each other, one was clean-cut and the other had longer, shaggier hair and a scruffy goatee. Both were blessed with square jaws, glossy black hair and warm chocolate eyes that crinkled at the corners as soon as she opened her eyes.

"Ah, welcome back, *bella*," the neater one smiled. "You had us a little worried for a moment there."

Daisy swallowed. She had clearly died and gone to heaven, but God only knew how that had happened. Perhaps she'd vomited herself to death?

On that note, though, she croaked out, "What happened?"

"You fainted," he told her. "I hope you don't mind—my brother Paolo carried you upstairs while I went out to the car and got my bag."

"No, that's—"

A new, younger woman bustled efficiently in from the hall, carrying a bucket full of cleaning supplies and a wet rag. She smiled and waved at Daisy, said something unintelligible to the men, then left again.

"Our sister Giada," her translator explained. "She says she sterilized the hall bathroom. Now she will go down and get you some clean sheets and towels."

Clean *anything* sounded amazing, but Daisy still shook her head. "She doesn't have to do that."

At that, Paolo bumped the side of the bed with his knee and clucked, scolding her like he would a toddler or a puppy. Daisy winced as another wave of nausea snaked through her.

Her genial rescuer waved the second man away, then pulled over the desk chair so he could sit next to Daisy's head. "It's done. Please don't worry. You are lucky, though. If we weren't here having dinner with our *nonna* tonight, it might've taken a lot longer to get you some help."

"Signora Magnani is your grandma?"

"She is," he twinkled at her. Daisy was pretty sure if she looked straight at him for too long, she could drown in those devastating pools he had for eyes. "You met my mother downstairs, my brother Paolo just now, and our sister Giada, of course," he continued. "My father is running late, or you would have seen him, too."

Daisy was at a loss. "Maybe next time," she muttered.

The man just grinned at her and patted her arm. He still hadn't given her his own name.

"And…you are…" she prompted, sounding grouchy.

He smacked his head and looked chagrined. "Ah! Forgive me," he said. "Dr. Luca Delledonna. At your service."

A doctor. Relief and gratitude swamped her, and humiliating tears sprang to Daisy's eyes. "I think I'm really sick," she whispered, announcing the obvious.

"Not for much longer," he soothed. "Now, why don't I check you out while you tell me what happened."

Dr. Delledonna reached into an old-fashioned black doctor's bag on the floor and extracted a stethoscope. He popped it around his neck, then procured a blood pressure cuff that he wrapped around her arm.

"I went out with some friends from school last week," Daisy said, watching his face while he took her blood pressure. "Maybe I ate something bad. I woke up the next morning with a fever and chills, and I haven't been able to keep any food down since. I'm so weak. I'm missing all my classes. It's hard to get out of bed."

Dr. Delledonna made a sympathetic sound and bent to listen to her heartbeat. He guided Daisy upright and gently supported her while she breathed and he moved the stethoscope over her back.

His cool fingers palpated her neck and jaw, then he dropped the cuff in his bag and extracted a small handheld device, which he ran across her forehead to take her temperature.

He gestured to the wilted, fetid sheet covering her body. "May I check your abdomen?"

Daisy nodded, and those capable hands of his were soon pressing on her hollow stomach and prodding at her sides.

At last, her doctor sat back, looking thoughtful. "Do you remember where you went to eat?"

"I can't remember what it was called. It was in the Oltrarno. A seafood place."

He nodded. "There's been an outbreak of *yersinia enterocolitica* around there. Your symptoms seem to point to that. I can take a blood sample and have it tested at the lab to be sure, but I expect you're nearly past the worst of it. Until we know for sure, I'm going to write you a prescription for an anti-emetic, so at least we can start getting some food into you."

"Thank you," Daisy said, even though the mere mention of eating had her stomach roiling once more. "I appreciate that. And I have insurance. I'm not sure how you usually bill people but —"

"You do not owe me for a simple kindness," Dr. Delledonna said stiffly, as if she'd offended him. "Rest now," he continued. "In the morning, my mother will bring the prescription, and Nonna will make you some pastina and broth. Go slow, but try to eat some of it, if you can. And keep drinking plenty of water."

"I will."

Dr. Delledonna smiled at Daisy again, gave her another friendly pat, and went to the door. He paused on the threshold, long enough for her to ask again, "Doctor, are you sure I can't pay you something? At least let me cover the cost of the medicine."

His eyes traveled over her face thoughtfully. "I'll make you a deal," he said at last. "Once you're back on your feet, you can buy me a coffee. That's all the payment I need. And please, call me Luca."

"Absolutely. Anytime," Daisy blurted out, before she really considered what she was promising.

Luca smiled broadly and let himself out. Once she heard his footsteps retreat down the stairs, she let herself sag into the mattress. As saviors went, getting stuck with a hunky heartbreaker did not suck one bit. And somehow, she'd even gotten herself an appointment for a follow-up visit.

Too bad she probably looked like a homeless person and smelled like a farmyard. Otherwise, she might have been tempted to flirt with the man, despite her sorry condition.

Soon, his sister returned, bearing a pile of fresh bedding and clean towels. Giada helped Daisy into the desk chair and kept a wary eye on her while she briskly stripped the bed and remade it in record time.

Before long, Daisy was wriggling out of her jeans, downing a few sips of cool water, and sacking out in utter exhaustion for the night.

LATE THE FOLLOWING morning, she'd just managed to wash her face and brush her teeth, and had gingerly changed into her last clean t-shirt, when there was a knock on her door.

As the good doctor had predicted, his mother and grandmother stood shoulder-to-shoulder in the hall, one brandishing a little pharmacy bag, and the other carrying a tray with a covered bowl and a plate of toast.

Signora Magnani immediately hustled Daisy back into the bed, where she propped a couple of pillows behind Daisy's back and arranged the tray on her lap.

Then, she sat beside Daisy and busied herself with ripping into the bag that contained the medicine her grandson had ordered.

While Luca's grandmother watched Daisy like a hawk to make sure she swallowed the first dose, his mother bustled around the room, loading all of Daisy's dirty, cast-off clothes into the laundry bag hanging on the closet doorknob.

"What are you—ma'am? Please, stop. You don't have to do that," Daisy cried.

The woman might not have spoken much English, but she'd obviously picked up on Daisy's tone. She shook her head and waved her off, letting loose a flurry of rapid Italian.

Luca's grandmother translated haltingly. "She know that," she said. "But if we no help each other, is no good life. Beside. Is no work. Two minute to load machine, and all done."

Daisy was struck dumb by the matter-of-fact recitation. Signora Magnani leaned in to lift the dishtowel off the tray, and revealed a steaming bowl of broth filled with tiny balls of pasta. It smelled absolutely delicious, and the simple motherly gesture made Daisy's eyes fill.

Even if it made her throw up clear into next week, she was going to choke down as much as she could for Luca's *nonna*.

"Your grandson is very nice," she told her, lifting the spoon. "He wouldn't let me pay him, though."

His mom smiled and dropped the bag of Daisy's laundry out on the landing.

"This no surprise me," Signora Magnani said. "He so honorable."

"He did say I could buy him coffee, at least. Once I get better," Daisy told her.

Signora Magnani froze in the act of handing her a slice of toast, and shared a quick, amused look with her daughter.

Luca's mother smirked. "*That* surprise me," she said.

"Really?" The pastina was going down better than Daisy had expected, and—courtesy of the fast-acting anti-nausea medicine, no doubt—Daisy's stomach was already feeling better than it had in a week.

She spooned up more of the salty, buttery goodness, while Luca's grandmother went on. "*Si.* He love his patients and they families very much, but he work too hard. Luca is good man and so handsome, but he never go out. Never see women. Is a crime. He too *esigente*."

Daisy shook her head, not understanding. In a moment, Luca's mother whipped out a cell phone, tapped something out, then announced. "Finicky. He too finicky."

Signora Magnani agreed. "Every woman he meet is too young, too needing, too something, something, something."

"Too married," Luca's mother added, rolling her eyes. Her own mother smacked her playfully on the arm.

"Is a losing game, trying to find the perfect woman. No one is great beauty, great, eh, mind, great cook, great lover, great mother…no all at once. He want too much. Is *ridicolo*."

"So…this coffee idea is a good thing?" Daisy asked carefully.

"*Si.* Very good thing. You buy Luca dinner instead. Then you wait. You two, you going to fall over for each other like two…eh, two trees in strong wind."

Daisy squinted at the tricky analogy, but decided it was probably better not to dwell on the details too much. "If Luca is that picky, I'm sure he'll find something wrong with me, too. It won't even be that hard."

His grandmother chuckled.

His mother grinned, too, and attempted to explain in her broken English, "This no *problema*. If you do not be sick—you so helping, *mia cara*—Nonna still, eh…"

"Fix," Signora Magnani supplied.

"*Sì*, Nonna fix you two up, eh, by the month. She keep talking Luca you. Since you be here."

Signora Magnani lifted her chin and tried to look innocent. She failed.

Unfortunately for Daisy, the pastina she'd been eating chose that moment to come back up again. Signora Magnani swiftly stuck the small trash can under Daisy's face and held back her hair.

"You no worry," she tutted, patting her on the back, "Luca be back soon and help, okay?"

Three

L UCA'S STEPS SLOWED as he approached the small trattoria where he'd arranged to meet his former patient. Daisy sat at a metal bistro table outside, wearing a faded denim jacket in the cool evening air. The setting sun outlined her reddish-brown curls in a golden halo, but her down-turned face was already falling into shadow.

As he watched, she reached down and pulled a large red and orange scarf from her bag and wrapped it around her neck. It looked soft and warm and would keep the damp chill away. Luca was glad she'd thought ahead—tonight, he'd rather stay outside where it was quieter, and he was less likely to run into someone he knew.

Now that Daisy was feeling better, he was looking forward to talking about more than her health with her, and he'd hoped to do that without constant interruptions from every neighbor and friend he'd spent the last thirty-odd years getting to know.

She'd just pulled out what looked like a school report when he strode up. "Hey, Doc," she said warmly. Her lips tipped up in a welcoming smile, and her gaze moved with interest from his white dress shirt, to his camel-colored blazer, to the tie he'd just removed and shoved in his pocket.

Luca wondered what scale he was being measured with.

"Can it really be you?" he marveled. Luca gestured briefly to the maître-de.

He came here often enough that what he wanted didn't require a lot of discussion, and when the man returned with two tiny glasses, Luca set one in front of Daisy with a flourish.

"I see you come bearing gifts," she smiled.

"Naturally. I hope you like limoncello?" He settled himself in the chair opposite her while she stuffed the student paper back in her big bag.

"I love it. Thank you."

Luca knew he must be staring, but he couldn't help examining Daisy's face and hair and clothes for signs of her returning health. Finally, he tossed up his hands happily. "Look at you! You look spectacular," he chuckled.

She really did. If he'd thought she was pretty before—albeit, in a wan, consumptive sort of way—Daisy was now a heartbreaker.

"Thanks. I'm feeling much better," she told him. As an afterthought, she added, "Obviously."

Luca sat back, more convinced than ever that this date was a terrific idea. "If I'd known two weeks ago that I was treating a goddess, I might've done things differently."

Daisy snorted. "I'm sure it probably seems that way, after the condition you found me in."

"I admit that was not, perhaps, your best look. Still, I hadn't expected…" His mouth was running away with his good manners.

Luca managed to blockade his stupendously amateur efforts to flirt, but only by knocking back his entire glass of limoncello in one gulp.

And, great—now the object of his incipient lust thought he was a drunk, in addition to a fool.

Daisy nibbled on the corner of her lip, eyeing him quizzically. Next to his feet under the table, she began rubbing one shoe slowly against the other. It was clearly a nervous habit she'd had for a while—her left shoe bore a dark smudge along the instep, as if she did the same thing all the time.

Her uncertainty was oddly endearing.

Luca's idiot mouth took advantage of his moment of distraction, spewing out more words and saving Daisy from having to come up with a suitable response to his prior lunacy.

"Italian women like to dress like rock stars when they go out," he rambled. "Like Donatella—with the heavy makeup, the tight, ragged clothes…" His hands flew around, sketching his dislike in the night air. "It's too much, with all the…the…" His gestures got a bit more direct.

Luca was beginning to remember why he worked so damn much. Socializing like a real human boy was definitely not a current strength of his.

"Cleavage?" Daisy guessed.

Scratch that. It was this woman, in particular, who made him crazy. "This is the word for…" Another rude gesture his grandmother would probably smack him with a spoon for.

"*Yes.*" Daisy flushed an enticing shade of pink. Luca had never wanted to kiss someone more in his life.

But suddenly, he wanted to tease her even more than he wanted to lock lips with her. He grinned, and a long-untapped well of mischief swelled within him.

Gone was the kind doctor who'd nursed her so gently back to health. Now he had a dark, tempting devil sitting on his shoulder, and it must have shown.

A little desperately, Daisy grabbed her mini wineglass and swallowed a mouthful of liquor.

Luca leaned in like he was imparting a kinky secret. "It's much sexier to leave some things to the imagination, don't you think?" He kept his voice low, but she heard him perfectly.

"*Oh*," she whispered. "Yes." Daisy was blushing like an adolescent with a flaming crush. He could lick up those rosy cheeks and still be hungry for more.

"Like that thing you are doing with your mouth," he murmured, pointing.

"Me?" she sputtered. "What am I…I'm not…"

"*Si*, that. With the one corner going like—" Luca tilted his lips up on one side, mimicking her expression.

Daisy supplied the word for him. "Smirking," she said.

He wondered if he was smirking, too. Luca *felt* like he was drooling, however, possibly in a very lovestruck-zombie kind of way.

"Ah, yes. When you do that, it looks delicious," he told her. And it did—it really did. He wished he'd thought to ask her for a whole dinner instead of just coffee.

Which they weren't even drinking, because he'd immediately upgraded them to cocktails, anyway.

Daisy sat back in her chair with an ungainly thump.

While she was mulling over his compliments, Luca tipped his chin at the waiter. For once in his life, it was a guy he didn't recognize.

Luckily, the man knew his job. He sailed in quickly to set a small red leather folder first in front of Daisy, and then in front of Luca.

"Are you hungry?" Luca inquired.

Daisy blinked rapidly, drawing his attention to her startling green eyes and the inky-black lashes framing them. Luca winked, and she let out a confused, "Um…"

"I, for one, am famished," he informed her. Then he cracked his menu and began whistling. After a moment, it dawned on him. *One Enchanted Evening.* How perfect.

Daisy grabbed at the waiter's sleeve a bit urgently. "Another limoncello, please."

She was off-balance. *Good.* So was he.

Luca grinned. "Make it two." Once they were alone again, he felt a little guilty for steamrolling her. "I'm sorry. We were only supposed to have coffee. Is this okay? Do you have the time?"

"No. I mean, yes—it's fine. I have time. I was just supposed to be the one asking you."

Luca shrugged. "You ask, I ask. In the end, it's all the same. We still get to eat and enjoy each other."

"Yes, but…I'm supposed to be thanking you for taking care of me. Remember?"

Luca had spent several days gazing down at a beautiful woman lying in a messed-up bed, falling for her smooth, creamy skin and tight caramel curls. He'd become spellbound by the contrast between her tough-talking, husky voice, and her sweet face. He'd been dying to learn more about her, even if it did fly in the face of the usual doctor/patient relationship.

And all the while, she'd looked up at him like he was her savior. As if he'd hung the moon. Pretty memorable, if you asked him.

"I remember," Luca told her. "And I assure you, getting to spend some time together without me worrying that you'll faint at my feet again is thanks enough."

At last, the sense of humor he'd occasionally spotted in her drifted to the surface. "What, you expect me to believe that women aren't swooning around you all the time? I wasn't born yesterday, Casanova."

He chuckled. "It's true. Not one woman has dropped like a stone in days. *Days.* It's bizarre. Might even be a sign of the Apocalypse."

"Give me a break. You probably have a whole swooning-woman protocol in place. Support the head. Administer smelling salts. All fathers, brothers, and husbands must keep back at least five feet..."

Yes, there was the woman Luca couldn't stop thinking about—the one he suspected would give as good as she got. Luca felt like a dog pulling at his leash, wanting to get closer to her.

"That last part is only because the woman needs air to recover sufficiently."

Daisy barked out a sexy, throaty laugh that warmed him from top to bottom. Sure, some points in the spectrum were significantly warmer than others, but that was the male body for you—always impractical in how it handled its blood flow.

Speaking of warm, though... "Are you warm enough out here?" he asked. "I'm sure we could move to a table inside, if you'd prefer. It's still early enough that they'll have room."

"Actually, yeah—that would be great."

They gathered their things and stepped into the small trattoria, where there were, in fact, several small tables available. Luca conferred briefly with the maître de and secured the most private one in the farthest corner.

Once they were settled in, he let his eyes roam over Daisy again. She unwound her wrap and let it fall back off her shoulders, then slipped out of her jacket, too.

Madre di Dio. Her dress. Her shoulders. Her *skin.*

Luca was abruptly certain he did not have the stones it would take to get through this meal without embarrassing himself. He could only pray that they'd bring him some bread or something, so he could act like he was slavering over that, instead of her.

"What a lovely dress," he managed to squeak out. Right, because women *adored* squeaking from the manly men they wanted to sleep with.

"Thank you," she replied. Daisy looked thrilled to have a conversational topic handed so neatly to her. "I wasn't having much luck finding a place to shop for clothes near my school or the pensione. But I spotted your sister in the hallway one time, and she agreed to help."

"That sounds suspiciously simple for Giada."

"Yeah. You know her better than I do, obviously. I expected her to give me a boutique recommendation. Instead, I got a sarcastic copilot who took me all over creation and really didn't pull her punches when she didn't like something on me."

"I can only imagine," Luca smiled. Giada knew him well. The dress Daisy was sporting was pure torture.

He needed to dial back his appreciation before he freaked Daisy out, though. She was looking down and plucking at her skirt self-consciously.

"You think it's okay?" she wondered.

Was the dress so different than something she normally would have picked out? Luca loved the way it skimmed her knees in front, then curved lower to brush her calves in the back. He liked the way the high neckline emphasized her breasts and the belt nipped in at her waist. The slinky material made every curve Daisy owned look slippery and touchable.

"More than okay," he assured her. "Though I may need to order a steak, just so I'll have a knife to fend off the hordes of men you're going to attract before long."

Then, Luca clamped his teeth together and forced himself to study the words marching around on his menu. If he kept staring at her like a caveman, Daisy wouldn't mistake the desire brimming in his gaze, and that seemed a little too hot and heavy when they hadn't even ordered appetizers yet.

She made a small sound that made him look right back at her, though.

"Why do you blush?"

A small shrug. Shards of candlelight darted like lighting across the surface of her dress when she moved.

"Daisy? Why are you embarrassed?"

She huffed. "I'm just not used to people looking at me like that," she muttered grudgingly.

"You're joking. You must see this look on men every day of your life."

Daisy shook her head. Quite, *quite* emphatically.

Luca frowned. It was not exactly polite, but he couldn't stop himself from reaching out and tugging on the perfect coil of hair next to her cheek. "American men have ruined an entire country of women for the rest of the world," he mused. "I'd forgotten that."

"Well, I can't argue with you, there," Daisy agreed. Her words were relaxed and easy, but her posture was not. She held herself carefully still, waiting for his next move.

Luca watched his hand go rogue and drop to her bare shoulder. Shocks of electricity shot up his arm and fired through his blood. Daisy shivered.

"This dress is going to drive me crazy all night," he informed her.

She snorted in that dismissive way he was rapidly becoming familiar with. "Don't blame me. Your sister is completely responsible for that."

Luca's eyes narrowed as he stopped to consider exactly what his sister's motives might have been. "As her younger brother, I maintain a list of complaints. I'll be sure to add this to it."

IT WASN'T TERRIBLY adventurous of him, but Luca ordered the bracciole. He *always* ordered the bracciole. And, lucky him, it was delivered with a ferocious-looking steak knife that would double as an excellent weapon should any other male even sneeze in his date's direction.

Daisy ordered a simple fettuccine dish, which she assured him was delicious. She was far more interested in his meal, however. Eventually, Luca broke down, cut her off a slice, and slid it across the table.

"It's my favorite," he explained. "I get it whenever it's on the menu, even though my *nonna's* is the best."

"Mmmm," Daisy hummed, savoring the taste he'd given her. "It's so good."

Luca made a really abysmal attempt not to connect the happy sound to all things bedroom-related.

If there was one thing guaranteed to stifle his cock's more enthusiastic impulses, however, it was thoughts of his grandmother. "Tomorrow morning," he announced, "If Nonna asks you how our meal went, you have to tell her I like her bracciole better. Promise me."

"Of course."

Another thought occurred to him, and Luca figured he should warn Daisy now. "She's going to want to teach you how to make it, you know."

"Seriously?"

"You wait. By the time you come back from class tomorrow, Nonna will be ready. She'll pull you into her apartment and have all the ingredients already arranged in the kitchen."

"But why would she want to do that?"

Why, indeed. Unfortunately, Luca thought he had a pretty good idea of what the women in his family were up to—not that he minded.

Luca smiled at Daisy's confusion. No, for once, he didn't mind his family's interfering one bit.

Four

I T WAS OBVIOUS that Dr. Harlan Green had been prepped ahead of time for his introduction to Luca. During their short conversation, the small, energetic man was more than ready to entice Luca to New York with a whole host of benefits.

New lab facilities. Only one class to teach during the coming school year, so Luca could get settled and comfortable in his new surroundings at his leisure. Green had even dangled the possibility of a department-head position, though Luca supposed that was a promise many people heard during the cocktail party stage of negotiations.

The one thing Dr. Green did not offer, was, naturally, something he knew nothing about—or rather, *someone* he knew nothing about. She would have been an impressive bargaining chip, if Green had known. There would be no resisting her allure.

Luca let his gaze drift over the smaller man's shoulder to the wall of windows beyond. In the early darkness of Manhattan winter, the lights of the city winked and pulsed in a glittering fretwork that stretched into the distance.

Absently, Luca wondered if Daisy really was out there, somewhere. How strange would it be if she sat mere blocks away, drinking her favorite coffee, and completely unaware that he was here? How awful would it be if this trip—this *move*—got Luca no closer to his ultimate goal?

He sighed and looked down at his companion once more. Dr. Green was beginning to fidget, growing flustered at Luca's distraction.

"You make a compelling case," Luca told him, in what he hoped was a congenial voice. "Perhaps we should meet again this week, to go over the details in a more conducive setting."

Green smacked himself in the forehead. "Absolutely! Of course. You're here to celebrate your friend's engagement, not to talk turkey with Joe Schmo." Luca blinked at the sudden burst of baffling slang, and Green transitioned into contrition. "In my eagerness to meet you, I'm afraid I got a bit carried away. I hope you'll forgive the lapse."

Luca waved his concern away. He was flattered that such an esteemed colleague had so much enthusiasm for his work. If he weren't feeling so morose about his stalled hunt for Daisy, he'd be more than willing to make conversation, engagement party or not.

It was only that, as the minutes of the fete wore on, the tiny hairs on the back of Luca's neck had moved into high alert, prickling in the oddest way every time the crowd shifted and reformed around him. Every time a caterer brushed his sleeve, or a guest bumped into his back, Luca felt himself holding his breath and searching their faces.

And then—it happened. Like a bullfighter's cape, a swish of red in his peripheral vision drew his eye, and Luca was suddenly, terrifyingly eye-to-eye with the woman he'd spent the last year searching for.

His shock at seeing Daisy's tall, lithe form across the party was considerable. In one of those moments of abrupt clarity, it made sense why Red had insisted he come here for this. Luca only wished his friend had prepared him as well as he had prepared Dr. Green.

Whatever surprise Luca might be feeling, however, was reflected tenfold in Daisy's face. If he'd been knocked off-kilter to see her, Daisy looked like a black hole had suddenly opened up in front of her. Obviously, no one had warned her, either.

"Luca," she mouthed, turning hospital-sheet white.

He nodded, a little giddy to be hearing her sultry voice again. "I can't believe it's you. I'm so happy to see you again. I've been—" Luca broke off, the rush of words piling up in his mouth and obstructing his breathing. Instead of continuing his babbling, he found himself simply shaking his head and throwing up his hands.

Dr. Green said carefully, "I'll just call you Monday, shall I?"

Luca couldn't bring himself to tear his eyes away, in case Daisy disappeared, like a mirage. "I look forward to hearing from you."

Daisy spun on her heels, her entire body angling away like she was about to launch herself from a cannon—in the exact opposite direction from where Luca stood. That made no sense.

"Daisy?" And then, when she didn't stop, "Daisy, no!" Luca lunged, grabbed for her hand, and held her in place. "Wait. Don't leave. What are you doing here? Are you—"

"Please. Let me go," she begged, lips quivering and staring over his shoulder like she was trying not to cry.

"But why? Is everything okay? I've been looking everywhere for you. I've—"

She stopped pulling on her hand and stared at him, confused. "What? You have?"

"Of course. I was so stupid to let you go so easily. I realized it almost immediately. But you never answered any of my calls or texts, and then your number stopped working altogether. I waited for you to contact me for six months before I really started searching. But I couldn't find you. I—" Luca hesitated and swallowed thickly, dismayed by the utter horror carved into Daisy's expression. Stupidly, he pushed on, though. "I've missed you."

A strangled sound emerged from her throat and she gave another weak tug on her hand. Luca released her.

So…okay. He was actually really terrible at this, it seemed. When he'd envisioned his eventual reunion with the woman who'd stolen his heart and invaded his dreams, it had looked nothing like this.

Luca had acted far more debonair, for one thing. And Daisy had been overjoyed to see him, for another. *Passionately* overjoyed.

This car crash was a scenario he had not entertained for even a second. Daisy shakily pushed her lush hair back from her face, and a sickening thought occurred to him—but no, when Luca's eyes sought it out, her ring finger was still empty.

She wasn't married yet. However, he supposed she could still be committed to someone else.

"Daisy, what's going on?" Luca asked.

"I thought we'd never see each other again," she whispered. She was so pale he was beginning to worry that she was going to faint on him. She did have a history.

Luca cast his eyes quickly around the room but didn't see any vacant chairs. He didn't dare go searching for one, though, because it was patently clear Daisy would take off the instant he did.

"I thought so, too," Luca admitted. "But I couldn't do it. I couldn't live without seeing you again. I had to at least try for something more."

A high-pitched squeak of disbelief popped out of her, and Daisy looked desperately around the room. No one was paying any attention to them. No one was coming to her rescue—no one but Luca, that was.

"You don't seem very happy to see me," he said, pointing out the obvious.

She bit her full, berry-painted lower lip, and a painful throb of longing arrowed through him. "Because I'm not who you think I am," she said, almost too quiet for him to hear. "I'm not the Daisy you knew in Italy."

That slapped him back a step. Luca wasn't precisely the man she thought he was, either. He was positive it didn't matter, though.

Daisy still looked like she was on the verge of tears, but he asked anyway, "Then who are you?"

Right then, with a characteristic bit of atrocious timing, Red strolled up to them like the lord of the manor, grinning idiotically. "Ah, look what we have here," he drawled, slinging a long, heavy arm across Luca's shoulders. "I see you've met my newest graphic designer."

Daisy could hardly escape now. Luca watched her shake off whatever was troubling her so deeply, then wrap herself in an unbreachable mantle of professionalism. "Believe it or not, Dr. Delledonna and I know each other already. We met last year in Italy."

"Is that so," Red smiled. "What a small world. He and I have been friends for twenty years." Red winked at Daisy, then turned to Luca. "Imagine if you'd refused to come to my little party," he said, barely repressing his smug chuckle.

"It's strange," Luca mused, "How much I want to kill you. It never takes long, does it?"

"Now, now," his old friend chided him. "Violence is not the answer."

"It might be," Daisy muttered to herself.

Red's eyebrows flew up and he turned to stare at her. "What was that?"

Daisy pretended not to hear him, hiding behind her wineglass as she gulped down a healthy mouthful of dark red courage.

"Might I have a few moments alone with Daisy," Luca inquired, as levelly as he was able.

At this, Red's charming fiancée Piper bounced up to their little group. "Hey guys," she said, eyes twinkling, "What's going on?"

Red transferred his full attention and his arm to his future wife. "Later," he told her, and steered her neatly away.

"Look," Daisy said, the instant they were out of earshot, "Some of these people are my colleagues. I can't do this here."

"What is *this*, exactly?"

She stared Luca down, fierce and indomitable. It was all he could do not to wrap his hand in her wild curls and bend her backward over his arm for a long, hot *bacio*.

"Fine. But meet me tomorrow," Luca managed. He was deeply conscious that he hadn't couched it as a question, but it *had* been a long twelve months of searching. He wasn't in the mood for debate, at the moment. "Take my number." And then a small dig, "You know, in case you lost it."

Daisy heard the edge in his words, alright. She winced and looked away, considering Luca's offer like the choice was a difficult one.

Thankfully, when she finally turned back to him, her eyes had softened a small amount. Her original dismay had evolved into resignation, and her shock into curiosity.

"You look good," she said quietly. It looked like it took something out of her to admit it.

Luca had no such problem. "You look like a dream come true."

Daisy sighed and then gave up the fight. "Okay. I'll do it. I'll see you," she agreed.

He felt guilty about winning, but if she thought that would change his mind, she was dead wrong.

It only took a few more heartbeats, a few more inhalations and exhalations, before the other guests had parted them again. Daisy introduced him to a friendly woman in glasses—Lyla, he thought she'd said—and then promptly walked off with her.

Soon, Piper had collared Luca and steered him into a conversation with a couple of other doctors who worked with Harlan Green. For the moment, their reunion was over.

THE PARTY DRAGGED on, and Luca obsessed about each glimpse of Daisy he got through the crowd. Now that he had her in his sights, he was desperate to be rid of all the small talk and socializing. He just wanted to be alone with her.

He wanted to find out what had happened, why she had left without a word—why she'd disappeared without a trace. He needed to know why Daisy looked so scared to see him again, and what she would think about him moving to Manhattan long-term.

Luca had a breathless moment of anxiety, thinking about his family and the patients he'd have to leave behind if he really intended to move here. The position Dr. Green was offering was an excellent opportunity to further his research, however, and Luca could find new physicians for most of his patients.

There was truly only one patient who—but no. Andrea would be fine without him. Luca would not simply abandon the young man to his fate. He'd consult by phone, and fly back to Florence if necessary, and all would be well. Besides, wasn't Andrea doing better now? He'd almost certainly stay that way.

With that resolved in his mind, Luca waded into the fray, searching for Daisy in earnest again. Enough of this waiting around. They had things to figure out right now.

He found her loitering at the edge of the room, trying not to get caught staring at him. Luca strolled up, winked at her, and watched a deep red flush flare across her cheeks. He did love those blushes.

Just like that, adrenaline spiked in his veins and his respiratory system kicked into frantic, exuberant hyperdrive. Now that Daisy was so close, his fingertips positively pulsed with the need to touch her.

Her expression was daunting, but Luca had come this far. He'd see this through, safe in the knowledge that this was the correct decision as long as he got Daisy at the end of it.

"Please," he said weaving his fingers through hers. *Madonna*—they felt like ice. "I thought I could wait to talk to you, but I was wrong. Isn't there somewhere here we can go? Just for a few minutes?"

He lifted her hand to his mouth and pressed a kiss to her wrist. Daisy's breath hitched, then she peeked around again, to see if anyone was watching.

"No one cares about us. Tell me where you've been."

"I have to get out of here. I'll call you tomorrow. I promise."

"If you'd actually taken my number earlier, I might believe you."

"Luca, please. You think you want to talk to me. But you don't. Don't humiliate me by making me prove it."

"Daisy, you keep saying things like that. Of course, I want to know what you mean. Why wouldn't I? Not too long ago, we were two people in—"

"Don't say it!" she cried.

Several people near them turned to stare. Daisy swayed on her feet, and blurted out, "I'm sorry. It's okay. I didn't mean—"

She wrenched away from Luca and walked quickly toward the apartment's front door.

"Daisy?" he called, lurching into pursuit.

"I can't—"

"Can't what?"

She turned and stared at him, and Luca caught his breath. Her face was a tortured mask of confusion, pain, and despair.

Something more was going on here. Something he did not understand.

Five

D*AISY*," LUCA BREATHED, aghast when he caught sight of her face. She could only imagine what she must look like. If even half of what she was feeling was on display, she was probably a ghastly sight.

Daisy backed up a step, and Luca paced forward the same distance.

She retreated again, attempting to maintain her distance, but like some bizarre choreographed tango, he still stepped toward her, a maelstrom of emotion brewing in his dark eyes.

"Stop," she commanded, holding up a hand. "Don't do this here." Daisy wasn't sure how much longer she could hold it together. Seeing Luca in the flesh again was far harder than she ever would've expected.

Worse was that she had no idea whether she wanted to give in and fall sobbing into his arms in relief, or run so fast and far that she was lost forever.

However, some of the people currently staring at them were Daisy's coworkers. And even though she'd been at Trident for months now, she still felt like the new kid. It still seemed like it would be so easy to screw up—to lose their respect—and then Daisy would be right back at square one again.

After twelve months of tumult, she was finally in a stable place. The thought of upending that, even for Luca, was unbearable.

Luca's head had snapped up at her harsh words, and he finally seemed to develop some situational awareness. He scanned the room, then nodded toward a dim hallway off to the side. It was cordoned off with a velvet rope slung between two brass poles. A purple velvet *rope*—like they were at a movie theater, and not an engagement party.

Luca pulled Daisy toward it, unclipped the thing as if he saw them in private homes every day, and then ushered Daisy through. His firm touch on her back sent traitorous sparks ricocheting through her. She darted ahead, but a sudden voice in the darkness froze her in her tracks.

"Looking for the restroom?" a caterer inquired. Daisy fumbled for an answer while Luca simply nodded.

"Around the corner. First door on your right," the man said. He was a garden-variety metrosexual, all hair product and groomed beard above his black uniform. Too pretty by half.

Unlike Luca. Luca was gorgeous, but looking at him, there was no doubt he was all man.

"*Grazie*," he murmured in his seductive baritone, then propelled Daisy forward.

The caterer took no more notice of them than he would a fly, so Daisy assumed this didn't look like a kidnapping. She doubted it looked like a tryst, either, but what did she know? It wasn't like she'd spent her adulthood hooking up at fancy parties.

Still, this was New York. A caterer in this city probably witnessed all kinds of weird-ass things, like bartenders and cabbies did. Daisy's little peccadillos wouldn't even rank on a scale like that.

Luca found the little jewel of a bathroom in short order and crowded her into it. Then, he closed them both in without even a ripple of concern crossing his placid expression.

Daisy took a deep breath, hoping it would steady her. Her heart was galloping a million miles an hour with him so close.

"So, yeah. I guess this is happening," she said. She thought she'd managed to sound suitably cavalier—her voice had barely quavered at all.

In the cramped space, it was easy for Luca to reach forward and run his fingertips lightly up her arms and across her collarbones. He cupped her cheeks gently.

"Am I dreaming?" he wondered softly. "Are you really here?"

Daisy refused to shiver. She also refused to let herself sway toward his tall, warm frame. Luca looked so good. He *smelled* so good. Like cedar and oranges and wild, unbridled nights of passion.

Perhaps not that last bit. Even if it were true, Daisy couldn't have him, anyway. Not this time—not once Luca realized what a liar she was.

Except…*wait one doggone minute*. He was a dirty, rotten liar too, wasn't he?

"You lied to me," she informed him, as if Luca didn't already know. "You told me you were only—"

"Now I know you're real," he interrupted. "And no, I never said whatever it is you're about to tell me. I never lied to you."

Daisy hesitated. "Fine, maybe not outright. But you did let me believe—"

"That is true. I—"

A sharp, loud rap sounded out against the door panels, making Daisy squeak and jump. Luca took advantage and pressed closer.

"*Un momento*," he barked, at the same time Daisy called out, "Coming!" Too late, she realized exactly how *that* would sound.

Obviously, the line that connected her mouth to her brain had jostled loose in all the recent confusion. She'd have to weld that shit back into place before work rolled around on Monday morning.

There was a laden pause, and then her boss muttered, "Ah, Christ," outside the door.

And...yep, Daisy definitely needed to find a new job now. *Crap.*

"Listen, you two—I don't know what you're doing in there," Red growled, "And I don't want to know. However, I can assure you that my engagement party is not the time, and my mother's guest bathroom is not the place to catch up with each other."

Daisy covered her face with her hands and tried not to moan out loud.

Her boss said, "Wrap it up. *Pronto.*" Then his dress shoes promptly tapped out a staccato retreat across the parquet floor. Guess that caterer suspected something was up, after all.

Daisy dropped her hands and looked at Luca. Was that the faintest glimmer of amusement on his face? He couldn't possibly see the same impossible hilarity in this situation that she did. There shouldn't be anything funny about this at all.

Except Luca chuckled, warm and smooth as honey. And then the suave bastard went and kissed her.

Daisy wasn't ready. He caught her off guard, and that was probably why she fell so easily into kissing him back.

In moments, her mutinous hands were threaded through all that thick, silky black hair, her chest was pressed tightly against Luca's, and her tongue was tangling with the wiliest—and best— kisser in all of Italy.

And New York. Probably in the whole world.

God, she ought to be thankful she hadn't thrown a leg or two around him, too.

Daisy told herself she was weak. That she'd felt out of place all evening at this ritzy party, that she'd been lonely for months, and hadn't had sex in a year. She pretended that any grown woman worth her stilettos would jump at the chance to lock lips with Doctor Sexy.

She was not making out with him—*Jesus*, was that *her* moaning?—because she had missed him.

Missing Luca implied that Daisy had been wrong to leave Italy as she had. Wrong to ghost him. Wrong to seize control by dumping him before he could dump her.

Everyone knew long-distance relationships never worked out, anyway. And, if the conversation she'd just overheard between him and Dr. Green was any indication, Daisy had been right to beat feet.

If the Luca she'd *thought* she'd been with wasn't a good pick for her, then this real, internationally-employable version was even less so. Once he figured out who she really was, he'd be walking on water to get back to Florence.

Daisy could do without seeing the inevitable, dismayed expression on his handsome Michelangelo face. She'd seen enough of that to last a lifetime.

Was it so wrong to want to keep her incandescent memories of their time together unsullied? To hold that pearl in her pocket, a precious tiny thing, to bolster her when she needed a boost? It couldn't possibly be selfish to remember, as long as Daisy didn't try to keep up the charade in the here and now.

Right?

Luca pulled his lips from hers to catch his breath. Daisy told him, "We have to stop this. We need to go."

"I know. I'm sorry. I couldn't help myself, though. It's been so long, Daisy. I was starting to lose hope."

Daisy shook her head. "I have no idea what you're even talking about."

"I know. That's why I want to see you tomorrow. You don't work on Sunday, right? Let's go somewhere quiet, so I can explain everything."

"Luca, I don't know. This…this isn't a good idea."

"So you've said. Just take my number, meet me, and tell me why."

Daisy sighed, but that only brought her right up against him again. Luca's fingers flexed against her waist and his jaw twitched, like he was fighting an internal battle of his own. She could only imagine.

He had no idea what he was getting into, but Daisy supposed one hour wouldn't kill him. She probably owed him that much, if he'd really been hunting for her as he claimed, because Luca was a decent guy. Maybe the most decent guy she'd ever met.

And he wasn't asking for much from her—not yet, at least. Daisy could go tomorrow, hear him out, and then give him a kind but firm cease-and-desist.

It could be closure for both of them. They obviously needed it.

"Will you come?" he prompted.

She wished Luca hadn't worded it quite that way. Up until tonight, Daisy had made excellent progress in not thinking about coming with Dr. Luca Delledonna.

"Yes," she relented. "I'll come. Get out your phone. I'll put my number in it for you."

He did as she asked, watching her carefully until she'd finished. Then Luca snatched his cell back and texted her, making sure she hadn't given him a bum number.

Her little red satin clutch dinged from its perch on the tank of the toilet. He nodded toward it.

He'd texted her, *Che ora?*

Daisy shrugged. "Whatever time is good for you. How long are you here for?"

Luca's gaze was direct and unwavering. "Indefinitely. Until I figure out this thing with Dr. Green, at minimum." But his look made it clear he intended to figure out a thing or two with Daisy even more.

She tried to stay on track. "Okay, then how about this. Where are you staying?"

"The Library Hotel in Murray Hill. It's close to Weill Cornell, isn't it?"

"Yes, I think so. There's a bunch of places over there." She tapped on her screen for a minute or two, then told him, "Okay, here's one with a table free at one. Can you do that?"

"I'll do whatever you want, as long as you'll be there, too."

Luca was insane, but maybe if Daisy was lucky, he'd be cured in his sleep overnight, and would show up tomorrow with a reasonable head on his shoulders.

"All right, look. I'm sending you the link to the restaurant. Are you sure you can find it?"

"Daisy, I lived here for years. I'll be fine."

"Oh." Well, that explained the mystery of how he'd ended up friends with Red, anyway. "So, I'm going to leave now, before we raise any more eyebrows or get in more trouble with my boss."

Luca pecked her lightly on each cheek. "You go out first. I'll wander around back here for a while before I go back to the party."

"Thanks. I'm just going to grab my coat and say goodbye to Red and Piper. I won't take long."

Daisy scooted around him as platonically as she could manage, even though every molecule of her body was screaming at her to rub against Luca like a cat in heat.

She cracked the door and peeked out into the corridor, but he caught her hand before she could leave. "Daisy?"

"Yeah?"

"It really is wonderful to see you."

"You, too," she said.

And damn, for a couple of liars, didn't they both sound so sincere?

Six

Eighteen Months Ago

IT'D TAKEN A couple of weeks for her to feel completely like herself again, but now that she did, Daisy was beginning to get out and about once more.

She'd gone back to teaching her photography students first, focusing on technical lessons in class until she recovered her strength enough to bring them on excursions around town again.

She was back to hitting up the shops and museums in her off-hours too, but she was still a little gun-shy about trying any new restaurants. That was okay, though.

At the pensione, Signora Magnani—Nonna, the woman insisted she call her—fed her like a boss, and Daisy had a nice collection of favorite cafés from before her illness that she could still visit without worrying.

Since their dinner together, Daisy had run into Luca around town a few times. Whenever it happened, his face lit up and he swooped in with kisses on both her cheeks. "Ah, my special patient," he always said. "When are we going to have dinner again?"

Daisy just smiled and put him off. Luca didn't *really* want to get together again. He was only being polite, since she was rooming with his grandma.

But today, when he strolled up the narrow stone sidewalk and spied her sitting outside of a little gelateria around the corner from the pensione, he stopped in his tracks and looked determined.

"*Ciao*, Daisy," he said, coming nearer. "How are you?"

"Great, thanks to you."

"Are you…" he looked quickly around. "Waiting for a friend?"

"Nope. It's just me and my second gelato."

Luca grinned. "May I join you?"

"Sure," Daisy shrugged. It was no big deal, she reminded herself. Italians spontaneously stopped for coffee or pastries with their friends all the time. There was no reason whatsoever for her pulse to tick at a faster pace.

As Luca wove through the other tables toward the entrance, he gestured toward her and asked, "What are you having?"

"Strawberry basil. You should try it. It's phenomenal."

He came back out several minutes later, looking smug. "No more strawberry basil," he informed her, parking himself in the other chair. "But perhaps that was for the best."

"Oh? Why?" Daisy wondered, eyeing his paper bowl with interest. "Which flavor did you get?"

"How do you say it?" Luca mused, casting his eyes toward the sky. "Orange. Uh…blood orange." He took a long, leisurely lick of the blob on his spoon and Daisy tried not to think about his tongue doing that anywhere else. Like…everywhere on *her*. "This is also phenomenal," he claimed.

She could only imagine.

Daisy polished off her second helping of the strawberry basil gelato and schooled her expression into something she hoped would pass for normal.

Luca watched her, then summoned a harried busboy who was clearing a table nearby. "*Un caffè americano,*" he told him. "*Inoltre…un espresso per me. Per favore.*"

The boy nodded and rushed off. When he returned, he slid a cup of regular coffee in front of her and placed a small white espresso cup in front of Luca, right as Daisy began to feel chilly. She pulled her sweater back on, marveling at his timing. Doctor Luca was one observant fella.

"Should I find us a table inside?" he wondered. "You're getting cold, no?"

His concern was charming, but it was also a little unnerving. Her ex Jason had never been half as solicitous.

"Nope," Daisy demurred. "I'm fine. Especially now that I have this." She toasted him with the coffee cup, took a big gulp, and promptly burned the top layer off her tongue with the scalding liquid.

Luca winced and chuckled at her watering eyes. "Let's not create a new malady before I've finished treating the first one, all right?"

Daisy wondered if he was only concerned about her because of what he did for a living. Maybe all doctors were like him, caring and kind, and looking out for random people they stumbled across in their daily lives.

She wouldn't know. Daisy could probably count on one hand the number of doctors she'd spoken more than three words to in her life. Her foster mom, Pam, hadn't been one to run to the clinic for much less than a massive headwound.

And her ex-boyfriend had only been an English professor—though, to be fair, Jason had been a wildly popular one. He'd had a certain rock-star kind of charisma that had drawn Daisy's attention right from the beginning.

She certainly hadn't been attracted to his mildly passé efforts to be cool, or to his chronic smoker breath. No, Daisy had fallen hook, line, and sinker for Jason's *intensity*. When Professor Parker took her hand and looked deeply into her eyes—in the beginning, at least—it was like Daisy was his lodestar, his one true north.

She'd never been that for someone before and she was still pissed at how well the ploy had worked on her. In only a few short weeks, they'd gone out together enough times that pretty much everyone in both their departments at NYU knew they were an item. Daisy had allowed herself to start thinking about the future—to start thinking big.

So stupid. Although, if she'd kept her wits about her, she might not be here right now. Her failed relationship with Jason was the reason Daisy now got to sit across from the ridiculously good-looking Dr. Luca, after all.

If Jason hadn't been slated to teach the fall semester of creative writing at NYU's study abroad facility in Florence, he would never have urged her to join him there.

Daisy would never have thought to ask if she could pick up one of the adjunct professor spots, even if it was only for photography. Why would they have wanted her? She'd been a nothing-special junior professor of graphic design, not an expert in anything important.

But if life had taught her anything, it was that it had a twisted sense of humor. Not one week after she'd landed the coveted slot, Jason's academic star had crashed and burned in a fireball of scathing public censure. Turned out Daisy's boyfriend was routinely sleeping with his students for grades and some of them had been underage. She never would've guessed it, either. *Go figure.*

However, it was her fourth doomed relationship in two years, and it stung like a mother on its way out the door. Jason had come after the guy who'd always pushed to move in with her—he'd been sleeping in his car while he tried to make it on Broadway—and *he'd* been on the heels of the chronically-late stockbroker with tattoo sleeves and a wife and kids he'd forgotten to mention.

The less Daisy thought about door number four, the better a place the world would be.

But Luca didn't have to know any of that. Here and now, the hot doctor looked perfectly content to be sitting across from her, smiling serenely while he licked his gelato spoon.

Daisy paused to wonder what *his* dark underbelly was going to end up looking like. All men had them. Would it be an addiction to prescription meds? Affairs with his patients?

Somehow, she couldn't picture Luca being that skeevy.

"It's nice here," she told him, pushing all thoughts of past mistakes aside. "I only found it a couple days ago, but I've been back about ten times. Their lemon flavor is my favorite, I think."

"It is nice," he agreed. "And even nicer with you here. But, how is it possible that I found you alone?" He gestured at the quiet side street surrounding the café. "I can't believe you don't have a line of men waiting on the sidewalk to talk to you."

Daisy shrugged. With the fiery way Luca was studying her, she'd rather die than have him find out the truth about her. "Oh, you know how it is. Sometimes a girl just needs a break from all the attention. Don't tell anyone I'm here, okay?"

Her words came out careless enough, but her shame was a visceral thing, writhing low in her belly. Most guys had no trouble whatsoever forgetting about her. Hell, most times they hardly noticed she was there in the first place.

Not this one, though. Not now.

"Anyway, I could say the same about you," she smiled. Luca snorted and waved her off, but she persisted, "What? Aren't the cute nurses allowed to follow you out of the hospital once in a while?"

"Nurses are too dangerous for me," he scoffed. Then, when Daisy arched an eyebrow at him dubiously, he explained, "All those needles. All that antiseptic."

She had to laugh at his silly, exaggerated shudder. As ridiculous as he was acting, though, his eyes never left her face. Searching, roaming around…Daisy tried not to feel uncomfortable, wondering what he was thinking—what he saw.

"Your eyes are very green, aren't they?" Luca said suddenly. He scooted his chair closer with a loud scrape across the stones of the sidewalk. "They were so bloodshot last week, I thought they were blue."

He was very close to her face, so close Daisy could feel his warm breath on her cheek. She studied the ancient façade of the building across the street, and hoped she wasn't turning too red. That seemed unlikely. She turned red when she even *thought* about blushing.

When Luca didn't immediately say anything else, Daisy darted a quick glance at his face. This close, his eyes looked like melted milk chocolate, and his smooth olive skin was impossibly touchable. She could see his dark whiskers coming in along his jaw, the kind of thing that felt rough on a woman's palm—or on her thigh.

Daisy forced her eyes away again.

If the dude's cheek looked like it felt that good, what would happen if she saw his chest? Or, even worse, Luca's stomach?

Daisy swallowed. Even in his perpetual khaki pants and button-down shirts, it was obvious he took care of himself. Without those modern trappings obscuring the view, she had no doubt he'd give the marble statues in the museums a run for their money.

Luca was rangy and tall, with broad shoulders and a taut belly. Hard arms. An ass that Did. Not. Quit. His scent wound around her, crisp and spicy. Daisy tried not to be too obvious about inhaling it, but seriously—was it fair for a guy to smell that good?

No, she decided, it was not. But Italy was a land of unholy temptations.

On the tail end of that thought, it became abruptly, eminently clear that Luca was dragging out his perusal of her irises for as long as he possibly could. Daisy knew they weren't *that* interesting.

And, honestly, once Scooter Ferguson had informed her that they looked "spooky" in the fifth grade, Daisy was a teensy bit sensitive about looking like a witch.

"Will you quit crowding me?" she laughed, pushing on Luca's chest. And, yeah—it was definitely as hard as it looked. "People are going to think you're trying to kiss me."

As soon as the words exited her lips, she wanted to yank them back again. Luca sat back and his face flipped through a cascade of expressions, none of them sticking around long enough to decipher. Before long, though, his easy, teasing grin was firmly back in place.

"Kissing? On the second date?" he sighed, acting all wounded. "I would never be so presumptuous."

Kissing on any date with Luca sounded like a fine idea to her, but now Daisy *knew* she was blushing. She felt that familiar heat bloom across her cheeks and neck almost instantly. It was so freaking frustrating, the way it flared up when she least wanted it to. So frustrating, in fact, that it took her a full minute to realize he'd said "date."

But that was insane. She and Luca weren't even in the same galaxy when it came to romance. Despite his casual compliments, he wouldn't ever want to date—or kiss—someone like her. Especially not after witnessing her retching up her stomach lining so recently.

She'd vowed not to ever think of that again, though.

Daisy opened her mouth to say, "Sorry," but she never got the chance.

Luca had ducked in again, lightning-fast, and set his hot, luscious lips against hers. And, *oh*—the man was a pro. The way he kissed her made it obvious that he loved it. That he reveled in it.

And it was equally clear that he especially liked kissing Daisy. Out here in the middle of the street, where anyone at all might walk by, he was happily making out with her like it was his favorite pastime. Luca's hands drifted up to cup her head, and a deep groan rumbled up the back of his throat.

Daisy was shocked, but she wasn't a moron. If the universe, in all its incomprehensible capriciousness, had seen fit to gift her with *this* little nugget of crazy, no way was she going to turn it down.

She clamped a hand around the back of Luca's neck, and kissed back.

THEY LINGERED FOR hours, laughing and kissing at the little metal table on the street. At last, however, the shop closed, the street emptied of pedestrians, and Luca offered to walk Daisy home.

He kissed her again on the sidewalk in front of Nonna's. When they eventually came up for air, Daisy spotted a brief flutter of white in the pensione's front window and knew his grandma had seen them.

"Shit. I think we're busted," Daisy murmured against Luca's lips.

He seemed reluctant to pull away. "Busted?"

"Nonna at the window," she warned, "Stage right."

Luca kissed his way to her ear. "So what?"

"Given what my last few weeks have been like, I'd prefer not to get poisoned by your grandma, if it's all the same to you."

"Are you kidding?" He pulled back and laughed at her. "Nonna won't poison you. If anything, she'll give you an award for service to the family."

AND LUCA WAS right. For the next several days, Signora Magnani vacillated between doting on Daisy and testing her. If she wasn't plying Daisy with coffee and fresh pastries at all hours of the day and night, she was feigning weak coughs to see if Daisy would get her some water.

On some afternoons, Nonna would sit down heavily in a chair in her kitchen, fanning her face while Daisy bellied up to the sink and tackled the lunch dishes.

Later, when dinner was safely in the oven, Nonna would make a miraculous recovery and dance Daisy and Giada around the room to old songs from the 1940s.

One day, when Daisy tried to give the woman a break from cooking by going out to eat at a bistro down the street, Signora Magnani grabbed her with two wrinkled hands—first by the arms, and then by the face.

She patted Daisy's cheeks. "You a good girl. You stay and eat with me tonight if you like." Her heavy accent added an extra *uh* to the end of some of her words, lulling Daisy into complacency.

Then she added, "We talk about my grandson. Luca—he like you,
I think."

Oh, Lord. Cupid had obviously entered the building. No one
but no one had ever tried to fix Daisy up with a family member
before. Daisy could feel herself turning fire engine red.

Nonna chuckled and patted her again. "I like-uh you, too," she
decreed.

Seven

Eighteen Months Ago

FOR YEARS, LUCA had gone over and over it with the women in his family. He still could not date the medical residents at the hospital, even if they were the only unrelated females he met on a daily basis.

For one thing, Luca had too much control over them for it to be at all appropriate. For another, the residents were so busy and tired all the time that dating them would be too much like taking advantage of drunk or unconscious women.

He flatly refused to date the nurses, either. None of them had yet managed to get past the awe factor that seemed to apply to him. They couldn't seem to see the man beneath the reputation. And Luca *was* just a man, with all the usual manly wants and needs.

He just needed to find a woman who could meet him at that level, and it was turning out to be a difficult proposition.

All of that, perhaps, explained why, when he met Daisy for the first time, Luca was entirely content to let her believe that he was some friendly neighborhood general practitioner. A family doctor, making the rounds of his grandmother's pensione like it was his regular job.

Even now, when Daisy was decidedly not his patient any longer, Luca neglected to correct her misassumption. All he wanted—all he'd ever wanted—was to be liked for who he was. And Daisy did.

She liked him a whole hell of a lot, actually. It was more addictive than an entire pharmacy of opiates. It was…transformative. In barely any time at all, he'd turned into a real, live human and she'd become his torrid summer obsession.

There was Daisy's beauty, to begin with—her head full of caramel-colored curls, some of them tipped with pale blond. Her impossibly creamy skin, that flushed for any and all reasons. The spray of freckles across her nose, her ripe, full lips, her light green eyes—all of it called to Luca. Sang to him. Ensorcelled him.

Luca was fond of Daisy's height, and how he barely had to dip his head when he wanted to reach her mouth with his. He liked her long, lean build, the way she always held herself just a little bit in reserve, and her quiet, sultry voice.

He loved the way Daisy talked and dressed tough, the contrast with all that sweetly feminine allure setting up a drumbeat in his blood that could only be quelled by holding her. Kissing her. Touching her.

Luca had been felled by Daisy like lightning felled an oak, and his condition was apparently obvious to everyone in his family.

Hence, the rampant match-making.

It wasn't bad enough, apparently, that he was making every excuse he could to spend time with her. No, Nonna, Mamma, and his sister simply had to get in on the action. And those were only the three he was sure were meddling.

Luca had his suspicions about Paolo and Papa, too. He simply hadn't managed to confirm things yet.

Even so, the combined efforts of *la famiglia* meant that Luca got to devote many of his non-working hours to playing tourist with his beautiful American.

Today, it was sunny and warm, so he'd brought her to the *Giardino Bardini* to see the pretty views of Florence.

Daisy had brought along a serious-looking camera, and as they wandered the paths, she busily snapped pictures of small details like fallen leaves and the corners of the low stone walls. She took photos of the vista, too, and occasionally of him.

"Are these pictures just for you?" Luca wondered. "Or do you need them for a school project?"

"Most of them are for me," Daisy admitted. "But we're doing some light studies in class next week, and I can use all those shadows by the wall for that."

Luca nodded as if he understood, but he didn't really know much about what went into taking a good photo. He could use the camera on his phone, that was about it. So he did.

"Smile," he told her, hoping to catch an unguarded expression to look at later.

The light was behind her, though, and Daisy's face came out shadowed. It was oddly appropriate, given the fact that Luca had been remarkably unsuccessful in finding out much about her life outside of Italy so far.

"What will you do after this?" he inquired.

"You mean tonight? Probably just lay around reading. What about you?"

"Probably, I will lay around watching you read," he joked. But he didn't want to let her divert him again. "That wasn't what I meant, though. I meant, what will you do when your classes in *Firenze* are over?"

Daisy turned and looked down the stairs that bisected the steep tiered hillside. Below them, the Arno was a lazy, glittering gray ribbon peeking through the buildings along its shore.

"I'll go back to New York," she shrugged, as if there was nothing else to consider. "I have some stuff I'll have to take care of. But this break has been good, you know? It's given me a chance to consider my options."

"Do you…" Luca was dying to ask, but suddenly afraid of what she might say.

She sidled closer, setting her camera on a bench and wrapping her arms loosely around his waist. "Do I what?"

Luca kissed those delectable lips, tasting on them the coffee she'd just had. "Is there someone waiting for you back at home? Someone who misses you in New York?"

Just like that, Daisy's content expression shuttered tight. "No. No one misses me," she scoffed.

"Are you sure? Manhattan's a big place. Someone in that city must wish you'd come back soon."

"Well…there is somebody," Daisy admitted. "His name is Jerome."

He knew it. Luca had *known* he couldn't be so lucky as to find a woman like her and have her be free for the taking.

"Ah," he said weakly. "How fortunate for you."

"He's my pet turtle."

"I'm sorry. You said he's a—"

She pulled her phone from her pocket and checked it quickly. "*Tartaruga?*" she sounded out. "He's this big." She cupped her hands into the shape of a small round ball of dough. "And greenish-brown. I'm pretty sure he's crazy about me, so it stands to reason that he misses me right now."

Luca's relief was overcome only by his fascination. Trust Daisy to go in a different direction than the usual dog or cat. "How can you tell?"

"Well, my neighbor who's watching him sent me a proof-of-life video last week. I think Jerome looks pretty sad in it."

"Do you still have it? May I see?"

Daisy motioned him over to sit next to her, then called up a short, 30-second video. In the glare of the sun, Luca could barely make out the small, dark, slow-moving blob at the bottom of some kind of aquarium. There was a branch in the background, and maybe some lettuce in there with it.

And that was about the extent of what he could make out. "What do you think?" Daisy asked. "He looks unhappy, doesn't he?"

"Oh, definitely." Luca set her cell aside and threaded his fingers into her soft, thick coils of hair. Her pulled Daisy's face close, tested the seam of her lips with his tongue, and groaned when she granted him entry.

Her taste exploded on his tongue—strong coffee and cocoa from their snack earlier, plus something tantalizing that was wholly Daisy. He wanted to taste her everywhere. Luca's dearest wish was to clear the premises of everyone else, so he could lay this woman out on the grass and devour her.

"How important is this reading you're planning on doing later?" he asked between kisses.

"So very unimportant," came her breathless response.

"Then forget about it. Come home with me instead."

"I can't stay late. I have class in the morning."

"It's okay. If we go now, we'll have plenty of time." There would never be enough time for him to get his fill of her, but Luca would have to make do with what he had. And what he had was this moment, right now.

She pressed her lips against his, lingering there like a promise. Like a poem. "Can we come back here again?"

"Any time you want."

"And will you make me that creamy pasta dish for dinner—the one with the peas and the prosciutto in it?"

"It's pancetta—and yes, I will. On one condition." Luca pressed his cheek against her head. Daisy's hair was warm from the sun.

"What's that?"

"Work up a healthy appetite with me first."

"You drive a hard bargain." Daisy bent over to pack her camera into the bag near her feet, so he pinched her ass as a little incentive. "Hey!"

Luca winked at her and grinned. There was more where that came from, and she knew it.

She narrowed her eyes like she was mad, but she was already up and moving, her feet carrying her rapidly toward the exit, and that was good enough for him.

HE MADE IT home in record time. No sooner had Luca parked his car and stumbled up the two winding flights of stairs to his flat, then Daisy was stripped to the skin and spread across his dove-gray sheets like a decadent pagan offering.

He was a lucky, lucky man and Luca was not one to take that sort of thing for granted. He gripped Daisy's knees and spread them wider, so he could enjoy the spectacular view while he shed his own clothes, and then Luca was on his knees at the foot of the bed, kissing his way toward the very heart of her.

Daisy's body stretched taut when he ran his tongue firmly up her soft pink labia. She didn't make a sound, though, and Luca wondered if he'd ever get used to that. The way she clamped her jaws together and held in every moan fired all his competitive instincts.

He thought he might try anything in an effort to get her to let loose one scream of his name. Just one, loud and heartfelt, to wake the neighbors.

FOR THE NEXT hour, Luca did his level best to reach that goal. He got a few gasps and one tiny murmur that could have been a whimper. It seemed like progress, and since Daisy ended up boneless and blissful across his chest—much like Luca himself was—he was willing to concede the field for the moment.

The setting sun made orange streaks across his ceiling. He watched them and wondered what kind of place she lived in at home.

"What are some of the things you'll have to do when you get home?" Luca asked.

"Mmm," Daisy murmured sleepily. "Find a new place to live, for one."

"They kick you out of the dorms when you graduate, right?" Daisy's languid body abruptly went stiff. He tried to understand where he'd gone wrong. "Or don't you live on campus anymore?"

Luca had liked college fine, especially with friends like Red and Tate to share it with, but he couldn't imagine living in campus housing at her age. Perhaps NYU had different facilities than Columbia had, though.

"Uh, no," she said eventually. "No, I have my own place. But my lease is almost up, so…I need to find a new one."

Luca was swimming in murky water, he could tell, but he didn't want to give up now. He switched gears slightly, and hoped he'd have better luck. "Will it be hard to find work as a photographer, do you think?"

"I…" Daisy may as well have been a marble statue beside him. She wouldn't quite meet his eye. "Actually, I'm in graphic design. I thought…" She hesitated, a vulnerable expression wreathing her features that knifed into his chest.

He stroked his palm down her arm. "What?"

"I thought maybe I would try to start my own business. See if I could hack it that way."

"You should. I'm sure you will do very well," Luca assured her. "You have such a unique way of seeing the world. Many people will appreciate that vision."

Daisy cocked her head and her eyes got suspiciously watery. "Thank you, Luca. That was really nice. No one's ever told me something like that before."

At least he had that going for him. He said, "Then shame on them. Maybe New York doesn't deserve you after all. Maybe Italy is the place for you."

Daisy settled back on her side, her head pillowed on her arm while she gazed thoughtfully at him. "Maybe."

Her irises were really the most extraordinary green. Light in the centers, and rimmed with darker, pine-green flecks. Luca stared into them and thought he could drown if he wasn't careful.

He must have dozed off.

He slept until Daisy's stomach rumbled so loud that it woke him again. Luca groaned and threw an arm over his face, feeling guilty for his bad manners.

"I'm sorry," he told her.

Daisy propped herself on an elbow, then leaned down to take his nipple between her teeth. She tugged, just a little. Luca growled in warning, but Daisy simply smiled angelically and swirled her tongue around his aureole.

"And I'm hungry," she announced.

"Yes, I heard."

"The pigeons in Rome probably heard. Don't you think you should feed me now?"

Sometimes, it was too easy. Behind his arm, Luca grinned. "I thought I just did that."

"You promised me pasta, not salami," she fired back.

Luca chuckled, "Ah well. Sometimes you have to be happy with what's in season." He rolled over and buried his face in his pillow, so she wouldn't see him laughing.

Daisy must have seen his shoulders shaking, though. She smacked him hard on the ass and barked, "Get up and make me some dinner, woman!"

Luca dove sideways, pinning Daisy beneath him while she squawked and wriggled. "*Woman*, did you say?" Luca ground his hips against her, lest there be any doubt about the appendage that made him decidedly all male.

"Yup," she giggled. "And don't forget your apron."

Dinner would have to wait.

Eight

*E*NTRANCING. LAST NIGHT, Daisy had looked positively entrancing. Well, except for her expression, which had been one breath away from outright panic. Something Luca still could not understand, given the fact that she was the one who'd left Italy so precipitously.

As far as Luca knew, he'd done nothing whatsoever to instigate such alarm. He'd done nothing but fall in love with her, and he didn't think he was such a poor catch that *that* would freak Daisy out.

Not unless she was hiding something important. Her behavior last night suggested she might be.

Luca flipped through the potential options in his mind. A violent husband she'd neglected to mention. A criminal past. A criminal *present*. A terminal disease…

Dio. He really hoped it wasn't a fatal disease.

Anyway, every inch of Daisy—from her hair to her toes and back again—had been even more gorgeous than he'd remembered. Which should have been unlikely, given how much Luca had built her up in his mind.

She kissed the same, too. Wild and desperate and hungry for more. He couldn't say how far he might have taken things if Red hadn't arrived to give him the "Down, boy."

His friend would only have done that if the happy reunion he'd engineered was drawing unwelcome or inconvenient attention. So Luca had capitulated and arranged this morning's meeting with Daisy.

He sat at a sunny table in the center of the bistro Daisy had told him about, nursing a weak cup of lukewarm cappuccino and wondering if she'd really come. Maybe she was delayed at the market with her husband and kids. Maybe she'd succumbed to her disease overnight, and Luca would not only not see her this morning, he'd never see her face again.

HE WAS TOO dramatic, of course. Daisy rushed in five minutes later, looking like she'd spent half the morning trying to cover up the fact that she hadn't slept a wink.

"Sorry I'm late," she said, nodding when the waitress bustled over and offered her coffee. "I couldn't get a cab."

Luca checked his watch. "Don't worry. It's only 1:15. I was just early, that's all."

She arched a brow at that. "Early? Have you ever been early before in your life?"

"Ah…no, I don't believe so. I guess I really wanted to see you." He had.

Luca had been up early, showered and dressed and ready to go, far ahead of the appointed time. He'd forced himself to wait around at the hotel as long as he could before giving up and walking over at 12:30. Luckily, they'd seated him right away, and let him nurse his coffee while he waited impatiently to see if he'd get stood up.

"God only knows why," Daisy muttered.

"You should know why."

"Listen, Luca. I told you last night. You don't have all the information. You might want to dial this happy reunion act back a bit, until you do."

"Okay, fine." Luca sat back and eyed her. "So tell me. What don't I know?"

Daisy shook her head. The tiny silver hoops in her ears caught the light. "I wouldn't even know where to begin. Have you seen our waitress? I'm starving."

"She's heading over now. Look," Luca said, pointing. "As far as where to start, why don't you begin with what happened to you when you left Italy."

"I came back to New York." And dropped out of sight.

Daisy paused her story while they placed their orders. Once the waitress disappeared again, Luca prodded her, "Did you graduate? Start your own shop, like you wanted to?"

She sighed. "Luca, I wasn't a student. I don't know why you thought I was. I was in Florence as an adjunct professor, *teaching* photography, not studying it. I was supposed to be there to spend time with my boyfriend, but we broke up before the semester even started. He worked for NYU, too. He was an English professor, but he got fired."

It was more background than he'd ever been able to pull from Daisy before, and Luca was fascinated. "But you must have known I was mistaken about your role there. Why didn't you correct me?"

Daisy blew out a long breath. "Because it was great to not have to be *me* for once." If anyone could understand *that* sentiment, it was him. "But it was a fantasy, Luca. It wasn't supposed to be real."

"It felt real to me," he told her, and even though she didn't reply, he knew in his bones it had been real for her, too. Daisy didn't have that kind of fakery in her.

He had the sense that he was pushing too far on that front, however. Luca tried a different angle. "How is your shop? Are you doing well?"

"No, I had to close it sixth months later. I ended up in Boston for a while after that."

Their food arrived, and they took a few minutes to taste their dishes, request various condiments, and order more coffee.

"So, you were in Boston," he said finally. "No wonder I couldn't find you."

"I have a friend from college who works for a contemporary art museum there. After I had to close up my shop, She hooked me up with a job doing the layouts for all the museum's pamphlets and publications and stuff."

"That sounds like a good fit." Daisy's expression said otherwise, though, so he asked, "Was it okay?"

"It wasn't bad."

Madonna, it was like pulling teeth trying to get her to talk more. "Why did you leave?"

Daisy toyed with her coffee mug. "Well, my friend's mother-in-law was in town at the time, and after a while…it got to be a bit much."

"She was unkind to you?"

Daisy laughed. "No, much worse than that." When Luca raised his eyebrows, prompting her to explain, she told him, "Her name is *Violet*."

He paused, glancing upward for a beat or two while he tried to unravel what she meant. Finally, he had to admit, "I'm sorry. I don't follow."

"Did I forget to mention that my friend is named Poppy?"

"You did. Yes."

"And don't you think three flowers is too many for one social group? Because I do. I think three women with flower names is too much for one planet."

"Daisy. Poppy. Violet," Luca muttered to himself. "How remarkable."

"Obviously, I had to hit the bricks." He blinked at her. He kept getting hung up these bits of slang he didn't understand anymore, and it was frustrating as hell.

"*Leave*," she said, seeing the problem immediately. "I had to leave and come home," Daisy clarified. "As it happened, your buddy Red's job came at the perfect time."

Luca perked up. "He and Piper told me you helped with his marriage proposal. That was very nice of you."

"No biggie. I'm all about those happy endings." Daisy must have realized that she sounded like an illicit massage parlor ad—she went pale, then flushed a vivid fuchsia.

She recovered only a split second after that. Perhaps she thought that Luca wouldn't get the joke again. "Anyway, Red and Piper seem like they're crazy about each other. So, there's that."

Luca nodded happily. "Surprising, but true," he agreed. "They've been helping me figure out how to manage the move here. They're very cute together."

"The move." Daisy sat back with a thump. "So, you're staying? You're taking that job?"

Luca shrugged. Was she serious? "Of course. How could I turn Green down when he's offering so much? Besides, now that I know you're here…" He left the thought open-ended, just to see what Daisy would do.

She tensed all over, looking ready to bolt. Was the suggestion that he might still have feelings for her really so difficult for her to comprehend? Luca couldn't bring himself to worry too much, though. He was in her orbit. For now, it was enough.

"Anyway. Red's real estate agent already found me a place to live this morning," he told her. "The hardest thing is done." That wasn't true, given the panic etched into Daisy's face, but Luca wouldn't call her out on it. Once she'd had time to digest everything, she'd come around.

He hoped.

Eventually, she managed to force out a few words. "That's…so convenient. I'm not terribly surprised, though. If anyone knows how to get things done around here, it's Red MacLellan."

"So I'm learning."

She fidgeted with her fork. "Where is the apartment?"

"East 40s. Top edge of Murray Hill." Luca tapped his fingers on the table, thinking. "It's quite nice, but it's too big for me. I asked them to find something simpler, but I was overruled. It happens," Luca shrugged. "This one is close enough to the hospital, I suppose, and it can be ready for me to move in by the time I get back."

"You're going home?"

"Just for a couple weeks. I have to close up my flat and pack my things to ship over."

"Hm," Daisy murmured, nodding along. "So, the apartment here comes furnished?"

"No, no. It was empty and echoing like a tomb when we saw it. But Piper said she could arrange for some basics while I go tie the strings."

He'd obviously gotten the vernacular wrong. Daisy's mouth twitched and her brow crinkled adorably, and Luca tried to figure out where he'd gone awry.

After a moment, she solved the mystery for him. "Do you mean *tie up loose ends*?"

"Yes. Sorry." Luca tried to gauge her mood, but it was hard. Unreadable emotions were racing across Daisy's face like an old cartoon flipbook. He commented, "Apparently, Red was right—I have been gone too long. But I think once I am here and speaking English regularly, the memory will return."

"I'm sure it will. And you really don't have to worry. You already speak it better than half the people who were born here."

"Thank you."

They fell into silence, and it stretched awkwardly. Luca's knee bobbed under the table as he took a few half-hearted bites of his eggs. Before, their quiet times had never felt strange. Of course, that was probably because they'd been occupied by kissing.

"Anyway," he said again. "Piper has assured me that I will be in possession of a bed and sheets, towels and plates, and a comfortable sofa once I return."

In contrast to many people Luca knew, his friend's fiancée had proven herself charmingly practical and efficient. Piper appeared to be resourceful and utterly without pretension, and, if she did even half the things she'd claimed she would, Luca's transition to New York would proceed nearly seamlessly.

He was sure that Piper's capable demeanor made her natural beauty even more entrancing to Red. Much like Luca felt about Daisy.

His Daisy. Sitting across from him and fidgeting like a schoolkid.

She cleared her throat suddenly. "Well, if Piper is going to be decorating for you, maybe I can help." Luca grinned at the unexpected offer, and immediately Daisy looked like she wanted to stuff her words back in her mouth. "I just mean, I could take a few things off her plate. She's got her new series coming out, and they're planning the wedding and whatnot, so I probably have more free time. If you're cool with it, you could tell me what you like, and I could make sure Piper doesn't get you anything weird."

He'd met Piper several times in the last few days. As far as Luca could tell, she was the epitome of unfussy class and refinement, with just the right dash of style. What was more, if his friend Red was going to marry her, Luca was willing to bet she didn't have a weird bone in her body.

But if Piper's involvement with his apartment meant that Daisy wanted in on the action, that was fine with him. The two women could outfit his new home until Kingdom come, if it got Daisy invested in him once again.

Besides, the project gave Luca exactly the excuse he needed to extend his time with Daisy today. Another victory he hadn't seen coming.

He tried not to let his triumph show. "Excellent idea." He checked his watch, but for a change, he really had nowhere else to be. "Why don't we look at some stores now?"

Daisy clearly hadn't seen that salvo coming. "Now?" she squeaked.

"Right now."

She gripped her utensils and stared down at her plate, while Luca agonized over whether he'd pushed her too far. When she looked up, she was grim.

"Why did you let me think you were some little small-town doctor? Why would you hide who you really are from me?"

She'd handed him his answer only moments earlier. "For the same reason you let me think you were a grad student," he said. "It was a relief to step outside myself for a time. To just be me, without all the expectations and misconceptions that come with being Dr. Delledonna."

Daisy sat and studied him, as she decided whether to believe his words.

"I don't blame you for doing that, Daisy, because I understand how it feels. I forgive you for it. Can you forgive me?"

She swallowed and stared off in space. Eventually, she nodded. "Yeah. I can do that." A deep breath. An adjustment of the linen napkin in her lap. "Fair's fair."

"Will you help me with the apartment?"

"Yes. I can do that, too," she said.

Nine

DAISY SPENT THE rest of their brunch looking at the photos Luca had taken of his new apartment that morning, then coming up with a game plan for the remainder of the day. She researched home stores on her phone and worked with Luca to figure out his budget. From there, they came up with the most likely candidates to visit.

The project gave them something to focus on that wasn't *What Might Have Been*. And Daisy didn't have to feel guilty that she'd come here this afternoon intending to tell Luca she wished him well, but couldn't see him again.

Somehow, her intention to make a clean break once and for all had turned into her team-decorating his new apartment while he went home to Italy to pack up his life. She fully expected *that* to turn into some other excuse to spend time with him once he returned.

Knowing the sorry condition her willpower ended up in after a few minutes in the man's company, it was a pretty sure bet that Daisy would fall back into bed with Luca in short order.

Hadn't she found herself tucked in a bathroom and sucking face last night, when she'd totally meant to flee like her ass was on fire?

She was so, so screwed.

"I HAVE A question," Luca said, halfway through the second furniture store.

Daisy nodded absently, scanning the living room mock-ups for something that would fit with his style. Luca kept insisting he really didn't care what they picked for him as long as it was comfortable and functional, but in reality, he was expressing very definite ideas about what he liked—mainly through complaining about everything he hated.

So far, Daisy had determined that he preferred soft neutral colors and fabrics that felt soft, too. Velvet was in. Shiny leather was out. Gray and taupe and white were a go. Anything red was a definite *no way*.

"Daisy?" he prodded. She made a note on her phone and glanced up.

"Hmm?"

"Why were you so scared to see me last night?"

And just like that, the room bottomed out. She fumbled for some pat explanation that she could use—some easy thing that would make sense to this man. Something that didn't involve thirty years of confusion, shame, and humiliation.

"I wouldn't say I was scared," she stalled, but she'd never had a very good poker face.

Luca looked dubious, and rightly so.

"Okay, yeah, I flipped out. I'm sorry about that. I kind of panic under pressure."

"Lots of people do. The part I'm curious about is why you felt pressure. And panic. And fear. I don't remember doing anything that would cause you to feel that way. Am I wrong? Am I forgetting something important?"

The poor man genuinely seemed to believe that the problem could be him, and not her. It would be laughable, if it weren't so utterly outrageous.

"No, of course you didn't do anything wrong," Daisy groaned, then flopped onto the nearest couch, a purple brocade number that barely gave an inch when she sat down. "You—and your family—were wonderful to me. You should know that."

Luca perched next to her carefully and made a disgruntled face as he attempted to get comfortable. Daisy made a mental note—no brocade and no stiff cushions.

"Then why?"

"Luca…" He looked so hurt, though, and Daisy couldn't stand to let him think it might have been his fault.

She'd forgotten the way he managed to slip under her defenses so deftly. It was totally unnerving, and at the same time, such a relief that she didn't have to pretend all the time.

"Maybe…maybe I just wanted you to remember me the way I was in Italy. I don't want you to know New York Daisy. She's a total mess."

He eyed her up and down. "You are not a mess. You look the same. Better, even."

"On the inside, Luca. I'm a mess on the *inside*."

He sighed and leaned back, then immediately sat back up again. "This sofa—I do not like this sofa."

Daisy grabbed his hand and led him away. "You don't have to get that one. We'll find you a better one, I promise."

He cast one suspicious look over his shoulder, like he thought the couch might try to follow him, and then stopped her once more.

"Here's the flaw in your logic, *cara*. Unless something really terrible happened to you in the last twelve months, then this messy internal situation was a preexisting condition in Italy. It sounds like it was there—and like you were just *pretending* it wasn't."

"That's…yeah. That's accurate."

"And I liked you that way, don't you see? I liked you so much, just as you were."

"But you didn't know—"

"I don't know everything, it's true. In fact, I have the sense that there are many things I don't know. But I want to learn them. I always have. Please give me a chance."

"You think you want a chance. But you won't say that once you know who I really am."

"Are you secretly a horrible person who is mean to people's grandmothers and tortures small reptiles in her spare time?"

"No! Of course not!"

"Do you secretly hate art and music and beautiful scenery and making love?"

Daisy sighed and went weak in the knees. "No," she whispered.

"Were you lying about loving books?"

She shook her head.

"Did your mouth and your hands and your body lie to me when we were together? Tell me, Daisy. Was *that* all fake?"

"You know it wasn't. No one can fake having chemistry like that."

"Definitely not you, anyway. And not me, either."

Daisy huffed and looked around the store one last time. "Everything in here is too fussy for you. I think we'll have better luck at the chain store in Midtown."

Luca gestured for her to go ahead of him, politely took his leave of the saleslady who'd been trailing them around, and held the door wide for Daisy to exit. Out on the sidewalk, he edged around a pair of teens in headphones and hoodies and marched to the curb to hail a cab.

She'd never seen one pull over so fast. It was that face of his—he was universally beautiful, no matter what you were into.

In the back of the taxi, she tried to pick up the thread of their conversation. "So…about what you said."

Luca didn't waste a minute. "Daisy, I know enough real information about you to understand what I want. I can learn all the less-important details in time, but they won't matter in the face of what I do know—that I want another chance to be together. To prove to you that we can be good anywhere we go. In any country. In any year."

Daisy was flabbergasted by Luca's blind faith. "How can you be so sure?"

"I think…" He paused and looked down, then took her hand and held it tightly on his thigh. "I think I can be so sure because the way I feel about you is different from anything I've ever experienced before. It's more—" He waved his free hand around, searching for the adjective he wanted, but only came up with, "More. And it hasn't diminished, hasn't gone away in a year of total separation. That's very telling, I think."

"It sounds like you've thought about this a lot."

"Every day for twelve months, while I got more and more frustrated that I couldn't track you down."

"I'm sorry, Luca. I shouldn't have left you hanging."

"You had your reasons. And it's done now. We can't go back and change it, but we can go forward in a different way."

"Won't your family be angry? After the way I left?"

"My family, you may remember, did everything in their power to get us together. They were disappointed to see you go, and a little hurt that you did not keep in touch, but they will be overjoyed to know that you are here, where they cannot be, looking out for me."

"That's very generous of them."

"This surprises you?"

Daisy smiled. "Actually, not at all."

"Daisy, the bigger question is not what anyone else thinks. Do *you* want to see where this fire between us will go?"

Did she? "I'm not sure," she admitted.

"Okay. There is no rush. You decide when you are ready. I will go home and settle things there, and then I'll return, and we can take each day as it comes. I don't want to push you."

"I appreciate that."

"I hope you will find me completely irresistible, however. I hope that I will be very, very hard for you to resist. Impossible, even."

Daisy had to smile. Luca could do that with his hands tied behind his back. He kissed the back of her hand, grinned back at her, and turned to watch the streets slip by.

BACK AT HOME that night, her turtle Jerome was his usual cheerful self, and ecstatic to see her. Daisy flopped down next to his aquarium, and he immediately crept painstakingly over to the corner closest to her, then sat staring up at her.

He was ready to listen. He might also be hungry, or asleep with his eyes open. Sometimes it was tough to tell.

"Jerome, what am I going to do," Daisy sighed.

Sympathy was written all over his small, wrinkly face.

"I mean, I never expected to see Luca again. It was only supposed to be something short and sweet you know? Get in, have some fun to expunge Jason's memory, then get out again. No one falls for anyone, no one gets hurt, everyone moves on with their life."

Jerome bowed his head. He knew what that was like, all right. He was a real turtle of the world.

"Except…"

Her pet peered back up at her, sensing the coming plot twist like he always did.

"Now that Luca is here, it seems like I was wrong about everything. That's not so surprising, right? So why do I feel so blindsided?"

Jerome, of course, was a born therapist—it was probably one of the reasons they got along so well. He had a knack for sitting quietly and listening when Daisy needed it most, and he was great at letting her answer her own questions.

Especially the ones where he knew Daisy already had the solutions. Jerome was no dummy.

Daisy groaned and smacked her head. "*Crap.* I've been kidding myself, haven't I? I'm so dumb." She'd never been the kind of person who could sleep with a guy and not feel anything for them. Daisy had fallen for all kinds of lousy romantic candidates that way.

Sweet-talk Daisy into the sack, Men. You'll get more than you bargained for.

But Luca wasn't like that. He was obviously a better prospect than Daisy could ever have guessed. A man with a terrific job that made the world a better place. A guy with a close, loving family and movie-star good looks—not to mention his sex-god skills in the bedroom.

By all rights, Daisy should have been terrified of the ruin he could wreak on her patchwork heart. She'd been blind, though. She'd told herself she was fine.

Now, Daisy had her doubts. Why else would she have lied to Luca about something as unimportant as what her job in Florence really was? Why else ghost the man, when he'd been nothing but kind to her?

Beside her, Jerome dropped his head and lurched a few inches away, turning his back in exasperation while Daisy came to her final, inevitable question: why pretend like she didn't still love Luca like crazy?

It looked like she'd moved on from him about as well as an office building downtown could change streets. "Jerome," Daisy whispered, "He came looking for me. He says he never stopped trying to find me. Who does that?"

Her turtle pawed at the edge of his tiny pool with his little clawed flipper-foot, then stared over his shoulder at her.

Daisy frowned. "I know. A man who cares does those things." She swiped at her cheeks and discovered that they were wet. "He said he wants another chance, Buddy."

Shoot. Now she was a mess.

"Well?" Daisy demanded. "What do I do? Do I give it to him?"

Jerome yawned and crawled away to hide under his big branch. It was his way of telling her that he was officially over her stupid questions. Daisy was going to have to figure out her love life for herself.

Dang it.

Ten

Twelve Months Ago

DAISY NURSED HER sweating can of *limonata* in the warm kitchen, and watched Signora Magnani making pasta for her weekly Sunday dinner with her children and grandchildren. The lady didn't have to invite her to hang out like this all the time, but Daisy was glad she did. She loved this part of the week.

Considering that she had come to Florence as a vengeful little *eff-you* to her ex Jason, Daisy was surprised by how much of her trip she'd managed to enjoy. As far as she knew, she'd never set foot outside of New York before this trip, but she'd liked every minute of it.

The architecture and the food, her bright, curious students, and most of all—the people. Next week, when she was back in New York and struggling through her regular reality, Daisy knew she would miss the way her landlady's easy affection, too-hard hugs, and crinkly smiles anchored her days.

She watched the woman kneading and rolling the dough on her sturdy kitchen table, and then, before she could think about whether it would be okay, she grabbed her camera out of the bag at her feet and began shooting pictures.

Daisy didn't trust her own memory much, since it couldn't even supply her with a single image of her real parents. For the next few days, she decided, she'd record all the little things she'd fallen in love with during her trip to be sure she remembered them.

Like the hands. So many capable, loving hands—of husbands and wives, aunts and nieces, cousins and friends. There was so much possibility in those hands, so much determination and hope.

Maybe once she was back to being the Daisy no one wanted, she could look at those pictures and remember that *belonging* was a real thing—a thing that happened to other people all the time, and which could happen to her at any moment.

It sounded so easy. So doable. If only that was true.

Next week, when Daisy had to say goodbye to all this, it was going to suck, big time. She had to remember that it was a fantasy, though. Luca, and all he promised, was a fantasy.

In real life, Daisy needed to go home, tie up all the unfinished business she'd left festering in her wake, and get on with living out the hand she'd been dealt.

She'd learned that morning that NYU wasn't renewing her contract for the second semester. It was a disappointment, but she'd suspected it was coming after the dustup surrounding Jason.

As Nonna worked and the camera shutter clicked away, Daisy decided it was definitely time to strike out on her own. She was tired of working for other people, letting them dictate her vision and her projects and the way she spent her days. If she set up a solo shop, she could rectify that.

It felt like the right step. Daisy had spent the last several months stepping out of her comfort zone and stretching her boundaries. She'd practiced how it felt to be different—bigger and stronger and more confident—and somehow Daisy would figure out how to carry that new skill home with her.

She lowered the camera from her face and met the kind, gentle eyes of Signora Magnani. She'd never known a grandmother of her own. That ship had sailed.

But maybe—maybe someday Daisy could be that person for someone else. If the time came, she'd want to be just like Nonna.

It was something nice to think about and kept her from dwelling too much on what was coming.

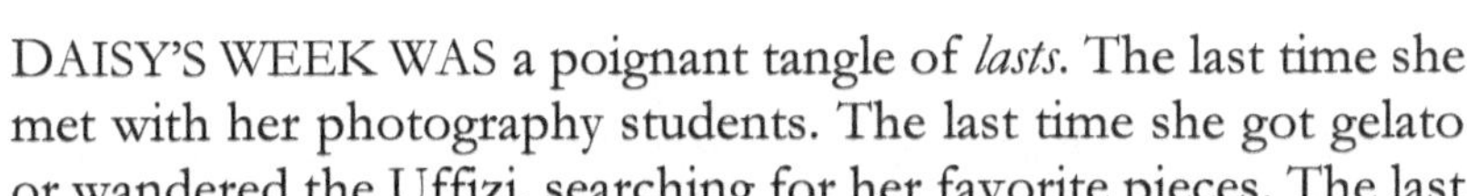

DAISY'S WEEK WAS a poignant tangle of *lasts*. The last time she met with her photography students. The last time she got gelato or wandered the Uffizi, searching for her favorite pieces. The last time Daisy cooked dinner and ate with Signora Magnani.

At least she was leaving Florence in December, instead of in those golden days of September or October. Italy felt different in the winter, reminiscent of New York in some ways. It would be easier for Daisy to make her exit.

However, before she could do that, she had one final task to accomplish. And so, here she was, making her way across town on an ATAF bus to Luca's apartment, while everything she'd brought from New York sat on the floor of her room in his grandmother's pensione.

Washed. Packed. Ready to go.

If only Daisy herself could be arranged so efficiently. Instead, her emotions were all over the place. She felt relieved and sad. Desperate and lonely. A little wild.

She felt guilty for not saying anything to Nonna or Luca or any of the others. Daisy felt even guiltier that she didn't plan to. How could she do it, otherwise?

If they knew when she was leaving, there would be such a scene—tears and hugs and promises to keep in touch. And, if there was one thing Daisy hated, it was an emotional goodbye.

She longed for the affirmation it would give her, but she hated how needy that made her feel. It was better to do it her way. Because if that family looked into Daisy's eyes, and cried with her, and vowed to stay friends—and then didn't mean it...

Daisy couldn't bear it.

Better to stop that crazy train in its tracks, before it could even leave the station. Luca's family would be fine, anyway. For one thing, they had each other. For another, they'd made it their whole lives thus far without knowing her from Adam and would likely never miss her.

Daisy would be fine, as well, because there really was no other option. She was always fine. She'd have her memories, too—those wouldn't go away just because she was back in New York.

Daisy could hold on to everything in her heart, a special miniseries outside the regular broadcast of her life. She could remember, and dream of a different existence. It was going to have to be enough.

The bus rumbled to a stop near the hospital where Luca worked. Daisy stared down at the book in her lap and tried to work on her equanimity. Tonight was going to be hard. She couldn't slip up for one minute. Luca was perceptive and he always saw things in her face that surprised her—things Daisy was sure were buried deep.

If she didn't perform her role flawlessly, he would know right away that something was up. So, Daisy had gone over and over it. What to do, what to say.

Hell, she'd even arranged for a cab to wait for her in the wee hours of the morning, so she could slip out while he slept and still get back to pick up her stuff in time to make her flight.

"Ten euros says my book is bigger than yours," a teasing voice said. It was Luca—as if Daisy had conjured him with her thoughts alone.

She looked up to find her handsome, dark-eyed doctor sitting across the aisle and smiling at her with a battered paperback already in his lap. She had no idea how he'd managed to board without her noticing him. Talk about being out to lunch.

Daisy arched a brow and smirked derisively. "That puny thing? I'll take that bet." And…look at her flirting like nothing was wrong. Where in the hell had she learned that from?

"Oh, no. Not this one. This is just my commuting book," he countered. "The one on my coffee table at home is what's going to win the bet for me." With his tan skin and thick wavy hair, Luca was already an unmitigated heartbreaker. The fact that he was an unabashed reader, too, seemed like overkill.

"Yeah, well—" she flipped to the back of her thick hardcover to check the page count. "It'd better have more than 726 pages if you expect to take my money." She'd need that many pages and more to make it through the ten-hour flight to JFK.

"Piece of cake," Luca said smugly. As always, his eyelashes looked impossibly long behind his glasses, the sooty fringes framing the sexiest pair of heavy-lidded bedroom eyes she'd ever seen.

After a few moments of riding in companionable silence, Daisy nodded at the book in his lap. "Do you have any trouble juggling the stories?"

"I'm sorry. I don't follow."

"I mean, is it difficult to switch back and forth between the two books?"

"Ah. No, not at all. Why? Can't you?"

"I suppose I can. I don't enjoy it, though. Usually one story ends up grabbing my attention more, and I have to put the other aside until I finish the good one."

"Which perhaps explains why you are lugging around a book the size of a paving stone."

"Pretty much."

"That's why I carry this one with me on the bus and leave the weighty one at home. Better for my shoulder and spares the other passenger's shins when my bag bumps against them."

"How very practical and thoughtful of you."

"I thought so."

Daisy scrambled for something else to say, to keep the conversation going in its current, unchallenging track. "I used to bring my e-reader to the gym and on the bus, but it died on me. I'm stuck with lugging bricks for now, I guess." Or until she got home and bought a new one, anyway. She ought to find a new job first, though.

The bus screeched to a halt, and Luca stood with a grin. "My stop."

Funny. "Mine, too," Daisy said, though of course he knew. She followed Luca down the stairs and they strolled along the street toward his house. For the first time she thought to wonder, "You know, your English really is perfect. Have you spent a lot of time in the U.S?"

It was a detail Daisy probably ought to have learned before she decided to skip out on their relationship like she was a teenager pulling a dine-and-dash.

"How kind of you to notice." Luca helped her over some uneven cobblestones with a gentle hand on her elbow, then explained, "And yes, I lived in New York for several years to attend college and medical school. I thought I'd told you."

That was a fascinating—and troubling—development. In his pressed slacks and pastel plaid dress shirt, Luca looked like he could have lived anywhere from Schenectady to Shanghai. Trust her to find the one Italian that knew *her* hometown.

"Small world," she mused. "I grew up there."

He brightened at that. "That is remarkable. Is that how you ended up at NYU?"

"Basically." Daisy left it at that. Come tomorrow, the less Luca knew about her, the better off they'd all be.

WHEN THEY GOT to his place, the first thing Luca did was point out the 1200-page medical encyclopedia sitting on his coffee table. Daisy sighed, dug through her purse, and tried to hand the man his money.

"Keep it," he laughed. "I cheated."

"Oh, no. You won it fair and square."

"You can make it up to me another way," Luca murmured, coming close and fondly running a hand over her hair. "But first, I'd like to have a quick shower, if you don't mind waiting. It's been a long day."

"Be my guest." Daisy sat at his kitchen bar while she waited, torturing herself with what she was about to do. She almost left, but the thought of going back to Manhattan without being with Luca one last time was too awful to contemplate.

He walked back into the room moments later, his hair still damp, black and shining like ink. Even in winter, his skin looked tanned, two or three shades darker than her own.

In a slight nod to modesty, Luca had donned a short pair of black boxer briefs, but they did nothing to obscure what he was packing underneath them. Moving around the kitchen, he was supremely unselfconscious, and as comfortable with his near-nudity as he would be in jeans and a sweater.

Luca was also hugely, proudly erect—not that he commented on it. Instead, he pulled a bottle of wine from the cabinet near his refrigerator.

"I picked this up yesterday. Would you like a glass?"

It was a pinot noir. Her favorite, and he knew it. Still, Daisy hesitated. A little wine might help her relax and enjoy herself, while not giving away her intentions. Too much, though, and she ran the risk of letting down her guard and confessing everything.

Once that happened, it was only a hop, skip, and a jump to begging him to let her stay. To giving up and letting Luca take care of her, instead of taking care of herself. Daisy could never afford to do that. Once he tired of her, she'd be worse off than ever.

She said, "Only a little," and forced a smile.

Luca winked and turned to pour, and Daisy admired his fine ass in those briefs without remorse. He slid her glass across the counter, took a sip of his, then stalked around the bar to stand behind her.

He set his hands beside Daisy, caging her in while he kissed the top of her shoulder, the side of her neck, the rim of her ear. His breath was warm and fast against her cheek.

"You smell so good," he murmured, then spun her stool around. Luca gripped Daisy's knees and pulled them wide, making space for himself between her legs. Her pleated wool skirt rode up high.

Luca kissed her softly, but she couldn't bear the tenderness. Not tonight. So Daisy licked and bit at his lips, and rubbed her thumbs across his stiff nipples the way he liked, until Luca gave up on gentleness and got hungry.

Desperate. Wild. Just like Daisy.

He gripped her skull in his hands, holding her in place so he could ravage every corner of her mouth. And then he clutched her hips so he could push his impressive length against her.

Daisy couldn't help herself, couldn't hold it in this time. She moaned into Luca's wicked mouth, and he broke off with a gasp, staring into her eyes. Then, he dropped his head back to stare at the ceiling, beseeching a higher power for deliverance from her.

"Oh, Daisy," he murmured, "You don't know what you do to me, *mia bella*."

He ran his hands up her thighs and his palms felt hot, even through her thick black tights. Luca's fingers reached the wide lace elastic at the top of her legs and hit the pale bare skin above. He stopped short. Tilted his head and looked down at his discovery.

He grasped her thighs tightly. Then Luca narrowed his eyes, pushed Daisy's skirt to her hips and ran the tips of his fingers along the damp panel of her panties. Even now, right on the edge of what was endurable, she wanted him.

He grunted and dove for her mouth again. Soon, Daisy was the one breaking off the kiss, to toss his words right back at him.

"Luca, you don't know what you do to me."

"I know what I want to do, my little bookworm. No doubt about it. Now lift up your lovely *culo* so I can get rid of this pretty scrap of lace."

"Not here," Daisy begged. She couldn't face him in the light. She needed the anonymity of his dark bedroom if she was going to keep her secret. "Let's go to your bed."

"As you wish." Luca scooped her up and hoisted her onto his shoulder, then prowled into his room and dropped her onto the mattress. Her skirt tangled around her waist and he eyed it with interest. "Off with those panties," he gestured. "But leave the stockings. Those I want to keep."

Daisy watched Luca's face as she peeled off her underwear, but his gaze was riveted to the white skin of her thighs, and the auburn hair between her legs. He readjusted himself in his boxers, and she had to swallow against the sudden rush of desire that shot through her.

He flipped her over, lifted her to her knees, and palmed her ass in one large hand. Daisy had never been so relieved as she was right then, when she realized she wouldn't have to face him while she silently said goodbye.

Eleven

Twelve Months Ago

WHEN LUCA RECEIVED the urgent summons from his *nonna*, he didn't think much of it. At the time, he was deep in conference with his trickiest patient, Andrea Vittini, going over an experimental therapy that Luca was eager to try in the man's fight against gastric cancer.

So far, Andrea hadn't responded well to any of the usual treatments, so when Luca had heard about the study going on in *Roma*, he'd followed up with the physician in charge right away. If Andrea and his wife agreed, they could get him enrolled in the study immediately—and Luca hoped it would be the thing that finally turned the tide for the young man.

Andrea was just getting started in life. He deserved a fighting chance, and Luca wanted to give it to him.

Besides, the call from Nonna could be about anything from a new guest giving her the evil eye to a leaking faucet in a bathroom. Neither particularly ranked as life-or-death situations.

So, Luca assured his grandmother he would come by as soon as he could and finished up that day's bevy of patient appointments. He headed up a departmental meeting the following morning, and then completed his rounds at the hospital. He advised one of the students who worked in his lab on which residency program might be the best fit for her.

Luca finally got to Nonna's pensione nearly thirty-six hours after her call. Once he arrived, he regretted his decision immensely.

He found Nonna sitting at her kitchen table—no big surprise there. A wrapped Christmas gift sat in front of her, which she was regarding somewhat forlornly. Nonna was none too pleased that he'd taken his own sweet time in getting to her.

"I'll be right back," Luca said, before she could lay into him. "I'm just going to run upstairs to Daisy's room and say hello, and then I'm all yours."

Nonna stared at him balefully. "Go right ahead."

Luca paused and squinted at her. There was a warning in those words. He went anyway.

He found Daisy's room on the third floor open, empty, and pristine. Not a single thing was in sight to indicate that she lived there. To show that she'd *ever* been there.

Luca pulled out his phone and texted her. *Where are you? Did you change rooms?*

His phone remained as eerily silent as Daisy's room, and it occurred to him that she hadn't responded to *any* of his recent texts. Luca scrolled through the thread and realized Daisy had gone dark the morning after their last date.

A chill stole through him. He spun and charged toward the stairs and when he burst back into Nonna's kitchen, she was ready for him.

Before he could say a word, his grandmother announced, "She left this on her bed." Then, she produced an envelope and added, "And this came this morning."

She handed Luca a letter from NYU's study abroad office there in *Firenze*. Luca slipped it out of its envelope and smoothed it out with shaking fingers. Enclosed was Nonna's final payment for the room and board of Daisy Montgomery.

If Signora Magnani had rooms available, they hoped to install a few new students or faculty members there at the start of the next semester. In *January*. When Luca had *assumed* Daisy would be leaving.

He looked up at her. "What does this mean?"

"I believe it means that Daisy's gone," she replied tartly.

His brain felt like toxic sludge. "Gone, as in, went to different lodgings?"

"What do you think?"

Luca thought he had a very, very bad feeling about this. The last time he'd seen her, Daisy'd had a fraught sort of edge to her.

He'd been anxious to bury himself to the hilt in her sweet warmth, his hunger for her barely held at bay, when he'd realized she might be fighting tears.

Luca had put on the brakes, carried her to his bedroom and stalled until he was sure she was okay again.

And Daisy had seemed absolutely fine after that, her usual passionate self—until Luca woke up the next morning and found himself alone, that was. He'd assumed she had an early class to prepare for. How to take photos of the rising sun, perhaps?

Daisy wouldn't have simply left without a word, would she? Luca was completely crazy about her, and he'd made sure she knew it. Daisy might not be as demonstrative or vocal about her feelings as he was, but Luca wasn't totally clueless or oblivious.

If she hadn't been head over heels too, he would've known it.

He would've.

Right?

Nonna snapped her fingers to get his attention. She gestured toward the gift. "What should I do about this?"

Luca forced down the bile trying to climb up his throat. "Who is it for?"

His grandmother pulled the small tag free of its ribbon and showed it to him. "It's addressed to all of us."

Nonna wasn't exaggerating. The tag said, "Signora Magnani and Family." Luca supposed that was meant to include him.

He flipped it over and read aloud, "*Dear Nonna, Teresa and Marco, Luca, Giada, and Paolo; Thank you for being so kind to me during my stay in Florence. I wish you all a Merry Christmas, and best of luck in the year to come. Fondly, Daisy.*"

Daisy had rolled Luca in with all the others, as if what they'd shared was no more important than cooking with Nonna or dress shopping with Giada. As if Luca was nothing more than a cog in the machine.

A gear, instead of a heart.

Luca pulled out a chair and sat with a sudden, uncoordinated thud. Filled with foreboding, he tipped his chin at the gaily-wrapped parcel. "What's in it?"

"I don't know. I haven't opened it. I was waiting for you."

He gestured. *Get on with it.*

Nonna removed the ribbon and paper painstakingly slowly—folding each beside her carefully before she lifted the lid of the box inside. A large frame encased a matted photograph of the whole family gathered around Nonna's dinner table. They were all laughing, happy to be together, in love with life and each other.

No one was taking the slightest notice of a beautiful woman wielding a camera in their midst. Well, no one but Luca, anyway. His face was staring right at the camera, with a small, secret smile playing on his lips.

Nonna tapped his face under the glass. "You love her," she said.

Luca shook his head. Did he, though? Could he love a woman who had simply left, just like that? A woman who could vanish into the night, like a breath of fog coming off the Arno?

Nonna tutted sadly at him. "Oh, Luca. What did you do?"

Porca Guida. He had no idea.

Luca had taken more time away from work than he had in years, so he could spend it with Daisy. He'd brought her to interesting places all over the area. He'd cooked for her and worshipped her body the best way he knew how.

He'd tried like hell to crack the surface and get to know the intriguing woman beneath. Maybe…maybe *that* was the issue. Maybe Daisy didn't want to be known.

"Daisy is young," he told Nonna instead, though it occurred to Luca rather abruptly that he didn't actually know if that was true or not. She was wise in a way that made her seem ageless— both old and young at once. "And her life is in transition. She needs time to get on her feet and find her way in the world, before she should saddle herself with man troubles."

Time to graduate school and find a steady job. Time to spread her wings, and also to grow accustomed to the relentless demands and responsibilities of adulthood. After a few years of that, then maybe Daisy would understand what it meant to commit to another person long term.

What a joke. Luca was thinking of words like *long term*, and Daisy hadn't even thought of the word *goodbye*.

Nonna scowled darkly at him. "You know what real man troubles are? When a man decides what is best for you, without even asking you what you think about it."

She pushed to her feet and stomped off, leaving him alone with Daisy's parting gift staring up at him.

Luca was obviously a first-rate ass. No wonder Daisy had left him.

He picked up the frame and stared at it for a long time, trying to remember the exact moment Daisy had taken the shot. She'd joined them for many meals, and her camera was never far from her side. She'd fit in so easily. Like she belonged there.

Luca shot out of his seat and went to find his grandmother. He found her in her front parlor, rage-dusting some figurines on her mantle with a rag she'd procured from God knew where.

"Nonna, I don't understand. Are you mad at *me*?"

"*Sì!* I am," she spat, setting a small milkmaid down with a bit more force than was strictly necessary.

"Why?"

"You know, sometimes you fool me into thinking you understand things. It's that bedside manner of yours. Too charming to be useful outside the hospital."

Luca took a deep breath. "For the sake of efficiency, why don't you spell things out for me."

"Okay, Man-Boy, I will. Number one—did you even bother to tell Daisy how you felt about her?"

"Of course I did. I told her all the time."

"Fine, then. Number two—did it ever occur to you to *ask* her what she wanted to do after her trip was over? To find out whether she wanted to stay with you, or—I don't know—stay here in *Firenze*?"

"Well, no. Not yet, anyway. I'm just as blindsided as you are by her leaving early. I thought I had more time to deal with all that kind of stuff."

"You thought you *had more time*," she mimicked. "She was supposed to leave in a matter of weeks. What were you waiting for? The last minute? Or maybe divine intervention?"

"No, I wasn't. But I thought I'd bring it up closer to the end, certainly."

"Right. Because young people make such terrific decisions under pressure."

"Nonna!" Luca was not used to her acting like this anymore. His grandmother hadn't been this sarcastic since he, Paolo and Giada were idiot teenagers. Like magic, her tone was definitely making him feel like one now.

He tried for a calm, placating tone, himself. "I realize that you are probably feeling hurt and upset by this. But Daisy taking off without warning is not my fault."

"It is if you did not give her a reason to stay."

"How could I do that, if I didn't even know she was going to do this?"

Like a puppet whose strings had been cut, Nonna's fury drained out of her, and she sagged suddenly onto her sofa.

"Why, Luca? Why did she go away, like a ghost in the night? Was I mean to her by accident?"

"Never." He went to sit next to her, so he could pull her into his arms. "This doesn't make sense. It's not like Daisy to be cruel. I think…" He sighed, wishing he could will his brain into finding some kind of logic in all this. "I think there must be something that we don't know. Some secret that unlocks the riddle."

"Will you find it out?"

"I don't know. I can try."

Nonna dropped her head against his shoulder and let Luca rub her back for a minute or two, then pulled away, stood up, and clapped her hands together.

The time for sadness had clearly come to an end. His grandmother now bore all the hallmarks of a woman on a mission. *Madre di Dio.*

"What we need is a plan," she announced.

Luca frowned. *Uh-oh.* "What kind of plan?"

"A plan to find her, so you can fix this. Now, what do we know?"

"She…was a student in the NYU study abroad program here. Right? They paid for her room and board."

"Yes. Good boy. What else?"

Luca wracked his brain, trying to remember any relevant details Daisy might have mentioned in their time together. "I think…I think she said she lived in New York."

Nonna waited, staring him down like a drill sergeant, until at last Luca had to throw up his hands and shrug. Knowing Daisy liked to read did not help at the moment. Neither did knowing what she tasted like when she was about to come on his tongue.

"And we know her name," his grandmother announced. "Do you think it's a very common name in America?"

"I have no idea, Nonna."

"This is not very much information."

"Don't I know it."

"Good thing you're a smart boy. You can use what we have to find out more."

His grandmother looked very confident. But was Luca smart enough to get the job done?

Twelve

LUCA WRAPPED UP things at the hospital in Florence first, sitting through a two-hour excoriation by his administrator for giving them such short notice that he was leaving, and then standing by while his secretary printed out letter after letter to inform all his patients of his defection to America.

Luca signed each one personally, and then—for good measure—called Andrea Vittini and a few of the others to reassure them personally that they'd be well taken care of.

There was a little party at the nurse's station on the oncology wing, on the last day Luca did rounds. Someone had made and brought in a cake from home, and even Luca got a little choked up saying goodbye.

He might not have wanted to date the nurses, but they were fine individuals, nonetheless—competent and efficient, intelligent and deeply caring. He'd miss their added insights and immeasurable daily assistance.

The residents and students who helped run his lab took Luca out for lunch, and peppered him through the whole thing with questions about what New York City was like.

After that came a cocktail party at Dr. Cassata's home, with several of his fellow surgeons and oncologists. Francesca, as well as her cardiologist husband, had both had surgeries earlier that day—so the food was catered and somewhat lousy, and the wine was abundant.

His colleagues were curious. Luca stayed longer than he should have, telling them about Dr. Green and his research, about the Weill Cornell facilities, and what Luca thought he could accomplish there.

WHEN IT CAME time to pack up his apartment the following day, he was tired and thin-skinned. Emotional, too. He was ashamed to admit that he needed help to get the job done.

Still, like a child, he called his parents, and naturally they both came running. Luca suspected they would have seized on any excuse whatsoever to spend a few extra hours with him. Maybe that was why he'd felt so overwhelmed, too—maybe he'd needed them there to reassure him that he wasn't completely crazy to do this.

At the end of the day, Luca had to concede that he felt better. Together, they'd made two towering piles of boxes. The larger one contained most of what he'd need right away in New York, and his parents promised to have it shipped to him in a couple of days.

The other pile would get stashed in his sister's basement, for delivery in a few more months if all went according to plan. The bulk of that included his summer clothing, non-essential books, and other odds and ends he'd acquired over the years. All of it could easily have gone into storage, but Giada had insisted on taking possession of it. He suspected it was his sister's way of being helpful and involved.

She'd also vowed to bring Daisy a wedding dress from Florence once Luca finally won her heart for good—an Italian gown for his American bride. Luca thought that was jumping the gun quite a bit, but Giada wouldn't be dissuaded from the idea.

In any case, his father ended up straining his back helping carry the boxes down Giada's narrow basement stairs. Luca had to park him in bed with some anti-inflammatories and a heating pad. They said goodbye like that, and something about bending over the mattress to hug his dad was eerily prescient.

What if one of his parents got sick while he was away? What if something bad happened to Paolo in his kitchen, or to Giada on her long drives to and from work?

What if the mystery man his sister had her eye on was no good for her? What if Paolo's wife had too much trouble getting pregnant?

Luca would not be here to help with any of it. He would miss big things and small ones once he left. The world would keep spinning, and his parents and siblings would get older. Luca himself would age, too.

There'd be weddings. Babies and christenings. Birthdays and holidays and perhaps even funerals. Luca might miss it all.

His throat got tight as the enormity of that finally sunk in.

Luca turned away from his father in that bed, and came face-to-face with his mother, standing nearby. As Mamma often did, she instantly read on his face everything Luca was feeling.

"You'll regret it for the rest of your life if you don't go," she said firmly. "If you don't try, you will never forgive yourself."

True. So true. "But can you forgive me?"

"There is nothing to forgive. Go and get your love, and don't worry about the rest."

Luca nodded, bent to kiss his father one more time, and then left for Nonna's pensione.

THEY WERE GATHERING at his grandmother's for one final farewell, before Luca boarded the redeye that would carry him back to New York overnight.

His father had to stay home in bed. His mother was running late, though, and Luca needed to get going in only two more hours.

"I don't like this," Paolo said, distracting him. "Packing up your entire life for some woman in another country is a bad idea."

"He's not moving for the woman. He's moving for the job," Giada said beside him at the kitchen table. "Daisy is simply a bonus."

Paolo fired back, "That explains why you're still single. Unreliability is not a bonus."

Now Nonna pitched in, whacking Paolo on the arm and scolding, "Your sister is still single because she's working so hard. Once she takes over from your Papa at the firm, her life will settle down again. Then she can find a man."

Giada had a glint in her eye that might've concerned Luca if he wasn't so busy dwelling on his own problems. "Or, maybe I'll take on a partner. Maybe I'll just marry *him*," she said defiantly.

Paolo snorted, but Nonna's gaze grew sharper. "You have someone in mind already?

"Maybe."

"Then bring him here."

Luca's brother wanted no part of his sister's marital prospects, however. He said, "Luca, think of your patients. What will happen to them without you?"

"They will be taken care of. I nominated Dr. Cassata to take my place as department head. Once she's confirmed, she will hire my replacement and transition my patients to the other doctors."

"But what if everything goes wrong?" Paolo demanded. "What if Daisy hates you, and you hate New York, and you want to come home? You won't have a job or a place to live anymore."

Luca already knew he enjoyed living in Manhattan. He was already excited about what he and Dr. Green might accomplish by conducting their research in tandem. The only wild card was Daisy, and that was hardly a surprise to him.

He shrugged. "I don't expect that to happen, and even if it does, it won't be for a long while. We'll cross that bridge when we come to it. There are other hospitals. Other apartments."

His sister pouted. "You can always live with me, but I'm going to miss you, Luca. It won't be the same here without you."

"I'll miss you, too. But I'll come visit. I promise."

Nonna was firm on her own requirement, "You bring Daisy when you come back. She needs us almost as much as you need her."

"Nonna, I can't promise that, yet. But I'll do my best. I'll try." Luca checked his watch again. "Where's Mamma? I hope she remembers that I have to check in earlier for an international flight."

Nonna clicked her tongue and got up to check the *bracciole* in her oven. "She'll be here soon. Don't worry. There's always traffic this time of night." To Luca's brother, she added, "Paolo I think this is ready. Will you pull it out and begin slicing it? We can start eating while we wait for your mother, so Luca won't be late."

While the two of them busied themselves with the food, Luca leaned over and whispered to his sister, "Who's this *stronzo* you're planning to set a trap for?"

Giada laughed at him. "You idiot. Do you even know how many things are wrong with what you just said?"

"Look, I only have a couple of hours, and I haven't even eaten yet. If I need to kill or maim someone, I need time to plan."

"Simmer down, Doc. It's early, yet. I don't even know if he likes me yet."

"How could he not?"

"I could say the same for you, Mr. *I Won't Promise To Bring Daisy.*"

She had him there. "Giada, you're my sister," Luca said, ruffling her hair. "You have to say that. You think everything I do is great."

Giada batted him away and retorted sourly, "Not everything, you caveman. And if you think like that with Daisy, you are not only going to fail, you're going to fail spectacularly."

Such ominous words. They followed Luca for the rest of the evening at Nonna's, to the airport, and onto his redeye flight to LaGuardia.

Would he fail? Luca couldn't say. And he didn't like the suspicion he had, that the outcome of this mission of his was not in his control.

BACK WHEN HE'D been in undergraduate school in America, Luca and his roommates had often bandied around a tired, worn-out phrase: *All's fair in love and war.*

But really, Luca had to wonder how fair it was to lump love in with war like that. Love, after all, was a healing, a genesis, a creation. And war was just destruction, plain and simple.

What was more, was it really true that anything was allowable when it came to love? Because Luca was absolutely certain that cheating wasn't fair.

Neither was lying.

For example, if one was, say, a professor of photography, teaching classes at a prestigious university abroad…one probably shouldn't pretend to be a student. Not if you were actually in love like you claimed.

Likewise, if you were an internationally-known expert in a rare form of stomach cancer, perhaps it was not strictly ethical to act like you were a small-time family doctor, just because you thought it appealed to a certain American young lady.

In his defense, Luca, too, had been in love.

He supposed that made him and Daisy even. But here and now, twelve months later and a thousand years smarter, he had to wonder whether anything about his passionate, summer-long affair with Daisy Montgomery had been real, or true, or honest.

They'd both lied, and they'd both entered into their relationship with the knowledge that it had an expiration date.

Except, during all this time that Luca couldn't get Daisy out of his head, he'd forced himself to acknowledge the one inextricable truth: beneath all the things that had been fake, there had been something real and rare between them.

It was why he was heading toward a new life in New York, ready to make a fool out of himself for a woman who was now nearly unrecognizable to him. She was not his Daisy, and yet she was.

Madonna, he was predictable. Luca had been a sucker for an enigma from the moment he was born. Luckily, it so happened that he was also a genius at solving riddles.

Luca would live through this.

No. His spine snapped straight. Simply living through the coming months was not enough. Luca had old and new patients to assist, innocent victims of the vagaries of fate, who were counting on him to help them live. He had an evil scourge of a disease to find a cure for.

He had an adopted city to become reacquainted with and old friends to enjoy.

But most of all, Luca had an incomparable woman to woo. Somehow, he had to convince Daisy that they were meant to be together, and he suspected it would not be an easy task.

Luca had to be better now than he ever had before. He had to be *il migliore*. The best.

Thirteen

DAISY WAS COMPLETELY stymied when Luca texted her his flight information a couple of days before he was due to return from Italy. Inherent in the message was the assumption that she'd want to know—like she was already his main squeeze again.

It reeked of serious relationship territory.

And then a day later, she received an email from Red, forwarding her the details for the car that was scheduled to pick up Luca from the airport. Again, the presumption was that Daisy was expected to *do* something with the information.

But was she?

Was everyone in their cozy little clique expecting her to simply don her girlfriend cape and get on the party bus? Daisy didn't know how she felt about that. She'd never been much of a joiner.

The sad and lonely half of her—the part that was starved for affection and the kind of love that other people seemed to trip over without even trying—wanted Luca in her life like it wanted to breathe. It wanted the coterie of people who came with him, too.

It was the suspicious, heavily guarded, *you-can't-hurt-me* half of Daisy that was throwing out flags, however. That part of her knew that a brief fling did not a healthy relationship make, particularly when both parties had been playing less-than-transparent roles.

So, even if Luca was insisting that they had enough compatibility to build something real on, Daisy wasn't as sure. Sometimes, she was so happy to love and be loved that she ignored her instincts—ignored warning signs that other people didn't.

Daisy couldn't afford to be sloppy like that anymore. She had more than enough sorrows to cry herself to sleep with at night, without adding heartbreak to the mix, too.

She couldn't kid herself like she did when she left Florence. If Daisy hooked up with Luca once more—and if he got a whiff of how screwed-up she really was and decided to take off—she knew she wouldn't handle it well. Daisy's sad, pathetic excuse for a heart would probably close up shop and move to Jersey.

The question she now had to answer was clear. Was the lure of more time with Luca—more kisses, more sweet-talking, more filthy Italian growled in her ear while he rocked her world—enough to make the risk to her well-being worthwhile?

She *didn't know*. Frustratingly, Daisy was no closer to figuring out that calculus than she'd been when he left two weeks ago.

She'd started to think of her feelings as a hotbed of unrest, like one of those infamous, unpredictable cities you read about sometimes in the newspaper. One day it was only another quiet trip to the market—and the next, the mob was throwing bottle rockets and looting stores.

How could Luca want any part of a woman like that? Daisy couldn't fathom it, and it was exactly like a bull-headed man to turn a deaf ear when she tried to warn him.

Her therapist's thoughts on the subject were kind, but succinct. "Daisy, we can't live without love, even when it feels like it would be easier. We also can't make ourselves *not* love someone just because *that* seems easier. Love is messy and hard sometimes, but I promise that it's worth it, in the end."

While Daisy tried to figure herself out, she waffled about the airport issue for two days straight. First, she decided she would go, because there really was nothing more depressing than getting off a plane with no one to meet you. Besides, an airport pickup was no big whoop. Friends did it for each other all the time.

Then, she changed her mind and resolved not to rise to Luca and Red's bait. It wasn't like either of them had actually *asked* her to go pick Luca up—they'd only *assumed* she would. But Luca was a grown man, and he wasn't helpless. He could get home from LaGuardia his own damn self.

DAISY WENT. GOD damn it all, she went to the freaking airport like a trained seal, and she even tried to look pretty for it. Hell, she'd checked her phone to see if Luca's flight was delayed before she even got out of bed that morning.

She wasn't quite ballsy enough to call the car company and have them pick her up on their way, but Daisy did grab a cab to Queens in plenty of time to reach the airport before Luca landed.

As she stood there in baggage claim, waiting for the infernal man to make his way through customs, she felt like a royal idiot, though. Had it really been necessary to buy new lip gloss for this errand? Wasn't the one from the engagement party adequate?

Other people were holding signs. Daisy didn't have one. There was probably some kind of rule about that, though. Once you'd done the dirty with someone more than, say, ten or twenty times, they had to recognize you in public. *No need for a sign, peeps, I know how to make him meow.*

Daisy sighed. Luca was going to read so much into her presence here. He was probably going to act like a total pain in her ass about it, like it was precisely the confirmation he needed to assume they were a hot and heavy couple again. She shouldn't have come.

She glanced around at all those paper signs people were holding near the exit, but none had Luca's name on them. Shouldn't his driver be here by now, too? What if the person didn't show? What if Daisy was supposed to confirm with the company or something, and it was her fault Luca had no ride?

She sighed again, more loudly this time. She was being a spazz.

There was undoubtedly still time to take off, with Luca none the wiser. There was still time for her to save face, to act cool and dignified and not like a lovestruck puppy. There was…

There he was. Striding down the concourse like a god plunked down among mortals—staggeringly handsome, tall and confident and as graceful as a panther. And Luca had eyes only for her.

He blazed a path through the crowd right for Daisy, like a dark and dangerous heat-seeking missile. Before she could smile, or flee, or muster up some clever welcome-back banter, Luca dropped his bag, wrapped his arms around her waist, and lifted her high into the air. Then he spun her around and around until she was breathless and couldn't help but laugh.

No one had ever done that to her before, not even when she was a little girl. Daisy covered her embarrassment with her usual bluster. "What is this? A sappy rom-com movie?"

Luca grinned up into her face. "I'm so happy to see you, *cara*. I didn't know you'd be here." He set her down, and Daisy felt her face flame hot.

"Was I not supposed to come? You texted me the time, so I thought…"

"Of course, you were supposed to come. You just never said you would, that's all."

"That's because I didn't actually decide to until this morning."

Luca took her face in his hands and planted a big wet kiss on her. "Well, I am very glad that you did."

Daisy shrugged. "You're kind of forgetful sometimes. I wasn't sure you'd remember the way to your new apartment," she mumbled. "Since you only saw it the one time, right?"

Underneath his tortoiseshell glasses, Luca arched a dubious eyebrow at her. He was so adorably nerdy-hot, Daisy was about ready to give the other travelers another show.

He said, "I did have the address, Daisy."

"Well, I have the keys. So why don't we go get your bags, and then we can find that driver Red supposedly hired for you."

"I like it when you say *we*."

"Luca."

He rolled his eyes, but he took the hint. "Okay, okay," he groaned. "But I brought a lot of stuff. I think we'll need one of those metal carts."

"Alright, you get that and head over to your flight's carousel. I'll run outside and see if the car is waiting out there."

LUCA WAS LEANING on the big metal handle of his loaded baggage cart when Daisy came back in from searching outside. The poor guy looked exhausted.

"I'm sorry," she said. "I don't think they're out there. Let me see if I can find Red's email on my phone. There's probably a number we can call on there."

A light might as well have gone on over Luca's skull. He immediately groaned and smacked himself in the forehead. "*Porca miseria*," he swore. "I'm so stupid, Daisy. I was supposed to text them once I landed, but I totally forgot. *Mi dispiace*. I'm so sorry."

"It's all right. Can you still do it now, or did they leave?"

He fumbled his phone out of his jacket pocket, messed around on it for a bit, and then announced, "Ah. Success. The driver's name is Teddy. He said he's circling around, and he'll be here in five minutes."

Daisy was impressed. "That's not too bad. Do you want to sit down while we wait?"

"I'm afraid if I sit down, I might not get back up again. I could use some fresh air, though. Is it very cold outside, or can we wait there?"

Daisy grimaced. "It's pretty cold. But even worse is that you aren't going to find anything breathable out there. Through those doors, it's unmitigated cigarette smoke and bus exhaust."

Luca deflated. "Gross."

"Don't worry. You'll be home before you know it. Your place has a big fire escape you can go out on if you want."

Luca's wrinkled nose told her exactly how enticing he found that idea.

"Or, you could go to the park later, after you've had a chance to rest. It's supposed to warm up a little bit this afternoon, and you're not too far away."

That perked him up. "Do you want to go with me?" he asked hopefully.

"I'm sorry, I can't. I have a yoga class." Which Daisy had signed up for specifically, so she could chill the heck out after this morning's angst-fest.

"I didn't know you did yoga." The thought clearly appealed to him.

"As I've said, there's a lot about me that you don't know." Such as the fact that Daisy's therapist had been the one to suggest she try yoga in the first place, when Daisy went through a rough spell after her move back from Boston.

Or the fact that Daisy even had a therapist at all. Her name was Rita. Daisy had been seeing her for at least ten years.

Luca jumped suddenly and peered down at his phone. "*Bene.* Teddy has arrived. Shall we?"

IF IT HAD been a weekday, they might have spent a good chunk of the next hour in morning rush hour traffic. As it was, however, they made it to Murray Hill in half that time.

Once Teddy had delivered them into the capable hands of Luca's new doorman, ensuring that the man loaded all of the luggage onto his gleaming brass hotel cart to Teddy's satisfaction, he bid them farewell and sped off down Lexington Avenue toward his next assignment.

The doorman ushered Luca and Daisy into the elevator, then helped them unload everything into Luca's small entryway.

The entire time, Luca's twitchy little neighbor futzed around the outside of her own front door down the hall, keeping an eye on them. She poked at an arrangement of fake flowers on a console and cooed loudly to her fluffy white dog, while Daisy tried to ignore her existence.

Once Luca's door was safely shut behind them, Daisy told him, "In case it wasn't obvious, you have a very nosy neighbor."

"I'm sure that will be delightful," he commented drily.

"She's also a total racist."

"Yeah, that's not delightful at all. What makes you say that?"

"Only the fact that she kept calling me your maid, even though Piper and I both told her I'm your friend."

"You're more than a—"

A firm knock sounded right behind them. Luca narrowed his eyes at the door, then threw it open and glared at the interloper.

"Oh, hello there!" his neighbor chirped. "You sure are a delicious hunk of handsomeness." She held out a limp hand like she expected Luca to kiss it, then retracted it sourly when he simply stared at her. "Now that you're here, I wanted to come introduce myself. I'm Ms. Atwood. I live right down the hall."

She pointed, in case he hadn't noticed her hovering two minutes earlier.

"Dr. Luca Delledonna," he replied, giving her a brief, brisk nod. "How nice to meet you."

"Oh, you're foreign!" she trilled, like it was some delightful bonus.

Daisy rolled her eyes. "He's from Italy, remember? I'm sure we told you that. Like…a hundred times."

Ms. Atwood paused as if she'd caught a whiff of something distasteful, then continued on like Daisy wasn't even there. "I know you're getting settled right now, but if you have a minute later, I was hoping you could jot down the name of your cleaning service. My girl just up and stopped coming the other day, if you can believe that. They're always so unreliable."

"I'm sorry. I don't have a cleaning service at the moment."

"Well, obviously, *this* one is exceptionally rude." She tilted her head almost imperceptibly toward Daisy and widened her eyes. "I wouldn't use her either. But you know you can always ask the agency to switch them out for a different girl."

"I'm standing right here, I speak perfect English, and *I am not his maid*," Daisy complained.

Luca looked calmly into her eyes. "May I take this one?" he inquired.

Daisy swept her arm out. *By all means.*

"You've obviously made a mistake," Luca told Ms. Atwood. "As I said, I have no maid. I do, however, have an intelligent and beautiful fiancée that I'm wild about. I believe you've met her several times." He slung his long, strong arm around Daisy's shoulders and pulled her close. "Right, *cara*?"

While Daisy tried to formulate some kind of adequate response that didn't involve choking or sputtering, Luca chuckled warmly and kissed the top of her head.

Ms. Atwood's smile was a thin, brittle thing, and completely devoid of good humor. "How very exotic of you," she drawled. "My ex-husband was the same. He liked them brown, too."

Daisy probably had the palest skin out of all three of them, not that it mattered right then. At least Luca was getting a crash course in one of the things she'd wanted him to recognize, however.

He might not give two shits that they were different, but not everyone on the planet was quite as evolved. People could make life ugly if they wanted to. Daisy knew that for a fact.

Luca paused a long moment, and then he announced, crisp and clear and barely accented at all, "It's suddenly quite clear to me why your husband is now your ex. Now, if you'll excuse us, we have the twenty-first century to rejoin."

And then he slammed his door in the woman's shocked face.

Daisy felt like her face was burning from her hairline to her collarbones. Luca turned and placed a whisper-soft kiss on the tip of her nose.

"Welcome to the neighborhood," she murmured.

"It's safe to say that I despise that little *folletto* quite—" He waved his hand around like he did when he was trying to come up with a word. "—quite viscerally. Did I handle it properly, do you think? Should I have been angrier?"

Daisy shook her head. "It wouldn't have mattered, anyway. You can't reason with stupid." Luca looked supremely dissatisfied with that answer, so she tried to divert him. "What's a *folletto*? I don't know that word."

He dug his phone out of his pocket and checked his translation app. "It says, 'goblin.'"

Daisy laughed. "Okay, I'm totally going to use that one. Now, let's forget about Ms. Goblin. There'll be plenty more where she came from. Are you hungry?"

"No, *cara*. Don't worry. I ate something on the plane." Luca thought for a minute. "I'm not entirely sure what it was, but it was something."

"Then do you want me to show you what we did while you were gone? Or should I just take off for now?"

"No, stay. Show me what mischief you ladies got up to."

They left his baggage near the door, and Daisy led him into the center of his living room. "As you can see, Piper had painters come in to get rid of all that white primer. It looks warmer in here, now, right?"

Luca nodded, then wandered over to examine the digital thermostat on the wall. Soon, the heat kicked on and balmy air began wafting out of the vents. "Now it will feel warmer, too," he smiled.

Daisy pointed like a game show hostess. "We got you a very comfortable couch and a good TV, and plenty of lamps so you can read anywhere in the room."

"Very good." Luca trailed after her toward his galley kitchen, but his eyes were fixed on her ass, not on his new furnishings.

"Eyes up here, Chief," she barked.

Luca did not comply. Instead, he inquired, "Daisy, are those the tights?"

Fourteen

W HAT TIGHTS?"

"*The* tights, *cara.*"

For lack of a better option, Daisy lied through her teeth. "I don't know what you're talking about."

"That's a lie. You know exactly which tights I mean—the tights you wore the last time we were together. When we fucked so hard, the headboard knocking against the wall woke my neighbors."

"What!" After a morning of blushing roughly every fifteen minutes, Daisy knew she must be absolutely crimson by now. Her face felt like it was a thousand degrees, and not because Luca had turned up the thermostat.

More gently, he added, "I'm sorry. You don't remember the part where they teased me for days afterward, do you? You were gone by then. Not that I'd realized it. Not yet, anyway."

"Luca, I'm really sorry," Daisy muttered, feeling every inch like the worm she was.

"No, Daisy, I'm sorry. That was unkind of me. If I say I forgive you, I shouldn't keep bringing it up." He looked around the room a little abjectly, then gestured to the couch. "Should we sit down?"

"Sure."

He bounced a little in his seat. "This couch I like," he announced.

"I'm glad. We tried to find you a good one that wouldn't take forever to get delivered."

"Thank you."

Daisy shrugged. "I'm just glad it works."

Luca's eyes were soft as he studied her. "Daisy, will you tell me why you convinced yourself that we were such a bad pairing? Because I simply don't see it."

She knew it wasn't fair to expect Luca to read her mind. And she and Rita had talked over why it was also unfair to expect someone with a completely different background to interpret things the same way she did. So, Daisy bit the bullet and spelled it out for him.

"Well, as your neighbor so kindly pointed out, you are white and I am obviously…not."

He sat back. "Do you think so poorly of white men?"

"Luca, don't be dense. You know as well as I do that you shouldn't write off whole groups of people just because their skin is lighter or darker than yours. All I mean is that some people think we shouldn't date each other, and they could make our life difficult."

"I'm not one of those people, and until I met my new neighbor I didn't know any of those people, either. I don't care what random strangers think of me. Some people don't like me because I'm a man. Some people don't like me because I'm Italian." He shrugged rather eloquently. "Not my problem. Theirs. Now, what other reasons do you have?"

"Well, what about the fact that I grew up in a scruffy little apartment in Brooklyn and have had to claw my way to adulthood, and you're this sophisticated and accomplished doctor who has good things just drop into your lap all the time?"

"Other than you dropping into Nonna's pensione, I've worked very hard for the good things in my life. Thank you very much for glossing over that."

Daisy swallowed. The man just would not listen to reason. "Fine. How about me being raised by a self-absorbed single mother, and you coming from a big, happy, well-adjusted family? You have no hang-ups, Luca—no emotional baggage. I have, like, a whole matched set and then some."

Luca merely shook his head mildly. "Daisy, I think perhaps not having siblings of your own led you to some misconceptions about bigger families. Maybe you learned what you think you know from television? Or the movies?"

He didn't wait for her to reply. "The truth is, when you have that many people living together, people bicker. Everyone has different personalities, and sometimes people have bad days and foul moods and decide to be petty for no reason."

"I think you're just saying that to make me feel better."

"Oh, really? Because Nonna and Paolo fight all the time about how things should be cooked. You didn't get to meet Paolo's wife Renata, but she complains routinely that Nonna oversalts the food. And when Renata and Paolo drink too much wine at dinner, they start telling each other dirty jokes. They say it's to make each other laugh, but they're really trying to shock Nonna and scandalize Mamma."

Daisy scrunched up her face, trying to visualize a meal that different from the ones she'd been a part of. "Seriously?"

"*Sì.* And Mamma and Giada always argue about whether Giada is getting too skinny, and whether she's ever going to cut back on work long enough to get married and have babies."

"I never heard them say anything like that," she protested.

"Yes, well—everyone puts on their best face when they want to impress guests."

Daisy peered at him, trying to figure out Luca's weird quirk. She couldn't do it. "What's your thing? What do you do wrong on Sundays?"

"Me?" Luca looked comically affronted. "Nothing. I'm the youngest, so I'm basically the perfect child. Everyone adores me."

"Bullshit."

He chuckled. "Okay, well…occasionally Papa tells us about crazy medical stories he's read in the newspaper. You know the kind—things like tropical fruits that cure thyroid cancer if you rub the juice on your toes. Octopus serums curing dementia. That sort of thing."

Daisy waited for Luca to elaborate, but he didn't. She poked him in the arm. "*And?*"

"And, when I explain why it's ridiculous and flies in the face of all laws of nature and the basic functions and capabilities of the human body—"

"Because, *science*," Daisy interjected wryly.

"Right, and then they all say I'm a snob and mean, and don't understand or respect holistic and natural cures that have been around for thousands of years. They say I can't think outside the rigid framework of standard Western medicine."

"Is that true?" He seemed awfully agitated about it.

"No! I took three whole classes on that stuff in medical school. Some of it can be verified through the scientific process and really does work. But Papa likes to needle me anyway, so he finds the strangest things he can."

"And it doesn't bother you?"

"No. And I suppose that's my point. Everyone on earth has their little oddities, even if they seem perfectly normal to you. So, when you find someone who fills you with joy—who makes you happy to be sharing the same air—you should hold on for dear life. Even if you think they are your complete opposite in every way."

"And there's another way we are different. You always sound so confident about things," Daisy said. "How do you do that?"

Luca scoffed. "It's a big act. I doubt myself all the time. I think everyone does. But you, of all people, should know how good humans are at hiding their vulnerabilities."

Daisy could only nod at that.

"*Cara*, it's really hard to carry burdens alone. I know you have your secrets, and I think you must be holding something very heavy. I hope…I just want to share the load with you. And I hope you'll trust me enough someday to let me."

"Luca…" She blew out a long breath. "If I trusted anyone, it would be you."

That seemed to be enough for him. He pushed to his feet and went to get a couple of his bags. "I'll go put this stuff in my bedroom, I think. What did you and Piper do in there?"

Daisy grabbed his carry-on and followed Luca down the hall. He stopped a few paces into the room and stood looking around.

"I should probably tell you a little bit about this bed," she said.

He turned to wink at her. "I think I can figure out how to use one, if you're interested."

She ignored the come on. "Not this one."

That gave him pause. "Oh? Why?"

"Let's just say, Piper and I had a perfectly normal mattress set picked out for you, and then Red caught wind of it."

He cocked his head. "I'm sorry. I don't follow."

"Well…he told us this whole story about helping you buy a mattress from a grad student at Juilliard, when you guys first moved off campus."

Luca chuckled. "I remember that."

"He said he and Tate had to listen to you bitch about it for the next three years."

"Hmm. That's—"

"Red then went out and bought you this bed himself, in case you're worried that Piper and I spent all of your money. I think Red's exact words were, *The world is a happier place when the prince gets his beauty sleep.*"

Luca put his hands on his hips and studied the bed, clearly miffed. "What's that?" He pointed at the small envelope resting against the pillows.

"I don't know," Daisy told him. "Red left it for you."

Luca walked over, grabbed the square of paper and tore it open. He scanned what Red had written, then burst out laughing.

"What's it say?" Daisy asked.

"*Enjoy your housewarming gift and your naps, you pansy-assed baby,*" he read aloud.

Daisy's mouth dropped open. "Jesus. This guy is your friend?"

"One of the best. Though I don't think I ever realized what a long and perfect memory Red has."

"It's actually kind of terrifying."

He grinned. "Don't be scared, *cara*. You and I know something about Red that most people don't—his weak spot."

"That man has no weak spots."

"He definitely does. And her name is Piper."

Daisy hissed in admiration. "*Shit.* You're right."

"Of course, I am." Luca smiled, "And I'm doing it on almost no sleep, so Red is obviously full of hot air."

She smiled back at him. "Well, he did get you a very fancy bed with a memory foam top. And, you can adjust the firmness in like six different zones, to whatever you like. We left the remotes in the night table drawer for you. Look."

Luca fished them out and held them aloft. "Should we test it out?"

Daisy squinted at him suspiciously. This could easily be a ploy to get her in bed with him.

He just grinned at her. "I'm serious—and tired. No funny business, I swear." He flopped onto the bed and watched her expectantly.

Daisy stepped closer, then gingerly laid beside him, close to the edge in case Luca reneged on his promise to keep it clean. She *had* been dying to try this thing out.

He handed her one of the remotes and she stabbed at a few of the buttons. Heck, it looked like the thing even had some kind of warming function. For a person with perennially cold toes, that sounded pretty clutch. No matter what she pressed, though, nothing happened underneath her. She checked the batteries, but they looked fine.

"Mine's not working," she complained. "Is yours?"

Luca was laughing at her. "Yours works fine." He reached over and switched remotes with her. "Try this one and leave my side alone."

Now she was making stuff happen. They laid side by side playing with the features for a couple of minutes, before Luca set his remote aside with a long groan.

"Red was right," he said, eyes closed tight. "This bed does feel amazing."

"I agree. I might need to save up for one of these babies." Daisy screwed around a little more, making her side of the bed nice and soft and warm. Luca stayed quiet and still. "You must be exhausted after that flight," she said after a while. "I should go."

Luca sighed quietly. She turned and looked closer, and realized he was fast asleep. He looked pleased and content, and like he'd dropped off right in the middle of staring at her.

Daisy crept out of the room and let herself out as quietly as she could. Mercifully, she was spared another run-in with Ms. Atwood, who probably would've accused her of stealing the silverware or something.

All the way home on the subway, the image of Luca's happy, peaceful face stuck with her, warming her belly with excited, hopeful flutters. It was going to take a lot more than an afternoon yoga class to get rid of those.

BY EARLY EVENING, Daisy was relaxed and fed and showered, and Luca was awake and texting her—profusely apologizing for falling asleep on her that morning.

He also claimed to have a gift for her from his mother, Nonna, and Giada, and he wanted to bring it by.

The first night in a new apartment by yourself could be weirdly lonely, Daisy knew. Nothing was familiar yet, and there were always a lot of strange sounds. She'd always hated going through it, herself, and maybe Luca did, too.

Nervously, Daisy sent him her address. Her place wasn't as nice as his, but she made decent bank designing book covers at Trident. She had nothing to be ashamed of—anymore, at least.

Thankfully, Daisy wasn't a particularly messy person, either. It only took about ten minutes of rushing around to straighten things up and wipe down her counters, and then she was buzzing Luca into the building and waiting for him to reach her floor.

When he came out of the elevator, he did indeed have a gift in his hands—as well as a huge bouquet of flowers he'd procured from somewhere along the way.

She held open her door and watched him look around, an alert and curious expression on his face. "It's a lot smaller than yours," she pointed out.

"I like it. It's very welcoming." He smiled widely, "It suits you perfectly."

"Thanks." Daisy accepted the pretty flowers and carried them to her kitchen to look for a vase. Or a bucket. Perhaps some kind of vat that could contain the floral bush she was holding.

Luca had stopped near her reading chair in the living room and was peering intently into Jerome's habitat. Daisy put the flowers and some water into a big glass hurricane she found under her sink and went out to join him.

They stood side-by-side in her living room, watching her pet turtle repeatedly tried to climb up the side of his aquarium, only to slide back down again.

"So, this is Jerome. I've probably mentioned him. Jerome, meet Luca."

Luca asked, "Are you sure that cage is big enough for him?"

"I think so?" Daisy shrugged. "I got the size that the pet store recommended, and he hasn't grown bigger. The thing is, four glass walls can't stop Jerome. He has big dreams."

Luca tilted his head as he studied the turtle. "How can you tell?"

"I just can. Jerome and I have a bond."

"Okay…"

Daisy sighed. She was probably playing this awkward conversational card for a hand too long, but she had no idea what else to say. "Poor Jerome. I think he'd like to be a world traveler someday. Unfortunately, he's stuck with me for now. And lettuce." She reached in to put a nice crisp leaf in front of him.

Her pet was obviously mad at her for telling Luca all his secrets. He snubbed the lettuce and pivoted around to give Daisy the cold shoulder, then stared resolutely into the darkest corner of his habitat.

Luca smirked, and she rushed to explain. "He's not trying to be rude. Jerome is just jealous that you've gotten to live in another country and he hasn't."

"Daisy. *Cara*, I think turtle brains are too small to come up with thoughts like that."

"You don't know that."

"But—"

"No, seriously. People are so arrogant. We don't even know what other *humans* are thinking, but we're so positive that we have the hopes and dreams of all the other species locked down tight."

Luca's forehead crinkled comically, and then he laughed. "Good point." And then, to her turtle, he said, "My apologies, *Signore*. Perhaps I can show you some photos of my home sometime."

"He'd like that," Daisy agreed.

"Not as much as I like you."

"Luca—"

"No, I mean it. I didn't get a chance to tell you earlier, but I don't want you to be in doubt for one second about why I am here in New York and what I plan to do with my time."

She swallowed nervously. "What do you plan to do?"

"You, *il mia amore*. I plan to do you. And before you assume that I don't know what I'm talking about, let me assure you that I understand the connotation perfectly. I've been trying to find you for twelve months. Trust me—that was more than enough time for me to conjure up all sorts of fantasies of what I would do with you once I found you. You *and* those tights you wore this morning."

Damn it, why *had* she worn those freaking tights today? And what kind of man recognized them after so much time?

"I think you better make sure you know what you're getting into, before you make too many promises you won't want to keep."

"I know very well what I'm doing. But you're being very foreboding. What's going on? Have you contracted something virulent since last we met?"

"I—yuck. *No.*"

"Neither have I." Luca's grin was wolfish as he sidled closer. "Lucky us."

Daisy would hardly call it luck. After all, it was hard to get a disease when you avoided dating like the…well, like the plague. Now, feeling the flutters Luca set off in her belly any time he came near, she understood why no other man had grabbed her attention since she'd been back in the U.S.

Because no one else could compare to Luca. Never had, and likely never would. Daisy wished she'd been born a different person, one who would be a good match for him. One he could be proud of over the long haul.

But she wasn't. And before long, despite his protestations, Luca was going to figure that out. The question Daisy had to answer was, did she stick around until that happened and maybe lose her heart in the process? Or should she cut him loose now, while she still had a prayer of surviving intact?

Luca dipped his head and placed precise kisses down the side of her neck, making her stomach swoop and swirl like snowflakes in a gust of wind. Maybe Daisy didn't have to shut him down right now. Maybe it would be okay if she waited a day or two. A week. No more.

Just, you know, to make sure she wasn't making any rash decisions.

Fifteen

L UCA SLEPT LIKE the dead for a solid seven hours, missing the entire day and waking to find it dark once again. He'd fallen asleep in his clothes, it seemed, and it was a struggle to fight through his disorientation to even find a lamp to turn on.

Daisy was nowhere to be found, but he could hardly blame her. Luca was groggy and sweaty and smelled like airports and hired cars. It was exceedingly strange to realize he was actually in New York again after his two busy weeks in Italy. Not only that, he was here for good.

If all went well, that was.

Luca scrubbed his hands over his face and pushed to his feet. It took some stumbling around before he could put his hands on the bag with his bathroom essentials, and another few minutes to figure out how to work the controls in the shower.

Eventually, though, he was standing under a pounding, scalding spray, and groaning at how good it felt. Speaking of good, the image of Daisy's cheerfully perplexed face as she played with his bed remote next to him was a sight he could easily fall asleep to every night. She was so much more adorable in person than he remembered, at turns sweet and uncertain and prickly.

And she'd laid beside him willingly, in that space-age bed. Christ, it seemed as hard to fathom as the fact that Luca now owned a bed that required not just one, but *two* remote controls. As Tate would say, *What the fuck?*

The mattress was as comfortable as anything Luca had ever slept on, however, so he was willing to excuse the craziness of it. Particularly if it got Daisy horizontal and next to him again.

Luca shut off the shower water, found a large towel to wrap around his hips, and brushed his teeth. Feeling reasonably human once again, he wandered out into the main rooms to get the lay of the land, turning on lights as he went.

Daisy was right to be proud of what she and Piper had accomplished. His new apartment had been greatly improved from the empty shell it'd been before he left.

Luca's walls were now a soft cream color, instead of the stark, chalky white they'd been before. He had a large brown couch of buttery leather and mounted to the wall across from it, a television that he would probably never have time to watch.

The larger of the two bedrooms held his big bed, which was covered in soft gray and white bedding. Luca thought about all the germs and general travel grime that must have been on his clothes when he'd laid down earlier and decided the duvet would have to be washed before he used it again.

The extra bedroom that he'd complained about before had been transformed into a tidy home office, with a solid-looking desk and an ergonomic chair that was nicer than anything Luca's hospital offices had ever had.

He grabbed his laptop case from the foyer and laid it on the desk, then strolled into the galley kitchen, discovering an assortment of pasta in the pantry, an artful bowl of tomatoes on the counter, and pots of basil, parsley, and rosemary under the window.

Luca sighed—they'd die of neglect before long, but for now they were a homey sight, and scented the air with a pleasant, herbal tang that reminded him of Nonna's garden.

He scanned the counter, his shoulders sagging in relief once he spotted the restaurant-grade coffee maker near the sink. Like his brother Paolo's, it had side-by-side spigots for drip coffee and espresso, and even a wand on the side to froth milk. It must have cost an abominable fortune—but Luca was glad for it even so.

It would probably take him a couple of days to get past the worst of his jet lag, and good coffee would help. Daisy and Piper had truly thought of everything, those angels. Even his refrigerator was stocked with basics he'd need for the next few days.

Luca grabbed some cheese and grapes from the refrigerator, some crackers from the pantry, and fixed himself a snack. A clock ticked somewhere in the house, slow and steady. The window was a little fogged from the cold air outside, and it made the city lights shining through it look blurry.

He wondered what Daisy was doing. She'd said she had a yoga class in the afternoon, so she must be done with it by now. Maybe she'd like some company?

Luca supposed he could ask her to dinner, but the thought of getting dressed up and going out somewhere didn't hold much appeal.

He set his plate in the sink and carried the rest of his stuff into the bedroom. He hung up his soggy towel, began unpacking his clothes, and threw on a clean pair of sweatpants in the process. Then, in the final bag, he discovered the perfect excuse to see Daisy again.

What you wanted was always in the last place you looked, wasn't it? There, in the dark recesses of his suitcase, sat the wrapped gift his family had sent for Daisy, and it was an excellent reason to ring her up and see if he could snare some more time with her.

Luca stashed his empty luggage on the top shelf of his closet, stripped the bedding from his bed, and went in search of his ever-disappearing phone.

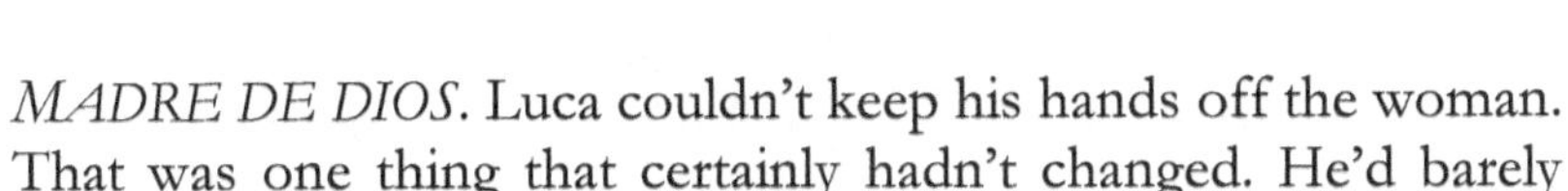

MADRE DE DIOS. Luca couldn't keep his hands off the woman. That was one thing that certainly hadn't changed. He'd barely been at her house for five minutes before they were going at it like a couple of teenagers.

Just like before, all it took was a couple of minutes in Daisy's orbit, and he was itching to touch and taste.

If she was catnip, then he was a tomcat, desperate to rub against her and mark her as his.

What *had* changed in the time they'd been apart was Daisy's response to Luca's ardor. Before, she'd been slightly confused by his attention—but amenable, nonetheless. Now, she was about as skittish as the feral cats who hung around Nonna's back door.

More with the cats. Luca clearly had *micia* on the brain.

Ever since he'd discovered Daisy at that party, she had been melting into his arms one minute—and tossing around every verbal and physical obstacle she could find to keep him at bay the next.

Luca had never been a big fan of mixed signals, so he'd been doing his level best to get to the bottom of her reluctance. So far, he'd determined that Daisy was healthy and single and gainfully employed, so no worries there. Unfortunately, she had concerns about her race, social station, and family background that seemed to be holding her back.

Luca did not share her concerns. He thought he'd been pretty clear from the beginning about that. Which begged the question, what was it about *her* situation, in particular, that made Daisy so sure he'd balk at it?

He'd have an easier time figuring it out if he could finagle more time with her, especially if she'd give him something more to go on. As it was, Daisy had only grudgingly admitted that she was the sole child of a single mother, and hadn't said much else.

Now wasn't the time to find out more, however. Now was one of those times when Daisy wanted what he did, and Luca didn't intend to waste a single second of it. Snug in her warm, cozy apartment, it felt like they had all the time in the world to get reacquainted.

So he kissed her neck, and inhaled the tantalizing scent of her skin, and let himself get carried away like he'd longed to do for all the months he'd been missing her. Soon, he was carrying Daisy in his arms to her tiny bedroom, in the hopes that it would lead to good things.

THE CLOCK ON Daisy's nightstand was as loud as a beating heart, echoing the one Luca had heard in his own house earlier. In comparison, Daisy was still remarkably quiet in bed.

Her silence should have been more memorable, he supposed, since in all his adult life, Luca had never made love to a woman who was that silent. Yet somehow, in the twelve long months that he'd been yearning for her, he'd forgotten that impressive detail.

The woman hardly made a sound, even when in the throes of passion. It didn't seem possible, given the amount of growling and groaning and dirty-talking Luca found himself doing, but what could he say? Daisy was inspiring.

Still, before she'd left Florence, he'd undertaken several weeks of careful, dedicated study of the situation, and Luca had eventually discovered many of the ways she gave herself away. She had tells, his Daisy, and tonight he loved finding them all again.

There were the hitches in her breathing, for one thing, when his lips brushed over certain spots. There was the way her fingertips pressed into the meat of Luca's shoulders, when Daisy wanted him deeper, closer, *more*.

And then—one of his very favorites—there was Daisy's clenched jaw and expression of deep concentration when she was about to come apart for him.

All the signs were still evident, for a meticulous student to read. Combined with Daisy's soft skin and even softer soul, it was a textbook that Luca was sure he would never tire of.

Continuing education was so, so important these days.

And after losing so much time with her, Luca knew he had to be vigilant going forward. He never wanted to lose his edge, or lose Daisy, again.

On the topic of edges, his fascinating woman seemed to have acquired a piercing in her navel since the last time Luca had been in bed with her. Curious, he touched it with his finger and watched her squirm.

"This is new," he pointed out, as if she wasn't aware.

Daisy propped herself up on her elbows. "Yes. I went with Poppy in Boston one time. I guess it's a little trashy, but I always wanted one. And I figured, I'm a grownup—why the hell not?"

Luca hummed, liking the glint of it against her ivory skin.

Before he could weigh in, however, Daisy announced quite definitively, "I like it. I think it's pretty."

"On principle, I should tell you about the risks of infection, but it's a little late for that," Luca smiled. "I assume you went to a safe place?"

"I think so. They were very clean and sanitary, and they used gloves and antiseptic and everything. Poppy said she and her husband had gotten tattoos there before, so…I trusted them."

Luca nudged the ring gently and the clear rhinestone hanging from it caught the light. Daisy had always seemed like a decadent buffet before this, but for some reason that little gold wire notched Luca's always-simmering hunger two levels higher.

"Do *you* like it?" she wondered.

Luca raised his eyes to Daisy's and held her searching, pale-green gaze. She looked worried and uncertain, and it tugged at his heart. He bent down and bit her hip.

"*Sì*," he told her. "I like it. I like you. Always."

Like. Ha. Such a weak, ineffectual word for what Daisy made him feel. That belly ring she was so worried about had sent Luca from horny to thermonuclear in about three seconds flat.

Lest there be any doubt about it, Luca levered himself up her body so he could capture her mouth with his. Daisy tasted tart and salty, and felt warm and solid under his hands.

She was a piece of art, all long, strong curves and secret melting places. She arched up to meet him, pressing her skin against his, and satisfaction roared through his veins. Perhaps she was as happy and relieved as he was to be in this position again.

Luca cupped one full breast in his hand, taking her dusky brown nipple between his lips and giving it a tug. That elicited a nice, loud gasp, so he tried it again on the other side.

Then, that little fake diamond beckoning to him like a siren song, he kissed his way downward, past her sternum, to her belly button again.

Luca licked the ring, and Daisy's hips bucked off the bed. He flicked it with the tip of his tongue, and she writhed. *Interessante.*

Luca gripped Daisy's hip to hold her in place and drew his free hand up the inside of her thigh. He toyed with the piercing with his tongue once more, then tugged on it gently—right as he slid two fingers deep into her silky wet heat.

Daisy jerked and moaned. It was soft, but it was unmistakable. "Forget what I said," he told her, lifting his head. "I don't *like* this thing. I love it."

Luca bent his fingers inside her, searching for that spot that made Daisy wild, and shifted his mouth from that devilish jewelry to more southerly climes.

When his tongue hit her clitoris, Daisy yelped. Luca froze in surprise. An anvil might as well have dropped on his head.

"Are you okay?"

"*So* okay," she breathed.

Tentatively, he flicked his tongue against her again, rotated his fingers just a tiny bit, and listened to Daisy moan. *What in the world?*

"Are you sure? Because—"

"Please stop talking. Just keep doing what you're doing. Please?"

Luca bent his head and gave her one long, strong lick, and Daisy sang, "Ohhhhh, yes."

He shook his head, braced himself on his elbows and stared up at her in amusement. "Who are you and what have you done with my quiet Daisy?"

"Are we really going to have this conversation *now?*" she demanded.

"*Cara,* you've never said a single word in bed before. And now…" he gestured. Now he was getting the play-by-play.

"And that's a problem?" she squawked, astounded. "Have you ever even heard yourself?"

"No problem. I'm enjoying it. I'm just curious what's changed."

"You know what they say about curiosity."

"I do. Now use all those words you've discovered and tell me what's going on."

"You have got to be kidding me." A quick, incredulous study of Luca's face clearly told her otherwise, so she huffed, "I just missed you, all right? I missed this. I didn't realize how much until that stupid party, but once you kissed me…"

Luca grinned. Apparently, absence *did* make the heart grow fonder. Or, at minimum, the sex glands. Color him surprised.

"What happened once I kissed you, *mia bella*?" Like he didn't already know.

He'd been burning and hungry for her ever since, too, lust gnawing at him like an infection. Luca flicked Daisy's belly ring back and forth and waited for the outburst he knew would come.

"I can't stop thinking about everything we used to do, okay? It's like it's all on replay in my brain, and I would really, *really* appreciate it if you would please get back to our previously-scheduled program!"

"I'd be delighted." Luca slid down her body and concentrated on making Daisy come quickly, because he didn't think he could wait much longer to sink inside her.

She'd been closer than he realized. In moments, Daisy was shuddering and whimpering a litany of prayers as she came apart, and Luca was peppering shaky kisses across her belly while she floated back down to earth.

She threaded her fingers through his hair when he pushed up and braced himself over her. Luca was pretty sure it wasn't healthy to be this hard, and he knew exactly what he wanted to do to take care of it.

"I want to be inside you," he told her, his voice coming out gravelly with need.

"I want that, too." Daisy's big green eyes were wide and trusting, making him swallow against the rush of emotion that engendered. She felt around on the mattress for the condom they'd left there and handed it to Luca with a quick urgent kiss.

Luca sat back on his heels, hissing at how sensitive he was as he tried to get the thing on himself properly. And then, mercifully, beautifully, he was sinking into Daisy's body and her legs were wrapping tight around his ass.

He groaned at the way she felt, moving in perfect tandem with him. This new Daisy might be pricklier on the outside, but she was still as stunningly hot and soft as she'd ever been on the inside.

He wondered if that was true metaphorically, as well—if she was still secretly tender-hearted and sensitive. He was going to learn. He was going to know her inside and out, if it killed him.

And then he didn't think at all, because Luca felt like he was coming home, not moving away, with her.

Sixteen

MADONNA SANTA, WINTER was cold in Manhattan. The blasting radiators in Daisy's apartment warmed the air well enough, but they also dried it out so much that Luca worried he might wash away from all the water he had to drink to stay alive. He had to rub olive oil on his lips so they wouldn't crack and rub her scented lotion on his skin so it wouldn't itch.

Those minor annoyances were worth enduring, however, given that Daisy looked unbelievably hot in her winter clothes. In the humid Florence weather of last year, Luca had gotten accustomed to seeing her in a variety of skirts and sundresses each day, her thick curly hair held off her neck with colorful scarves, and her painted toes peeking out of strappy Italian leather sandals.

Here in New York, Daisy's style was decidedly more urban. When she'd walked him out of her building so he could catch a cab home that morning, she'd worn a leather motorcycle jacket the same dark red as a nice chianti, painted-on black jeans, and a soft gray scarf wrapped around and around her neck. It'd tickled Luca's cheek when he kissed her goodbye on the sidewalk.

She'd blushed like every last person on the street knew what they'd been up to for the last several hours. Luca had really, really missed those eternally pink cheeks of hers.

When he'd fallen for her in Italy, Daisy had been unbearably sexy, Luca reflected on the way home. She was still that, but she was also fierce here. In her chunky lace-up boots, she looked like some kind of dirty motorcycle princess, and Luca wanted to kiss the holy hell out of her while she straddled him like he was the ride of her life.

That made him laugh out loud, which merely made him look crazy as he walked into his new building and caused the doorman to give him the side-eye. Who was Luca kidding? Kissing was the least of what he wanted to do with Daisy.

He dwelled on some of the more interesting options as he rode the elevator to his floor and let himself into his apartment. He'd been granted an unexpected, but welcome, start on his amorous plans last night, but there was so much more to consider.

And he knew, if Daisy began to trust him with more of her heart, the sex would only get better. Maybe she'd even get louder. If Luca could convince her to *love* him, hell—Daisy might turn into an outright screamer.

At this early stage, it seemed like too much to hope for. He'd barely been in New York for a full day yet.

His thoughts were pulled right out of the gutter they were wallowing in by the distant chiming of his phone, however. Luca must have left it here last night, in his rush to get to Daisy's.

He tracked the sound to his small sunny office, and eventually discovered the annoying device under his laptop and the medical journal he'd been reading on the plane. Luca grinned when he saw who it was.

"Tate?"

"What's up, Doc?" his old friend quacked.

Luca was pretty sure it was a comical voice Tate was putting on, and not some new strain of Middle Eastern throat malady. He remembered—there was a wise-cracking cartoon rabbit who said exactly that phrase.

"*Mio amico*! *Ciao*," Luca replied, and immediately felt guilty. "I'm sorry I haven't called. It's been so busy with the move and wrapping up at the hospital—"

Tate cut him off. "Dude, stop. I get it. I've been absolutely killing myself out here every day, too. Fighting bad guys, you know. They never stop. But we cool."

Luca suspected, as he often did with Tate, that he was being teased. But before he could figure out how to volley something back, Tate went on.

"I just wanted to make sure you got back to New York okay. Red said you found a place to live already?"

"Yes, thanks to him. I took an open-ended sabbatical from the hospital in Florence, my flight was uneventful, and *mia famiglia* did not chain me down so I wouldn't leave them." Then Luca sighed, "This apartment is too big, though. I really don't need all this space."

"Spoken like a true European," Tate groaned. "You realize that space is a commodity where you are now, right?"

"But—"

"Luca, I've been sleeping on the rocky, *spacious* fucking ground for years. I think you'll survive. Embrace the space. *Be* the space."

"Well, at least Red and his bride have thought of everything. You should see the bed that *stronzo* bought me. It has remote controls, but I sleep like I'm comatose on it."

"So, I heard. And I also heard that Red and Piper weren't the only ones kitting out your new pad."

Luca ignored that salvo for the time being. "They even set up some kind of food delivery service for me." Likely because Red knew perfectly well that Luca occasionally forgot to feed himself.

"I think it must be run by Italians. The first delivery, they brought rapini." He'd found it in the vegetable drawer of the refrigerator.

"Christ, not rat weed?" Tate grumbled. "You better eat that shit fast. The only thing worse than *fresh* rat weed is——"

"——rat weed that's gone bad. Yes, I'm aware." Luca smiled at the memory.

His old roommate had routinely been appalled by the food that Luca had inadvertently allowed to go to waste all those years ago, but nothing had disgusted him quite as much as the wilted, rotting bags of rapini leaking into the bottom of the refrigerator.

Tate chuckled, but then he wondered, "What's Piper like, anyway? I've talked to her a couple times, but it's hard to get a read on her over the phone."

"She's…" *Worthy*, Luca thought. She'd be the making of their old friend, of that he was certain.

In the short while he'd known Piper, she'd already proven herself a friend to him. In time, she'd no doubt be like a sister, as much as her intended was like Luca's brother.

Given the opportunity, Luca had no doubt she'd adopt Tate someday, too.

"She's perfect for him," Luca said at last. "I've never seen Red act so human."

"That's good to hear. What about you, though? You've tracked down your inamorata, right?"

There was a loaded pause, in which Luca realized something momentous. "You knew, didn't you? You both knew she was here all along?"

"We only suspected. What are the odds, right? It's a small fucking world."

Luca nodded, remembered that Tate couldn't see him, and said aloud, "Yes. It really is."

It wasn't small enough, though. It had still taken him far too long to find Daisy, and it was possible that in all that time, whatever love that had flared between them had died of neglect.

He didn't think that was the case, and last night seemed to confirm his hope. But if Luca couldn't fan the ember back into a healthy blaze again, then he would have left his home and his family behind for nothing.

"And? What's the status? You have her locked down yet?"

"Daisy is…trying to get over her shock at seeing me here, I think. But I have some reasons to be hopeful."

"Dude, you'll do fine. If Red could find some honey willing to hitch her wagon to his, you should be shacking up by the end of the month."

Luca paused, trying to make sure he'd understood the gist of what Tate had said. "That might be a little ambitious."

"You forget, I've seen you in action, Romeo."

Luca groaned. "I wish you would forget. That was a long time ago."

"Come on. It's like riding a bike." And then Tate snickered. "Riding something, anyway."

"Grow up." Luca shook his head, deflecting, "What about you? Have you seduced anyone there? A fellow soldier, perhaps? Or a lovely girl in a nearby village?"

"Have you been writing yourself too many prescriptions? I'd rather not get my nuts shot off, if it's all the same to you. I like those babies right where they are."

Luca snorted. "You're right. Maybe just write a few letters to a nice girl back in…" He wracked his brain for the name of some rural state in the middle of this vast country but could only manage to summon the name of Tate's home, "…Ohio."

Maybe that was out in the country. Maybe not. Luca had no clue, and now it was Tate's turn to scoff.

"And do what? I can promise a girl exactly nothing right now."

"You're not a machine, *amico*. None of us are."

In a nonsensical, robotic voice, Tate intoned, "Russian machine never break."

Luca sighed. It was useless trying to get him to be serious. "Well, if you get tired of sleeping on the ground, come here. You can stay with me—and my new couch is really comfortable."

"Aren't you sweet. But nice try, asshole. I've done my time cleaning up after you. If you want a maid, you're going to have to hire one."

Luca told him, "I think Piper said she's trying to find me one." He doubted his friend heard him, though. An enormous commotion had erupted in the background.

Tate muttered, "Fuck, fuck, fuck," breathing hard like he was running. "Gotta jet, dude." And then the line went dead.

Dead. What an unfortunate word choice. Luca winced, said a quick, fervent prayer for his friend's safety, and went to sauté that rapini for his lunch.

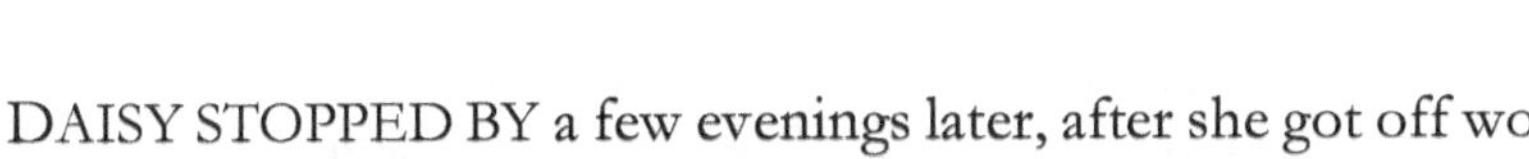

DAISY STOPPED BY a few evenings later, after she got off work. Luca had only worked a half day, as he had all week, but the process of finding his way around the new facility, getting all his credentials, and meeting everyone *and* their cousin was definitely debilitating.

He'd made it home and onto his couch every day, but that was about it.

Daisy stopped short at the sight of the boxes in his foyer. "What's all this?"

"Clothes and other things from home. My parents were only supposed to send half of it, but apparently my sister went rogue and mailed all the ones I stored in her basement, too. She said she was already sick of them taking up space, but I expect our mother told her I was complaining about the cold."

"You haven't opened any of them?"

"There's no rush," Luca shrugged. "I brought what I really needed on the plane with me."

Daisy cocked her head. "How long have they been sitting here?"

Luca shrugged. "Not long." There were a handful of medical journals and some other mail on top of one box, and a coffee cup on another.

Daisy stepped closer, peered inside the cup, then showed Luca the dried-up brown sludge in the bottom of it. "Want to try again?" She walked it into his kitchen and filled it with water.

When she returned, Luca attempted to nail down the timing. "I'm not sure," he frowned. "Two days, perhaps? Maybe three, though."

"Don't you want to open them? Maybe they sent you a warmer jacket."

Luca felt vaguely embarrassed, standing there like a blockhead next to such glaring evidence of his organizational failings. "I'll get to it. I started working this week, though. Remember?"

"Okay. But you're not working tonight, and I'm here now. Why don't we grab a quick bite and tackle it after dinner?"

He flopped onto his couch—Daisy really had done a fantastic job picking out the couch—and sighed dramatically. "Can we order something in? I promise I won't always be this pathetic. I think it's the jet lag, though. It won't release its evil grip on me."

"Yes, that sounds great. And FYI, you might want to use melatonin for a couple nights until your body recalibrates to this time zone."

Luca nodded. He probably ought to have thought of that himself. "I don't think it would be so bad if it wasn't getting dark at 4:30 in the afternoon. It's dark when I leave for the hospital, and dark when I get home. I feel like I'm going through my residency again. Or like I've become a vampire."

"I'm beginning to see why Red insisted on getting that bed for you," Daisy grinned.

Luca winced. "I'm whining like a three-year-old. That's awful. I'm sorry. Maybe you should back out of the apartment slowly and come back next week, when I've grown an adult-sized pair of testicles."

Daisy just laughed and pulled her phone out of her pocket. "Settle down, tiger. How's Indian food sound?"

LATER, SHE COMPLAINED hotly when Luca insisted that she leave a shelf empty in his closet, and drawers empty in his bureau and the bathroom cabinet.

"But Luca, *why*? It's much easier to find things when you spread out more. You wouldn't lose stuff so often if you were more organized."

"For you, *cara*." He'd thought that would've been obvious. "So you can leave some things here, if you want."

Daisy huffed at him, "Would you stop being nice? You don't have to make space for me!"

"I want to. And if I do, maybe you'll decide to fill those spaces." He winked and waggled his eyebrows, hoping to soften the message a little.

Daisy blinked, stunned into inarticulateness. "That is…that's…"

Luca barged ahead, not waiting for her to finish. "Daisy, to be completely clear—I'm leaving space in my heart and my life for you, too. I'm also hoping those will get filled."

"This is unreal. You're being preposterous," she muttered, then spun away.

"Why is it so crazy that I like you? You, and no one else, mind you. Why is it so hard to believe that I want you in my life?"

"It just is."

Luca moved behind her and set his hands on her shoulders. She was trembling. "Daisy," he murmured, nuzzling into her hair. "Don't worry. It's going to be okay."

After a long minute, she took a deep breath and relaxed back into him. "God, I hope you know what you're doing."

"I'm doing my best. I only need some direction from you, to make sure I'm not traipsing all over what *you* want."

She nodded, then whispered a soft, barely audible, "Okay."

Luca took a chance and wrapped his arms gently around her, and reveled in being able to hold her warm, lovely figure close to his heart. Her body fit him so perfectly, it was like they were made for one another.

Daisy's thoughts were clearly not heading down the same path his were, because she asked rather abruptly, "Did Piper say whether their housekeeper could help you, too?"

Luca was thinking of all the ways they fit together, and Daisy was thinking about how messy his apartment was? He blew out a resigned breath. He was getting worse and worse at this.

"Mrs. Markham? No, she's not taking on new clients. It's okay, though. If it gets really bad in here, I can call an agency." He grinned into her soft curls. "I'm sure my neighbor will know a few."

Daisy growled, "Yeah, and they've probably all blocked her number. But listen—why don't I just help you? We both know I'm going to be here anyway."

Luca turned her in his arms. "Absolutely not. You have your own home and job to worry about. You don't need to worry about me, too. Besides, I'm a grown man—I'm perfectly capable of taking care of myself. I just need to remember, that's all."

"Maybe make yourself a schedule," she offered, accepting that. "Set reminders on your phone."

As tough as Daisy pretended to be, she obviously cared deeply about her friends. When she spoke about them, her stories often involved her doing the mothering—looking after them and making sure they were okay—even if she didn't realize she was doing it.

And right now, she was sweetly concerned about *him*. Luca smiled at the compliment and dropped a peck on her nose.

"That's a very good idea. And if me doing a better job cleaning up the place makes you feel more comfortable here, then it's an even better incentive."

"I just thought you might be happier if everything was neat."

"I'm happy when you're happy. So, get ready to see how tidy I can be."

Porca miseria, if his brother could see him now—Paolo would shit a brick, and then probably die from laughing.

Seventeen

THEY HADN'T MANAGED to get together since they'd cleared out all of Luca's boxes from home. It had taken them a couple of evenings, but now, despite his game efforts to stay in touch, Daisy worried that Luca was already working too hard, trying to make a good impression at his new job.

She had started getting flirty texts from Luca every afternoon, once he was back in his office doing paperwork, or in his lab trying to hire assistants, or getting his equipment up and running.

After spending a few nights with him, she'd had to give up on the preposterous idea that she could keep the man at arm's length. Luca was just too freaking wonderful to keep away from. He acted like he adored her, for one thing, and he had an irresistible, magnetic combination of bravado and vulnerability that slayed her every time.

Also, Luca kissed like it was his superpower. Daisy was basically fucked.

Ha. Nothing basic about the fucking. She'd just have to deal with the eventual heartbreak—but that could wait.

LUCA HAD ASKED Daisy to meet him at the hospital after work that evening, so they could go directly out to dinner from there.

He'd heard about a restaurant nearby there from his new coworkers and wanted to try it with her.

It felt strange to be walking along hospital halls without being sick herself, or worried about someone who was. The same anxiety she would have had in those situations settled into Daisy's bones anyway, however, simply from breathing that antiseptic-scented air.

After a couple of wrong turns, she found Luca behind his desk in a small, cluttered office at the end of the oncology wing. She knocked tentatively on his open door and peeked in.

Luca was wearing a blindingly white button-down rolled up over his elbows, and his usual pair of nerdy-chic tortoiseshell glasses straight from the pages of Italian GQ. With his black wavy hair and almond eyes, olive skin and husky voice, the good doctor was devastating to behold.

And then he opened his mouth and busted out that silky accent of his. "Ah, there you are. I was going to come hunting for you soon. I know it's like a maze back here."

Daisy checked her watch. "I'm only ten minutes late! By your standards, I might as well be half an hour early."

Luca chuckled. "That's true, but I missed you, so it felt like a thousand years." He came around his desk and kissed her to make his point, with probably more enthusiasm than that office had seen in years.

Daisy wondered suddenly what percentage of his patients were young and single. Hell, if she'd had any idea doctors like him existed, she would definitely have been clocking in at those recommended checkups more often.

She might even have developed a raging case of hypochondria just to see Dr. Luca more often.

Once he released her, Daisy looked around Luca's office—at the books and files, the old desk and even older chair. Next to his phone sat a single framed photo. Curious, Daisy picked it up and found her own face smiling back at her.

"Where was this taken?" She'd never seen it before.

Luca's smile was nostalgic. "From the *Giardino Bardini*. Do you remember it?"

Daisy did. They'd had a great time there, and the photos she'd taken that day had turned out beautifully. "I do. I didn't know you were taking pictures of me, though."

Not only that, but Luca had printed it out and framed it, then put it on his desk at work, where anyone could see it. Daisy took a big breath. She was in deep.

"Do you mind?" he wondered.

"No," she shrugged, playing off her surprise. "At least it came out good."

"They all came out good. And it was nice to have them. You know. *After.*"

Daisy nodded. She'd spent plenty of time in the last year looking at Luca's picture, too. But she'd brought a different one to give him now.

"Anyway, now you'll have two pictures here," she said, reaching into her bag and handing him her small gift.

Luca unwrapped the photo of his Nonna, standing near the front door of her pensione with a happy grin on her face. "Oh, it's perfect," he breathed, smiling down at it. He set it down carefully next to Daisy's picture and adjusted the angle. "What prompted this?"

"I wanted to thank you for the gift you brought me from Florence. I keep forgetting to tell you—but I opened it after you left that first day."

"Oh, really? What was it?"

"Don't you know?"

"No, the ladies wouldn't tell me. They just told me to deliver it."

Daisy smiled. "Luca, they gave me a binder full of your family's recipes. It's amazing. They even attached pictures, so I would know how everything was supposed to look when it was done."

"See? I told you they liked you. They would never have done that for someone they didn't care for."

It did seem like they'd put a lot of effort into it. Daisy told him, "I love that it's all handwritten, too. There must be three or four different people's writing, but some of them are in Italian. You'll have to help me translate those."

"Of course," Luca said. "The Italian ones are probably Mamma's. She's a little better at speaking English than reading and writing it."

Daisy nodded, "That makes sense."

Luca rocked on his heels and looked out the small window behind his desk, but he couldn't hide his curiosity. "So…which dishes did they include?"

The poor man looked so excited. In a flash, Daisy realized why his people had given her that particular gift, and why they'd inscribed inside the front cover, "Take good care of him for us."

In Luca's family, food was love, and with that cookbook they'd handed Daisy the tools she would need to be good to him. It was one of those presents that was bigger than it seemed—not that she'd enjoyed many of those.

Daisy wished she'd been as lucky in the family lottery as Luca had been, but this was no time for crying about things she couldn't change. Instead, she'd take their thoughtful gift and do her best to carry out their wishes.

So, she told Luca, "Well, the first and most important one was obviously your grandma's recipe for bracciole. If you'd like to come over this weekend, I can make it for you. Nonna showed me how when I lived with her. But now that I have the recipe too, I'm pretty sure I can do it justice."

Luca looked ready to fall at her feet. "Daisy, I'll be there if I have to move mountains to make it happen. Just name the time. I'll even bring dessert."

"Just bring yourself," she told him, laughing. "With any luck, dessert will take care of itself."

ON SATURDAY, THE sun had been down for hours and her meal—that Daisy had put together with meticulous, exacting precision so she wouldn't screw anything up—was very close to being ruined.

Luca was late. And not simply Italian-Late, but Something-Is-Wrong-Late. He wasn't answering her texts, either, which could mean a number of things. He might have forgotten his phone at home or forgotten to charge it.

Or he might have been mugged halfway to her apartment and be lying in an alley somewhere. How was Daisy supposed to know? She decided she was clearly not cut out for this.

Out of nowhere, though, Luca was calling from the lobby and asking to be buzzed in. He was breathless as he walked from the elevator to her door and enfolded Daisy in an apologetic hug.

"*Perdoni*," he said. "I would have been here sooner, but this strange *puttana* stole the only free cab. I had to take the subway instead."

Even Daisy knew *that* word. "Luca! You can't call people that."

"Why?" he wondered, trying to look innocent and mostly failing. "You swear all the time."

"It's different," she told him. "Bad words sound much different coming from you."

"I don't think that's true at all. Why would you say that?"

"Because you're much more sophisticated, that's why. Don't argue."

"I think this box you have me in feels very…" Luca shifted around with an adorable half-frown, "…restricting."

"Tough. Deal with it," Daisy told him.

"Besides, I was not trying to assault the woman's character. I was just stating facts. I really think that might have been her profession." Luca shucked off his jacket and hung it on the coat tree near her door, then jammed his hands in his dark jeans.

Daisy rolled her eyes and sighed heavily. "Well, where were you when it happened?"

"Eh, near Grand Central, on 42nd. Sort of. Close to there. I was rushing and too frustrated to note my exact location."

"Look," Daisy said. "I suppose it's possible she could've been a hooker. But she could just as easily have been an actress or a street performer."

Luca shrugged eloquently, then grinned. "Same thing, no?" Like the distinction between a prostitute and an actress was immaterial.

"No!" Daisy cried, in utter exasperation. "For all you know, she was just a regular woman who likes tight clothes."

"Or not a woman at all."

It was then that Daisy noticed the evil glint in his eye. He'd been baiting her again. She groaned, "Oh my God, you infernal—"

Luca snatched her wrist, pulled it toward him, and began biting along the meat of her forearm—none too gently—all the way up to Daisy's elbow. "Minor deity only," he said against her skin. "But you can pray loudly through this next part. I won't mind."

Daisy whacked him on the arm with her ladle.

"Ow! Hey," Luca complained, rubbing at his cashmere sleeve.

"You're an hour late, Doc. The special dinner I made you almost burned. Now, you have to eat it *before* you break out all your rusty seductive wiles."

"I'm sorry, grouchy woman. You're just too edible when you're angry."

Daisy threatened him with her spoon again. "My *food* was edible. *Forty-five minutes ago.*"

Luca just laughed, the ass, but at least he started walking toward the table. "Don't hurt me, please. I promise I'll be good now."

"You'd better be."

"Just point me toward the bracciole, *cara*, and I'll do whatever you ask."

AN HOUR AND a half later, Luca had eaten more of her homemade lentil soup and bread than seemed humanly possible—plus, devoured her first attempt to make his favorite food, and pronounced it delicious.

Once he was full, they relocated to Daisy's couch to watch a movie. However, with the volume on low, he'd stretched out with a long sigh beside her and fallen asleep with his head in her lap in only moments.

So much for Daisy's dessert goals.

She laced her fingers through Luca's wavy midnight hair, fascinated as always by how it could be so shiny and silky without any apparent product help. If she didn't moisturize the hell out of her locks, she'd probably look like a scarecrow.

Luca murmured when she touched him, turning his head to kiss her thigh.

"When did you go into the lab today?" Daisy asked quietly. The little clock on her bookshelf said it was barely nine now, not to mention the weekend.

"6:30."

"A.M.?"

"*Sì.*"

"And tomorrow?"

"Also 6:30."

"Why?"

He didn't answer. Luca had lapsed back into sleep.

Daisy gazed down at him, looking like a fallen angel in her lap—albeit an exhausted one. Even tired, he'd still trekked to her apartment without a single complaint or whine, so she could feed him her reheated soup and bread, and his favorite family meal.

No way had Luca done that for himself. Her bread was too salty, and despite what he'd told her, she knew her first attempt at bracciole had turned out so-so at best.

There was any number of restaurants near the hospital where Luca could have gotten take-out on his way home. He would've been perfectly justified, too, telling her he had to get some rest and couldn't make it.

But no, Luca had come here for her, so that Daisy could play at being his girlfriend. So she would feel useful—like her weak attempts to be good enough for him had a prayer of making a difference. He'd done it because he knew it was important to her.

Even when it would've been way easier not to come. It was hard not to read all kinds of things into that, and at the moment, Daisy didn't even try. She simply let an earth-shattering notion wash over her.

For the first time in her life, she actually wanted to take care of someone besides herself. Was there any possible way that wouldn't go bad?

Eighteen

ONE THING THAT hadn't changed since last year? When Luca woke up in Daisy's bed on a Sunday morning, he was still as frisky as they came. She couldn't exactly complain though—her handsy doctor knew lots of ways to wake her up, and pretty much all of them left her on cloud nine for the rest of the day.

This time around, Luca had bagged the idea of going into his lab before he'd even finished round one of Project Alarm Clock. And once Daisy's growling stomach had rousted him from her sheets long enough to eat breakfast, he came up with a totally different plan.

She nursed her second cup of coffee and eyed him warily, while Luca dug into a plate of leftovers from the night before.

"It's a great idea," he told her around a mouthful of meat and bread. "We have the whole day, and the weather is supposed to be good—at least until tonight, anyway. Let's do it."

"I don't know why you want to, though. It's going to be boring. And dumb."

"Nothing to do with you is dumb, Daisy. And I want to see it. I think it will be interesting."

Which really was the problem with talking too much in bed. One person got creative with their tongue, and the next thing the other person knew, they were spilling all kinds of unhelpful details about the neighborhood where they grew up in Brooklyn.

Daisy longed to take back every reckless word she'd uttered earlier, lounging around with Luca. She ought to have known he wouldn't simply let her stories stay stories. The researcher in him wanted context. It wanted details, and visuals. *Proof.*

Luca wanted to see her old neighborhood in person. The problem was, Daisy hadn't been back there in years, and she was completely unsure whether she wanted to go there today.

"Daisy?" Luca prodded. "Can we please go see it? We don't have to stay long."

"Just tell me why," she said, stalling for time.

"I suppose…" he shrugged and wiped his mouth with his napkin. "I don't know. You've seen where I grew up. I guess I want to see where you grew up. I want to see the place that formed you. Why is that wrong?"

It wasn't wrong. It was a completely normal thing that other people did all the time. And Brooklyn was a busy place—the odds were good that no one would even know who Daisy was if they took a quick walk down a couple of streets there. She could get in, show Luca what he wanted to see, and get out again.

Easy, right?

"Okay," Daisy relented. "I'll take you. But afterward, we're going to that new photography exhibit at MOMA, and you better act interested."

Luca's face was shining as he promised, "You have my word."

SHE'D BEEN SO close. One more block, and they could have stepped onto the subway, settled in for the ride back to

Manhattan and gone on with their lives. Luca wouldn't have been terribly impressed with the scruffy streets he'd seen, but the situation was still tenable.

Daisy could've recovered from it. But no—she should've known the whole outing had been way too easy.

Instead of making their escape, she and Luca had been stopped in their tracks by an all-too-familiar voice, raspy from years of smoking. It called out to Daisy from the door of a little Brazilian restaurant she didn't know. Daisy strongly considered ignoring it.

If Luca hadn't peered down at her curiously, then looked over his shoulder to search for the voice's owner, Daisy might've kept walking. She might've pretended she didn't hear it or acted like it was calling to someone else.

She couldn't do it, though. She had to turn and look, and when she did, Daisy made very unfortunate, but very definite eye-contact with the woman who'd raised her. She hadn't laid eyes on her in ten years.

"Daisy? That you, kid?" Pam said again.

"Hey, Pam."

Her foster mother muttered a few rushed words to someone inside the restaurant, and then she was shuffling across the sidewalk, wiping her hands on her apron and smoothing back her frazzled, graying hair.

"I wasn't sure it was you. I saw you walking by, and I thought maybe, but…" Pam stopped and gave Luca a suspicious once-over. "You said you were living in Manhattan now."

Daisy wished the sidewalk would open up and swallow her, but that seemed unlikely. And it meant there was no getting around the introductions. "Pam, this is my friend Luca. Luca, meet Pam."

Luca's eyebrows shot up at Daisy's description of him. She knew what he was thinking—*friends* didn't usually stick their appendages where his had been. Quite recently, as a matter of fact.

"This your new man?" Pam asked, eyeing Luca dubiously. Daisy wasn't sure whether her foster mother thought Luca was too good for her, or the opposite. Either way, she clearly assumed the pairing was a dodgy one.

Daisy sighed. *In for a penny.* "You could say that. And like I said, his name is Luca. You can even speak to him directly."

"How do you do?" Luca said, then extended his long, elegant surgeon's fingers into the tense air separating them. He looked impossibly urbane next to Pam's squat, dumpy frame and her stained t-shirt with the restaurant logo screen-printed on its pocket.

Pam hesitated before making contact. "Oh. You're foreign," she said, "What are you, one of those Latin guys?" She shook his hand like she thought she might get scabies from it.

"No, he's Italian," Daisy put in, before Pam came up with anything more insulting than she already had. "I met him when I lived in Florence last year, but now he's moved to New York for work, so…" she shrugged.

Luca gave Pam his most charming smile, and it went over about as well as a lead balloon. Daisy's foster mother had decided he was shady, and that was that. The harder the man tried, the worse she'd think he was.

It was only a matter of time before she brought up the mafia.

Luca asked, "And how do you know Daisy?" Right, because regular people might have offered that information already—as one did in polite conversation.

Pam scowled darkly, and Daisy just knew she was about to blurt out something mortifying. She jumped into the abyss with the slightly-less-humiliating truth before that could happen, "Luca, Pam is my foster mother. She moved away about ten years ago. I had no idea she was here."

Even as his hand grasped Pam's, Luca's eyes shot to Daisy in surprise.

Yes, she wanted to say, *one of the unpleasant secrets I warned you about. I told you, you should never have followed me to America.*

"It's a pleasure," he said smoothly.

His gaze moved back and forth between them, and Daisy figured he was seeing what everyone did—Pam's shortness and Daisy's height. Daisy's skin, paler and smoother than Pam's ruddy complexion. Daisy's tight caramel-colored curls, and Pam's lank, bleached-blond bob. Daisy's nose. Daisy's lips.

It was obvious there was no biological connection between them. Pam was as whitebread as they came, and Daisy was…something else.

They barely had an emotional link—even the hot dog guy at the cart down the block could see that. And now Luca could, too. It was utterly humiliating.

Now really wasn't the time, but Daisy couldn't help muttering, "So…you're back from California, I see."

Pam had taken off for the west coast a week after Daisy's graduation from high school. Daisy was forced to crash with friends for months before her freshman year at BU, and then had to beg and wheedle her way into campus jobs that offered housing every summer.

By spring break of her junior year, Daisy had saved up enough money to try visiting her foster mom out west. She'd wanted to see what was what—make sure the woman was okay and not strung out or living out of her car—but Pam had put her off.

She'd claimed she didn't have the room to put Daisy up. Daisy offered to sleep on the couch, or the floor, but Pam wouldn't budge.

Daisy hadn't thought the woman had the power to hurt her anymore, but that had stung. Remembering it now, it still did.

It was no wonder Daisy was so flustered to find the woman here in Brooklyn again, two blocks from where they used to live together, on the exact day Daisy had brought her boyfriend over the bridge to see her old neighborhood.

What were the goddamn odds? Had to be a one-in-a-million coincidence.

Talk about unlucky. Par for the course for Daisy, though.

Pam said, "Yeah. Things weren't working out anymore," but her eyes slid guiltily away.

Daisy wondered what *things* the woman was referring to. She never had gotten a straight answer about what precipitated the move to begin with, or what Pam had done once she landed out there. Not like it mattered.

"Sorry to hear that."

Pam made a face. "Pshhh."

Poor Luca. His eyes ping-ponged back and forth between them, searching for clues to what was going on. He was clearly at a total loss.

"Okay, well," Daisy clapped her hands. "We should probably get going. Good seeing you."

Pam blinked like she hadn't expected such a sudden departure. "Oh. Yeah. Okay."

Daisy gripped Luca's arm and pulled, trying to muscle him along the sidewalk. His feet were planted, though. Maybe he'd refuse to budge until he figured shit out, but if so, he'd be standing there alone. Daisy was so out of there.

Pam piped up again, "Hey—you still got the same number? We should get together sometime. I mean, like not on the street. I found a place to live, a couple blocks from here. You could come over one of these days."

Daisy had zero intention of doing that. The absolute last thing she needed right now was some tweaked reminiscing about the 'good old days.'

"Sounds good," she said blandly. "My number's the same. Text me and we'll figure something out." She felt safe offering, knowing that even if she did want to meet, Pam would almost certainly drop the ball. No harm, no foul.

A busboy ducked his head out of the restaurant Pam had materialized from and waved his arm to get her attention. "Pam! Rodrigo's looking for you. We got customers."

"I gotta go," Pam said. "I'll call you, okay?"

"See ya," Daisy said.

Pam waved and scurried back to work. This time, when Daisy yanked on Luca's arm, he moved.

IT WAS TOO crowded on the subway to talk. *Thank God.* Daisy's thoughts were spinning around in dizzying circles, and her heart was lodged in her throat like a multivitamin that had gone down the wrong way.

Luca stood in front of her, using his bigger body to buy Daisy a little breathing room. Every time the train banked around a curve or rocked on its tracks, her nose smashed into the hollow of his neck.

He smelled so damn good, it hurt. She could feel him staring down at her, could feel the gears turning in that remarkable scientific brain of his. He was sifting through what he'd seen,

Daisy knew, comparing it to things he'd already found out about her.

Lining up the evidence. Measuring it. Weighing the implications. Developing theories. It was what the man did, and by all indications he did it very well.

Before long, Luca was going to identify the cancer. He was going to isolate the tumor, and then he was going to excise it from his life.

Daisy stood there and tried to decide whether she was glad she'd caved in and played girlfriend and boyfriend for the last couple weeks, or not. Was it better to have snatched a few more nights from Luca, before he broke things off? Or had Daisy made the inevitable worse for herself?

His utter, heart-rending perfection was so much fresher in her mind now. That didn't seem ideal. At least before, time had dulled the edge of her longing somewhat. Daisy would have to go through Luca withdrawal all over again, now.

She wondered how he'd do it. Would Luca use work as an excuse? Say he was far too busy to keep getting together and make a clean break of it?

Or would he simply call less and less, and cancel dates more and more, until their connection died a slow, agonizing death from neglect?

Would one method hurt more than the other? It was impossible to decide. Still, Daisy had known all along that Luca would find out about her eventually. Yes, it had happened sooner than she'd anticipated, but it hardly came as a surprise.

Now, she simply had to get through the conversation that was bound to follow Luca meeting Pam. Daisy choked back the sob that tried to climb up her throat. She wished, impossibly, that the train would never arrive in Manhattan—that it would keep on going and she'd never have to meet Luca's eyes again.

Then she'd never have to see the revulsion she knew would be there.

Nineteen

DAISY WAS QUIET as the grave on the train back to Manhattan, and Luca knew she was agonizing over that stiff and awkward meeting with her mother.

He still hadn't decided whether she'd known the woman lived in Brooklyn and had only hoped not to run into her—or whether she really had been as surprised as she seemed.

Lord knew it was the last thing Luca had expected. As he thought about it, he realized that he really hadn't formed any theories about what kind of family Daisy came from—and that was likely due to the fact that she'd never shared any stories or details about any of them.

Still, having met this woman Pam now, Luca could say with conviction that she was not who he would've picked as Daisy's mother. Aside from a certain shared prickliness, they were nothing alike.

Luca was dying to know more, but it was obvious Daisy wasn't ready to fill him in yet. He assumed they'd head on to the MOMA exhibit as they'd planned, and hoped it would take her mind off things.

"I'm not really in the mood anymore," Daisy said, when he checked with her. "But I am starting to get hungry. How about you?"

"I can eat," Luca agreed. He could always eat.

"Then let's get off the train at Washington Square. I know a good place near NYU and I think they have live music tonight. Does that sound good?"

"Any time with you sounds good, *cara*."

When she smiled back at him, her eyes were unbearably sad. Luca tried not to read too much into it and resolved to wait and see what the evening brought.

DAISY WALKED BESIDE him on the sidewalk, but she didn't hold his hand—that wasn't always her way. Luca would've liked the connection, however, and not only because he wasn't feeling too sure about what frame of mind she was in.

She brought him to a dimly-lit bar full of red leather banquettes and sketchy-looking people. They wandered around the place with their tattoos and piercings and hipster clothes, apparently finding the whole Rat Pack schtick to be eminently chic.

Luca stuck out like a broken bone in his cashmere sweater and Italian boots, and *merda*, did they all notice. He would be lucky if he stayed in possession of his wallet, and suspected he'd be humming Sinatra for the next week on top of it.

He'd been noticing that deeply ingrained association with Italian-American culture that many New Yorkers seemed to have now that he was back here. It was slightly Italian, Luca supposed, but also wildly alien—like something a theme park might concoct for its "Taste of Italy" attraction.

Like the love child of actual immigrants and those who'd seen too many Hollywood mafia movies.

Luca must have had quite an expression on his face as he thought about it, because Daisy snorted as she jostled his arm. "What's the matter? Not your kind of people?"

"Not really." There was no use hiding it. "And I can't stop wondering about all the tattoo needles these *cretinos* have used. Were they sterile?" Luca shrugged. "I don't know. I hope so, for everyone's sake."

Daisy laughed and tried to offer him some hand sanitizer from her bag. He waved it away—he had to smell the harsh bite of antiseptic nearly every day of his life. No need to have it associated with Daisy, too.

"No, thank you. I'll go wash my hands in the bathroom once we order."

"You sure? The bathroom might be even worse," she grinned.

"Sure. That stuff is actually terrible. Overusing it contributes to the mutation and drug-resistance of viruses." And…there Luca went sounding like a finicky ass again. It was hard to believe Daisy wanted to be seen at a place like this with him.

It was lucky he'd grown into a tall man by the end of his teens—it was probably all that was keeping him from getting bullied for his lunch money right about now. Maybe even by Daisy herself.

Daisy peered down at the small bottle of sanitizer like she'd never seen it before. Luca's mouth kept emitting non-romantic—and possibly pedantic—words at a breakneck pace. "A healthy immune system needs to be exposed to germs to function well. It needs to build resistance to what's around you so it can protect you from illnesses."

Her mouth twitched, and he couldn't tell if she was amused or annoyed. "Thank you so much for mansplaining that to me, Doctor. What would I do without you?"

"Feel sad?" Luca tried.

He took in her abruptly blank expression, and his mouth went insurmountably dry. Daisy was hiding something. Something important.

Where was that drink he'd ordered, anyway? They'd probably had to go out and find more ice, he guessed, despite it being winter. Every drink in this country seemed to require ice and more ice.

For something to do, Luca grabbed the little carafe of olive oil from the salad dressing caddy, poured a dot on his finger, and smoothed it over his lips.

Daisy's expression grew stranger. "I'm sorry—did you just use olive oil as lip balm?"

"Yes." Of course, he had. Who didn't?

She tilted her head. "Does it work?"

"Very well. My mother uses it on everything. Dry skin. Dry hair…"

"Pasta?"

Now she was teasing him. "That too."

Up on stage, a raggedy-looking bunch of miscreants was congregating, tuning their instruments and consulting with each other periodically.

Daisy sat up straight and elbowed him enthusiastically, but her smile still didn't quite reach her eyes. "Wait till you hear these guys," she told him. "They're a lot of fun."

LUCA TRIED TO enjoy the music, he really did. But it was loud and it was fast, and it wasn't the least bit conducive to enjoying his surprisingly-delicious carbonara.

It also made it impossible to have much of a conversation with Daisy. Maybe she'd planned it that way, though. Maybe it was what she'd needed.

Once the performance ended, however, it was a relief to be able to slide in next to Daisy on her side of the booth and put his arm around her. She leaned her head against Luca's shoulder and toyed with her coffee cup. Over near the bar, there was an American football game being played on the television.

After the excellent pasta, he'd had high hopes for the cannoli, but it was sadly soggy and cold as ice. The coffee was better, and it was nice to linger over it now that the majority of the strange people had left.

Luca kissed the crown of Daisy's head and took a lock of her hair thoughtfully between his fingers. He stretched it straight, then smiled to himself when it sprang back into its natural coil. Like a princess's hair, instead of an ordinary woman's.

"So…your father must have been the one of African descent," he said, thinking of Pam. "Do I have that right?"

Daisy's fingers froze on the table. "No, he…I don't know, actually," she said.

"But Pam—"

"Was only my foster mother."

"Yes. The woman who married your father," Luca confirmed.

"You're thinking of step-parents. I have no biological relationship to either Pam or her husband," she clarified.

Pam was married? Luca went silent while he considered what Daisy was telling him.

"Scared yet?" she wondered bitterly.

"Daisy, no." Luca turned to face her. "Of course I'm not. I just want to understand, that's all."

"Well, foster care is when the government removes a child from their biological family because that family is unfit to raise them, or is neglecting them somehow. Then the government gives the kid to total strangers, who get paid to take care of them."

A light went on, and Luca sat back. "Ah," he said. It was hard to hide his shock. He'd never considered that Daisy might have something like that in her past, and he ached for how hard that must have been for her.

"Bet you're reconsidering dating me now, aren't you?"

Suddenly, much of her reluctance became crystal clear to him. She'd seen his close family, compared it to her own, and decided she didn't measure up.

"What kind of person would I be," Luca wondered aloud, "If I judged you by the choices other people made? Choices you were probably far too young to participate in or understand? Things that weren't even your fault?"

"Still," Daisy insisted brusquely. "Those are my genes. Those are the kind of people who made me—who raised me. I can't change the fact that it affected me."

"Why do I suspect you mostly raised yourself?"

"Because you've talked to me for longer than five minutes?"

"And now I've also met Pam." Luca shook his head again. "How old were you when Pam got you?"

"I was two. Pam and her husband were apparently my third foster family, but I don't remember the others. She always liked to say, 'third time's the charm,' though, so I remember that part."

"And how long were you with her?" If Daisy was in a sharing mood, Luca was going to take advantage of it, and find out as much as he could.

"Sixteen years."

That was stunning. "So long?"

Daisy snorted. "You'd think that would be a good thing, right? Pam and her husband Ray took me in, intending to adopt me if they could. But then Ray took off. Pam never gave me up, but she never went through with the adoption either."

"So you were hers…" Luca began.

"…but not," Daisy finished. "I've never belonged to anyone but myself." Luca must have looked like he had something to say about that, because she rushed on, "I put it all together when I was fourteen."

He contemplated that tidbit, then asked, "What do you know about your biological family? The authorities must have told Pam something, no?"

"If Pam ever knew anything about my history, she's long since forgotten it. Which means I also know nothing." Daisy shrugged, and it was almost studied in its callousness. "That's in the past, anyway. I've moved on."

"Have you?"

"I had to. I had no choice," she said. "Not if I wanted to keep living a life I could value. Not if I wanted to be able to look myself in the eye at the end of the day. Wallowing in your misfortunes gets you exactly nowhere. Busting your ass to be the person you want to be is a lot more productive."

What an incredible woman she was. Luca kissed Daisy softly and murmured, "Was she kind to you, at least?"

"Pam was fine," she sighed. "People probably thought we were like any other single mom and her kid, until I got older and mouthier."

"Except, she made you call her Pam? Not Mamma?"

"No, that was all me. I stopped calling her 'Mom' when I was fourteen."

"When you 'put it together.'" Luca frowned. "What happened?" He couldn't believe she was finally telling him all of this.

Daisy said, "I got accepted to a performing arts high school in Manhattan, on a full scholarship. When Pam brought me over to register me, that's when I found out I wasn't actually hers. I mean…I guess I knew she hadn't birthed me, but I'd always just assumed I was adopted. Turns out I was only some stray she got paid to feed."

Luca didn't attempt to convince her of anything rosy or optimistic. He only said, "That's a very difficult age to find out something like that."

"You think?" Daisy was acting abrasive, but it was like she couldn't help herself. It was as if her tender parts had been exposed to the elements, leaving her raw and defensive.

He wished he could hold her—comfort her, *somehow*—but Luca didn't think she'd accept it. "Had you ever asked Pam about your father before then? You must have been at least a little curious, after Ray left."

"Yeah, of course I was. But Pam was always so cagey about it. I started to think…" Daisy fell silent. "It sounds so sordid."

"What?" What harm could a child's speculation from so long ago do? It changed nothing about who she was now.

Daisy admitted, "I started to wonder if maybe she'd been raped. If I was the product of that."

"Oh, *cara*." Luca's heart felt bruised, just hearing it. How much worse had it been for Daisy to feel it?

"Awful, right?"

"*Sì*. I'm so sorry you had to go through that."

"Well. You know—it is what it is. I'm better now. Less angry," she said.

"And you have no desire to know the truth about your real parents now?" Luca would be searching under every rock on the planet, if he were her.

"What good would it do?"

It wasn't a rhetorical question. Daisy looked genuinely curious, as if she'd never come up with a single compelling reason to try to find anything out about herself. She seemed to think that she was who she was, and her conception of herself wouldn't change if she knew a few more details about her infancy.

"Perhaps…" Luca cupped her cheek gently, then slid his hand down to rest over her beating heart. "Perhaps knowing would give you peace. Understanding."

She scoffed, "Believe me, I understand plenty."

Poor Daisy. Evidently, this was one of those reasons she didn't think he'd want her. Luca didn't believe for a minute that she understood things, or that she'd moved past them, but now was not the time to dispute her assertions.

It was time to change the subject. Big time.

Daisy apparently agreed. "For example," she said, edging closer, "I think I understand how to turn that frown of yours right upside down."

"I think—" She stopped Luca's words cold when she slid one hand onto his thigh and squeezed the meat of his quadriceps. Daisy raked the short, polished nails on her other hand across his stomach, and a third nearby part of him became quite noticeably interested in the proceedings.

Daisy purred in appreciation. "I think you should let me," she said. "Want to get out of here?"

"*Gesù Cristo.*" Luca tossed an unsteady hand into the air and waved over their server. "The check, *per favore.*"

Twenty

I T HADN'T TAKEN very long for Red to decide that Luca's stress levels were hovering at unacceptable levels—which was awfully ironic, coming from him. Between running the large conglomerate his grandfather had started, and planning his wedding to Piper, Luca's friend was as highly-strung as anyone.

Even so, Luca had only been back in New York for a matter of weeks before Red began making something of a project out of him.

There'd been weekend invitations to arts events around town, introductions to people Red and Piper thought Luca might like, and helpful suggestions about where he could find the best markets and coffee shops.

There was also, sadly, a lot of exercise-shaming taking place—and his old friend's emphasis on physical fitness was becoming even more stressful than the *agida* it was supposed to vanquish.

Seriously, Luca was a doctor. He knew he was supposed to stay active. But why did it have to take such ridiculous forms? What was so wrong with a stroll around the block at lunchtime, or a dignified, nightly walk after dinner?

He supposed nothing, if one actually managed to *take* that daily walk. Luca, however, was not good at remembering to do so in a timely fashion, and Red knew it. By the time it did occur to him to get moving it was often too dark and too late at night, and Luca was more likely to get pick-pocketed than to lower his blood pressure.

The situation had led, quite clearly, to his current predicament.

Today, presumably as some sort of reward for good behavior, Red had decided to take Luca for a run in the park, reacquainting him with a trail they'd last set foot on together in their early twenties. The sunny, cold morning was perfect, Red said, to get some fresh air.

Luca sighed. Maybe it would have been better, if he hadn't been up half the night, alternately making love to Daisy, and reassuring her that he had no plans to cast her off just because her foster mother was more salt-of-the-earth than fairy godmother.

At least he and Red might get to have a conversation while they trotted around the park like a couple of panting stallions. True, they'd be sharing the path with all the other vain and fitness-mad New Yorkers, but between Luca's new job and Red's, there wasn't as much time for simple talking as there'd been before. He'd accept what he could get.

UNFORTUNATELY, BY THE time Luca had donned a pair of track pants and his newest pair of sneakers, then hailed a cab to find Red at the appointed entrance off 5th Avenue, his *amico* had clearly been at the sprinting thing for a while already.

"Did you *run* here?" Luca demanded, aghast. Wasn't the scheduled route bad enough, without Red adding on to it by galloping all the way from his and Piper's loft in Chelsea?

"Of course. How else was I supposed to get over here?"

Luca gaped at him, and his breath made a cloud of steam in front of his face. "Like I did. By taxi."

Red groaned, "God, I forgot what a fucking baby you can be. Come on, hop to it. I clearly have more work to do on you than I thought. You went soft in Italy."

Luca felt around on his stomach, but his abdominal muscles still seemed reasonably firm. He executed a few half-hearted stretches, then reluctantly fell into step beside Red.

The winter air felt jagged and sharp as it sawed in and out of his lungs. Luca thought with longing of the fancy blue enamel coffee maker sitting on his kitchen counter at home, and how nice a hot cup of cappuccino would taste right then.

"This is not efficient," Luca griped, once he saw which way they were heading. "By the time we're done, I won't be anywhere near home. And you will be even farther from yours."

"Think of it this way, Princess. You might not be in your neighborhood anymore, but you'll be very close to Daisy's."

That was…interesting. And not in the unpleasant way that running at dawn was *interesting*. If Daisy had slept in, as any right-thinking human would have after the night they'd shared, she'd be all warm and snuggly when Luca reached her. Her guard would be down. She'd be sweet.

And then he could wake her up. Luca sighed, thinking of it. He did love morning sex with a beautiful, sleepy woman, and morning sex with Daisy was absolute heaven times a thousand.

Red was peering at him like Luca had three heads, however, instead of the two in current usage. Luca heaved another beleaguered sigh. "Lead on," he said, gesturing to Red. "You win. I'll chase after your little carrot."

As Red grinned and raced away, impossibly long legs pumping, Luca did, indeed, feel like a slow, plodding mule chasing a carrot lure.

Maybe the hospital had a gym somewhere he could use. A trainer to whip him into shape. A pill they could prescribe, to suddenly transform Luca into a superhero, instead of the carbohydrate-loving man he was.

THERE WERE DIFFICULTIES, naturally. Red was not the only resident of Manhattan who'd chosen that spot to get his exercise, and so, there were plenty of witnesses to Luca's abysmal attempts to keep up and look manly at the same time.

He'd assumed he was in reasonable shape, all things considered—he ate well, and being on his feet most of each day kept him lean. Red, however, was in excellent shape. Prime health. Top form.

It was exceptionally humbling.

Perhaps worse than that, however, was that despite the frosty temperature, Luca was soon perspiring like the racehorse Red was trying to make him into. Which meant that when they finally wrapped up this farce, Red would likely step into the climate-controlled luxury of a chauffeured car for his trip home—and Luca would set off on his quest to find Daisy looking like a flushed and sweaty refugee from a sanitarium.

He spotted an empty bench near the pond and plopped onto it in frustration. Once Red realized his running buddy was no longer dogging his heels, he paused, circled back, and stood trotting in place. Scowling darkly, of course.

"What's wrong, sweetheart? All tuckered out?"

Luca huffed, peeled off his fleece, and mopped his face and neck with it. The cold air made his sodden t-shirt feel twice as cold as before, and he hated how clammy it felt against his skin. So he peeled that off too, and tossed it on the bench beside him. Shivering and half-dressed, he leaned forward to retie his shoelaces.

Red whistled, long and mocking. "Jesus, Luca. What the hell happened to your back?"

Luca shook his head in confusion, but Red's expression said it all.

"Tangle with a tiger recently?" his friend prodded mercilessly.

In a sudden rush, Luca was back in Daisy's bed, nipping at her neck while her nails scored his skin and she moaned loud enough to wake the dead. He felt his face get warm. Well, *more* warm.

Red studied his expression and groaned in dismay. "That is so much more information than I wanted to know about one of my employees, you horny fuck."

"You brought it up," Luca muttered, fighting to remain calm so he wouldn't instigate further teasing. "Don't think about it." And then, considering the situation a little more, he pointed at his friend and added, "Don't think about *her*."

"Settle down, Adonis. You may remember I have my own woman to worry about. I can assure you Piper consumes one-hundred-percent of my thoughts."

He didn't have to look so smug about it. "Adonis was Greek," Luca pointed out, and then he reluctantly struggled back into his now-frigid clothes.

Maybe if he removed the sight of Daisy's passionate scratches, Red would deign to remove them from the conversation.

Luca couldn't go see Daisy like this, he thought. It was one thing to work up a sweat *with* the woman. It was quite another to show up on her doorstep at some ungodly hour, looking like a derelict before she'd even had her morning coffee. His mother would die of shame if she ever found out.

He pushed to his feet and trooped after Red while he considered his options. Luca could bring Daisy the coffee she'd undoubtedly need to endure the sight of him, but he was not completely sure how she took it and he didn't want to get it wrong.

As for himself, he'd almost consider a career change to Proctology if it meant someone would hand him a cup of hot caffeine in the next few minutes.

Red cast him an amused sidelong look. "The Romans called him Adonis, too, FYI."

Luca shook his head. "Why do I agree to do these things with you?"

"Because you know it's good for you," Red retorted. "Now, if you're a good little boy and pick up the goddamn pace, I'll buy you breakfast afterward."

"I can't go out to eat like this," Luca protested. "Look at me." Red, on the other hand, looked fresh as a daisy, his fair skin barely flushed and his hair not even damp.

"Relax. It's just a little shithole diner," he said. "Trust me, we'll be overdressed."

"So, you make me run around out here in the name of health, and then you undo all my hard work with a plateful of grease? How is that helping?"

"Who's working hard? Not you."

"*Stronzo*," Luca muttered.

"Out of the two of us, one of us is acting like an asshole, and the other one is me. Now come on. You love bacon. You know you do."

Red had him there. And it could be worse—at least Luca wasn't a smoker like Dr. Fitz or addicted to diet soda like Dr. Green. Using that scale, a couple of pieces of bacon here and there hardly seemed to rate.

It did appear like a visit to Daisy's was out, however. Unless—

"I don't suppose you have a shower at your office I could borrow," Luca mused. If he had his bearings and remembered correctly, the PKM headquarters would be right around there somewhere.

Red laughed outright. "Oh, man. You can't even visit her without getting cleaned up? You've got it *bad*, Luca."

"You know," Luca pointed out, "Not too long ago, I was the one listening to your drunken, lovelorn ramblings. You might remember that when you're making all your jokes."

"Oh, yes. Let's talk about that. Because your asinine advice was *so* damn helpful," Red said drily.

Maybe Luca should just stop talking. It would have the added benefit of preserving his air, since Red seemed like he might be intending to run until they hit Harlem, at this point.

His supposed friend punched him in the arm, knocking him off his stride for a step. Luca growled. It was getting to be more of a struggle to keep up with Red's longer legs.

"God, you big baby. Would you chill out? I'll call PKM security from the diner and let them know we're coming."

Luca nodded, and concentrated on not dying of asphyxiation.

"For the record, this was supposed to be fun," Red said.

Luca looked at him and had to smile. In a peculiar way, it *was* fun. Back in Italy, he had siblings and cousins, and neighborhood friends that he'd known for so long they were like family. But no friends had ever been quite like Red and Tate.

It was wonderful to be together again, making jokes and needling each other. And as much as he loved his home in *Firenze*, Luca had missed this. Missed his old roommates. Missed New York.

It was nearly unfathomable that Daisy should turn up right in the middle of all that. But that was fate for you—always getting creative and kicking you a ball you weren't expecting.

Luca wasn't going to ignore the signs, though. If the universe meant for him and Daisy to be together, then so be it. Luca was going along for the ride, and happily.

BY THE TIME he got to Daisy's house, he was full of bacon and eggs and appropriately caffeinated. He was also freshly showered, courtesy of the luxurious bathroom connected to Red's corner office and wearing a fresh set of gym clothes his friend had had in the closet.

Luca would've preferred a dress shirt and some slacks, but Red's pants were about four inches too long, and his shirts were a bit too narrow through the shoulders. It didn't end up mattering.

Daisy answered the door in a t-shirt and a pair of running tights. Her face was glowing, and her breath was coming fast. Luca might have thought she was aroused just from the sight of him, if it hadn't been for the treadmill he spotted in the corner of her living room.

"Oh, *cara*. Not you, too," Luca groaned sadly.

She walked over and released some lever with her foot, then tilted the deck of the treadmill up to free up floor space. "What's that supposed to mean?"

"It means you don't need to act like a hamster to look nice. You're beautiful as you are."

"That's very nice to say, but you clearly have no idea what my ass would look like if I didn't work out."

"Bigger? Rounder?" Luca guessed. "Because I would be happy with either of those."

Daisy merely rolled her eyes. "You think you would. But you're not imagining the cellulite involved."

"Trust me. I just spent the morning racing around after Red in the park. If having more meat on you is the price you'd have to pay for not going through that kind of torture, then do it. Pay that bill. I won't complain."

"You know, it gets easier the more you do it."

"Maybe."

Daisy examined him critically. "Do you actually expect me to believe that you went running and you look like *that*?"

"I showered at Red's office. You would not want to have seen me in the condition I was in, once we were done."

Daisy grabbed a towel from her kitchen and wiped off her face. "I don't get it. If you don't usually run, then how do you stay in that kind of shape?" She made a hasty circle with her hand in his direction. Perhaps she meant he was as round as a watermelon, but Luca dearly hoped not.

He figured a little bluster might not go amiss, though. "Italian genes, *cara*. They're the best in the world."

"Oh please. Italian ego, more like."

"Whichever. Just please don't start making me run 5Ks with you."

Daisy walked over and put her arms around him. She seemed lighter since they'd gotten the family conversation out of the way—more like she'd been in Florence. "You're kind of crazy, you know that?" she asked softly.

"Aren't we all?"

Luca was crazy for her, anyway. She was tough, yet fragile. Beautiful, but scarred. Moody, and still kind. Daisy had no comprehension that her differences were the very things that made her so incomparably unique.

Luca had never met another woman like her, and she made every one of his synapses fire and flare with longing.

Twenty-One

ULTIMATELY, DAISY WAS forced to concede that maybe she'd been wrong about Luca. She hadn't given him enough credit. Because—other than expressing a genuine non-irritating sympathy for her family history—he had been blithely unconcerned by it all.

He'd simply accepted the information, and then moved on. No disgust or repulsion in his voice. No change in the way he treated her at all. Which was sort of mind-boggling, after the way Daisy had built it up in her mind.

Her therapist would probably remind her at this point that half the things Daisy worried about never came to pass. Still, not having that embarrassing disclosure hanging over her head was nice.

Instead of acting like a landmine simmering under the surface of her days, her history as a foster kid had morphed into uninteresting landscaping—a bush beside the path of her life. Something you walked right on by.

Imagine that. It was a good part of why, when Daisy rolled into work come Monday, she felt better than she had in a long time. And her mood improved even more when she realized which project she got to start work on that day.

After lunch, Daisy had scheduled the first design meeting for her next big job, a plum assignment that everyone in the department had fought to win. She'd been shocked to be the one who eventually won the author over, but Daisy had worked hard to do so.

While all the others had created their cover mock-ups from the same roster of models Trident had been using for years, Daisy had taken a chance and gone out to haunt the college coffee shops around the city—and she'd found several fresh new faces for Tabitha Lovell to gush over.

Daisy had gotten lucky, but she'd also known that many art and photography students were short on cash and happy to make an extra buck doing some modeling for their peers.

They were more than happy to help out a fellow professional who was already out of school and might someday give them a job lead.

So, where the other designers made do with tinting the skin and hair of mostly white models, Daisy delivered the needle-in-the-haystack visage of an extraordinary young woman she'd discovered on the subway one day.

Sarah, as it turned out, was a member of the Blackfeet Nation—and she was modeling to put herself through the pre-med program at Columbia.

She was also so sick of her own face and the attention it garnered her at this point, that once she was done with school, she'd probably never look into the business end of a lens again. Or a mirror. Or even her reflection in a puddle.

Daisy had never met someone less at risk for developing a selfie addiction. But Sarah was refreshingly candid and whip-smart to boot, and she'd readily agreed to pose if Daisy landed the project.

Sarah was only the jewel in the crown, though—the capstone in a full cast of beautiful men and women Daisy had assembled to win over the inimitable Ms. Lovell.

It was a daunting prospect, not least because Daisy was a big fan of her work. Lovell's last erotic romances had been set in a Chicago warehouse sex club, and Daisy had devoured every-smoking hot title.

That series had put Tabitha on the map, but she was a force of nature in her own right—a rising star in the industry, and an unflinching champion of diversifying the stories that got told and sold and read.

Red had been ecstatic to woo her over to Trident, and they were all positive that her new series was going to be an enormous hit. Daisy did not intend to be the weakest link in the chain of people determined to make that happen.

She was going to take Tabitha's kaleidoscope of Wild West characters—formerly enslaved people, Mexican immigrants, Native Americans, and East coast outcasts among them—and turn them into book covers that readers would drool over.

Daisy had to bring to life a whole rowdy town of vividly-real couples in order to do justice to Ms. Lovell's vision. Tabitha's work was always a mad, colorful carnival of all kinds of love stories, and Daisy's brain was swimming with rough Western backdrops, a full spectrum of humanity, and steamy embraces.

All the embraces. She could not wait.

BY THE END of the day, Daisy was both euphoric and immensely frustrated. Tabitha was a dream to work with—bursting with creativity and ideas that Daisy could definitely incorporate into her designs.

However, the sticking point was that the penultimate book in the series, the culmination of so many seeds planted in all the other titles and the set-up for the dramatic finale, was still a bit of a gray area for the author.

For both of them, actually.

Daisy took a deep breath, determined to get to the bottom of it. "Tell me again what this book's about." There had to be something she could use, some detail that would unlock an idea for the cover design.

"This is about the daughter of the couple from book two. Remember? The hero escaped from his abusive plantation-owning father and came out to Fortitude to find the girl he'd been in love with since he was four years old."

"Ah. Right. The enslaved girl his father had sold off. Maggie, right?"

"Yes, but she escaped after that."

"And by the end of their book, she's pregnant, isn't she?"

"Exactly!" Tabitha enthused. "And by the time *this* book takes place, that baby is all grown up and getting her own happily-ever-after."

"Naturally," Daisy nodded, totally approving of the inevitability of that development. "Now tell me who she's getting her HEA with."

"One day, when Maggie's daughter is doing inventory in her parent's saloon storeroom, a new man arrives, wanting to sell her tequila."

"Just any kind of tequila, or…?"

Tabitha chuckled. "Of course not. It's his family's special label."

Daisy probed for more, "And…?"

"He's Mexican. And super hot."

"And selling tequila."

Ms. Lovell rubbed her hands together with glee. "Yes!"

Daisy tried once more to envision a possible cover. "Uh…can you give me *anything* else?" In her mind, she was seeing a dusty storeroom and open boxes of booze, but…would that be too similar to the stables and saloons of some of the other covers they'd devised?

Tabitha's face fell. "Not yet. Don't spread it around, but that's actually all I've got so far."

"Seriously?"

"Yeah, I really want to get it right, so it's been tricky," she sighed. "But…oh! Wait—his horse's name is Ronaldo. He's going to be really funny. Does that help?"

Daisy held up her hands. This was going off the rails rapidly. "Okay. Okay, we have to focus. So…Jose Cuervo should look…how?"

"Tall, obviously. Dark. And—"

Daisy laughed, "Let me guess. Handsome?"

"Pshhhh," she scoffed. "*Yeah.* Goes without saying."

Daisy flipped through the photos of the men she'd found so far, searching for a possible match among the ones they hadn't earmarked for other covers. As she looked at the headshots, she prodded Tabitha, "And Saloon Sally—what about her?"

"Lighter complexion than some of the others, I'd say. Don't forget, her dad is a redheaded Scottish immigrant."

Daisy nodded, thinking. She'd seen one girl, a photography major at NYU, who might fit the bill. Except then Tabitha's face scrunched up and she stared right at Daisy with a strange expression on her face.

"I don't suppose you ever do any modeling?" she asked.

"No. Never," Daisy laughed. She was *not* the type.

"Okay, but can I—?" Tabitha sat back, then leaned right forward again. "I know this is weird, but can I take your picture?"

"Why?"

"*Duh*. Because your face is amazing. I'm totally using you for inspiration. Hey—maybe I can even name her after you!"

"*What?*" Daisy squawked. She was a behind-the-scenes worker. She had no business whatsoever being in the foreground.

Tabitha was already laughing and cheerfully tapping on her phone screen, though. "Come on, don't worry! It'll be our secret!"

"Ms. Lovell," she groaned. "That's a terrible idea."

"Trust me. It'll be *fine*."

—————————————◇—————————————

THAT NIGHT, HELL must have frozen over, because Pam called Daisy's cell phone. *Guess she hadn't lost the number after all*, Daisy thought, settling into the armchair next to Jerome's tank while she tried to figure out *why* her foster mom was calling.

After a few minutes of insanely awkward and unenlightening small talk, she decided to bite the bullet and ask a question that had been nagging at her ever since her conversation with Luca.

"This probably a dumb question," Daisy announced. Why was she even bothering? It wasn't like knowing was going to get her anywhere.

"You always say that. But I don't think you've ever asked a stupid question in your life."

"I...thanks." *What the hell?*

"It's not like it's surprising," Pam said. "You always were sharp as a tack. Even when you were just a tiny thing."

Daisy paused and bit her lip. "Anyway...I was talking to a friend the other day and it made me wonder something." *There.* Better to blame this little burst of crazy on Luca. Then maybe Pam wouldn't give her shit for it.

"What's that?"

"How come you never adopted me? You had me all those years, and you used to say you were going to, and then you never did."

The words came out in a mortifying rush, and once they were hanging in the air between them like a putrid green cloud of stupid, Daisy wished she could cram them back in again.

Pam didn't say anything for a long moment. "That's not so dumb a question. You probably deserve to know." There was some rustling over the line, and then Pam added, "I should have."

"Why didn't you, though?"

Daisy could hear her foster mother swallow in the quiet. "Couple reasons, I guess. For one thing, we found out it was more expensive than we'd thought. We'd always planned to save up together, though. But then, once Ray left…"

"You didn't want me anymore?"

"No, nothing like that. I just thought…" Pam hesitated painfully. "It sounds blockheaded now that I'm saying it out loud, but I convinced myself that if I waited to go through with your adoption until Ray came back…"

Daisy waited, so long she thought Pam wouldn't actually finish.

"…then maybe he *would* come back," her foster mom finally said. Her voice caught on the last word, and she coughed to cover it up.

"But he didn't."

"No, he didn't. And by the time I figured out he wasn't ever going to come back, it was too late. You were grown and flown, as they say."

"Did you ever find out where Ray went?" Daisy wondered. "Maybe something happened to him."

"Oh, I don't know. I mean, how would it matter? The only important part seemed to me to be the part where he was gone." Pam was dismissive. *Too* dismissive. Maybe this was harder for her to talk about than she let on.

"You must have missed him," Daisy said, trying to understand. "Didn't you?"

She hated to be a buzzkill, but the truth was the truth. "Not really. I barely knew the guy. What was I? Five or six when he left?"

"Six, I think. You'd just finished kindergarten."

"So that's four years with Ray, give or take, right? I don't really remember him being around much, even then. And I think I only remember his face because you used to show me his picture sometimes."

"Ray worked a lot," Pam explained, "Drove a cab and worked as a busboy when we needed the extra dough. He got a kick out of you, though. Thought you were so funny when you got mad."

A scared, upset kid didn't sound very hilarious to Daisy.

Pam said softly, "He was really good at talking you out of your tantrums. He'd make faces and jokes until you stopped yelling long enough to listen, and then he'd explain things so you could understand. He was much better at it than me. I just seemed to make you madder."

Daisy had never heard any of this. And Ray actually sounded like kind of a nice guy. "I'm sorry he never came back," she said.

"Not your fault," Pam fired back in a rusty bark.

"Are you sure? Maybe Ray didn't like having a grouchy kid around all the time." Daisy hadn't ever thought of it like that before, but hell—maybe Ray leaving *was* her fault.

"Yes, I'm sure, Daze. He never complained about you. Not ever."

"But maybe inside—"

"No, kid. He loved you. He loved us. Why the heck do you think I spent so much time hanging around, hoping he'd come back? If Ray had been some knucklehead loser, I would've moved on with my life and never looked back. Okay? Stop trying to borrow trouble that ain't yours."

Right. That was exactly what Daisy's therapist liked to say. Just because someone acted in a way that was less than ideal, didn't automatically make it her fault, or her responsibility. Daisy took a deep breath, and let her exhale clear out all the garbage stewing in her brain.

"Anyway, thanks for telling me," she said to Pam. "I know you don't like dredging up stuff, but sometimes it helps me to fill in the blanks. Helps me understand."

"I get it." Pam seemed to be done and then some with their little chat. "Hey—call me anytime, okay, kid? If you think of something else? Or if you decide you want to hang out?"

"I will. Thanks."

"All right. Talk soon." And Pam hung up, just like that.

Daisy massaged her forehead, trying to work some sense into her brain. Why had she done that? All the old stuff didn't matter. It never had.

Except, for some reason…it did, now. And a dangerous thought began to take root, one that could only lead to trouble. Damn Luca and his probing questions.

Who *were* Daisy's real parents anyway? And why had they lost custody of her?

Could Daisy actually find out, now that she was an adult with resources and people who could help her?

Did she actually…want to?

Twenty-Two

DAISY GAVE HERSELF some time, to see if the new idea that had floated into her brain decided to shimmer right back out again the same way it had arrived.

Instead of doing that, the notion settled into a solid weight that basically threw on its parking brake and refused to budge.

It was blocking traffic up there in her head. Double-parked in the middle of a busy intersection and not going anywhere.

Annoyed with herself, Daisy sat at her laptop one night after work, when Luca had stayed late at the hospital, and started doing internet searches. There were no fewer than six public and private entities that currently handled foster care in the Brooklyn borough.

It was impossible to know if they were the same ones that had been operating thirty years ago, when she'd been born. Six was a lot, too—Daisy didn't know if she could endure one phone call to ask for what she wanted, much less half a dozen identical ones.

She couldn't stop thinking about it, though, so one day on her lunch break she took the plunge and texted Pam at the number her foster mother had used to call her the last time.

It went through.

Don't suppose you recall the name of the agency that placed me with you and Ray, Daisy wrote, heart in her throat.

Three days later, Pam finally texted back, *You're on a roll, huh? Not sure, but I think it was something religious. Maybe Saint something?*

Daisy couldn't fathom how someone didn't have that kind of detail tattooed indelibly on their brain, not to mention how they wouldn't have kept scrupulous records of the information pertinent to a real live baby's life.

Daisy rechecked her list to see if any of the places fit Pam's recollection. In the religious category, there was an "Our Lady of Hope Child Services" and an "Angel of Mercy Baby and Child Services."

However, there was also a "Saint Street Child Care." And while it appeared to only function as a church daycare facility now, maybe its mission had changed over time.

Daisy decided to start there but naturally, she got nowhere fast. The first receptionist she spoke to was friendly enough, Daisy supposed, but she didn't know anything that helped. However, she swore she'd have someone else call Daisy back that afternoon.

When that call came through, Daisy was on her way down the stairs into the subway, heading home from work. She retraced her steps up to the street, garnering a slew of pissy comments from the other commuters annoyed by her backtracking, then tucked herself against a bagel shop's front window so she could hear what the Saint Street woman had to say.

"I'm looking for information on my own foster care placement," Daisy explained woodenly. "Or, actually—trying to find out about my biological family. The one I was removed from. I'd like to come in and look at my file when you have time."

She'd been coaching herself to deliver that spiel firmly and professionally. It was harder to walk all over someone who was confident and decisive—a lesson it had taken Daisy years to learn.

"Name?" the woman intoned.

"Daisy Montgomery."

"Spell that for me, please."

"Daisy, like the flower. D-A-I-S-Y. Montgomery. M-O-N-T-G-O-M-E-R-Y."

"And that's your legal birth name?"

Daisy blinked. *Was it?* She said, "Y-yes," but she had no idea if she was right. Could Pam and Ray have been creative enough to give her a nickname that stuck, or even have changed her name altogether?

"Date of birth?"

"July tenth."

The woman waited for a beat. "I need the year, too, ma'am."

"Shoot. 1989," Daisy told her.

There was complete silence over the line, and Daisy rubbed one boot against the other. The temperature outside was dropping now, and far above her, between the tops of the buildings near Trident's main offices, the sky was turning a deep, steely gray.

It smelled like it was going to snow soon. True, the sidewalk where she was lingering also smelled like pee, but *welcome to New York*, right?

The woman's voice came back abruptly. "So, you were eighteen in what year? 2006?"

"No, 2007," Daisy corrected her. What did the year she'd aged out of the system have to do with anything?

"Oh, then I can't help you. We got a new computer system about eight years ago, and all the old data from before then was archived."

"But what if someone needs it? How do you get to it?"

"I don't know. But your stuff might've still been in paper records, anyway. I know those were put into storage at some point, but I have no idea where."

"Well, who would know? Can I talk to them?"

"Lady, I've been here for donkey's years. Even the pastor is younger than me now. If I don't know, no one does."

"So, that's it? I'm just shit out of luck?"

"Seems so. I'm sorry."

Daisy gave in to her frustration and disappointment. She didn't even know if she was calling the right place, to begin with.

She growled, "Yeah, you sound like it," and hung up.

"HEY, FLOWER CHILD," Poppy said, when Daisy called her a few nights later to chat. "How's life?"

"Good. It's good."

"Two 'goods'?" Poppy drawled. "This will be interesting."

"Why do you say that?"

"Never mind. Just tell me where I need to meet you, so we can hide the body."

Daisy laughed. "No body. Yet. But I'm really freaking confused, and I'm not sure where to go from here."

"All right, well—that happens to all of us periodically."

"I know." It didn't feel like it, though. Daisy sat like a lump and watched Jerome investigate some moss in his aquarium.

"You remember how it works, though, right? You tell me what's up, and I deliver clever ideas you haven't thought of yet?"

"That's weird. I remember you being more of a 'let's get drunk and go pierce something' kind of girl. I must have misdialed."

Poppy snorted. "How about you get comfortable with that one piercing for now. I'll attempt to be a decent listener for the rest of this."

"All right. Here's the deal. I'm dating this new guy, right? Well—actually old guy. Not *old*, old. Former. *Crap.* Just—I had a thing with him back in Italy and now he lives here and is driving pretty hard to the hoop."

Poppy processed that. "Got it. I think. Proceed."

"Luca is really normal and shit. I tried not to get involved, because you know I'm the exact opposite of that. But for some reason…he *likes* me. A lot, apparently."

"Imagine that. And I bet you held out on him for all of—what? Two days? Three?"

"Not even. But that's not the point."

"If you say so."

"It's just that he met Pam." Daisy's words landed like an elephant in the middle of their conversation, and Daisy could almost feel Poppy sit up and take notice.

"You don't say."

"Afterward, we had a long conversation, and Luca said some stuff that got me thinking."

"About what?"

"About…" Daisy gulped and pushed on, knowing Poppy wouldn't freak and make a big thing out of it. "My birth family. So, I tried to do something dumb."

"Wait, let me guess," her friend said. "You finally burned down Brooklyn." Poppy sighed, "I know it was a long time coming, Sweet Cheeks, but that's a lotta damn bodies to hide."

Her friend was only trying to joke her into feeling steady, but Daisy still had to get the last part of the story out.

"Pops, I tried to find the agency that placed me with Pam. I don't even know if I was barking up the wrong tree or not, but they basically refused to help me."

"Why?"

"Some a-hole lady said my records were too old."

"Well, that sucks."

"It felt like it, anyway. But what if she's right? What if I waited too long and now it's too late?" Poppy didn't say anything for a long time. Daisy groaned, "That's what you think, isn't it?"

"No…" her friend murmured, drawing out the word. "Actually, I was scheming."

"That's slightly more encouraging. What do you—?"

"You remember my sister-in-law, Meg?"

"Yeah."

"Her best friend Molly is a lawyer down south. She's married to one, too. I think they both do estate law, but I bet they'd know of something you could try."

Daisy winced. "Lawyers, Pop? I don't know if that's—"

"Relax, I'm not saying you should sue someone or anything. But maybe Meg's friend will have an idea. It's worth a shot, isn't it?"

THAT PROBABLY EXPLAINED how Daisy found herself printing a letter emailed to her from the Alexander & Alexander law firm in Wilmington, North Carolina ten days later, which she then slipped into an envelope and dropped in the postal box on the corner of her block.

It didn't quite explain why she then felt as exposed as if she'd forgotten to put on her skin one day. Daisy wasn't threatening to sue the Saint Street agency, after all. Molly and Jake had simply offered to pen a strongly worded, official-sounding letter on her behalf, demanding that the agency confirm Daisy was one of their foster kids—and if so, find her records and hand over a copy.

In the end, it would either work or it wouldn't. It wasn't like she had to face a firing squad or even sit through a final exam.

Daisy would simply read a piece of paper with some thirty-year-old names on it, or she'd be told to go pound sand.

She couldn't stand to tell Luca what was going on, though. What if nothing came of it? What if her records were truly gone and the only thing left of Daisy's history was a sixteen-year trail of payments to Pam and Ray Lee, for the care and upkeep of a kid they'd never tried to keep.

Not for the first time, Daisy wondered if it really had been about the money for the Lees. Pam liked to act as if it wasn't, but was Daisy a fool to swallow that line?

After all, her biological family hadn't wanted to keep her, either. Besides her actual parents, there had to have been grandparents, maybe, or aunts and uncles who could've taken her in. Cousins, perhaps. Even…siblings.

Daisy hadn't been such a wreck since she was fourteen years old. Not exactly the best mental space in which to conduct a romance, that was for damn sure. Good thing Luca was on his game—because Daisy was turning into a head case from the waiting.

Twenty-Three

LITTLE BY LITTLE, Luca was getting his act together here in New York. At home, he'd finally unpacked all his boxes from Italy, so his new apartment was beginning to feel a bit less alien.

He stood in the living room and looked around—Daisy had whipped his place into shape, no doubt. She'd ensured that everything Luca owned had a dedicated place where it belonged—and that Luca knew where that place was.

It made staying neat easier, and Luca definitely got less flustered when his possessions were exactly where he expected to find them on a regular basis.

Likewise, his new job was starting to seem less like an inscrutable game show, and more like an IQ test that he had a prayer of scoring well on. Luca was learning people's names and finding his way through the halls of the medical center. He was seeing a few patients, and his new lab was coming along nicely, too.

After several insightful conversations with Harlan Green, he'd come to the conclusion that he'd been on the wrong track slightly with his research in Italy. However, since that work now belonged to his former hospital in Florence, Luca was free to start fresh.

He had some interesting new ideas about how they might approach the CAR T-cell therapy, to maybe tackle the pesky HER2 mutations that proved so tricky in treating some gastric cancers. Luca let his mind wander down that path and set about straightening up the room.

Red and Piper had been incredibly generous with their time and support, so Luca had invited them over tonight to thank them the best way he knew how—with good food and amiable company.

Tomorrow, he would entertain Daisy, cooking a dinner for her that his mamma had assured him wasn't included in her new binder full of family recipes.

Luca owed it to Daisy after he'd had to cancel a date several days ago, so he could interview a couple of potential research assistants after their last classes of the day.

Daisy had been very understanding, but Luca suspected the students' timing had had more to do with scoring a free meal than with actual scheduling difficulties. That was okay, though. He'd been in their position once, too—he got it.

As Luca wielded a duster he'd found in his linen closet—a decidedly unmacho explosion of vivid purple feathers that his intrepid decorators had undoubtedly purchased to torment him—Luca began to notice the artwork on his walls for the first time.

He'd lived in this apartment for weeks. Sure, he knew there was some framed photography in the short hall that connected his bedroom and office to the living room. He could probably have even told someone that the frames themselves were narrow and silver in color.

However, given that he normally navigated that small space in the dark, exhausted after a long day at work or a sleepless-but-worth-it night at Daisy's…Luca wasn't in the habit of stopping to look around all that much.

He might not have done it this time either, if he didn't have guests coming over soon. So here he was, overhead light on, linen closet found and pillaged, and eyes drawn stage right—to an artfully arranged gallery of artistic photography.

In particular, Luca couldn't help staring at the enlarged picture of an old woman's hands kneading dough on a scarred wooden counter. Her wedding ring was too tight, and her knuckles were gnarled with arthritis. His heart thrummed painfully beneath his ribs at how much the image reminded him of his grandmother.

Except…*wait*—it *was* his Nonna. It had to be. Luca knew that mole on her wrist like he knew the nose on his face. Her knew her wedding band, and her blouse, too, barely distinguishable in the background. How was this possible?

Quickly, Luca searched the other frames, finding close-ups of his parents' linked hands, his sister's shoulder and hair, and his brother's intent jawline. He discovered stones from the foundation of his parents' house and a bistro chair from the gelateria where he and Daisy had once lingered over dessert and coffee.

He found other things, as well—hyper-enlarged views of his *Firenze* home and the people he loved—and there was truly only one way these images could have come to be in his Manhattan apartment.

Daisy.

Whose boss was scheduled to arrive in less than twenty minutes. Luca had gotten distracted again, and he had no doubt Red and Piper would be on New York time—not the hazy interpretation of hours and minutes that Italians tended to employ.

With one more hasty glance at his wall, Luca rushed into his bedroom to take a lightning-fast shower before they arrived. The food was warming in the oven and ready to serve. He just needed to make himself presentable.

While he got dressed, Luca thought about his discovery. If that truly was Daisy's work, she was a much better artist than he'd realized, and he was a complete pig for not having noticed it sooner.

He wondered what Red and Piper would think—or if they already knew. Maybe his friends had been here when Daisy hung the pieces. Maybe they'd all discussed it, and Luca was the only *testone* who hadn't yet caught on.

IT TOOK A while to get to the subject over dinner. First, Luca wanted to address an issue that had come up when he was paying bills that afternoon. He'd set up the rental company in his online banking app, filled out all the fields to pay his first month's rent…and promptly realized that the name of the company he was paying rent to sounded awfully familiar.

MacLellan and Whittier Properties. Luca looked it up online and discovered right away that it was a company held by Red, Piper, and some other man he'd never heard of.

He ought to have known they'd found this place a bit too fast and easily. People didn't just stumble across the perfect apartment in New York like that, even when they had the money to pay for it.

So, Luca swallowed his mouthful of bread and asked them, "Care to explain why I'm paying rent to you two sharks, instead of some other faceless landlord on the Upper East Side?"

"It's just an investment," Red said, waving him off. "Remember when I told you about that guy who bought Piper's family's house in Maryland? Eric Whittier?"

"I have some vague recollection."

"Well, after the miracle he worked there, and on our new place out on Long Island, my clever little bride had the idea to partner with him. Turns out he's a contracting genius. We're flipping houses and apartments all over New York and Maryland and using veterans to do it."

Luca's confusion must have been obvious, because Piper leaned in to put a hand on his arm. "We take old houses and fix them up with crews of former soldiers. Then we sell them for more than we paid for them."

Red's pride was evident. "A lot more. If you don't end up wanting to stay here, we'll sell this place for a nice profit. Assuming you don't trash it, that is."

"Ah, I see," Luca said.

"Eric's sister has been running the main office in Maryland," Piper chimed in. "That's who he bought my old house for. You should see how well she's doing. She's an organizational mastermind. The guys all love her."

Luca marveled at how they were able to juggle so many different types of businesses successfully. Red had always had a knack for it, but together, they seemed to have the Midas touch.

Luca, on the other hand, couldn't even make an edible salad for a casual dinner with friends. He pushed a tomato-like wedge to the side of his plate, and muttered, "I'm sorry about this salad. All of the lettuces were very sad at the market. And these things— they look like tomatoes, but they do not taste like them."

"Luca, it's winter," Piper chided him. "Unless you're eating squash and potatoes, pretty much all the produce stinks right now. We're used to it, trust me."

He sighed and drank some wine. That, at least, was palatable.

"Don't worry," Piper said. "You have a nice big fire escape. In the summer, I bet you could put some tomato plants in pots out there and have fresh ones whenever you want."

Did people do that? Luca was dismayed. "That doesn't seem safe. If there was an emergency, people could trip and hurt themselves trying to get to the ground."

Red groaned and rolled his eyes. "Oh my God. Could you be a bigger ninny? Now you've started worrying about injuries that haven't even happened yet."

Luca smiled in apology at Piper. "The truth is, I'd probably forget to take care of the plants anyway. They'd die of dehydration." The only reason the herbs in his kitchen were still alive was that Daisy had taken pity on them.

Piper shrugged, unconcerned. "Then you'll buy some tomatoes at the store, or ask the food service to bring you some. Or maybe you and Daisy can go to a few farmer's markets—you'd probably love that. Red and I go and eat ourselves stupid every other weekend during the summer."

"Don't spread it around," Red muttered.

Daisy. Luca had meant to ask them about Daisy. "Listen, have either of you seen the photography hanging in my hallway?"

"You mean the ones Daisy did?" Piper asked.

Oh, yes—Luca was definitely a *testone*. "*Sì*," he said. "But did you happen to also notice how good they are?"

Red set his napkin carefully beside his plate, then wandered over to examine the pictures. "Piper, honey—come here a minute."

Soon, all three of them were standing shoulder-to-shoulder in the little hall, gawking at the gorgeous snippets of Italy—of Luca's home.

"When she brought them over, I told her she should try to sell them," Piper said.

"Maybe not these ones specifically," Luca grinned, "But I'm sure she has others. She never went anywhere without her camera last year."

"If Daisy has shots from New York, too…" Red mused.

"I'd bet good money on it. I wasn't sure if I was just impressed because I like the subject matter, or because of the fact that Daisy took them," Luca explained. "But if you two agree that she's as talented as I thought, then maybe I'll encourage her to ask around at some galleries."

Piper nodded. "Definitely encourage her. These are really impressive."

"In fact…" Red said, narrowing his eyes as he leaned closer to inspect one photo.

"Do you know someone she could talk to?" Red's family had supported the arts in New York for as long as Luca had known him. Odds were strong that he'd come across a gallery owner or two in his adult life.

Piper snorted and gave her fiancé a little shove. Suddenly, Luca knew exactly what Red would say.

"Your mother?" he wondered.

"Afraid so, *compagno.*"

Luca said, "I'm meeting Daisy tomorrow. You see what your mom thinks about it, and I'll try to soften up the artist. I suspect she's going to take some convincing before she'll agree."

Red pulled out his phone and snapped a few careful pictures, and then gestured them back toward the table. "Luca, you could convince a fish to give up water. I'm sure you'll think of something."

THE APARTMENT WAS still in good shape from the cleaning he'd given it yesterday for Red and Piper, but Luca took one extra step in preparation for Daisy's arrival.

Since she was as enamored of Luca's high-tech mattress as he was, and since he fully expected them to end up in his bed shortly after dessert, putting fresh sheets on the bed seemed like the gentlemanly thing to do.

Luca gave himself far more leeway to shower and shave this time and did his best to make things look romantic. He lit the candles he'd bought at a Duane Reade around the corner and set *Traviata* to play softly on the speakers where he docked his phone.

While he waited for her to arrive, Luca wondered if Daisy would like to go see an opera in person one day. It was one of his favorite things to do, and for that reason, at least, he hoped she'd be interested. In the meantime, he could ask around and see what was available this time of year.

As for her artwork, Luca resolved to mention it over dinner. Daisy was usually pretty reluctant to accept compliments, and if she even admitted the photographs were hers, she might need time to think about showing them. Or she could even refuse to consider the idea outright.

Perhaps the home-cooked food on the stove would soften Daisy up and convince her to acknowledge her talent. Or maybe Luca could do the honors himself—on those clean, pressed sheets.

Either way, if Daisy confessed, he *had* to convince her to do more with her work than simply hang it in a hidden location in a private home. Daisy's art was extraordinary. It should be shared.

If she hung those photos in a gallery show, collectors would go absolutely wild for them, and Luca suspected that might do her some good. It was far too easy for her to roll her eyes when

Luca complimented her—she knew he was smitten, and therefore biased.

But total strangers with no vested interest in her whatsoever? Surely, Daisy couldn't discount what they had to say?

WHEN SHE GOT to his apartment, however, Daisy was immediately diverted by the museum gift shop bag on his counter. Luca had meant to put it in his office earlier but had gotten sidetracked by the changing of the sheets.

"You went to the museum?"

"Just for a little while," he told her. "They had some frescoes from an Italian palazzo, and this was the last weekend."

"What did you buy?"

"I got the book with all the paintings in it. I wanted to show them to you, since I think the exhibit will close before I can bring you back."

"Luca, that's really sweet." Daisy picked up the bag, presumably to peek inside, and inadvertently revealed the box beneath it.

Dannazione. Now he'd have to explain that, too. His forgetfulness was truly going to be the death of him someday.

Daisy's eyes went wide and she grabbed the toy, picking it up and shaking it around. Inside, all the little plastic building blocks rattled like the filling of a maraca.

"And then, I see you went toy shopping, too."

Luca sighed, feeling about five years old. "It sounds silly, but I really like this toy. It kind of reminds me of cells and DNA— the way the small blocks do not look like much on their own but when they stack together, they build something special."

"Such as the Statue of Liberty," she said, examining the cover of the box.

"Precisely. And the sets for adults are really challenging. They take concentration to build, and they take my mind off work. It's relaxing, you know?"

Daisy smiled, like she'd learned something adorable about him. Luca supposed that was better than her making fun of him.

He blurted out, "Also, they were my brother's favorite, so they have happy memories for me."

"Do you miss him?"

"Yes. Every day."

She sighed, "I miss his bread. God, that stuff was good. Although, it's probably better I don't have regular access to it anymore. I'd weigh 800 pounds if I did."

And that's when Luca realized Daisy thought he meant *Paolo*, the brother she'd met. The chef who'd come to Nonna's pensione every week, along with the rest of them, for Sunday dinner.

Of course. Why wouldn't she? Luca had never mentioned the fact that he'd once had another brother, and he didn't intend to infect the mood of their evening by doing so now. What would it matter, anyway?

Matteo was gone, and he wasn't ever coming back. Someday, if Luca and Daisy's relationship progressed the way he hoped it would, he'd have to tell her what had happened. For now, they had passable cannoli to eat and love to make.

Luca had to convince her that her artwork should have an appreciative audience, bigger than him, Red, and Piper. Bigger than this apartment.

The past was the past, and tonight it could rest quietly in its grave and wait.

Twenty-Four

ONE THING LED to another, as it usually did, and dessert led quite handily into Luca chasing Daisy around the apartment in a sexy game of cat and mouse. She was in a teasing mood and proving elusive—hence the chasing.

Luca had been looking forward to this evening for days, and he stalked toward her, drawing out his approach like a beast cornering its prey. Good thing they were at his house—at Daisy's tiny apartment, he would've accomplished his goal in about three steps, and where would be the fun in that?

She giggled, a fizzy, effervescent sound bubbling out of her that Luca attributed one hundred percent to her three glasses of prosecco. He unbuttoned his shirt and let it drop behind him, getting that detail out of the way, at least.

"Take it off," she laughed, "Take it all off!"

Luca's eyes narrowed as his gaze traveled up and down Daisy's fully clothed state—which for a late winter evening in New York meant thick fabrics and multiple layers. However, every time he got close to divesting her of one of them, she sidled out of his grasp.

"Stop moving," he told her.

He left his hand in place at his belt, and Daisy made a rolling, hurry-up gesture to get him moving again. He could hardly complain—he *was* an established and unabashed exhibitionist.

Daisy was more of a lights-out kind of girl, but that didn't mean she didn't enjoy a show.

"Come on, tiger," she laughed. "Release that kraken. Show me what I've been missing all week." She shifted sideways, angling toward the little hall leading toward his bedroom like she was about to bolt.

His belt hit the lovely herringbone wood floor with a troubling crack, but at Daisy's demand, Luca's fingers froze on his zipper.

"*Scusi?*" He was utterly befuddled. "What is a kraken?"

Daisy groaned. "Never mind! No language questions right now. I'll tell you later."

Luca gripped himself through his charcoal gray dress pants and gave himself a squeeze, taunting her. "Oh, no you don't. If you want to see this, then you have to explain what you just said."

"I don't just want to see it," Daisy purred. Luca knew she could see that he was fantastically hard and ready for her.

And Daisy knew he had a thing for her mouth. So she licked her lips, trying to distract him.

"Daisy," he warned. "Talk. Now."

"Oh my God, you are the worst!" she blurted out, giving up. "A kraken is a mythological sea monster. Like a giant squid. It drags unsuspecting people into the briny deep and eats them alive. Like I was hoping you'd do with me!"

Luca's eyebrows shot up and his breath rushed out in a sudden burst of laughter. "*Really?*"

"Yes, really. Now stop asking questions! You're killing the mood."

"Heaven forbid. But I have one more to ask before I let loose this beast, as you call it."

Daisy rolled her eyes and groaned again. "Fine. What is it?"

"How do you prefer your seafood? Because if anyone is getting consumed, it's going to be me."

"You…you…" Daisy sputtered, peeking down at him again.

"Unless you prefer eggplant to kraken."

Now it was her turn to laugh in shock. "So, you got that text, then? I wasn't sure you'd understand it."

"Message received and comprehended, *mia bella*. English might be my second language, but I'm not an imbecile." He dropped his pants on the floor and stepped over them, advancing on her once more.

Daisy edged closer to his bedroom door, openly admiring Luca's physique. "And what if I had sent you a peach emoji, instead?"

"Oh, believe me—we'll get to that, too. Now take off your clothes."

Shockingly, his command worked. Daisy whipped off her heavy turtleneck sweater and the slinky camisole she'd had hidden underneath, flashed him a glimpse of her black lace-covered breasts and darted into his room.

She was struggling to wriggle out of her boots and tight jeans when Luca reached her. He lifted her up, tossed her on his mattress, and dropped down beside her. Her belly ring winked in the lamplight, and Luca groaned.

That thing was going to kill him.

Daisy finally got her jeans off and tossed them aside, and Luca saw that her panties were made of the same sheer lace as her bra. There was something about the contrast of that sinful black material against her creamy skin—and all the tiny little bows and artful seams. It obliterated his control.

Luca pulled her on top of him and filled his hands with her spectacular ass. Daisy ground against his deep-sea creature and moaned, "Oh, God. You have the best hands. They're huge."

"I'm glad you think so. Now, I'd like to introduce you to my mouth." He urged her up his body until her black lace panties were only inches from his face. Daisy hovered over him, her strong thighs bracketing Luca's head as she braced herself on the wall.

She peeked down at his face, curls coming loose from the clip in her hair to frame her pretty face. "Luca, please," she whispered.

"Come a little closer," he told her, pulling her down. That lace was softer than he expected against his tongue, silky and already hot with her desire. He spent some time toying with it, giving Daisy just enough friction and pressure to wind her tighter.

She tasted better than any wine, and the sounds coming from her made him hotter than the surface of the sun. Still, Luca waited until Daisy was rocking against his face, desperately seeking the angle she needed, before he slipped two fingers beneath the elastic of her panties and inside her sweet, slick body.

Madre di Dio, he nearly came right there. She was so close. Luca let go of her ass, yanked down the front of her underwear and brought her clear over the cliff with only a few strong strokes of his tongue.

Daisy's legs quivered and her head fell against the wall behind the bed. Luca gently kissed her thighs until she stopped shaking, then eased her to the side. She smiled loopily up at him.

"Have I ever mentioned how much I love peaches?" he asked her.

"Not recently. But I applaud your devotion. In fact," Daisy pushed up on her elbow and looked down at the rather obvious and insistent evidence of Luca's love of stone fruit, "I have a pretty good idea of how I can show my appreciation," she said.

"You can pay me back later, if you want," Luca told her, batting her devious hand away. "If I don't get inside you in approximately one millisecond, I might go mad."

Daisy giggled again, so uncharacteristic and so cute. "And here I thought that was a myth."

"Wrong. It's completely, scientifically, absolutely proved and true," he intoned, while peeling off his boxer briefs and hunting in his bedside drawer for a condom.

"Hmm, sounds a little bit suspicious." Her eyes were glued to Luca's hands, rolling the latex over his cock. He hissed at the sensation.

"You can trust me," he gritted out, climbing over her and nudging her legs wide with his knee. "I'm a doctor."

"Oh, well, that changes everything."

Luca held himself steady by the thinnest of margins. "Daisy, tell me you want me."

"As if it isn't patently obvious."

"*Tell me.*"

She stretched up and pressed her glorious mouth to his, then sucked his lip between hers on the retreat. "Yes doctor, I want you. So much."

Luca pushed inside and could've sung an aria about how she fit him so perfectly. Daisy sighed out a whimper of longing and bent her knees, seating him even deeper. He pulled out slowly, then pressed in again, over and over in long, strong strokes.

He wanted to howl with how good, how *right*, it felt. Instead, Luca dropped his forehead to hers and wondered, "What if I hadn't found you when I did? What if Red didn't know you, and I was still searching, and longing, and wishing for you?"

"But you did find me," she murmured.

"I'd be half a man."

"You could never be half of anything," she said, and nudged his face up for a kiss.

"And you're all I want." Luca rolled his hips, wedged a hand under her ass to keep her close, and this time when Daisy came apart, he was right there with her.

SOMETIME LATER, AFTER they'd both cleaned up and then dozed for a little while, Luca propped himself on his pillows and Daisy laid her head on his chest. He played with her hair while she drew patterns on his arm with her fingertips.

"I have something to tell you," she said softly.

"What is it?"

"I did something this week. Something big."

Luca frowned. Her voice was shaking. "How big?"

"After we talked, I couldn't stop thinking about my real family. I kept wondering why I got taken away, and why they never got me back. I know it seems nuts, but I actually…" She swallowed and blew out a long breath. "I actually asked Pam if she remembered anything."

For someone who claimed to not care, that *was* big. Luca asked, "And? What'd she say?"

"She barely even remembered the name of the agency, but there's a place in Brooklyn that might fit the bill. Only problem is, they said my records were too old and they couldn't help me."

Luca sat up straight, dislodging Daisy and making her sit up, too. "But that's not fair. If they know something, they should tell you."

Daisy took another deep breath and met his gaze with a meek one of her own. "Which is why my friend Poppy suggested I do what I did next."

Luca knew it couldn't be anything too bad—Daisy simply had too kind of a heart for that. He thought it probably came from being all too aware of how easily callousness could hurt someone. "What'd you do, *cara?*"

"Well, Poppy's sister-in-law has a friend who's a lawyer. Her name is Molly, and she and her husband have an estate law practice in North Carolina." Daisy plucked nervously at the duvet with her long artist's fingers. "They, um…" She bit her lip, blinking at Luca like admitting it out loud was going to cause an eruption.

He tried to look as encouraging and even-tempered as he possibly could, but on the inside Luca was at the edge of his seat, willing her to tell him what he guessed was coming next.

"Luca, they wrote a letter for me to mail to the agency. Essentially demanding them to find my records—if they even exist—and give me a copy."

"Oh, Daisy." Luca sagged against the pillows and blinked back the sudden dampness trying to leak out of his tear ducts. "Did you mail it?"

"I did." She looked like she might be on the verge of tears, herself.

In all his years of practicing medicine, he'd seen a lot of scared people fight through a lot of tough situations. But he couldn't remember being prouder of any of them than he was of this woman, right now.

He told her so. "*Cara*, I'm so, so proud of you. I know that had to be difficult for you."

She nodded. "I'm kind of freaking out. They might not find anything."

"True. And if that's the case, you'll be no worse off than before."

"But what if they do find something? What if it's really bad and I don't want to know?"

"I suppose that's a possibility. What can we do to protect you from something like that?"

"What if…" Daisy gnawed on her lip, thinking. Then she shook her head and flopped backward, staring at the ceiling in dismay. "I can't think of anything."

Luca had an idea, but he didn't want to overstep. Very carefully, he took her hand in his. "Daisy, I won't be the least bit offended if you say no, but if you do get something back from the agency, maybe I could scan it first. To make sure there is nothing too bad in it, before you read it."

Her eyes snapped to his. "You would do that?"

"Of course I would."

"And it wouldn't be too weird?"

Luca was going to bank on the odds, and hope her history wasn't too awful. "I don't think so. But I will say, since life can surprise us in strange ways sometimes, that if that file contains something really troubling, we should probably give ourselves an exit."

"Like what?"

"Like…making sure a therapist is in the circle with all this."

"Yes. Right. I will definitely make sure Rita is *in the loop* with the situation the next time I see her."

"In the loop." *Right.* "So we have a plan?" Luca was incalculably relieved to know that Daisy had a therapist already in place, in case they were needed. It was the kind of smart and practical decision she made all the time, and never gave herself credit for.

Daisy's face lit up like a Tuscan sunrise. "We do. Thank you so much. I was so afraid to tell you, in case nothing came of it," she said, "But it was too hard to keep it a secret from you."

Luca liked the sound of that. "Can we talk about one more thing?"

"Anything." Daisy climbed into his lap and snuggled against him, a soft, warm, armful of beautiful woman. It did have a way of taking the sting out of the dark and cold of winter.

"Will you think about what we talked about over dinner? About maybe asking around at some galleries, to see if they'd like to show your photos?"

"Luca, I'm flattered, but I really just take them for myself. It's a hobby."

"I know that's what you said. And you don't have to change your mind anytime soon. Just…consider the idea. Like I told you, Red and Piper feel the same. We think a lot of other people would, too." Luca stroked his fingertips down the long hollow of Daisy's spine, then followed the ladder of her vertebrae back up again.

"I mean—it might be kind of cool, I guess. But I honestly wouldn't know where to start."

"That's where Red comes in."

"How do you figure?"

"His family does a lot for the arts all over town. Always has. But his mother, especially, knows people everywhere. If Elaine MacLellan didn't know where to begin, no one would."

"Luca, she's my boss's *mom*!" Daisy protested. "I can't ask her that."

Luca squeezed her tight. "What if someone else already did?"

Daisy pulled back—way back—and glared at him. "Someone like *who*?"

"Like Red?" He pasted a winning smile on his face, but it only made her scowl harder.

"You did not ask him to do that for me. I am going to kill you."

Luca held up his hands, in case she decided to act precipitously on her murderous threats. "It was his idea. Not mine."

"Well how does that help me? I can't kill my boss." She squinted at him thoughtfully. "I'll just have to send him a message by killing you."

Luca couldn't resist the pop culture reference. "Will you stick my severed head in his bed like in *The Godfather*?"

"Probably," she spat, trying not to laugh. "And you don't have to look so happy about it. Piper is going to be really pissed."

In a rush, Luca admitted the truth. "I should also tell you that Red already showed his mother some pictures of your work and Elaine emailed Red a list of names. He forwarded it to me this morning—ten people she thinks you should talk to. She might be calling a few herself. The stone is already rolling, *cara*. Please don't kill me."

"The *ball* is rolling, you big, interfering lunkhead. Now, tell me. How would you like to die?" Daisy feinted toward him.

He chuckled. And Luca couldn't help it, but bantering like this with her had his cock doing its best impression of the Leaning Tower of Pisa.

Naturally, Daisy noticed. Mother Teresa probably noticed, and she'd been dead for decades.

When Daisy lunged for him the second time, she went straight for the goods. "Not the eggplant," Luca yelped.

Daisy just said, "Shut it, you," and set to work torturing him.

Twenty-Five

T HE LETTER FROM the Saint Street Episcopalian parish arrived midweek, far sooner than Daisy was expecting. She propped it on her kitchen counter and basically treated it like it was radioactive until she had a chance to show it to Luca.

He opened it for her carefully, one night after work. Eyes moving over the page, he read the whole thing twice before telling her, "The pastor says he tried his hand at some of their old computer files. He was able to confirm that you were one of their foster children. Eh…" Luca frowned. "Unfortunately, the old memory drives they had the material archived on were corrupted. He was only able to pull four names, he says. The two families who had you before Pam, then Pam and Ray—"

"I don't care about those," Daisy told him.

"…And the name of your birth father." Luca looked up. "Daisy, there's a name here. The name of your real father."

All the blood rushed out of her head. "Really?"

He nodded, eyes bright.

Daisy was blinking rapidly, trying to understand how it could have been so simple, when her knees buckled and she sank to the floor right where she stood. Luca looked a little concerned, but it was probably safer for her to stay put where she was.

"Do you want to know what the name is?"

Daisy couldn't find the words. She just nodded.

"Your dad's name is Leonard. Leonard Bosu."

"*Leonard Bosu*," she breathed. "What kind of name do you think that might be?"

"I don't know. But it's a place to start, isn't it?"

"Yeah, but how? What do I do? Search for it online, or…how do I know…what if there are a lot of them?" Daisy asked. "How do I know which is the right one? Do I…Should I go to a library or something?" She was the child of a guy named Leonard Bosu. *Holy shit.*

Luca looked thoughtful, though. Still holding the letter in his hand, he got down on the floor next to her. "I've been thinking about that, and I think I know what you could try. You won't like it, though."

Daisy peeked at the paper he was holding but couldn't bring herself to touch it yet. "Will I like it more or less than Elaine MacLellan trying to find me a gallery?"

Luca twinkled at her. "That's a very good question, *mia bella*. This might perhaps be equal."

She groaned. "You want me to ask Red, don't you?"

"He has a private investigator he sometimes uses. I know he wouldn't keep going to the same person if he didn't think he was trustworthy and reliable."

A private investigator would almost certainly know what to do with her father's name, Daisy thought. She could probably learn if Leonard was still alive, or maybe even where he lived right now.

"That's not a bad idea," she conceded. "But please don't call Red for me. I have to do this for myself."

"Of course."

"Can I see it?" Daisy asked. Luca knew exactly what she meant. He turned the letter toward her and pointed out the name.

Leonard. Leonard Bosu—her real father.

<hr>

DAISY LASTED ONLY one day before her need to know trumped her reservations about involving Red in her personal life even more than he was already. She climbed on the subway and headed downtown to the PKM Conglomerates building, where Red had his office.

She'd called ahead and was waved in by his assistant, but Daisy still knocked and poked her head in Red's door warily. "Mr. MacLellan? Wayne said you might have a couple minutes for me to run something by you."

Red looked up from his work and scowled. "Daisy, I swear to God…"

"Ugh! Fine!" she growled and stepped inside. "*Red*—do you have a minute?"

He shut his laptop, smiling insolently. "Sure do. How goes the matchmaking trade?"

"Not gonna lie. Things are pretty grim." When he gestured to the large armchair in front of his desk, she walked over and perched on the edge of it. "I haven't been asked to assist in a marriage proposal in *hours*. It's almost as if word has gotten around about me."

"You were the one who refused to give up your day job."

"Yeah, well, I can hardly get my own love life in order. Why should anyone else trust me with theirs?" Too late, she realized her mistake.

Her boss frowned. "Dr. Delledonna giving you trouble?" He reached into his top drawer, pulled out his cell, and put it to his ear. "Maybe I should call him. God knows Luca needs more people keeping him in line. His family treats him like the second coming, for crying out loud."

"No!" Daisy cried, holding up her hands before he could dial. "It's not that." Red lowered the phone slowly, narrowing his eyes at her. "I swear. This is about something totally different."

"All right. Hit me."

"You said if I ever needed anything…" she said, and then faltered. Maybe this wasn't a good idea. Red oversaw the entire Trident Publishing operation. Should she really be trusting him with such personal information?

He had a reputation for being pretty hardcore. If she pissed him off someday, he could easily use what he knew against her. Daisy's heart thumped around in her chest like it was enjoying its first mosh pit.

She took a deep breath and tried to center herself. This wasn't the freaking mafia—she designed romance novel covers for a living. As long as she kept doing a good job, there was almost nothing she could do in a professional sense that would turn this man against her.

And even if he was strong-willed, Red was still ethical. If Daisy and Luca had a dramatic flameout, Red would never take it out on her at work. He'd simply never talk to her again, which would be easy enough for a man in his position.

Besides, Red had said over and over that he owed her for her help in his proposal to Piper. Now, he could even the score.

"Daisy," he groaned, "I said I had a few minutes. Not a few years."

She snapped to attention. "Right. I have this family thing, and Luca said you might know someone who can help me."

"With what?"

"Finding someone."

He gestured impatiently with his hands. "I beg you—please don't do the two-words-at-a-time thing. Give me more details. All the details at once, please."

Daisy took a deep breath. When she let it out, she pushed the humiliating words out with it. "I was a foster kid when I was little. I've never known anything about my real family, and the agency wouldn't give me my records when I called recently. So, a friend of a friend who's a lawyer sent them a letter, and now—I have a name. For my father. And I want to find him."

To his credit, her boss did not change expression at all. Red did not wince, flinch, or otherwise shy away from her in any way. All he said was, "You want to borrow my private investigator? He really knows his stuff."

That was suspiciously easy. Daisy wondered if Luca had called Red after all. "Um. Yeah. If you're okay with sharing."

"What's mine is yours. Got a pen?"

Daisy held up her phone, the notes app already cued up and ready to go. "Fire away."

Red rattled off a name and number from memory, then sat back and waited.

Daisy thought of something important. "Do you, uh…know what his rates are like? Is this dude really expensive, or…?" In complete and utter embarrassment, she admitted, "I'm sorry. I've obviously never had to use someone like this before. I don't have the faintest idea what they charge for jobs like this."

MacLellan jerked his chin at her. "Don't worry about it. It's on me."

"No, Red, don't be ridiculous. This is my thing. I can take care of it. All I needed was a recommendation of who to use. And a sense of what I'll be on the hook for."

"I realize that. I'm offering because I want to."

With his usual uncanny timing, Red's assistant buzzed in on the intercom. "Mr. MacLellan? Mr. Bigham, your ten o'clock, has arrived."

"Thanks." Red checked his watch and rolled his eyes, telling Daisy, "Asshole is always early. I'm beginning to think he has a thing for me."

Daisy smiled and shrugged. If it was the same Mr. Bigham she'd met at Red's engagement party, then he was eighty if he was a day—and he was definitely carrying a torch for her boss.

"Go on, get out of here," Red smiled. "I can handle him. I'll let my guy know you'll be calling, later. And Daisy?"

She paused at his door, one hand on the knob.

"Good luck."

"Thanks."

She took a step out the door, and Red called out again, "*Shit.* Wait a sec. I almost forgot."

"What's up?"

"Stop at my assistant's desk before you go. My mother heard back from a gallery owner she knows, someone who had to cancel a show they had scheduled in a couple of weeks. They want to talk to you. Wayne's got the details."

"Really?" Her voice did not squeak. It did *not*.

"Happy trails, Ms. Montgomery. Just look over your shoulder and remember us little people when you get famous," Red smirked.

Daisy groaned, "You've never spent a day of your life being little."

Now he grinned outright. "Don't I know it."

Mr. Bigham had gotten to his feet when he spotted Daisy emerge from Red's office, and now he ambled over, looking eager as puppy faced with a treat. Daisy glared at her boss one last time, then went to find Wayne.

LUCA WAS WAITING for her when Daisy got home that night, leaning against the brick wall of her building and completely oblivious to the stares he was garnering from passing women.

Nannies. Moms. Young professionals and teens. None of them appeared to be immune to his charisma.

He smiled when he spotted her, ditching his phone in his pocket and wrapping her in his warm, strong arms.

"*Cara*, you're home late today," he said. "Long day?"

Daisy didn't want to launch right into how heavy thirty-year-old psychic baggage was, or her fears about troubles that were so new she didn't know what to make of them yet, so Daisy only shook her head and told him, "Little bit. Nothing major."

Luca's gaze sparkled as he looked into her eyes. He trailed a finger down the slope of her nose, then dropped a light kiss on the tip. Before Daisy could even react to that absurdity, he was suddenly peppering her whole face with a barrage of quick, light kisses—dropping them on her cheeks and chin, nose and forehead.

In front of her doorman, for God's sake. Her cheeks went hot, and Daisy figured she was probably neon red already. She pushed on Luca's chest. "Stop it!"

He wasn't offended. Luca merely drew back and lifted his hands, like they were in one big, happy stickup.

"I'm sorry," he chuckled, suave as ever. "Sometimes, you're too delicious to resist. Everywhere I look, there are all those soft curves. I want to—" He gestured spastically. "Eat them up."

Daisy felt like she'd walked into some weird, kinky fable. She hustled Luca into her building and across the lobby, before he could say anything else embarrassing.

"Don't be fooled," she warned him. "I may look soft on the outside, but I'm all broken shards on the inside." She'd meant it to sound offhanded, but even she could admit the wording hit a nerve.

It was all this drama with her dad. It had her completely off-kilter.

Luca didn't seem the least bit put off, however. In the elevator, he simply informed her, "That's no good. Sharp edges can cause grave injury."

Like Daisy didn't know that. In the elevator, she rolled her eyes and muttered, "I'm used to it."

"Then I'll be the sea," her determined swain declared. "And smooth out all the glass." He worked his hands up and down her arms and his gaze turned sultry. "It might take some rubbing. A lot of rubbing together, so we don't miss any spots. We should be very, very thorough."

"Someone ought to," she murmured. She could not understand why Luca was finding this conversation so damn entertaining. Daisy was clearly telling him how broken she was, for God's sake—it wasn't supposed to be *endearing*.

"It's the nature of relationships," he said, turning serious. "Someday, you'll do the same for me."

Once they reached her floor, Daisy led him down the hall, unlocked her door, and pushed into her apartment. She scoffed, "Oh, right. Like you have any awkward edges."

When Luca moved in on her this time, his approach was direct and devastating. In moments, he'd kicked her door shut and folded her close. His hot, gifted lips wreaked havoc against the shell of her ear.

"*Cara*, I'm a man. My entire being is made of awkward edges." There were no more light, teasing kisses, now. Luca pressed his mouth along the hyper-sensitive skin below her earlobe, and Daisy gasped, despite herself.

Oh, he was a man all right—and there was nothing awkward about him. Daisy managed only one very shaky, breathless word, "Bullshit."

"No, it's true," he insisted, pulling back to look her in the eye. Luca's big hands kept hold of her hips, preventing her from fleeing too far. "I think you assume that you're the only one with imperfections. You see all the good in everyone around you, and all the worst in yourself."

Daisy scrunched up her nose. "That's not true. I don't…" She stopped. Started again, "Wait—"

"Think of it this way: Walking around, you notice all the pretty shells of people and think they're so much more complete than you. But you never consider the messes they're hiding inside. Entrails and blood and the disgusting by-products of so many biological functions. They have broken hearts, disordered minds, and chaotic emotions on top of that. Like me. Like you."

Daisy stared at him, willing her sluggish brain to catch up with her ears. Luca was still casting around, searching for a way to say what he wanted, so that she would understand.

"It's like your photographs, *sì?* You look at everyone else's finished pictures—the ones that have been filtered, cropped, and adjusted. Put in nice frames and hung on gallery walls."

Daisy's cheeks felt damp. She quickly wiped away whatever betraying moisture *that* was, then kept her arms between them in case she had to force Luca to back off and give her some space. Not yet, but maybe soon.

"Daisy at least compare like with like. Don't judge your raw, discarded candid shots against other people's professional photoshoots."

"You…" He—he had a point. Daisy realized with an uncomfortable flash that she *did* do that.

"Be fair to yourself," Luca urged quietly. "Surely you've earned that much."

There were no words to frame what a gift that idea was. Daisy simply nodded and hoped it would be enough.

It seemed to be. Instead of locking lips with her again, Luca simply gathered her close and hung on.

While she squeezed him back, her brain spun out and her heart thumped wildly. There was no good reason for Luca to want her, but he did.

Even it was only for now, Daisy figured she must be the luckiest woman in town.

"They want me," she whispered into his shoulder, still amazed by what had happened earlier. Still astounded.

"Who? I'll murder them all," Luca fired back.

"A gallery near work. That Mrs. MacLellan really works fast. She found this place near Trident that had an event that fell through. I stopped by on my way home and showed them some stuff I had on my phone—that's why I was late. They want me to fill the opening, Luca. I need to frame thirty pictures in two weeks."

"*Cara*, that's wonderful! Congratulations!"

"No, it's crazy! What the hell have you gotten me into? How am I even going to handle something like this, with everything else I've got going on?"

"With help, Daisy. You have friends, and you have me." He kissed her soundly. "And I am going to be beside you, holding your hand, every step of the way."

"Promise me. There's no way I can do all this by myself."

"Of course, you can. You don't have to, though. If it's help you want, then it's help you'll get."

Twenty-Six

R ED'S PRIVATE INVESTIGATOR worked fast—he sent Daisy his findings only three days after he took the job. Daisy wasn't sure if that indicated how good he was at his job, or how exceptionally easy the job had been. Still, he'd found her dad, and that was the important part.

The email stated that Leonard Bosu was now a guitar teacher at a small private school in the Village. Not only that, but the PI had actually talked to him—and Leonard had begged him to convey his fervent hope that Daisy would make contact as soon as possible.

The investigator included Leonard's home address, home phone, work phone, and cell phone, and told Daisy to reach out if there was anything else she needed.

Daisy was completely paralyzed. Should she call? What if Leonard was crazy? He'd been a horrible enough parent that his child had been taken away from him permanently.

And what about her mom? Why wasn't there anything about *her* in the report?

In that calm, reasonable way he had, Luca came over and talked Daisy through the main points. He held her hand while she placed the first phone call, and agree to go with her the following day, when her father had arranged to meet her at a cute little coffee shop they both knew in Midtown.

Leonard showed up in a tweed blazer with a faded black concert t-shirt underneath, nerdy black-framed glasses and a battered leather briefcase. He was tall and lanky, with a deep voice and an infectious grin.

It was impossible to see him as anything other than a friendly, likable middle-aged man. Daisy couldn't have kept her distance even if she wanted to. He drew her in like an industrial magnet.

Once he let her go, Leonard led with, "Jesus Lord you're a dead ringer for your mom." In an aside to Luca, he added, "Joy and I were high school sweethearts. I can still picture her like it was yesterday."

Daisy immediately wondered if Leonard would think she was strange if she started taking notes. *Joy*, she repeated to herself. *Mom's name was Joy.*

She and Luca had rehearsed what she wanted to know, and sorted things into levels of priority, in case Leonard proved forgetful or unwilling to talk much. After their brief phone call, Daisy doubted he'd be either of those things, but the exercise had helped to settle her nerves and gave her something to do while she waited for their meeting.

After a round of nervous small talk while they found a table, got settled, and ordered, Daisy finally worked up the nerve to ask Leonard one of her most pressing questions. "If you don't mind me asking, what *am* I, exactly? I've always wondered."

"Beautiful," was his succinct reply.

She could feel the flush wash over her cheeks. "No, I mean—"

"I know what you meant," her dad chuckled. "I'm sorry. I'm seriously trying to keep it cool, but no one prepares you for this kind of thing, you feel me?" He ran an unsteady hand over his graying hair and then patted the table. "Anyway, uh…let me see. Most of my people came from Ghana originally. My uncle figured that out at some point. Except for my grandma on my mom's side. She came from Thailand."

Daisy sat and contemplated that. It didn't seem like the right time to inquire whether his people had come from Ghana willingly or not, but maybe she could ask that some other time.

"Oh!" Leonard exclaimed, "And my dad's mother always claimed she had Cherokee blood. But I gotta be real with you— I'm not sure that's true."

"And my mother? J-joy, you said?" Daisy pushed back at the shame that blew through her for stumbling over her own birth mother's name, but she'd only learned it five minutes ago, after all. "You said she came from Jamaica?"

Leonard nodded, seeming pleased. "Yes, but she was almost comically pale. We were kinda like photo negatives of each other." He laughed, but it was tinged with sadness. "I think Joy was a mutt, too. Scottish and Irish, and maybe some Welsh originally? I don't know how her family ended up in the Caribbean. It was so long ago. It's hard to remember."

Daisy clung to those new details, measuring them against what she knew about herself to see how they felt—to see if they fit.

"So, basically I'm nothing," she murmured, confused by what someone was even called when they were half Ghanaian and half Scots-Irish.

"Not nothing," Leonard chided, "You're a bit of everything. Like everyone else in this city." He shrugged and cast his blinding grin on Luca. "Welcome to America, right?"

Luca grinned right back, "The great soup pot!"

His enthusiastic blunder loosened something in Daisy's chest, enough so that she could smile, too. "It's *melting pot*. But, yeah. Pretty cool, either way."

Her father leaned forward to fist bump her, saying, "Yeahhhhh."

Daisy tried to picture a pale girl from the tropics and came up blank. "What did Joy look like?" she asked.

Leonard burst into flustered activity. He chugged some coffee, grabbed for his beat-up leather attaché on the ground near his feet, and rummaged around inside. "I brought some pictures," he said. When he extended the crumpled envelope, his fingers were trembling.

Daisy slipped the old photos out and stared down at the young woman whose DNA had helped create her. Joy was only a girl—impossibly young and happy in her striped t-shirt and Converse sneakers. She touched her mother's face, transfixed by her freckles and her unruly mane of hair.

"She—her hair was really red."

"Yeah. It was so bright, people thought she dyed it." Leonard fidgeted a little, then added, "I have a lot more pictures. I can scan them and email them to you, or I could bring them the next time we get together. If you want them. I mean—"

"That's great. Either one of those would be…" Daisy had reached the final photo in the stack and let out the breath she'd been holding in a sudden *whoosh*. There was her mom in a hospital gown. And there, in her lap, was a wrinkled little baby almost totally hidden by a blanket. "Is that—"

Luca leaned forward to peer over her shoulder.

Leonard bit his lip. "You bet it is. That's you, Miss Thing. Only two days old."

"Oh my God. My hair." Thick orange fuzz covered the top of her head.

"Carbon copy, man. No kidding."

Daisy tried to think about some of the other questions she'd had, but her mind had gone blank and she couldn't take her eyes off the young girl holding her in that photo. "How tall was she?"

"Um…about medium, I guess?" Leonard glanced around, and eventually pointed out a businesswoman walking by. "About like her, I'd say."

"So, around 5'5 or 5'6?" Daisy confirmed.

"Just about."

"I'm 5'9," she pointed out, ever the captain of the obvious.

Leonard smiled. "I noticed. You get that from my side, for sure. All the Bosu gals are Amazons. My mom always said it was because of the Native American blood, but like I told you—no one's ever managed to confirm that."

She tried to hand the photos back, but her dad held her off, saying only, "Keep them."

Daisy met Luca's eyes, tried to absorb some of his calm and strength, and steeled herself for what she had to say—what she had to know. "Leonard," Daisy asked, "What happened?"

His dark skin took on a grayish look. "Joy died. Toxemia," he said. "They tried like hell to fight it, but it killed her so fast. Within a week after you were born. I tried to keep you—to be a dad to you. But…" Leonard sighed. "Jesus, I was nineteen and a hothead. I was fucking up right and left and with Joy dying so suddenly, I just kind of…went off the deep end, I guess. By the time they took you away, Joy's parents had given up and gone back to Jamaica. Her grandma was the one who reported me to Family Services. I heard later she tried to get custody for herself, but they denied her. Said she was too old and frail to care for you."

"Her plan backfired," Daisy frowned.

"Yup. By then, the damage was done, though. My family was scattered all over and no one stepped up, so they put you in the system, and I…took off." Leonard's voice broke on the hard truth, and he struggled to keep his composure.

Daisy looked at Luca, wondering how much he was following. Judging by the sympathy on his face, he'd understood enough.

After a few painful minutes, Leonard looked like he had pulled himself together, so she asked softly, "What then?"

"I'd been playing guitar in a ska band for a couple years, just little gigs around town, nothing serious. But after that summer, we pulled up stakes and went out west. Did the L.A. scene for a long time." He smiled a little sheepishly. "They called me Big Daddy Bosu."

Daisy smiled back. "That's pretty cool. Would I have heard any of your songs?"

"I doubt it. But we had a ton of videos and stuff on YouTube." Her dad fumbled his phone out of his jacket pocket and tapped at the screen. "Here. Look."

Daisy and Luca watched the grainy recording of young men leaping and thrashing around the stage for a minute. They weren't half bad, if a little over-enthusiastic.

"You cut your locs," she said.

"Yeah, well. I got old. I wanted to look more respectable when I got out of rehab, so…" He stopped when he saw Daisy's face. "I, uh…I used to hit the sauce pretty hard for a while there. I didn't like to think about shit. It was easier to raise Cain than to worry about where you might be—whether you were even okay. But I figured, wherever you were had to be better than the crap life I could've given you."

Daisy didn't want to pry into yet another painful area, so instead she asked, "Have you been in the Village a long time? So close?"

"Oh, no. Only a few years. Well—five. I was in Cleveland before that. It was when I realized that you had to be getting close to the age your mom and I were when we had you, I thought…I wondered what you were up to. Where you were. What you'd…think of me."

Leonard shook himself. "Anyway, I cleaned myself up and checked into rehab soon after. Had some stops and starts, for sure. But once I got the idea that I could try and find you, I couldn't let the program go. I kept at it, working the steps, and eventually the steps started working."

"And then you came back here."

"Only after I was convinced the sobriety thing was going to stick. I couldn't come home until I knew for sure I was on the right path."

"Are you? On the right path?" Daisy wanted to bite back the words as soon as they left her mouth. They sounded harsh, and it wasn't her business.

But Leonard sat up straighter and took a deep breath. "It hasn't been easy, but I'm five years sober and feeling really good. I still go to meetings, and I see a therapist once a month, just to talk things out. You know—trying to find you and not having much luck…it's been a *thing*. I didn't want to risk backsliding again. Not when…" He stopped and reached for his water glass.

His hand was shaking again, along with his voice. "Not when I might get lucky and finally get to meet you." If the man sitting across from her was faking all that emotion, he ought to be on Broadway.

Luca cleared his throat and spoke up, giving them both time to gather themselves. "You've worked very hard. You should be proud of yourself."

Leonard nodded. "I owed it to Joy—and to Daisy. I'm just so sorry I didn't realize how much time was passing before it got to be too late."

"It's never too late," Luca reassured him. Under the table, he squeezed Daisy's knee.

Daisy looked between them. "That's right," she said, "Hell, you're not even…" But then she stopped. "Actually, I don't know this. Are you even fifty yet?"

"Soon," Leonard smiled. "Day after Valentine's, I'll officially be an old man. If your mom was still alive, she'd probably tease me to death about it."

"What was she like? Could you tell me some more about her? I mean, I know what she looked like and where she was from, but…"

Luca laced his fingers through hers. Daisy latched on tight, then immediately tried to loosen her death grip so he wouldn't lose sensation in the appendage. At least it wasn't his operating hand.

Leonard's melancholy lifted immediately and his whole face lit up like a sunrise. "You remind me so much of her. Joy had the whitest skin you've ever seen, and that vivid red hair. It was so thick—it used to fall in these messy waves in her face all the time. She was always complaining that it was too heavy for those clips and elastics that you girls always use."

"Did she have a Caribbean accent?"

"Lord, yes. When Joy washed up in my middle school one day, I thought it was so funny that she was so pale. It was literally impossible to imagine her in a bikini on some tropical beach. Thank God for sunscreen, man."

Daisy felt like she was blinking way too fast and wondered if anyone else noticed. After a lifetime of not knowing anything about her real parents, the sudden deluge of detail was hard to process. She didn't want to miss a thing and didn't want to forget, either.

Luca stepped in once more, keeping the ball rolling. "Do you know what brought Joy's family to the United States?"

Leonard shrugged. "Her dad's work, I think? I really don't remember. I'm sorry. Mr. Montgomery wasn't very talkative."

Daisy tried to picture the girl her father had described, eighteen years old with an infant daughter already. She tried to conceive of how someone so young, with their whole life ahead of them still, could die so suddenly. "Did she get to hold me much? Before she…you know."

Leonard barked out a laugh. "Are you kidding? Joy wouldn't put you down. She was freaking gobsmacked by you. We both were." He sank into thought for a moment. "I wanted to get married, you know, when we found out she was pregnant. But Joy wanted to wait. She wanted to look nice in her wedding dress, she said, not like some washed-up whale."

Daisy smiled, but her eyes were unconscionably watery.

"After you were born, I was happy she'd insisted. We were so damn excited that you were going to get to be a part of the wedding."

Daisy's damn eyes spilled right over at that. "Except there wasn't time."

"No." Leonard choked up, too. "We never expected…" He pulled out a handkerchief and mopped at his eyes, then jammed it back in his pocket. It was an oddly old-school affectation, given his rocker history. "Anyway…" he grumbled.

Luca patted his shoulder. "I'm so sorry for your loss."

Daisy watched her boyfriend and wondered how many times he'd had to utter those same words. How many times in a week? In a year? And yet he still looked like he really meant it.

When Leonard said, "Thank you," his grief did not seem to have been dulled by the intervening decades. Not in the least.

He shook off his sorrow with difficulty. To Daisy, he said, "I brought you something. I'm not sure if you'll want it, but um—" He extracted a tissue-wrapped packet from his blazer and fiddled with the tape holding it closed. "We didn't get a chance to tie the knot, but Joy and I did buy our rings before she passed."

He thrust the gift at Daisy. "I'd like to keep mine, if that's okay, but this one's hers. You can have it. If you want."

Daisy took the package in both her hands and stared down at it as if it were a ticking bomb. It weighed almost nothing, and the pink tissue had clearly been crumpled a few times before it was smoothed flat again for this purpose.

She tried to unwrap it carefully, but the delicate paper tore on her first attempt. Inside, was a narrow silver band, studded all over with small diamond chips like stars. Leonard eyed it and looked uncomfortable.

"It's nothing special. I got it from some guy who used to sell jewelry from a table near our high school. He said the stones were real diamonds, but they probably aren't. I promised Joy I'd get her a better one someday."

Daisy shook her head and slipped it on. Perfect fit. Exactly her style. She exhaled and glanced up at Leonard, but he was staring at her fingers.

"You have her hands. She refused to even try it on before we got married. Too superstitious, I guess. But it looks…on you, it looks…"

"*Perfetto*," Luca smiled.

Daisy was positive she must be beet red. "I'm probably not as pale as she was," she managed weakly.

Leonard chuckled. "Guess you got some part of me, after all."

Luca leaned in and pointed, "More than some. Daisy has your eye shape. And your nose and chin."

"I do?" Daisy swayed in shock.

Leonard searched her face, then turned to Luca in glee. "Dude, I think you're right. Hey—would you take our picture?" Immediately, he sagged, however, second-guessing himself. "I mean, if that's okay with you, Daisy?"

Oh, God. The man actually looked worried that she would say no. That somehow, after all this time, she'd *reject* him. *As if.*

Little did Leonard know, Daisy would probably cling to him like grim death from here on out if he was even a little bit nice to her.

It seemed impolite to point that out, however. "Lean in, Big Daddy," she grinned. "Let's do this thing."

Twenty-Seven

S EVERAL DAYS AFTER the meeting with Daisy's father, Luca was back at her place, sprawled in the comfortable little chair next to her bed while she tried on the dress she'd found to wear to her upcoming gallery show. It flowed over her tall, lean frame like a deep green river, and Luca wanted to slide his hands over the surface of it, to test how it felt.

But Daisy was prattling on about how she should wear her hair, and which color of lipstick would look best with that shade of green. He was supposed to paying attention to that, not searching for the faint edge of her thong at the top of her luscious backside.

Was she doing this to torture him on purpose? Twisting and turning from side to side, checking all the angles in the mirror on her closet door—did women even understand what it was like for a man to watch the process of them getting dressed up, and not just be presented with the final, glamorous outcome?

It was like getting a peek behind the curtain. An intimate, only-for-him peek. And…now Luca was hard again. Story of his life around Daisy.

"So," he said abruptly, trying to refocus. "It sounds as if you will be deploying all the war paint at this show, *sí?*"

Daisy eyed herself in the long mirror and shrugged. "I have to."

"But who are you planning to do battle with? The art critics? Almost everyone else there will be your friend, and I'm sure they don't want to fight."

She turned to face him, and the hem of her dress flared slightly around her calves. Luca took a moment to appreciate the glimpse—Daisy did have especially nice calves, toned and shapely and excellent to nibble on.

"Those critics are beasts, though, Luca. Truly. I only get one chance to make a good impression."

"You will. Just treat them like small, angry children." And then, because his mouth disconnected from his brain the second she whipped that heavenly green dress back over her head and ducked into her closet, he added, "Someday, we'll have those, won't we? Little beast children?"

Luca wanted to smack himself the instant the words left his mouth. Daisy never liked him to get too far ahead of where they were, but what could he say? He liked to dream, especially when the dream starred her.

She surprised him, however, her voice easy and light when it drifted from within her closet. "Sure. And, knowing me, they'll probably end up being savage, rambunctious devils."

Daisy emerged again wearing a sleeveless black gown that skimmed her gentle curves. It had a high neck and reached down to the top of her feet. Luca frowned—he'd liked the green one better.

Daisy braced herself on the doorframe as she slipped into a pair of suede heels that made her several inches taller. Luca would've liked to see them paired only with that peekaboo thong, but resigned himself to saving the image for later.

He sighed, returning to the topic of children. "I blame myself. If I'd only fallen for a nice Italian girl like Mamma wanted, I wouldn't have to worry about such things."

"Well, what can you expect?" she laughed. Luca leaned forward so he could watch her paint her soft, full lips a bright red. "If your judgment had been better, you might have found a better broodmare."

"True. Though I doubt that kind of woman would have been as fun in other respects."

As Daisy hustled past him to her dresser, fussing with a pair of dangly, sparkling earrings, Luca got his first real view of the back of her dress. Or rather, the complete lack of one.

The scoop of it plunged deep, nearly to the top of her ass. No way could Daisy still be wearing either a bra or panties under there. Where would she hide them? No wonder he hadn't been able to find any evidence.

Luca swallowed thickly, got to his feet, and moved in.

She smirked at him in her mirror, maybe guessing the direction of his thoughts. "I suppose I do bring certain talents to the table."

He bent to bite her earlobe but was stymied by the bulky earring. "About those talents."

"Uh-uh," Daisy protested, "None of that. That car you ordered is probably already outside. If we don't leave right now, we're going to be late."

Right. *La Traviata.* With all the visual stimuli floating around, and the bantering about procreation, he'd forgotten they were supposed to go to the opera tonight. And, since it was Daisy's first time, Luca wanted it to be perfect.

They'd have to get better acquainted with her bed afterward.

IT WAS AN exceptionally good performance. As often happened to him at the opera, Luca found himself transported by the singing—that extraordinary thing some people could do with the same set of mundane parts that most humans were issued at birth. How could a simple pair of lungs or a routine voice box create such beauty?

It defied reason and yet, there it was. Beside him, Daisy was rapt, too, and Luca was thrilled that she seemed to be enjoying herself. They sat side-by-side, silent and still, and let the magic envelop them.

He'd arranged ahead of time for drinks and a light snack at the intermission, so when the curtain came down, Luca brought Daisy downstairs. While she sipped a glass of champagne and nibbled on caviar, she looked as if she'd spent a thousand evenings like this—and her adaptability was frankly amazing.

Luca wondered, "What do you think so far?"

"Isn't it obvious?" she laughed. "I love it. I wish I'd thought to try it sooner. I could have been coming here for years as a student."

Luca shrugged. "Sometimes we don't know what we're missing." Once you found what you were missing, however, living without it was the worst. He ought to know.

"It's got me thinking about the whole nature versus nurture debate, I've got to tell you," she mused. "I mean, I've always been creative—coloring and drawing and playing with paper and clay and stuff long before I ever held a camera. It was just the way I was made. But I never understood where it came from, because Pam wasn't that way at all."

Luca could see that. "Perhaps Pam never had the opportunity."

"Maybe not. But then I met Leonard. And I realized tonight, while I was watching that performance, that the man who gave birth to me has been a lifelong musician. Plus, he says my mother was really artistic, too. So, did I get my creativity from them?"

Before they'd parted ways, Leonard had told them all about Joy's skill at drawing—about the awards she'd gotten in school for her art, and the way she could capture the likeness of a person or an object with only a few hasty lines on a page.

He'd seemed like a decent man, Leonard—kind at his core, and gentled by what had to have been some hard-fought years. Luca was happy that he'd been so delighted by Daisy. She deserved it.

He told her, "Could be. Genes are really incredible in what they transmit from parents to children. They do so much more than simply pass on eye color and the family nose. And, we still don't know all their secrets."

Daisy nodded and went back to her food. She was so lovely, her smoky eye makeup and red lipstick making her even more breathtaking than usual. Luca wanted to let her hair down, slip her gown off her shoulder, and kiss the tender skin at the hollow of her neck.

The bells began chiming for the next act, and reluctantly, Luca set aside his longing for a little longer. He didn't want her to miss a minute.

Midway through the last act, however, Daisy's fascinated gaze shifted from the stage to him. She turned toward Luca, gently touched his arm to get his attention, her eyes were huge and soft.

Luca looked into her upturned face, the aria swelled and soared all around them, the soprano hit a high note and drew it out, and…

His eyes fell to Daisy's mouth. He couldn't resist her spell a moment longer. In the middle of the Met, he cupped her velvet cheek and kissed her with his whole heart.

It went on and on. Tangled tongues and stolen breath, cardiac muscle banging around in its bony cage, cock standing tall in his tuxedo pants and demanding center stage.

The old woman beside Luca huffed and muttered her disapproval.

It was only when the crowd around them surged to its feet to applaud the cast, that Luca could tear himself away. Daisy looked shell-shocked.

"I love you," he whispered against her trembling lips.

"You're completely crazy," she said.

"I'm not. I'm sober and sane and I love you. Do you believe me?"

"Shockingly, I kind of do." She didn't say it back, but he'd expected that. Daisy would likely need to mull things over before she jumped on the train with him. Still, the emptiness on her side of what ought to have been a balanced give-and-take stung.

After the cast took its bows, Luca guided Daisy out to where the hired car was waiting to take them to a late dinner, and he wondered how long he'd have to wait before he heard *I love you* back. Would he ever? Was he kidding himself that they'd really get some kind of happy ending?

She'd joked earlier about having rowdy children, but maybe that had only come easily to her because Daisy considered it a preposterous notion—a completely unlikely farce. Something laughable. Something outrageous.

Before he'd met her, Luca hadn't thought of himself as such a bad prospect. It figured that the one woman who could level him would be the one he couldn't easily entice.

Daisy broke into his gloomy thoughts with a sudden question. "Luca, it didn't occur to me when we met him, but do you think I should invite Leonard to my gallery show?"

"Why not? He'd probably be thrilled."

"I don't know. You don't think it's too presumptuous?"

"Daisy, in case you failed to notice, Leonard was ecstatic to be breathing the same air as you. You're his daughter. He obviously wants to get to know you. He'd probably feel honored to be asked."

"Maybe he already has plans, though. It's pretty short notice."

"There's only one way to find out. If he can't make it, then so be it. At least you tried."

"He's pretty artsy, though, right? I bet he'd get a kick out of it."

"I think he would."

"And we wouldn't have to tell anyone who he was, if he felt uncomfortable."

Luca cocked his head. "I can't imagine that would be the case, but…would *you* feel uncomfortable? Because if you invite Leonard, and then introduce him as your friend to people, that might hurt his feelings."

And, now Luca was right back to feeling sorry for himself. Here he was, the man who didn't get an *I love you* back, championing the feelings of others. *Terrific.*

"Hmm. You're right. I guess I can ask him beforehand. Find out what he prefers."

"You can. But you should also decide what you want, too, so everyone is on the same page."

Daisy took a deep breath and watched the storefronts race by the car window for a while. It was late—many places were closed for the night in this part of town. There was still enough ambient light to see her profile, however.

Such a pretty face, and Daisy was almost entirely unaware of it—blind to the effect she had on the people around her. That was what happened when you were so wrapped up with what was going on inside your own head.

Like Luca was now.

He asked her, "Are you nervous about the show?"

"Yeah. I really am. I don't want to look like an idiot. I mean, my boss and his family will be there. Coworkers. Friends. You. Maybe even my father. What if they get there and think it's all a big joke?"

"That's not going to happen. Red would not have called his mother about you, and she would not have called around to galleries, if they did not believe in your work. What's more, the gallery people would never have invited you to show at their place if your photos weren't up to par. You said you knew the place, right?"

"Yeah, I walk by it all the time. They do a really nice job."

"There. So you've been vetted by professionals. And that's good enough. After that, as long as you put in your best effort, you can't control anything else. Not what people think and not what people say."

"I know. And objectively, I get that everyone is entitled to their own opinion. Art is really subjective."

"It is. They may like your work, or they may not, but that doesn't mean what you're doing doesn't have value. It doesn't change whether you are talented or not. Those things exist outside of their personal opinions."

"Thank you," Daisy said softly. She turned back to him and Luca took her hand.

"Do you think inviting Leonard will make your show harder to handle?"

"No, I don't think it will. At least he'll be a friendly face."

"And I'll be another. I know this is a big step, and it's scary, but I'm really proud of you. You're doing the right thing. And I'll be right there with you, cheering you on, okay?"

"You promise? I don't think I can get through it without you there."

"I promise. I said I love you, didn't I?" Luca winced inside at the way that reminder held a bite, like he was trying to goad her into saying it back. "What kind of man would I be if I left you high and dry on your big night?"

"Not the kind I want or need," Daisy said.

"Exactly. And you can bet that I want to be both, for a long, long time to come."

Twenty-Eight

THE CALL ABOUT Andrea Vittini came from Italy around nine in the morning. Luca was sitting at his desk, nursing the last few sips of a nice cappuccino that he'd brought from home, and glancing at some patient charts before he went on his rounds.

He knew instantly that something was very wrong. His former colleague, Francesca Cassata, was using too apologetic a tone as she described Luca's favorite patient coming in for his regular checkup the day before.

He'd complained of tiredness and a lack of appetite, Francesca said, and had looked thin and pale. His wife had sat beside him, worried and quieter than usual—as if she'd known the truth in her bones.

Luca listened with the phone pressed to his ear, as Francesca described taking the man's vitals, then sending him for the standard labwork and ultrasound of his stomach.

Luca begged to know why no one had called him sooner with his heart in his throat.

Dr. Cassata simply said, "*Dottore*, honestly—there was no time."

Andrea's labs came back showing alarmingly high levels of cancer markers in his blood. Even worse, the ultrasound indicated a definitive return of the young man's gastric tumors.

Luca was crushed. When he'd left for New York, his patient had been doing so well. Vittini had gotten accepted to a promising research study and was reporting steady weight gain and a return of his strength and stamina.

In addition, his wife was newly pregnant with their first child.

"Take a biopsy right away," Luca ordered. "And stabilize him as best as you can. I'll be on the next flight there, and we can operate as soon as I land. With some changes to Andrea's regimen—"

"No, Luca, you don't understand," Dr. Cassata cut in. "We admitted him immediately. Carlo opened Vittini up last night."

Luca had probably been in bed fucking Daisy at the time, as if he didn't have a care in the world—or, at minimum, like good people in two countries weren't counting on him for their very survival.

The sour bile of shame rose in his throat. If his colleagues hadn't phoned him until now, then the prognosis couldn't be good.

"What did he find when he went in?" he asked.

"Carlo wants you to know that he did his best. He got what he could, but he had to close up without getting everything."

"What the hell is that supposed to mean? Carlo is hardly fresh out of school. If he couldn't get everything—"

"It means no one could." Francesca's voice brooked no argument. "Not even *il grande Delledonna*. The tumors have spread, Luca. We've told Vittini to settle things in his life, because he doesn't have long."

"So, that's it then? You're all just giving up on him?"

"It's what Andrea and his wife want."

No. That couldn't be right. Andrea was a fighter. He'd never throw in the towel, especially not before he got to lay his eyes on his first child.

"Luca," Francesca said, "Listen to me. I know how special Vittini is to you. If you want to say goodbye, you should call him. I think he'd like to hear from you."

Fury billowed into his blood, hot and red as lava. "Oh, I'm not going to say goodbye," he growled. "I'm going to do far better than that."

"What's that?"

"I'm going to save him."

"Dr. Delledonna, stop and take a breath. Think about what you're—"

Luca cut the call and marched out of his office, going on the hunt for Dr. Green.

HARLAN GREEN HAD been practicing oncology for decades longer than Luca, but he had the same kind of soul. He understood a thing or two about those special patients who came along once in a while—the ones who stepped right past the professional distance doctors tried to maintain and rooted themselves deep inside your heart.

So, when Luca explained the situation and asked for some time off, only weeks into his tenure at Weill Cornell, Green didn't bat an eye. He simply launched into action and did what needed to be done to make it happen.

Shooing Luca off with promises to rearrange schedules and call in favors, Harlan sent him on his way and wished him godspeed.

An hour later, Luca was whirling around his apartment like a veritable dervish, frantically throwing clothes into an overnight bag and arranging for a car to take him to the airport.

On the ride to LaGuardia, Luca began calling airlines, searching for the next available flight to Italy that still had a free seat.

In short order, he landed a spot in coach, on a three p.m. with a brief layover in Frankfurt. With any luck, Luca could be at the hospital in Florence by breakfast time tomorrow.

He had just enough time to make it through security and get his butt in his seat before they closed the airplane doors. While Luca waited for takeoff, he texted his family, letting them know when he was coming in and arranging for Paolo to stop by the hospital tomorrow to pick up Luca's bag and ferry it to Nonna's.

He also called Andrea's wife, getting some background and listening to her accounting of the last few days. He let her cry her heart out before he told her he was on his way.

Once the plane was in the air and the pilot allowed the use of electronic devices again, Luca was right back to work—setting up a group chat with Francesca, Carlo, and the other doctors helping to care for Andrea.

He interrogated them for as long as they allowed, gleaning every last detail from their impressive brains and the breadth of their collective practical knowledge. When they finally shut him down, Luca knew everything they did.

He used that information to scour his brain and the internet for something—*anything*—that might help Andrea Vittini. There had to be something new. Something they'd missed. Any holy grail at all to change that poor man's fate.

When Luca could no longer think, when he couldn't read the words swimming across the screen in front of his face any longer, he loosened his tie, closed his laptop and his eyes, and tried to sleep.

There must be something he was missing, Luca thought, drifting into a troubled, restless slumber. There had to be something else.

GIADA SHOWED UP at the airport, bleary-eyed, but apparently ready and willing to bring him to the hospital as they'd planned. Luca offered her a dejected, *"Ciao,"* and kissed her on both cheeks.

His sister eyed him dubiously. "Come home and shower first," she told him. "You'll feel better, and you'll certainly look more respectable."

"No, I can't," Luca said. "There's no time."

"Luca. Don't view it as a gentle suggestion. Consider this a firm and inviolable command."

He frowned at her. "Do I really look that bad?"

Trust an older sister to give you the unvarnished truth. "Yes," Giada claimed, "You do. A shower and some espresso will put you right, *fratello*. Don't fight it."

Luca looked down at his crumpled clothes, then took off his glasses and tried to polish them on the hem of his shirt. "Nonna's is closest to the hospital," he conceded.

"I know that. Can't you see I'm heading there?"

He hadn't noticed. The juxtaposition between *Firenze* and New York already felt surreal.

Giada prodded, "Did you call Daisy to let her know you arrived safely?"

The way his family had been begging for news of his and Daisy's relationship for the last few weeks, you might have thought Luca was starring in a hot and heavy soap opera on TV.

Luca's head, however, felt like a pile of muck that'd been scraped from the bottom of the Arno. *"Scusi?"*

"Daisy. You remember her? Your woman?" His sister hit him on the arm, like she would a vending machine that was withholding snacks. "You *did* call her to tell her you landed safely. Correct?"

The bottom fell out of Luca's soul. "*Vaffanculo*," he muttered foully. He checked his watch, tore it off his wrist, then reset it for the six-hour time difference. "What day is it? I don't even know anymore."

There might still be time to salvage things, but he had a sinking suspicion he was far, far too late.

"It's Saturday, *idiota*. Are you even okay?"

"No, I'm not okay. My favorite patient is at death's door, Giada, and it's all my fault." Not to mention the fact that his relationship was probably also at death's door right now.

"How is that your fault?"

"I left him. I went chasing to America after a woman and look what happened to Andrea."

"Luca, that's—"

"*And*, what's more—" Luca choked on the words backing up in his throat and couldn't force them out.

He'd missed Daisy's gallery show. Over and over, he had promised her that he would be beside her and he'd broken that promise. He'd left, hadn't called, nothing.

It was a terrible thing to do to her, and there was almost nothing Luca could do to fix it for a week or more, depending on how things went with Andrea.

Daisy knew he loved her, at least—there was that. Luca was thankful, now, that he'd had the sudden and irrepressible urge to tell her during their visit to the opera, even if the fact that she hadn't returned the favor had felt ominous and grim at the time.

God willing, Daisy would take his love into account when she judged his absence. She'd have to realize that he would never have done such an awful thing unless he'd been stuck between a rock and a hard place. Unless it was an absolute, life-or-death emergency.

Except, he hadn't *really* been stuck, had he? He'd taken the call, and he'd left without a thought. Luca had never once stopped to consider what he was supposed to be doing last night, while he'd been thousands of miles over the Atlantic.

And furthermore, was this really a life-or-death crisis? Or was Luca just acting like a headstrong *stronzo?*

"Luca, if you did not call Daisy, you should do it now. Before you forget. She'll be worried about you otherwise."

Maybe she would be. Or maybe Daisy had already planned out all the ways she could murder him, reanimate his corpse, and then kill him all over again.

That was the best-case scenario. The worst-case? Today, poor Daisy would be listing for herself all the reasons why she should expect to be treated so badly—and why she and Luca could never last.

She'd decide all over again that they were never meant to be in the first place, despite the improbability of their meeting in *Firenze*, and the unlikelihood that he would ever have found her again in New York.

Porca Giuda, they'd been making so much progress, too.

With shaking hands, Luca pulled his phone out of his jacket pocket. He wasn't sure if he should call, or text, or email. What could he say, and how could he make Daisy listen? His mind was a blank, gray haze.

It didn't matter anyway. When he attempted to turn his cell on, he discovered that his battery was dead. All that mid-flight research, no doubt.

In about thirty more minutes, they would be at Nonna's pensione. Luca could charge his phone while he got cleaned up, and maybe by then, he could come up with some magic formula—some spell to transform himself from the ass he'd turned into when he boarded that plane, back into a man.

Twenty-Nine

O N THE DAY of her gallery show, Daisy took time off at work so she could finish up a few last-minute tasks. If she was being honest, though, she also did it so she might have a prayer of holding it together for the long hours until showtime.

She'd combed through her photos from the last few years to come up with a good selection to hang on the gallery walls. She'd cropped and she'd filtered and she'd corrected for light and shadow on her computer, long into every night.

Thankfully, the gallery had been able to suggest a lab that some of their regular artists worked with, and the place had handled Daisy's printing specifications easily.

The tricky part had turned out to be getting everything framed on time. Daisy had to split the work between three different shops, pay an arm and a leg for rush jobs—and she'd still had to beg Luca to lend her the pieces hanging in his apartment, just to fill things out.

He'd been willing, but adamant that no matter how many signs they had to post, those pictures better not be sold by accident to someone else. Luca had vowed to patrol that wall of the gallery all night, in case anyone showed too much interest.

Under no circumstances would the images of his home and family take up residence with some random stranger. They were his, and he wanted them to stay that way.

It was flattering that he was so attached to them, but he hadn't seen the little surprise Daisy had cooked up for him yet. She suspected that Luca would like it even better than the art he already owned, if anything because there was no way he'd be able to look at it and not know how much she cared about him.

Which reminded her—she had to get going if she was going to pick up the last four pieces and get them to the gallery on time, so they could be hung before the show. They'd reserved one whole wall for them, linking the Italy pictures to the New York ones.

The frames were really big, and they were going to be heavy. Daisy was standing in her kitchen, trying to decide if she should call Luca for help, when the lobby call-box buzzed.

"Hello?"

"Delivery for Ms. Montgomery."

"Really?" That was weird. She wasn't expecting anything. "Okay, I'll be right down."

Daisy grabbed her purse and her keys and hit the elevator. She could always call Luca on the way and ask him to meet her at the frame shop—he'd said he didn't have much going on at work that day.

At the front door of her building, a young woman in a lime green windbreaker was shifting from foot to foot. When Daisy opened the door, the girl asked, "Ms. Montgomery?"

"That's me."

"Here you go. Enjoy." She shoved a big box into Daisy's hands, had her sign a form, then took off on her courier bike.

Daisy wrestled the box back inside where it was warmer, set it on the stairs, and pulled the delivery note free.

You can do this, it read. *You really can.* – L

Two dozen red roses and a one-line pep talk. Daisy sighed in contentment, buried her nose in the cold, beautiful blooms, and hiked back upstairs to put them in water before she left.

She didn't need to call Luca now. Somehow, she'd figure out how to take care of this errand herself. Daisy would rather wait to see him until later anyway—when she'd be primped and polished and looking more his speed.

Then she could thank him properly for such a thoughtful gift.

Luca loved her. He'd told her so, in unequivocal, easy-to-comprehend English. And he'd been telling her so in a multitude of other ways, as well.

So…did Daisy love him back? She cared for him immensely, it was true. But she had no idea if this sweeping, swooping, nerve-jangling feeling she got whenever he was near was love or infatuation.

Daisy didn't even know if she was capable of love—not the kind that kept people happily married for fifty years, anyway. Luca would want nothing less.

Could she love like her father, a man who'd pined for his high school sweetheart for decades after she'd died? Leonard had never married anyone else, and had never gotten rid of his costume jewelry wedding band, despite not getting to speak his vows to begin with.

Maybe that chip was broken in Daisy and had been from the moment her family handed her over to complete strangers to be raised. Maybe Daisy was faulty in critical ways. She'd certainly always felt like she was.

Weren't you supposed to *know* if you were in love? Wasn't it supposed to be obvious, like it was in books and movies—where it coursed through people with the force of a lightning strike?

Daisy didn't know. And her questions would have to wait until tomorrow, anyway, when she would have made it to the other side of the craziest, most thrilling, most terrifying night of her life.

THE PROCESS OF getting the big frames into the back seat of a cab, and from there into the gallery, proved just as frustrating and time-consuming as Daisy had feared.

There'd been no getting around it, though. These last pictures were the centerpieces of her show, and Daisy wanted them to be perfect. She'd splurged for special mats and frames and had crossed her fingers that the shop wouldn't let her down.

It'd made for a white-knuckle timeline. By the time Daisy arrived, the gallery folks were standing around their ladder, breaking a sweat next to the last bare wall—and that was really saying something since the temperature outside had been dropping steadily all day.

It was a frosty eighteen degrees in town by the time they finally kicked her out. They stowed their ladders in the gallery's back room and instructed Daisy to have a drink—or twelve—before she came back for her show.

They meant it as a joke, but Daisy was strongly considering it. She'd broken three of her already-short nails during the delivery, and she didn't even want to know what her hair must look like.

As she stood on the curb waiting for a taxi, Daisy tried to think of a way to salvage the situation—and eventually decided that Poppy would know what to do. Because Daisy's college buddy had suffered from panic attacks for years, she was a veritable encyclopedia of relaxation techniques. Daisy took a chance and texted her.

I'm a wreck. What can I do for the next hour that will both calm me down and help me look better for my show?

Poppy's reply came quickly. *Girl, you're a lost cause. Go get a mani/pedi. And spring for the gel polish so you won't chip or smudge it while you're getting ready.*

And you think that will help?

My soul cries for you. You've obviously never gotten a spa pedicure before.

If Poppy said pedicures cured nervousness, then Daisy believed her. *Okay, I'll try it,* she typed.

Good. I'm gonna lose reception here in a minute – knock 'em dead later, ok?

Daisy stepped out of her second taxi of the day and looked curiously around the block she lived on. She knew she'd seen someplace around there…someplace nearby…

…and *there*. Right on the corner was a nail salon, its windows brightly lit and plastered with posters of perfectly manicured hands. That could be her. That *would* be her. Daisy marched inside like she knew what the heck she was doing.

When they parked her in a massage chair, stuck her feet in the water, and asked her what color, Daisy thought instantly of Luca's flowers.

"Red," she told them. "Bright red."

While the warm, fragrant bubbles of the foot spa worked their magic, Daisy pulled out her phone to check in with Luca. He'd enjoy knowing where she'd ended up, she just knew it.

However, there was a text waiting from her father that probably required her attention first. Daisy must have missed it somehow, in all the confusion at the gallery.

Would it be okay if I brought someone to your show tonight? he'd asked. *She's begging to meet you.*

Daisy stared at the words. She? Her mind reeled with the possibilities. It could be a friend or a family member, she supposed, but it could also be a significant other.

Leonard hadn't mentioned seeing anyone, but that didn't necessarily mean anything. For all Daisy knew, her father could have been shacking up with someone for the last twenty years.

She typed, *The more the merrier*, and shrugged. The nail lady had started massaging her feet and her legs, and Poppy was so right—stress didn't stand a chance in the face of those capable hands.

She was shuffling after her new favorite salon professional, toward one of the manicure stations at the front of the place, when her phone rang in her pocket.

Daisy grabbed for it, hoping it was Luca, but ended up with Pam.

"Hey, kid," her foster mom said. "So—this thing tonight."

Daisy wanted to groan. Someone had invited Pam? *Holy hell.* The woman was going to be completely out of her element.

"Pam, you really don't have to come if you don't want to. It's no big deal."

"What are talking about? I got someone to cover my shift at the restaurant and everything."

"But do you really want to truck all the way over here? It's freezing out. And it might go late."

"I think I'll live. But the reason I called is because I don't know what people wear to shindigs like this. I don't have too many reasons to get dressed up anymore, you know?"

Daisy looked down at her newly glossy toes and bit her lip. She knew for a fact that Pam couldn't own more than one or two dresses, and those would be hopelessly outdated and reserved mainly for weddings and funerals.

"I don't think you need to worry. Some people might get dressed up—" Like Daisy, for example, "—but some won't."

She said it as if she knew. Daisy had never been to opening night at a gallery show, though.

"So, like, church clothes, you think?"

Best to keep things simple, Daisy thought. "Yeah. I bet church clothes will be perfect."

"All right. And I'll probably eat dinner before I come. In case the food is strange, or whatever."

"Good idea," Daisy told her, even though the invitations hadn't mentioned anything other than cocktails and hors d'oeuvres. Weird food for Pam could mean anything from kale to caviar, however. If eating first made her feel more comfortable, then so be it.

Daisy was hardly one to talk. She was the one sitting here letting a woman paint her nails for her, when she was perfectly capable of doing it herself—and that was just as much of a coping mechanism as anything Pam was going to do.

DAISY PULLED HER hands out of her mittens almost immediately, so she could admire her glossy, cherry-red nails as she walked along the icy sidewalk back to her building. All the slush from earlier in the day had frozen over in the frigid weather. Darkness was falling and the Friday evening rush hour was in full swing.

She pulled her hat down tighter, feeling a little queasy from the butterflies fluttering around in her stomach. The nail thing might not have been completely effective as a sedative, but at least she was going to look nice tonight.

She had flashy nails, a pretty dress, and really excellent shoes she'd found earlier that week. Daisy had friends coming to cheer her on and talk her up to any critics in the crowd. She had a gorgeous man who loved her, to stand sentinel at her side.

No wonder she was giddy. On a whim, she ducked quickly into the little gift shop halfway to her building, hoping to find something special she could give Luca later to thank him for all his support.

In the back corner with all the toys, she found the perfect thing: a building block set like the ones he'd talked about, made to look like the Trevi Fountain once it was complete. The shop gift-wrapped it with newsprint and a big floppy ribbon, and she knew Luca would love it.

Besides, she thought, shivering a little as she continued on her way, it wasn't like she had to face a firing squad at the end of the night. All she had to do was stand around for a few hours and be polite. Smile for a few pictures, answer a few questions, shake some hands—and then she'd be home free.

She could drag Luca back to her place and have her wicked way with him.

Daisy managed to talk herself into a reasonably calm state by the time she hit her lobby, and it held steady all the way up to her floor and into her apartment.

She hung her coat on the rack, ditched her bags on the counter, and went into her kitchen to down a quick bowl of cereal and a spotty banana. After roughly three seconds of contemplation, she also drank a quick shot of tequila for courage. Then Daisy headed into her bathroom to take a nice, hot shower.

In the mirror, she caught sight of the wild mess that had once been her clean, conditioned hair, and wanted to drop right there and cry.

Crap. There was no time to rewash it, and not much hope of salvaging it, either. Daisy ran her fingers through the curls and tried to untangle it as best as she could, pinned it up under a cap while she showered, and mentally ran through her options.

Barrettes, clips…maybe a scarf, wrapped around her head and tied with a cute knot? It might look a little more bohemian than she would've liked, but hell—she was going to an art gallery. If there was ever a place to rock that look, it was there.

By the time she dried off, she knew just the scarf she'd wear, too. She'd bought a silk floral one in Italy one day, with Luca's sister Giada. It would pick up the green of her dress and the red of her nails, and even though Daisy would probably end up looking like a Christmas tree, she had a feeling Luca wouldn't mind.

She smirked, imagining his reaction. If he was a very good boy tonight, Luca could unwrap her like a present when they got home. And, if he ended up having to resuscitate her because of a bad reaction to too much socializing, then it would probably only make things more fun.

Daisy kept the thought of playing *dirty doctor* front and center in her brain while she finished getting ready and called a cab, and she let it calm her as the minutes to show time ticked down.

Thirty

ULTIMATELY, LUCA'S FORCE of will was no match for Andrea Vittini's. The young man approached dying with the same fortitude and resolve that he had once applied to living. He'd made his decision and would not be swayed from it.

Luca admired it, but he still couldn't figure out what had changed in such a short amount of time. The human spirit was an incredible entity, though, capable of so much more endurance than seemed possible—and capable of choosing not to persist anymore, as well.

Sometimes, just like a boxer, the spirit took one too many hits, and simply refused to get up and keep swinging any longer. It seemed like that was what had happened to Andrea. Francesca hadn't been exaggerating when she'd said he didn't have long.

Luca found out on his third day in Italy that Vittini's wife had lost the baby she'd been carrying sometime since he'd moved to New York. It was her third miscarriage in three years—a crushing blow.

The knock-out punch, as it were.

When Andrea requested it, the medical team disconnected him from all the tubes and wires keeping him alive and kept their vigil in the hall outside his room, while his wife and parents held his hand and watched him leave their lives.

Luca hoped that someday he would be as sanguine, when it came time for him to meet his maker. He hoped there would be loved ones close, to wish him well. To love him.

THE FUNERAL WAS a grim affair, gray and raw with cold. Luca sat near the back of the church, flanked by Francesca and Carlo, who'd rushed over during their lunch break at the hospital to lend him their support.

In the wavering candlelight, the deceased looked far too much like his brother Matteo, for Luca's peace of mind. It was undoubtedly a trick of the light—Andrea was older than Matteo had been, for one thing, and had lighter, shaggier hair.

But Luca knew, with sickening clarity, that one of the reasons he'd grown so attached to Vittini was that his easy smile was exactly the same as his brother's had been.

Matteo had been only twenty years old when he'd succumbed to the same, hideous disease. It had taken him so quickly—in barely two years, the eldest son in the family was lost to all of them.

Luca, a naïve, sheltered twelve-year-old, had been utterly powerless to stop or change any part of it. He could only sit by and watch as his parents and siblings were devastated—as he was devastated.

Times were different now. Luca had knowledge and skill at his disposal to fight the scourge. Usually, anyway.

Sometimes Death still won, and each time it was no less a bitter defeat.

SOMEHOW, LUCA ENDED up at his parent's house afterward, in his childhood bedroom. As he changed out of his dark gray suit and into a sweater and jeans that he found in his old closet, he noticed that his phone was dead again.

He had no idea how long it'd been that way. Was it newly dead, or had it been dead since Luca had landed in *Firenze*? There was no telling.

Fortunately, he didn't have to battle with the grim reaper to revive a phone. He only had to find the cord and plug adaptor in his attaché case and connect it to an outlet to charge.

After a few minutes, the screen glowed into life, and Luca saw with a sinking heart the calls and texts from Daisy. From Piper. From Red.

He dropped his head into his hands and groaned. He'd never texted them back. Not once.

Luca's father found him that way, crushed and guilt-ridden and immobilized by his own stupidity.

"Son? What's going on?" he asked.

Luca explained about Andrea and the funeral that morning, leaving out the critical fact that while he was trying to fend off death itself, he'd missed the most important event in his girlfriend's life.

His father saw the connection to Matteo immediately, of course. "Gianluca, you've done good work. The best," he sighed. "Your brother would be so touched by your enduring love for him. So proud of what you've accomplished."

"It's not enough, Papa."

"It's always enough. Our love is always enough."

"But I can do more. Next time, maybe I will save someone's father. Someone's brother or son, if I just work harder."

"Maybe yes, you will help others. I hope that is true. But sometimes you will fail, too, because a higher power is in charge of our living and dying. Not you. And putting your own life aside will not bring Matteo back. More than anything, he would want you to find peace with that."

"I have," Luca argued.

"Have you? Have you made enough time to be with Daisy, while you've been working so hard, like a good American?"

Luca flinched—how could he not? He'd been swept into a culture that valued excess over substance. It had been easy to make time for Daisy when he'd first moved to Manhattan, but as his duties increased and his days got longer, he'd steadily slid back into old habits.

He'd been aided and abetted by coworkers who admired such behavior and hadn't had his family near to remind him of what was actually important.

And then, when the chips were down, Luca abandoned Daisy without even a second thought.

Perceptive as ever, his father moaned, "Oh, no. What have you done?"

"I… came here so quickly," Luca stuttered, "And then I was at the hospital and…"

"Luca—"

"I missed something very important to her, Papa. I haven't spoken to her, and I'm worried that I've hurt Daisy badly. Too badly to recover from."

"If you're worried about it, you almost certainly have."

"I could not have done things differently. It's best Daisy learns that now."

Although, in retrospect, the decent thing to do would've been to call her right away. *That* was something Luca absolutely should have done differently.

But he told his father, "If Daisy doesn't understand how I feel about my job, then maybe we aren't right for each other after all."

"You sound very certain of that."

Luca shook his head. He was certain of nothing. Realizing how little he knew about anything—while he was so busy strutting around like a peacock in his lab coat and stethoscope—had him tearing up.

Unfortunately, once the waterworks began, they rapidly turned into a messy, biblical flood. Luca broke down in a way he'd never done, shoulders shaking uncontrollably and painful sobs ripping from his throat. He'd avoided this for days, but *accidenti*—he hated losing to Death. Despised it, with every fiber of his being.

His father sat close beside him, running a gentle hand over his head like he had when Luca was small. He patted Luca's back and waited until his heartache fizzled out.

"Better now?"

Luca mopped at his face and croaked, "Daisy may not forgive me for this, Papa. And then I will have lost two people important to me, not one."

"What Daisy does is not in your control," his father retorted. "But when you explain to her what happened, you must remember—for a woman to see a man grieve like that…it is not something she can ever set aside and forget. If you are not sure that Daisy is the one you will spend your life with, if you don't know yet if her love is true and everlasting, then spare her your sorrow."

"I'm sorry, what?"

"I'm saying that if Daisy is still making up her mind about you, she might not be able to recognize the strength beneath your emotion yet. She might be afraid to trust you to take care of her when she feels sad or vulnerable, if she's worried about your weaknesses, too."

Luca gaped at the man. "Are you seriously counseling me not to *cry* in front of Daisy? After everything else that's happened today?"

His father simply shrugged. "I'm an old man, Luca, but I know a thing or two about women. When the time comes, remember what I said."

Luca sat back and could almost hear Tate's voice in his head, squawking, *"Dude, that's wack."* Because it was—it really, really was. His father's advice was strange, it was suspect, and it was almost definitely unreliable.

What would Red tell him to do? Luca couldn't venture to guess. Red made no bones about his utter adoration of Piper and it was clearly working for him. Perhaps he ought to take directions from that quarter instead.

"I love her," Luca found himself admitting. "I do want a lifetime with her. But Daisy already has so much hurt in her past. What if I've ruined everything by giving her more of it?"

"You're a good man, Luca, and Daisy is smart. She'll understand and forgive you."

"I'm not so sure."

He looked up and saw his Nonna, silently watching him from the doorway. Luca quickly swiped at his face again and tried to give her a brave smile, but she shook her head and waved his weak effort away.

"I like Daisy," she announced, stepping into the room. "Once you've made amends, you will propose to her, *sì?*"

Luca shrugged. "I'd like to. If she'll let me. I think it's going to take some time, though."

Nonna nodded. "She will let you." She shuffled over to the bureau in the corner, rooting through the years-old detritus on top until she found a small enameled jewelry box she must have stashed there at some point.

His grandmother carried it over, then sat heavily next to Luca and his dad on the bed. He watched her hands crack open the box and thought heavily of the photos Daisy had hung in his New York apartment—and of the woman who'd taken them.

He'd made her promise not to sell them to someone else at her gallery show. When he hadn't shown up, had she decided that all bets were off? Luca dearly hoped not.

Nonna pushed her fingers through the tangled mess of baubles in her box, and retrieved a ring with a happy, "*Ecco*! Here it is."

Beside him, Luca's father took one look at it and chuckled.

"What's that?" Luca wondered. Judging by the single diamond solitaire, it was someone's engagement ring, but *he'd* certainly never seen it before.

"It's my wedding ring." His grandmother turned it back and forth so the stone caught the light. "I stopped wearing it when your Nonno passed on. Too flashy for the pensione. I didn't want anyone to get ideas about me."

Luca knew she was extremely careful about who she allowed to stay in her rooms but she was right to be careful, since she was alone with her boarders so much of the time.

He studied the ring his grandmother held. The white gold band was simple, but it looked rich, and the oval diamond was quite large. Nonno must have spent a fortune on it.

His grandmother tried to slip it on her finger but couldn't get it past her swollen knuckle. With a sheepish shrug, she handed it to Luca. "Now I can't wear it, but Daisy can. You take it for her."

Luca stared down at the ring in his palm and tried to envision sliding it on Daisy's finger. His throat went dry and stomach flipped. Could he dare hope for such a thing, after what he'd done?

"You should keep it," he told his Nonna, offering it back. "You'll miss it if I take it. If Daisy ever forgives me, I can buy her another."

Nonna held him off, shaking her head. "No, trust me. This is the one. It's *perfetto*. Daisy will know as soon as she sees it."

Luca sighed. It *was* perfect for her, wasn't it? Simple, classic, enduring—and exquisitely beautiful. Like her. "You're sure?"

"*Sì*. Bring her back once she says yes, so I can kiss her."

Luca's eyes began watering again, as he imagined doing just that. Daisy would forgive him. His elderly grandmother would live long enough to witness a wedding at least, and maybe even a great-grandchild. Luca would be with Daisy—really with her—in New York, and Italy, and everywhere in between.

"*Grazie*," he choked out. Even if it never came to pass, the dream of it was a beautiful gift.

His dad patted his back again, and Luca hunched over the ring in his hand, shaking with the enormity of it all, and his utter inadequacy in the face of it.

He had to go back to New York, now. He had to fix this.

Thirty-One

LIKE SOME KIND of simpering idiot, Daisy spent the first hour of her gallery show worrying, fully expecting Luca to come galloping in with his lab coat flapping like a cape, as he apologized for being late in frenetic, charmingly-broken English.

He often slipped into Italian when he was worked up about something, and she wondered if he'd do it tonight. It was confusing and adorable all at once, and it would be difficult to resist. She wouldn't try to.

Luca would feel absolutely awful about his tardiness, anyway. Hadn't he said it himself? *"Wouldn't miss it for the world,"* he'd claimed. That was his proof, straight from the horse's mouth.

The only problem was, the horse was looking more like an ass with every passing minute. Sometime during hour two, Daisy gave up wringing her hands, plastered a wide, fake smile on her face and doggedly refused to look toward the gallery entrance anymore.

It was bitter cold out there. She focused instead on all the warm people inside who had actually shown up to wish her well—the people who were shocking her right and left with their thoughtful kindnesses.

Friends. Colleagues. Old art teachers, even. Who had figured out this guest list? Daisy couldn't even begin to guess. They'd added scores more to the simple one she'd drafted.

She didn't deserve all this attention, but it was a welcome distraction from the gaping black hole of Luca's continued absence. The yawning maw of emptiness into which her texts to her boyfriend kept disappearing. The desolate steppe stretching toward a horizon of misery, where…

"Daisy! There you are," her boss boomed from somewhere over her head, cutting off her exceedingly unproductive train of thought. "How goes your total domination of the art world?"

She tilted her face up to Red's and lied with a smile, "Excellent. Everyone seems to be having a really good time."

"An open bar will do that for you," Red said.

His fiancée Piper was enthusiasm incarnate, however. "Are you kidding? This thing is a blast! Thank you so much for inviting us."

Daisy could've hugged her for it, if she was the hugging type. Instead, she scoffed, "Well, it definitely helps to have some friendly faces in the crowd, that's for sure."

As awkward as it could be to act all chummy with the guy who oversaw all of Trident Publishing and then some, Daisy had discovered she had no such qualms about the man's future bride. Over the last few months, Piper had rapidly become one of her favorite friends.

"I don't know," Piper mused now. "There seem to be a lot of people here who want to be your buddy. If that's you stacking the deck, then you are way more popular than I ever was."

Daisy rolled her eyes. "I doubt that." Piper was exactly the kind of smart, cool chick everyone wanted to know. Daisy on the other hand…

"I wanted to buy a couple of the prints," her friend confessed, "But they had tags saying they were on loan from a private collection. How do you already have collectors? I thought this was your first show."

Daisy snorted. "Don't get excited. Those are only the ones from Luca's bedroom. But the gallery thought *On Loan* sounded better than writing *Not for Sale*."

"Did you hang those in his apartment when we decorated?" Piper looked thoughtful. "I didn't get a good look at them."

"Yup, that's them." Daisy looked around for someone to save her. She could not stand here casually talking about Luca for one more second, or she was liable to stab something with a cocktail fork.

"You think Luca wants to keep them?" Piper prodded.

"Well, they're shots of his family and he was pretty adamant. So, yeah…I think he probably does." Of course, Daisy couldn't say for sure, because Luca was *not there*.

Before she could even consider how to cut Piper's fiancé off at the pass, Red scanned the crowd, scowled down at her, and demanded, "Where the fuck *is* Luca?"

Daisy managed a shrug, breezy as you please. "Couldn't tell you," she said, even though her heart was fracturing in at least a hundred places. Luca wasn't coming. *Obviously.*

Now Piper was frowning prettily, too. "That doesn't sound like him."

"No, it doesn't," Red agreed. "Something must have happened at the hospital."

At first, Daisy had thought that too. "Well, whatever it was," she told them, "It…" Quickly, she turned the lock on her big mouth, before she could utter what she'd been thinking—that Luca's reasons, assuming he had them, were clearly more important than she was.

Hell, all kinds of things probably trumped Daisy for a man like him. Cabbie strikes. Weather events. Sophia Loren movie marathons.

In the face of Luca's consequential life, Daisy's silly gallery show was probably barely a blip on the radar. However, since she'd never made a habit of acting pathetic in front of people, she wasn't about to start now.

So, she forced herself to finish her sentence with her head held high. "I'm sure it was important to him." Every word felt like sand in her mouth.

Her boss asked, "Did you try calling him?"

"No, I—" She'd texted a weak, *Everything okay*? and then an *Are you dead?* before she'd given up.

Red whipped out his phone and tapped it a few times, then listened to it with a far-off look on his face. Piper gazed at Daisy sympathetically, and the desire to hug her abruptly shifted into irritation. Daisy liked Piper a lot, but she couldn't take her pity right now.

Red muttered a few words under his breath, then dropped his phone back into his pocket. "Voicemail," he intoned.

Precisely why Daisy hadn't attempted to reach Luca that way. If she had to listen to the man's rushed, all-business voicemail message right now, it would crush any last remaining embers of hope that might still be lurking in her chest.

"God, Daisy. I'm so sorry," Piper said. "This stinks. Luca must be so upset right now."

"Yeah, well," Daisy replied, then paused.

Luca would be upset—not Daisy. Because these two people, however well-meaning they appeared on the surface, were actually some of Luca's closest friends. They weren't hers.

They didn't actually care about Daisy any more than Luca apparently did. She'd do well to remember that.

"Anyway, I should probably mingle some more," she told them. She had to get away, and she had to do it *now*.

"We'll keep trying him," Piper called after her.

When Daisy walked away in her sky-high platform heels, she kept her ankles straight, just like the guy in the store had instructed her. Like ice-skating, he'd told her, as if that made any sense. How would he know?

His eyebrows hadn't been perfect enough for him to have been a moonlighting drag queen, but maybe he'd still liked to try on the wares. Maybe after that shoe store closed for the night, he pulled out all the size elevens and walked around in them.

Shoe Guy *had* seemed like he knew what he was talking about, though, and Daisy didn't relish the thought of adding a twisted ankle to her list of woes tonight. And so—straight ankles. Spine long. Upper lip stiff. Head high.

Daisy was indestructible, tonight and every night. No dumb doctor with velvet hands and a masterful tongue was going to dent her armor. *Screw that mess.*

Tonight, Daisy had photographs to sell. Fans to create. Critics to schmooze and wine to drink. There'd be plenty of time to rid herself of lame-ass men later.

DESPITE HER INTENTION to remain aloof, Daisy noticed at some point that she was keeping a running tally in her head, of all the things happening that Luca should have been there for.

First came the unveiling of the show's centerpiece, four large framed portraits of Luca himself. Two from the *Giardino Bardini*, and two from a walk they'd taken in Central Park a few weeks ago. He looked impossibly handsome and remote, with his sophisticated glasses and pensive expressions. Daisy had edited the light to make it extra moody, and it'd worked like a charm.

The gallery owner gave a whole spiel about how people acted as bridges—between past and present, between cultures, between countries. She explained how the individual depicted in the photos was a bridge himself, between the images set in Florence, and the ones in New York.

When she explained that, sadly, the works were from the artist's personal collection and would not be sold that evening, a long, tortured groan rose from the gathering, and Daisy wanted to scream, *No!*

She needed to sell them. She needed to lock those things in a storage shed somewhere in Alaska, so she wouldn't ever have to look at them again. They were supposed to have been a surprise for Luca. Now they leered down at her and made Daisy feel like a laughingstock.

Red cruised by with a knowing smirk, and out of the corner of his mouth muttered, "I'll pay any price."

Daisy retorted, "Five bucks and they're yours."

Her cheeks were burning with humiliation, but there was no time to dwell on it. Over in the corner, her foster mother was deep in discussion with one of the gallery employees. Pam was holding her battered checkbook and gesturing toward one of the smallest pictures, a tiny shot of some fencing at the park.

Daisy rushed over as fast as her feet would carry her. If Pam was trying to buy one of the pieces in the show, she was about to get a nasty education in art pricing.

"Hey," she said, out of breath but hopefully in time to avert catastrophe. "What's going on, here?"

"The lady said we could pay for the one we want tonight, and they'll ship it to us when your show is over. So, I told her I want that one."

Luca, Daisy's heart screamed, *Luca* would know what to say. The picture in question was priced at hundreds of dollars. Even if Pam had somehow amassed that kind of money, there was no way on earth Daisy could let her pay it.

"Are you sure that's the one you like best?" she asked.

"Yeah, it's great. I looked at all of them a couple times just to make sure. Is it okay for me to buy it? It wasn't picked by someone else already, was it?" *Oh, man*—Pam really wanted it.

"Nope. That one is all yours." Daisy nodded at the gallery employee who'd been tasked with taking names and arranging payment. "But don't worry about paying now. I'll give them your information later, okay?"

"But…how will they know not to sell it to someone else?"

The employee gave her a wink, walked over, and placed a discreet red dot on the placard.

"That's how," Daisy said. She would tell the folks later that she'd pay for that one herself, if they didn't want to just deduct the price from her earnings.

"Oh." Pam tucked her checkbook back in her purse and smoothed her hands over her black slacks. "So, did I do okay with the clothes? I don't stick out too bad, do I?"

"You do not stick out at all," Daisy reassured her, even though her foster mom kind of looked like one of the caterers. "They always say you can never go wrong in black."

"That's true. Anyway, you look great. Are you having a good time?"

In her own gruff way, Pam had seen Daisy through a lot of life. So, it was easy to admit to her, "It's a little nerve-wracking. But it's good."

Pam peeked around the room again. "That guy's not here, is he?"

"You mean Luca?"

"Yeah, the one I met, right? Shouldn't he be here, too?"

Daisy went for the easiest, most unassailable lie she had. "Oh, he had to work," she said. If anyone would understand that problem, it was Pam.

"Oh well." The fib seemed to jog her memory about her own schedule for the night, but didn't raise any red flags. "Anyway, you seem to have things in hand here. I think I'm going to head out, if you don't mind. I'm opening at the restaurant tomorrow. You wouldn't believe what kind of breakfast rush those people have."

"Totally understand. Are you all set getting home? Do you need me to get you a cab or anything?"

"No, I'm all right, kid." Pam gripped her in a rare, clunky kind of hug. "Good job tonight. I'm proud of you."

"Thanks, Pam."

Leonard walked up at exactly that moment, with a beaming smile on his face and a lovely woman at his side. "Did you say Pam? Could this be *the* Pam, by any chance?"

Mentally, Daisy added this to her Luca Missed It list. She wasn't sure yet whether she intended to use it to fill him in once he gave her an unassailable excuse and she forgave him—or whether she was going to roll it up like a newspaper and beat Luca over the head with it.

Gritting her teeth, Daisy smiled and introduced the man who'd given her up to the woman who'd raised her instead. "This is, in fact, *the* Pam," she agreed. "Leonard, allow me to introduce my foster mother, Pam Lee. Pam…this is my birth father, Leonard Bosu."

Pam's face went slack with shock, and her demeanor didn't improve much once Leonard gave a happy shout and wrapped her in a big bear hug. "Ms. Lee," he said, "I do not have the words to thank you for taking care of my baby girl for her whole life. But her mother and I are so, so grateful."

"You…she…" Pam said. She looked at Daisy in complete consternation.

"We just met," Daisy said gently. "Only a couple weeks ago."

Pam nodded in sudden understanding. "You found him? After what I told you?"

"I did."

Pam looked back and forth between them, and then her eyes lit on the third woman. "Are you Daisy's mother?"

The woman's skin was just as dark as Leonard's. If she was Daisy's mom, then Daisy's skin would've had to be a throwback to some previous, ghostly-pale ancestor. However, it was clear the gears were turning in Pam's brain, while she tried to decipher the clues.

"No, I'm not," the woman said, grinning and stepping forward. "But I'm nearly as good."

What was nearly as good as a mother? Daisy wondered. And could any other conversation in this room be as strange as this one? If Luca were here…but he wasn't. Daisy had to do this herself.

Leonard put his arm around the woman and explained to Daisy, "I told you she was dying to meet you, and I wasn't kidding. Daisy, meet your Aunt Alisha. My baby sister."

Alisha was also a hugger, and since she was nearly as tall as Daisy, she almost knocked her off her heels when she pulled her into her arms. She laughed into her ear, "You are just as gorgeous as I knew you would be. And so talented! Girl, I want to buy every picture in this place."

"Thank you. It's so nice to meet you," Daisy managed.

"I'm not going to bombard you with questions and stories and everything tonight. But here—take my card. It has all my numbers on it, and we can catch up later this weekend if you want. Okay?"

Daisy looked down at the business card Alisha had pressed into her hand, and saw that her aunt was a voice teacher, based in the Village like her brother.

"Okay," Daisy said, reeling from this new, unexpected connection. She realized abruptly that she had absolutely nowhere to put the card, though. Her dad had figured out the same thing.

"Gimme that," he said, then took a photo of the card with his phone. "I'll text it to you, all right?" He handed the card back to his sister, who looked sheepish.

"Where's your guy?" Alisha chirped. "Lenny told me all about him, and I've been looking forward to hearing that smooth Italian accent for myself."

Pam snorted, making *her* position on foreign accents quite clear.

"He couldn't make it," Daisy told her aunt, and immediately hated that her first interaction with the woman hinged on a lie. "But you can check out his picture right over there."

Leonard gave Daisy a nod, said goodbye to Pam, and led Alisha toward the portraits.

Pam grimaced at their retreating backs. "I have to say—that is not at all how I pictured him. I've been worrying that he'd be some derelict crackhead or something."

"No, not at all. He was just a kid in a bad situation, Pam. That's all. Leonard seems really nice now."

"Well, that's a relief."

"Tell me about it. Anyway, why don't I walk you out? I could use some air."

OUTSIDE IN THE frigid cold, Daisy watched the taillights of her foster mother's taxi recede down Madison Avenue, and thought maybe she'd been going about this night all wrong.

For whatever reason, Luca hadn't come tonight, and he hadn't told her why. Instead of bemoaning all the things that he was supposed to be there for—all the things he'd fervently promised to help her get through—maybe Daisy should recast the tale.

Because in his absence, Daisy had tackled her very first gallery show all on her own. She'd done a nice thing for Pam, and she'd introduced Pam to Leonard. She'd even met another family member that she hadn't known existed.

Daisy had sold her artwork to several people. She'd posed for pictures, and she'd given a few little interviews. There was no way to view the night as anything other than a screaming success.

For crying out loud, people had even loved the scarf in her hair.

And sure, maybe all those things would've happened exactly the same way with Luca in the room. But maybe Daisy would've played her part differently. If she'd had his hand to hold, would she have been as brave?

Perhaps not. She'd never know, now.

One thing she did know was this: Pam might've said she was proud of her, but Daisy was really fucking proud of herself.

Thirty-Two

LUCA WOULD'VE PREFERRED to do anything other than show up on Daisy's doorstep looking like death warmed over, but given that she hadn't answered a single one of his texts or calls since he'd gotten back, he was fresh out of other options.

He knew she'd be there. She never went anywhere before noon on Saturdays, if she could help it.

One of her neighbors was exiting the building when he got there, and let him in without complaint It wasn't exactly safe, but he was grateful.

When Luca knocked on her door and it swung open, Daisy looked incandescent—the glow from the sunlight streaming through her living room windows limning her silhouette in an otherworldly aura.

"You look like an angel," Luca murmured. And he felt like hell.

Daisy's eyes narrowed in a distinctly unheavenly way. "Oh, it's you," she said. She made a show of checking her watch, but Luca got the sense that she had already rehearsed her next words quite carefully. "Only six days and nine hours after my show. I know Italians like to show up late for stuff, but that's a bit extreme, don't you think?"

Luca blew out a long, exhausted breath and began with the obvious. "I'm sorry." When he realized she wasn't going to offer, he then asked, "May I come in?"

Daisy snorted. "Why not? Hey, in case you were wondering, my gallery opening—you remember, the one I was so worried about? It was a smashing success and I was a wreck through the entire thing." She spun and stomped off into her apartment, tossing a casual, "Fuck you very much for asking," over her shoulder.

Luca stepped inside, closed and locked her door behind him, and followed. "Daisy," he began. *Madre di Dio*, he was so inexpressibly tired, suddenly. He didn't want to argue.

Once she reached her kitchen, she turned on him. Her laugh was dry and cold. "But, you know—I guess that's on me. Why I thought someone like you would ever consider me more than a convenient piece of ass is beyond me. I mean, shame on me, right? You'd think by now I would know better."

As her words filtered into his murky brain and their meaning began to coalesce into something understandable, Luca froze. "I...don't think I appreciate what you're accusing me of."

"Oh, don't you?" Daisy was obviously spoiling for a fight. She was aflame from the inside out with righteous fury—exactly like the angel he'd thought of when he first saw her.

Except, instead of a celestial messenger sent to comfort him in his grief, she looked like her avenging sword would be separating him from his vital parts very, very soon.

"Daisy, I adore you. You know that. And trust me when I say, you are not a convenient piece of anything." It was clearly the wrong thing to say. Luca braced himself for an onslaught.

"I beg to differ. It doesn't get more convenient than this. You move to a new country for work, but no worries—you don't even have to break your 'no nurses' rule. That would be unbearable.

And God forbid you have to visit a single bar, but luckily you don't need to. Because you just happen to have a honey already in place. What do you doctors like to call it? *In situ?*"

Luca shook his head, trying not to rise to her baiting. Daisy was understandably upset, and her hurt was simply making her lash out. The storm would pass, though, and then he could explain everything.

"Daisy. *Bella.* May I sit down? I'd like to explain what happened."

"By all means." She gestured expansively toward the small table and chairs in the corner, then patted the top of Jerome's aquarium while Luca got settled.

Even angry, Daisy must have noted how exhausted he was, because she immediately began opening cabinets and setting up the coffee maker to brew a pot. Luca wanted to find hope in the fact that she was using the Italian beans they'd bought together a couple of weeks ago, but he knew that was foolish.

Leaving as he had, on her big night, was unforgivable—but it had felt like the only possible thing he could do. If only he'd told her that before he left, instead of trying to do it now, so far after the fact.

Luca cleared his throat and watched her, but Daisy didn't get any less stiff, and she didn't come to sit on the chair opposite him.

Eventually, he decided to just start talking. "I have a patient," he said. "A young man, back in Florence. He has a new wife and a baby on the way." Luca was using the present tense, but that no longer applied to Andrea or the baby, did it? "Had," he corrected painfully. "I had been treating him for many years. I thought he'd turned a corner—that we'd finally bought him a future."

Luca had to stop right there to regroup. He swallowed past the enormous boulder lodged in his throat and searched for his composure. Daisy turned slowly and her eyes found his. Behind the anger, there was something else. Fear, maybe. It was difficult to tell.

"What happened?" she whispered.

All Luca could hear in his head was his father's stupid advice. He didn't want to lose this woman's respect, and he never wanted Daisy to fear anything ever again. Not with him. So, he pushed down the tears that were threatening to spill over and held them in his gut with all his might.

"I was wrong," he said, and the admission almost undid him. He waited through three slow heartbeats before he could continue, "When they called me, I rushed home as fast as I could. I thought I could still save him. That maybe I had some magic that would fix whatever had gone wrong since I'd left. But when I got there, Andrea was already..."

Daisy slid a perfect cup of espresso in front of him, but Luca didn't think he could drink it, even if he wanted to. "He was gone within days," he told her. "I stayed for the funeral. I had to."

She sighed, and finally—*finally*—sat down. "I'm so sorry. That must have been hard for you."

Luca touched the little cup's handle. "You have no idea. I care about all of my patients, obviously. There's an intimacy that happens, shepherding them through such a devastating disease. But every once in a while, there's one who I...I can't explain it. They mean more. They take hold in a way the others don't. And Andrea was that way for me. He mattered so much. He felt like family."

So much like family, that when Luca had sat in that church and looked into the casket, he may as well have been suffering through his brother Matteo's funeral all over again.

Daisy nodded as if she understood, but then asked Luca the strangest question. "When you left..." A small shake of her head.

A slight twitch of her eye. "When you left, did you let Dr. Green know you were going?"

"Of course. I—" Luca was lucky he didn't have to teach any classes until the fall semester. It would have been harder to arrange coverage for those sorts of things. As it was, his lab was still getting off the ground, but he had a bevy of residents and colleagues who had been able to cover the care of his new patients for him.

"And the airline? You would have had to arrange your flight. Maybe even call a car service to take you to the airport, I bet."

With a sudden, nauseating wave, Luca began to see where Daisy was going with this inquiry. He nodded numbly.

"One more call, Luca," she said softly. "That's all it would've taken. Just one more short call to tell me you were leaving, and why."

"There was no time," he whispered again, but even he could tell it was weak and untrue. Somewhere, in all those trips to and from airports—in all those car rides back and forth from the hospital, the morgue, the cemetery—he could have called the woman he loved.

It wasn't like he hadn't been thinking about her. So perhaps Luca hadn't wanted to taint her with his sorrow—she had so much of her own already. Or maybe he'd been felled by exactly the kind of smug self-importance he so despised in other physicians.

Daisy emitted another sigh. This one was heavier, and it took something important out of her when it left. "Here's the thing," she told him. "I've spent my whole life being an afterthought to the people who were supposed to care about me. I can't...I can't be that anymore. Not for someone who supposedly lo—*cares*—about me. Not ever again."

Luca winced at the way she refused to utter the word *love*. Up until that moment, he'd believed, completely and unwaveringly, that his actions had been justifiable. Now, he could see how wrong he'd been.

"Daisy, this was a very unusual situation. You're right that I should've called, and I'm so heartbroken that I missed your big show—but I was in such a panic trying to get there and think of something to do, that it didn't cross my mind until it was too late."

He'd told himself that they had a connection, that they understood each other. If that was true, though, shouldn't Daisy have realized immediately that Luca would never stand her up like that unless it was an emergency?

Flatly, she repeated, "It didn't cross your mind."

"In retrospect, I suppose I expected you would at least give me the benefit of the doubt."

Her anger swooped back in, small red flags burning high on her wide cheekbones, leaving the rest of her face white instead of gold. Luca began to feel the first stirrings of some anger of his own.

"Look, let's be honest here. You are married to your job," she said. "You probably always will be. And there are plenty of women out there who will understand you and support you for it. You do good, important work, and that's something to be proud of. But…"

Luca was being let down easy. *Gesù Cristo*, Daisy was breaking things off with him. And he deserved it, because he was a self-absorbed pig—so obsessed with his little God complex that he hadn't thought to take two bloody minutes to exercise some basic manners. One phone call. That was all.

Luca didn't deserve her. *Merda*, but he wanted her.

"Daisy, please don't say it."

She rolled her eyes, but she looked sad. "I deserve better than playing second fiddle to your job for the rest of my life. I've earned that much, I think."

It was the first time Daisy had admitted to entertaining any serious thoughts whatsoever of a long-term future between them. Luca wanted to cry even more now, but he also wanted rear up and roar. To yell and throw things.

He wanted to kiss Daisy hard enough that she'd *have* to acknowledge the passion between them. It shouldn't be tossed away over one stupid mistake, but that was exactly what was happening.

Still, she was right. She *did* deserve better—she deserved the world. The moon. The stars. Luca passed a shaking hand over his face, dropped it to the table with a boneless thump, and promptly knocked over his espresso.

Daisy leaped into action, swiping the roll of paper towels from the counter and mopping up the spill before it could leak onto her lap.

"Give me another chance," Luca said grimly. "I promise it won't happen again." Such a smooth lie, like honey on his tongue. There would, of course, be other patients. Other emergencies.

When she smiled, he knew she'd seen right through it. "No. No, actually I can't see you anymore. I, um…" A pause while she summoned her unbelievable, glorious courage. "I can't do that. But I do hope you find happiness, Luca."

He shook his head, denying the possibility.

Daisy's voice was deceptively calm, but something about those red patches on her face and the taut tendons in her neck made Luca realize, without a shadow of a doubt, that she was a volcano on the verge of eruption.

Even in his desperation, he couldn't help but be impressed with her grace under pressure. Her bravery. She must have been just as incredible at her gallery show.

When she said calmly, "I think you should go," Luca did as she asked.

He rose to his feet, walked the thirteen unlucky steps to her front door, and put his hand on the knob. He could feel her, like the fleeting wisp of a wildflower's scent, close behind him.

"I will love you for the rest of my life," he told her. "Until I am dead and buried in the ground, and probably long after that, too." And then, before Daisy could refute or deny it, Luca let himself out.

"No. You won't," she said, and shut the door behind him.

She was wrong. Luca just had to find a way to prove it to her.

Thirty-Three

DAISY SAT IN the chair next to Jerome, holding the Trevi Fountain building set she'd gotten for Luca, and trying to decide what she should do with it.

On the one hand, Daisy had never tried building something like this before, and there looked like there were a crap-ton of pieces involved. It was obviously not meant for children or beginners.

Daisy suspected it would make her impatient and frustrated, instead of relaxed, and that it would take her twice as long to complete as a garden-variety normal adult.

That translated, unfortunately, into twice as much time for her to think about Luca while she played with his toy. Daisy sighed. *Oh, no.* She was never going to get to play with Luca's toy again, was she? How in the hell was she supposed to get over *that?*

All of her anger and powerful-woman platitudes drained right out of her, leaving Daisy a glum, mopey drag. She should just donate the thing. Someone, somewhere would benefit from the blocks more than she would.

On the other hand, Luca had seemed pretty confident that things like this worked wonders for stress relief, and she could certainly use some of that—it'd been a long, weird week to say the least.

EVER SINCE HER gallery show, Leonard and Aunt Alisha had taken it upon themselves to fill Daisy in on family history. It was clearly meant to explain why no one else had taken Daisy in thirty years ago, but the cumulative effect was only that it made Daisy's foul mood worse.

So much tragedy, and struggle, and heartache. It was a wonder the Bosu siblings were still standing, much less doing so well now.

Daisy was coming to understand that she had sprung from some pretty hardy stock, and their offer to help her track down any remaining relatives from her mother's side only made her admire them more.

However, to further complicate matters, Pam had been hounding her since the gallery show to get together again. Daisy had no idea where her foster mother's newfound interest in her was coming from. She only knew that the topic of Luca would inevitably come up during any meeting, and there was no way she could sit through one of Pam's diatribes on the inadequacies of men.

Not this week, anyway. Daisy kept putting the woman off and hoped it would work long enough for her to at least get in another visit to her therapist Rita. She always felt saner and steadier after those.

Finally, to round out Daisy's week, she'd managed to somehow get involved in an unusual situation. Tabitha Lovell, author extraordinaire, had reached out and inquired if Daisy would be willing to read a very rough draft of the book that was giving them so much trouble.

Tabitha said she hoped it would give Daisy some ideas for the cover, which was good. But she'd also asked if Daisy would share her thoughts on the direction of the story and how she felt about the characters and their chemistry.

Daisy had been open about the fact that she'd read the galleys for all the other titles in the series. Ms. Lovell had seemed to enjoy hearing her opinions as they'd hashed out the final covers for those books.

But giving opinions after the fact was one thing. Being an early-stage beta reader was another. It felt strange. The only thing that remotely qualified Daisy for the task was that she was a fan of Tabitha's, and that she liked to read romance.

What if she did it wrong? It would be so easy to screw up. If Daisy said too little about the story, it wouldn't help Tabitha at all. However, if she said too much, maybe Tabitha would be offended and think she was overstepping.

Daisy had no idea why she'd agreed to the arrangement, except…that first day back at work, post-Luca, had felt very lonely. She'd kept thinking of how empty all her nights and weekends were about to be, and she'd gone a little mental trying to come up with new ways to fill her time.

And so, she got to be a beta reader. And she'd added free weights to her treadmill routine. She'd visited the library twice after work, ended up in some deep discussions with the night librarian, and as a result, had started watching an involved new historical series on the BBC.

All to fill the time.

Daisy tilted the toy in her lap back and forth, and listened to all those little plastic blocks rattling around inside. She sighed again and turned to study Jerome.

Here she was, basically turning into Eeyore before his very eyes, and her pet turtle hadn't even noticed. Some friend he was.

Daisy blew out a long breath and made her decision. She marched over to her table, pried open the box, and dumped its contents out. Let the relaxation commence.

HALF AN HOUR later, Daisy had to admit there was something absorbing about following those building directions, step by step. There were small statues, and columns, and lots of clear blue pieces that looked like water. There were even cute little horses to affix to the set.

She was carefully trying to get one in position when her cell phone began ringing in its charger over on the kitchen counter.

Rats. It was Piper—Daisy had been trying to avoid her, in addition to Pam. But suddenly, she kind of wanted to talk to her.

"Hey, Daisy. How's it going?" her friend said when Daisy answered.

Horrible. Awful. Tremendously, "Not bad," she replied. "You?"

"Meh. Red had to go to L.A. on business. So, I've got a little writer's block."

Daisy frowned. "Those things are connected?"

"More than you'd think."

"Huh." Good thing Daisy wasn't an author like Piper. Her career would be in the dumps right about now.

"So anyway," Piper hummed.

Here it comes. Daisy braced herself for the stab of pain.

"We heard about you and Luca."

"Oh no," Daisy objected. "We are not talking about that. I know you guys are friends with him but trust me when I say—I had very good reasons for breaking things off."

"I know, but hear me out," Piper told her. "I'm not saying you weren't justified in your reaction to him blowing off your show. All I'm saying is…well, I talked to Red and it sounds like there might be some mitigating circumstances."

Oh, for crying out loud. "I know about the patient in Italy," Daisy groaned. "Luca told me about him."

"Yeah, that was really sad. But that's not what I'm talking about."

Daisy set down her miniature white horse and stared at it. "There's something else?"

"It seems so. Red knows more about it than I do, though. We'd like to have you over for dinner when he gets back in a few days, so he can fill you in. What do you say?"

Daisy struggled to decide what her answer should be. Luca could've put them up to this, she supposed, but it wasn't exactly his style. It was just as likely that Red and Piper were only trying to help.

As his friends, they'd want Luca to be happy. And, if he was even half as depressed as Daisy had been, then that would definitely prompt an intervention from them.

But what if this new detail turned out to be nothing? What if Daisy got her hopes up, and whatever they told her made no difference at all? Her depression was liable to tank into outright despair.

However…it was also possible that Red and Piper knew something about Luca that she did not. Red's friendship with Luca went back many years. He would've learned things about the man in all that time.

Big things. Possibly secret things.

Daisy had been on the receiving end of too much unfair treatment in her life to ever want to be the one dishing it out. And if, by some chance, she hadn't given Luca a fair shake, she'd hate that.

For all she knew, Luca had come to her apartment that day intending to tell her more than he had. Maybe he'd only explained about his patient, and not the rest of the story, because her attitude had been so pissy.

What if he'd given up on Daisy before he'd gotten to the most important part, and it was all her fault for being surly and rude?

She let out her breath. "Okay," she told Piper, "I'll come. Can I bring anything?"

"Just an open mind," Piper said. "All right? I know you want to ditch Luca, and I totally get it, but maybe don't do it quite yet. Not until you hear Red out, at least."

Her friend had it all wrong. Daisy didn't *want* to give up on him—she *had* to. "Piper, I can't promise anything. But I will listen."

"It's a start. And thank you for agreeing. I know I haven't had much time to build up any real friendship cred with you yet, but I wouldn't ask you to do this if I didn't have a good feeling about it. I appreciate you not rejecting me out of hand."

Daisy had no idea what to say about that. "Yeah, well—I guess I'm a sucker for anyone who likes shoes as much as I do."

"Whatever gets me in the door," Piper laughed. "I'll take it."

IF DAISY HAD expected Piper's fiancé to be more forthcoming than his future bride, she was sorely mistaken.

A few days later, at their loft in Chelsea, she sat across the table from Red and Piper and listened to Red say, "There are things you don't know about Luca. I believe they will put his behavior into perspective for you."

"Yes, Piper mentioned that. But so far, no one has told me what those things are."

Red grimaced. "The thing is, it's not my story to tell."

"Then why, may I ask, did you drag me here?" Daisy rolled her eyes. Piper smirked and looked at her groom-to-be with a commensurate *Yeah why, Einstein?* expression.

He narrowed his eyes at her, then turned to Daisy. "PKM Conglomerates recently gave Weill Cornell a sizeable donation.

They're going to establish a new gastric oncology department around Luca's research, and his colleague Harlan Green's."

Daisy sat back. "Wow. That was really nice of you guys."

Piper explained, "Now Cornell is having a per-plate benefit dinner to drum up some more cash. Dr. Green is going to give a speech, but so is Luca."

"We thought that all would be made clear to you, if you'd consider going to the dinner with us."

"How so?"

"Let's just say," Red said, "I might have heard some details about Luca's speech."

While Red and Piper launched into a coordinated, full-scale effort to cajole her and wear her down, Daisy blinked down at her plate.

Luca had often talked about his work in general terms, but he'd never told her many details. Daisy was insanely curious to know more about what he did, and maybe this was a better way to do it than the usual internet stalking.

If she went, it would also be a chance to see Luca's face again. Just the once—maybe it would cure Daisy of missing him so much and stop her from doubting what she'd done. Maybe it would enable her to own the decision she'd made and move on with her life.

Making a clean break had been a hasty choice, made in the heat of the moment. It had arisen out of Daisy's hurt feelings and the stupid, damaged-girl thought pattern she'd worked so hard to leave behind.

It wasn't really true any longer that no one loved her or cared for her in the least—even if it felt that way sometimes. Daisy had spent so much time dwelling on how she always came in second place for the people who were supposed to put her first, that she could list the ways without thinking: second place to her father's grief for her dead mother, second place to Pam missing her absentee husband, second place to Luca's job.

The truth wasn't always so simplistic, though. Luca had been correct, in that Daisy *hadn't* given him the benefit of the doubt on the night of her gallery show.

Even once he returned to New York, she hadn't remembered that he wasn't usually a careless or thoughtless man—only an occasionally forgetful one.

She'd never tried to understand *why* he'd made the choice he had, only fixated on the fact that it had hurt her. Except…the whys were so important, weren't they?

Six months ago, for example, Daisy never would've thought she could forgive her parents for giving her up when she was a baby. But now, she knew that it was a vow she'd made in ignorance.

Leonard, and by extension her Aunt Alisha, had helped Daisy remember that there was far more to people's stories than just the bare outlines. There were all the details, too—the colors and feelings and songs—and that was what brought the templates to life.

Luca had never once assessed Daisy's value based on the quick-sketch version of her background—former low-rent foster kid, current moody witch, and one-time liar about her job. He'd only accepted her exactly as she was.

And in return, she'd done the exact opposite for him.

"Okay," Daisy told her hosts now. "I'm in. Tell me what to do."

Thirty-Four

L UCA STOOD AT the window in his home office, staring out at the ugly, gray buildings arrayed before him. Without regular infusions of the heady elixir Daisy brought to his life, Luca had discovered that he was only steps away from turning into a melancholy drudge of a man. The fact that it was winter helped not at all.

It probably explained why his speech for the benefit dinner was turning into such an emotional sob story. Luca thought he probably needed to rein things in, so he'd sent Red at least four drafts, hoping for some input from a man who delivered these kinds of talks fairly regularly.

Instead, over and over again, his friend had merely replied with a curt, "Sounds good."

It was maddening, really. Wasn't it bad enough that MacLellan had put him in the awkward position that he had? Now he couldn't even deliver some constructive criticism?

Mixing friendship and money was a well-known recipe for disaster for a reason. However, Luca also knew that no researcher on the planet would turn down the kind of cash Red's company wanted to throw at him and Harlan.

His choice had been clear. Luca couldn't let his fellow doctors and future patients down and refuse the money—and, he couldn't bear to disappoint Red by not producing something great for that money.

So, his course was set. PKM Conglomerates would invest a staggering sum of money in Weill Cornell's gastric cancer research, and Luca would work as hard as he could to find a breakthrough.

Now, they'd gone a step farther and decided to name the new department after Luca's brother Matteo—and Luca figured it wasn't too much to ask for Red to at least tell him whether he was going to humiliate himself when he stood up at that podium on the night of the benefit dinner.

Gesù Cristo. Talk about potential disasters. Making Luca give a speech about his brother and his research had all the earmarks of a debacle in the making, especially considering the sorry frame of mind he was in.

The more he thought about it, though, the less Luca realized that he cared. Without Daisy to anchor his days, he was only as good as an automaton, anyway. What did it matter if a room full of people thought he was a maudlin fool?

Luca was going to put it all out there—string all his family laundry out on the line and to hell with the consequences. He turned away from the dreary scene outside and sat at his desk, cracking open his laptop, and starting a new speech from scratch.

He missed Daisy so much. He longed for the sight of her, and he ached for the particular combination of strength and vulnerability that she brought to the world.

Luca yearned for the taste of Daisy on his lips, and for the different perspective she gave whenever she weighed in on the odd world around him.

How could he have gone so wrong? How could he have been so stupid as to lose her? He still had no idea how to begin mending what was broken between them.

THOUGH IT FELT like torture, one night after work Luca's curiosity got the best of him, and he made an appointment at the gallery where Daisy's work was still hanging.

It wasn't the same experience as it would've been on the opening night of her show. With only him and a couple of employees haunting the space, it felt more like the hushed, otherworldly atmosphere of an after-hours museum.

Still, as Luca wandered from frame to frame, he hoped for inspiration—some clue that would tell him how to win Daisy back.

So many of her beautiful pieces had *Sold* stickers on their placards, and Luca was pleased to see them. He was also humbled to discover that the pictures from his apartment were still marked as 'on loan.'

Daisy wasn't the one who had a problem keeping promises, though—Luca was.

There was one part of the show he hadn't been prepared for in the least, and that was the portraits of *him* that Daisy had included. When Luca was unexpectedly confronted by his own faithless mug—staring down at him in quadruplicate like a small squadron of judgmental clones—his heart froze in his chest.

Poor Daisy must have waited all night for him to see what she'd done, and he'd never arrived. Luca wanted to shrivel into a ball of shame in front of the two gallery workers, hovering like spindly black crows on the sidelines to see his reaction.

The Luca in those portraits was a man in love. He was a man who'd somehow stumbled clumsily into the best relationship of his life—*twice*, for crying out loud—but had still managed to keep his woman happy.

The Luca standing on the ground in front of those portraits, however, could do no such thing. As easy as it had been for him to land himself in Daisy's arms, he'd just as easily flunked his way back out of them again.

To console himself, Luca searched the entire gallery for a single photograph that included some part of Daisy in the shot, but came up blank. Instead, He had to settle for buying a couple of the others that were still available, simply because they reminded him of dates they'd gone on together.

The gallery refused to part with the works until Daisy's show was over—no surprise there. It did seem fitting, however. Luca's whole life felt like it was in stasis, too, standing still until some magical solution crossed his brain that would convince Daisy to give him another chance.

He only hoped it would be soon. Much more of this and he'd be no good to anyone.

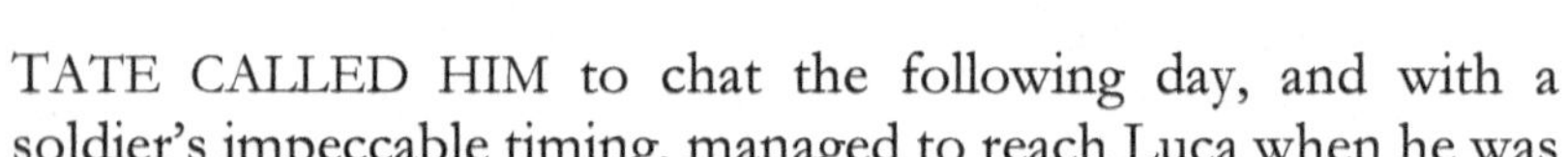

TATE CALLED HIM to chat the following day, and with a soldier's impeccable timing, managed to reach Luca when he was sitting in his office between appointments.

"Tate, *mio fratello*, how are you?" Luca asked, happy for the distraction. "Staying alive, I see."

"That's the plan. You doing okay in the Big Apple? All your new friends sharing their beakers and centrifuges?"

"Yes, everything is going very well." Well, *almost* everything.

His old friend wasted no time whatsoever getting to the one thing Luca did not want to discuss, of course. "And how's *il Bel Fiore* these days?"

The Pretty Flower—what a nickname. Trust Tate to come up with it *now*. "Who, Daisy?" Luca asked, playing dumb. "Still beautiful. I assume."

"What's that supposed to mean? Don't you know?"

"No, I do not," Luca huffed. "And don't pretend like you don't know what's going on—Red must have told you."

Tate said, "I haven't talked to him recently. Anyway, what happened? Trouble in paradise?"

"Manhattan is hardly a paradise, and yes, you could say that. Daisy and I are *finito*. She broke things off with me."

"Romeo! Say it isn't so," his friend gasped. So melodramatic. Luca wished Tate was within punching range.

"Why does everyone refer to Shakespeare in times like this?" he wondered. "You know that little *testa di cazzo* killed himself, right?"

Tate could probably tell that Luca was at the end of his rope, because he relented far faster than usual. "Shit, I'm sorry, dude. What the hell happened? Last I heard, you two were sporting heart eyes all over New York together."

"It's a long story, but essentially—Daisy had cause to decide that she wasn't a priority in my life. She said she didn't want to be anyone's second-best, which was very fair. And then she left me."

There was a long, heavy pause. Then his old friend groaned, "Luca, you moron. What the *fuck* did you do?"

"Would you like the highlights? Because here they are: I got a call that my favorite patient was on his death bed back in Italy, I dropped everything to fly there immediately to see if I could do anything to save him, and in the process I completely forgot to call my girlfriend and tell her I was not coming to her very important gallery show party that night."

"What—"

"To be clear, she was a nervous wreck about the party, and I promised her I would be there so she wouldn't have to do it alone. Oh, and my patient died, so there's that."

"Okay, seriously?" Tate demanded. "I am essentially a caveman with a gun, and even I know not to go haring off to another country on a mercy mission without saying goodbye to my woman."

Luca said sullenly, "As I said, everything happened very fast."

"And once you got there? What then? You couldn't text the girl? Call her? Send her flowers? Hell, the flight to Florence must be ten hours long, Shit-for-Brains. You could've managed *all* those things on the way. *And* gotten in a decent nap."

"I was worried about my patient, I guess. I was working to find a solution and it didn't occur to me to call Daisy. And then, once I was there…"

"You forgot you had a girlfriend? Luca, you're a smart dude, but that's dumb as *cazzo*."

"This seems like a good moment for me to regret teaching you bad words in Italian."

"And, now you're deflecting."

"Tate, what do you want me to say? Do you think I'm happy about any of this?"

"Look, man—you searched for this chick for, what? A year? Why are you rolling over and dying now?" Tate demanded. "You said she was the one!"

Luca agreed, "I thought she was. She is."

"Are you sure? Because sometimes you get dramatic about women."

"No, this time there is no doubt."

Tate growled in frustration. "And you're still fucking around crying? You need to be out there swinging for the fences with this girl. Not moping around, sipping Chianti and cursing your bad luck."

"It's ten in the morning, soldier. No one is sipping Chianti."

"Focus, motherfucker."

"For what?" Luca bellowed. Then, in a calmer voice, "I can't make Daisy love me again. She's made up her mind. A gentleman would respect that."

"So, stop being a gentleman. All's fair in love and war, remember?" Tate taunted. "Besides, gentlemen are boring. Channel your inner alpha male and go change the woman's mind."

"I don't think I have one of those," Luca said glumly.

"Go ask Red. I'm sure he'll give you some tips."

Luca had had about enough of other people pointing out his inadequacies. He said, "Can we please stop talking about this? How are *you* doing? Are you eating well?"

"I mean…no one's cooking me carbonara when I feel homesick or anything. But the calories are going in and out like they should."

Luca smiled. At one time in his life, he'd made carbonara for his roommate on many occasions—usually when Tate was drunk and sentimental at three in the morning.

"Are you homesick now?" he asked him.

"Always, dude."

"Then come home and visit. Surely you are due some leave time at this point. Stay with me and I'll cook you anything you want."

"It's not that easy, bro. If I leave them alone, the boneheads I'm in charge of here are liable to get their asses shot off."

"Someone else can take care of them for a little while. Try and come home."

"Tell you what—you go win back your lady and I'll look into it, okay? Red's wedding—"

"—is not for another year. Come sooner and we can all have an *addio al celibato*."

Luca's idea for a stag party flew clear out the window, however, at the unmistakable sound he heard next. *Gunfire.*

"Tate? Everything okay?"

Luca heard panting. Running feet. Yelling.

"Tate!"

There was an explosion, and some rustling around, as if his friend had shoved his cell phone in a pocket without cutting the connection. Luca pressed the phone against his ear and listened in morbid fascination as the sounds of war filled the silence in his office.

He listened for an eternity, it seemed, until finally there was only static, and he forced himself to hang up.

Before Luca returned to his duties, however, he made one more call.

Red picked up on the second ring. "*Ciao*, Luca. *Come stai?*"

"Okay, but…I just talked to Tate."

"Oh, yeah? How's he doing?"

"About the same. Only, the call ended a little badly."

"Shit, was there shooting in the background? I really hate when that happens. Totally freaks me out."

"Me too. But this was more than guns. It sounded a lot more serious, I'm telling you."

Red hesitated. "Well, what did Tate say?"

"Nothing. That's the problem," Luca told him. "I'm worried, *compagno.*" In fact, Luca had a writhing snake of fear trying to nest low in his belly, and that had never happened with one of Tate's calls before.

His friend seemed to pick up on the issue immediately. "Okay. So, what do you want to do?"

Merda, they were halfway around the world. What *could* they do? "I think…we wait for now. If you hear from him, let me know, of course, and I'll do the same. Otherwise…"

"We can try calling his mom," Red suggested.

"We can, but I'd rather not worry Mrs. Monroe."

"Yeah, me either. But if anyone would understand, it's her."

"That's true," Luca agreed. "We'll give it a few weeks, and if neither of us hears anything—"

"You can call her," Red said.

"No, *you* can call her," Luca retorted. "I had to sit through the war zone call."

"All right, you fucking baby. Fine. I'll call. Now tell me how your speech is coming along. How many times have you rewritten it now? Twelve? Fifty?"

Luca groaned.

Thirty-Five

DAISY WASN'T ABLE to hold out on Pam forever. Eventually, her guilty conscience got the best of her, and she agreed to meet her foster mother for lunch at her apartment in Brooklyn the following weekend.

When she got there, Daisy wasn't surprised to see that Pam's new place was small. She still kept it tidy, however, and even though Pam had never been one to accumulate many possessions, the home seemed even emptier than usual to Daisy.

All that moving around, she supposed. As she looked around at the second-hand furniture and the scuffed walls, it was hard to imagine one of her framed photographs hanging in such a place.

Once, this had been Daisy's life, too. She'd spent her entire childhood in apartments just like this one, and the tired, suffocating air had always made her want to scream and claw her way free.

Daisy was a different person now, though. She'd put herself through college and read books on financial literacy, so she'd know what to do with the money she would earn when she graduated. She'd borrowed books on social etiquette from the library, too, so she wouldn't embarrass herself in front of her coworkers.

Those things had made her more comfortable in her daily life, and the healthy income she pulled in these days allowed her to live in a safe neighborhood. Daisy had nice clothes, and plenty of things whose only function was to look pretty.

She'd even gotten the chance to live in another country for a semester, and in doing so, had met an extraordinary man unlike any other.

Through all of that, the restlessness inside Daisy had ebbed. She'd learned contentment. Her heart became, for lack of a better word, *receptive.*

It had welcomed Luca in, and then, in an excess of goodwill, had made room for Leonard and Alisha, too.

Now, it seemed that Daisy's heart had softened toward Pam, as well. Instead of feeling closed-in and antsy, sitting here eating tuna sandwiches with her foster mom simply felt calm and normal.

Comforting, almost. Pam didn't expect much from her—only that she be present, and real.

As Daisy looked at her, she realized her foster mother had aged significantly in the time she'd been away. Her hair showed gray at the roots, and her skin had a crepey texture that seemed new.

And, as much as she'd dreaded coming here today, Daisy was suddenly glad she had. Pam was trying, in her way, to make their lunch special.

Once they'd polished off their chips and sandwiches, Pam said, "I'm glad you were able to come over, kid. There's something I've been wanting to talk to you about."

"Really? What?" Daisy couldn't begin to imagine.

"Well, seeing you with that boyfriend of yours got me to thinking." Pam paused, then tacked on, "He's really crazy about you, ain't he?"

Not anymore, he wasn't. Luca probably wanted to curse the ground she walked on these days. Rather than explain that to the other woman, though, Daisy just nodded.

Out of nowhere, Pam asked, "Did I ever tell you why I went out to California?"

"Not really, no. You told me you wanted a change of scenery and that you were sick of the snow. But…" she trailed off rather than point out what an obvious lie it had been.

Pam merely chuckled, catching on. "I could tell that you weren't buying it, but I appreciate that you pretended to."

Daisy had been too hurt at being left behind, and too worried about how she was supposed to support herself, to do anything else. She said, "No problemo."

"Anyway, the real reason I went out there was to look for Ray."

"*Ray*? Seriously? What made you think he was out in Cali?"

"I'd heard from some friends that he'd been headed there. Then I worked a job with this guy who used to have beers with Ray sometimes. He told me that Ray had concocted this whole fool-headed plan to go out to Hollywood and become a stunt man in the movies. He thought he was going to make it big and then come back here and dazzle us all with it."

"You're kidding," Daisy said.

"Crazy right? I can't imagine what gave him the idea— probably some Dirty Harry movie or something. But then I thought, since you were off to college and didn't need me anymore, that maybe it was time to go find the idiot and bring him home."

Pam had been in California for ten *years*. To Daisy, that sounded like an awful lot of searching.

Her foster mom had fallen silent, lost in thought as she absently picked at her paper napkin. Maybe she thought the same thing.

"So, what happened?" Daisy prodded.

"I found places to stay. I got jobs waitressing and cleaning houses, and even, one time, making pizzas. And when I got a little extra money and had time off, I looked for Ray."

"You were gone a long time," Daisy pointed out. "Did you ever find him?" She tried to picture Pam and Ray on a beach somewhere, enjoying themselves while Daisy studied and ate in dining halls, but couldn't do it.

"I found hints here and there," Pam said. "I started hanging around the studio lots and went to the places where the grips and the set people hung out. I met people who knew of him, but I never ran into Ray."

"Do you know if he ever got work as a stunt man?"

"If he did, I never heard of it."

"Is that why you came back to New York again? Because you never found him?"

"Yeah," Pam admitted, "That and because I'm not exactly a California kind of person. I mean, the weather's nice and all out there, but the people are strange."

"I've heard that," Daisy agreed.

"But, kid—that's not the end of the story."

"What is?"

"After I went to your gallery show, I kept thinking about what a kick Ray would've gotten seeing you like that. So, I went to the library after work on Saturday, and I got on one of those computers they let people use."

Daisy grabbed her foster mom's plate, stacked it on her own, and carried them both to the sink. "What'd you do?" she asked.

"I started searching for public records and stuff. I don't know why I never did that out west. I guess out there, it always seemed like I was one day away from tripping over the old fool."

"You found something, didn't you?" Otherwise, why tell her?

Pam didn't appear to have a dishwasher, so Daisy squirted some dish soap on the sponge next to the sink and began washing the dishes.

"Yeah, I sure did. Would you believe Ray went and got himself killed in a motorcycle accident six freaking years ago? There were newspaper articles and everything. He was hit by a delivery truck."

"Oh, no." Daisy put down her plate and went back to sit next to her. "Pam, I'm so sorry."

"You always think you'll know if they die, but you don't." Pam's voice cracked, but she struggled on. "I had no idea at all that Ray was gone. I feel so stupid, thinking of all those years I was out turning over rocks looking for him, and all for no reason."

Would Daisy know if something ever happened to Luca? Until now, she would've thought she'd feel something like that deep in her bones, even if they weren't together anymore.

But maybe that was just a lie all women like her and Pam told themselves. A little white lie to make it through the hardest times. *We might not be together right now, but it isn't permanent. Until one of us is dead, there's still hope.*

"Christ, kid," Pam said sadly. "I wasted so much time. I should have done things differently."

"Pam, you…" Daisy realized that the woman who raised her might not have done everything right, but she had earned some forgiveness. "You did all right. Don't beat yourself up about it."

"I could have gone through with the adoption though. Given you that, at least."

"I'm really okay. I promise. And now that I've met my real dad and heard his story, I think I'm going to be better than okay." It was the truth.

"And he seems like a decent guy? He's not demented, or whatever?"

"Leonard's fine. I told you. It sounds like he and my mother were just really young."

Pam looked thoughtful. "Like Ray and I, I guess."

"Maybe."

Her foster mom pulled her purse from the back of one of the chairs, rooted around in it for a minute, then popped a piece of nicotine gum in her mouth. She said, "You saved my life, you know."

Daisy doubted that—she'd always believed Pam was about as tough as a tire iron. But she still asked, "How so?"

"There were a lot of shit days, kid. Let me tell you. A lot of days when knowing I had to get home and take care of you was the only thing that kept me going."

Daisy sat back and blinked at the other woman, seeing her— *really* seeing her—for the first time in many years. "I know I didn't make it easy on you," she admitted. "I'm sorry for that."

"Don't be. You know what? You were this fierce, unstoppable, tiger of a kid. You made me be better, just so I could rein you in. If you hadn't been so hard…hell, I'd probably have given up long ago."

"No, you wouldn't have."

"Trust me," Pam chuckled darkly, her voice raspy and low from years of smoking. "I'd be in a gutter somewhere. Not you, though. You're a force of nature, and you always have been."

Daisy grabbed her glass of ice water and gulped some down so she wouldn't lose her cool. Without even meaning to, she blurted out, "Thanks, Mom."

And fuck if Pam didn't go and tear up. *God damn it.* Daisy gave in to the crying, too. As her shoulders shook and ugly sounds crawled their way up from deep in her chest, she hugged the woman who'd raised her.

Talk about shit days when you weren't sure you could keep going. This one had to count.

"Pam…I broke up with Luca," she confessed. "I didn't want to. But when he didn't come to my show and didn't even call…"

"It hurt your feelings," her foster mom said.

"Well, yeah. He promised he'd be there."

"Did he have a good reason not to be?"

"He did, but…" Daisy couldn't quite get the rest out. It seemed small to point out how Pam had often made her feel as a kid, when the woman had just been trying to do her best, like everyone else.

"But, what?"

Daisy shrugged, feeling about three inches tall.

"You know what I think?" Pam asked. "I think you're scared shitless by that guy. I think you really like him—maybe even love him—and you're afraid if you admit it, it'll give him too much power over you. I bet you think the hurt you felt the other night is small potatoes compared to what he could do, if he really set his mind to it."

Jesus, when had her foster mother gotten so perceptive? It was downright eerie how well she'd read Daisy's mind.

She said, "How on earth did you figure all that out from one shrug?"

"Because, kid—it's exactly what I'd be thinking in your position. But you know what? I've figured out that you just can't live your life based on the *what-ifs*. There's too goddamn many of them. You may as well sit in your house all day watching other people through the window."

"I don't want to be that person," Daisy told her.

"Then don't. You've spent all your life being brave as hell. So, go out and do what you do best. Be brave, kid."

"Pam, it's really hard."

"Don't I know it," the woman said. "But the flip side is even harder."

Thirty-Six

T WENTY YEARS. HOW was it possible that it had been two decades since his brother Matteo had succumbed to a particularly nasty form of stomach cancer? The oldest of the four Delledonna children, Matteo had been quick with a smile and a joke, but kind, nonetheless.

Everyone in the family and the neighborhood had loved him.

Luca was the youngest of the brood, though that distinction mattered much less these days. Back then, however, being twelve had felt like such an indignity. He couldn't drive his brother to his many doctor's appointments, and later, he couldn't take his Nonna to the church or the gravesite.

His parents and siblings had barely seemed to notice him as they'd stumbled around in their grief. For a long time, Luca had only his books and Alma, the family cat, for company.

Now, as they all sat in a line, taking up the entire front pew at the church where Matteo's funeral had once been held, Luca was no longer the useless one—he was the one who was making a difference, as he'd vowed to do.

He'd studied all the time for years to get to his current position. Luca had gone to America for college and medical school, and had graduated at the top of each of his classes. He'd won a prime residency and mentored under some of the brightest minds working in oncology today.

Every day at work, Luca was saving the lives of other gastric cancer patients, even if he hadn't been able to save Matteo. He was keeping other families from having to suffer as his had done. It felt good to be needed. Good to help.

He thought about all of those things, holding his Mamma's hand while the memorial mass droned on and on. He wondered what Matteo would think of it—whether his spirit was still somewhere in the ether around them, guiding Luca's hand in his practice and his research.

Perhaps one day, his brother would help him make a discovery that would lead to a cure. Luca dearly hoped so, because as much as he liked helping, he hated seeing his patients suffer every day just as much.

LUCA SAT THERE and thought of other things, too. The patients he had scheduled for appointments in the coming week. The oncology nurse named Lucia, who'd been hinting for weeks that she'd like to go out with him, despite Luca taking rather extraordinary measures to avoid her station every day.

And Luca thought of Daisy, the American boarder at Nonna's pensione. With her wild amber mane of corkscrew curls, long, mouth-watering legs, and tart manner, she was a lure that he couldn't seem to resist.

And why should he? Luca was the textbook example of all work and no play making for a very dull boy—and at the moment he was very, very tired of being dull. If Daisy fired his blood and set all his nerve endings jumping with desire, then that seemed like a good thing.

As long as she wanted him back, there would be no harm in a small affair with her. They could have some fun, and there would be no awkward expectations on either side. She was, after all, only in *Firenze* temporarily, a graduate student studying abroad.

And, it would be a relationship with a very definite end date, since Daisy would no doubt be heading back to America at the end of the semester. Luca could come alive for their brief time together, and it would keep him sane through all the hard work he had coming up at the hospital in the next several months— maybe even the next several years.

Luca kept an eye on the priest, gliding slowly up the aisle in his heavy, embroidered vestments, and held his breath so he wouldn't get a lungful of the incense the man was waving at them.

Once Daisy left, Luca would effectively go back to living as a monk once more, just like that man of God over there. It would not be fun, or conducive to having a family someday, or at all helpful in assuaging the concerns of his mother or grandmother.

Not acting like a social butterfly was, however, necessary if Luca expected to stay focused on his research. He wouldn't make progress if he only showed up at the lab whenever he felt like it.

Thanks to his studies, his brain was now a honed instrument, but it could hardly be expected to make connections and links between all the data they were gathering if it were mired in pheromones and addled by infatuation.

His body simply needed to fall into line with the scheduled program. Right now, Luca suspected it would do that better if it was given a brief holiday.

It was why Daisy made the perfect dating prospect. Physically, she was straight out of a fever dream, checking every box Luca had ever had when it came to women, and even some he hadn't thought up yet. The attraction component was not going to be a problem.

Neither was attachment. Daisy threw off all kinds of reserved signals, too. She might like to go on a few dates, or she might not—but she was definitely not the type woman who was going to get clingy or want to take things to the next level any time soon.

No husband-hunter, that Daisy. Luca liked her a lot already.

His grandmother turned to him and gave him a misty-eyed smile. "That was a nice tribute to Matteo, wasn't it?" she asked.

"*Si*," Luca replied guiltily. "Very nice." While he'd been ruminating, basically resolving to seduce a student staying with his grandmother, the mass to honor his brother had apparently ended.

They all rose and filed into the aisle, walking toward the open doors at the back of the church while the rest of the congregation looked on sympathetically.

Behind him, Giada muttered to Paolo, "At least we have good weather for the cemetery today. Remember how awful it was the day we buried him?"

Luca remembered. It had poured all morning, a cold and raw rain that worked its way into your joints and extremities, and no amount of hot, homemade soup could abate. It had mixed with the tears of Matteo's wife and baby and chilled them so thoroughly that they'd moved to Chiavari soon after and never returned.

Today, when they all straggled back to Nonna's for Sunday dinner, they might be a little windblown, but at least they'd be warm and dry. To look at the assembled family, no one would probably even be able to tell how they were feeling on the inside.

They reached the cars, and spent some time milling around deciding who would ride with whom and which passengers would carry the bundles of flowers Mamma had bought at the market yesterday.

Procrastinating, as it were.

There was no delaying sadness, however, not on this day. So, they drove to the cemetery and marched across the grass like they did every year. Luca's parents helped each other over the uneven terrain. His brother and sister kept to themselves in stony silence, and Luca lent a hand to Nonna, moving more slowly behind the rest of them.

At the gravesite, they arranged their flowers around the headstone, stood blinking back tears in the bright sun, and remembered that integral part of their family, who each person missed terribly in their own way.

BACK AT NONNA'S later that afternoon, the family's spirits were slowly lifting, helped along by his grandmother's manicotti and an excellent Brunello that Paolo had brought from his restaurant.

Paolo's wife Renata was late joining them, and Luca wondered if she even would. Sometimes she preferred to sit this particular meal out, so they could be together and reminisce without having to worry about her feelings.

It was just as possible that she was home nursing a grudge, however. Luca knew his brother loved his wife to distraction, but he'd never been able to understand the woman's occasional petty hurts and fits of temper.

Someday, if he ever found a woman he wanted to marry, Luca hoped she'd be more easy-going than Renata. Who knew if that would ever really happen, though? The heart was a hard-working muscle, but it had about as much sense as the pasta he was eating.

Luca was just as likely to fall head over heels for a complete lunatic, and if family history was any indicator, he'd probably be just as blind to his woman's faults as Paolo was.

He sighed. Even more reason to try to keep things simple on the dating front.

Right on cue, though, Luca heard steps in the pensione's front hall. He had been listening for them and had chosen his seat at the table specifically so he could keep watch on who was coming and going.

On this day of the year, Matteo always felt like he was lingering close by, and Luca's big brother must have been looking out for him now. When Luca leaned back in his chair, he saw that it was, in fact, Daisy out there in the foyer.

He rose, set his plate on the counter, and excused himself quietly. His parents and siblings were embroiled in some heated discussion about politics and didn't notice him slip out of the room.

Nonna was too busy pushing ricotta sadly around her plate to care what her youngest grandson was doing, either.

Luca paused at Nonna's open door to listen but didn't hear steps heading up to Daisy's third-floor room. So, he turned and stepped onto the front stoop and just caught a flash of that fantastic head of toffee-colored hair turning the corner up ahead.

No doubt heading for that gelateria she was so fond of, Luca mused. It took only moments for his long stride to catch up with hers, and luckily, Daisy looked happy to see him.

"Is it too much to hope that you might be heading out for something sweet?" Luca asked her.

Daisy groaned. "God, you have me pegged, don't you? I'm trying to limit myself, but I could probably eat that gelato every day of my life. I have nightmares that they're going to think I'm stalking them and throw me out."

"I'm sure they're perfectly happy to take your money, as often as you want to give it to them," Luca laughed. "But what you obviously need is an excuse to go again."

"Obviously. Do you happen to have one?"

Luca threw his arms wide and bowed. "Yes, I do. I have not yet had dessert tonight, and I am desperately in need of some. You must bring me to your favorite place immediately."

"Not bad," Daisy admitted wryly. "I would almost be convinced, if I didn't happen to know how hard your grandmother worked on the torte she made you guys for Sunday dinner."

"Damn it. How did you hear about that?"

Daisy grinned, all rosy cheeks and white teeth and full, kissable lips. "I'm the one who stopped at the market and bought her sugar for it yesterday, when you had that *patient emergency.*"

Luca winced. "She didn't believe me?"

"Nope."

"To be fair, Nonna needs to get out and walk a little more. It's good for her to get some exercise, and if we do everything for her, she won't do it."

"She had to make a bunch of beds yesterday!" Daisy cried. "Her back was hurting!"

Luca rolled his eyes. "Nonna's back is as strong as an ox's. It's her knees that give her trouble sometimes. Don't tell me you bought that line?"

"Of course I did! Little old ladies aren't devious."

"That's where you're wrong. They're the most devious people on the planet. She got you to make the beds for her, didn't she?"

Daisy flushed crimson, and Luca wanted to kiss her cheeks so he could feel that heat on his lips.

"Now I feel stupid," she said.

"Don't. Nonna wasn't trying to get one over on you, she was probably just trying to test you."

"Well, did I pass or fail?"

"You obviously passed. She hung around talking to you the whole time, didn't she?"

"Yes."

"And Nonna probably asked you to have lunch with her this week, too."

"Wow. You're good. And I'm apparently a total sucker."

Luca laughed. "Not a sucker. Just a nice person."

He held the door of the gelateria wide for her and thought about what she'd told him. If Nonna was trying to figure Daisy out—to get to know her better—then perhaps she was more aware of Luca's interest than he'd assumed.

He'd have to be careful not to get his grandmother's hopes up. If he was reckless, Nonna was liable to start matchmaking, and before long, she'd draft Mamma and Giada to aid her cause.

Luca might have a chance of standing firm against one of them. He didn't have a prayer of holding off all three at once.

Up at the counter, Daisy squealed in delight, doing a happy little dance in her sandals. "They have lemon!" she told him. "It's my current favorite. Do you want one too?"

Luca perused the offerings. "Yes, I think I do."

"*Uno grande, per favore*," she told the employee. She asked Luca, "What size do you want?"

He stood there like a statue and watched her accept her cone and take a long, blissful lick. His phone buzzed in his pocket, and he couldn't even move a muscle to see who it was.

"Luca? Do you want a small or a large?"

He started, held up a finger and pulled out his phone to see a text from Giada. *Papa wants to know where you went. Are you okay?*

Just stepped out for a minute. I'll be back soon.
Better hurry—Nonna wants to serve her cake now.

Luca looked back at Daisy. "Better make it a small. They've realized I'm gone, and I'm going to have to fit in cake and coffee when I go back, too."

"Two desserts? You bad boy," Daisy grinned.

Luca winked at her, then stepped up and paid for their cones. He'd left his family dinner on the saddest day of the year, to go flirt with a woman he had no intention of staying with.

As he saw things, he was more than just bad—he was likely the worst of boys.

Thirty-Seven

Eighteen Months Ago

DAISY FOLLOWED DR. Luca out to the little tables on the sidewalk, even though the evening was beginning to cool off. Couples and families were out and about, enjoying the nice weather with an after-dinner walk.

Daisy wasn't ready to head home just yet, though. She asked Luca, "Do you have enough time to sit for a minute before you have to go back to Nonna's?" He didn't look eager to return either, that was for sure.

She wanted him to know he could stay here with her, if he wanted.

"I do. *Grazie*," he said. Luca sank onto a free chair with a long, tired groan. The poor guy looked whipped.

"Rough week?" Daisy wondered.

"Yes, very. I actually did have a patient emergency—it just wasn't yesterday."

He didn't tell her more, so Daisy pondered for a few minutes what kind of emergency he might have to deal with. Some person with gout? A kid with a broken arm?

Looking Luca over, she probed, "So, were you one of those people who always knew you wanted to be a doctor, or what?"

"Not always," he told her. "I did get interested in it when I was pretty young, though." Luca smiled and hesitated, then took his wallet out of his pocket with one hand and pulled a worn photo from it to show her.

Daisy peered at the old black and white snapshot. Luca looked so serious, a child with an adult's face, holding a real stethoscope to the body of an enormous sprawled-out tabby cat. A teenaged girl who must have been his sister looked on.

"Is that your first patient?" Daisy laughed. "I'm not even a medical professional and I could probably diagnose at least a few problems there."

"Yes, our pet was my patient. Besides Nonna, Alma was the only one who would still for my examinations. She loved…how do you say…*erba gatta*? Makes cats act strange when they smell it?"

"Catnip?"

"Yes, exactly. The catnip toys were always her favorites, but they tired her out quickly. And obviously, she was quite obese, too—she ate all the time, lying on the ground next to her bowl like some ancient Roman *principessa*. Or…like she was at one of those ridiculous buffets on cruise ships, with all the enormous portions. She might have made a good American," he teased, elbowing her.

Daisy smirked. "All right, enough of that. We'll get you hooked on supersized fries soon enough. Just give us time."

While Luca shook his head and put the photo away, Daisy sat there and marveled at what kind of man would choose *that* picture to keep in his wallet. A sweet one, probably. A sentimental one.

He broke into her swirling thoughts abruptly. "And you?" Luca prodded. "As a little girl, you wanted to grow up and be what?"

"Well…" Daisy remembered the stilted conversations with her foster mother and the way Pam had never quite understood Daisy's desire to be something *more*.

For Pam, what she was, was good enough. Rich people and educated people had their own problems, she'd always say, different from Daisy's, maybe—but still problems.

How could Daisy explain to Luca the longing she'd felt as a child—that ever-present yearning to belong to something larger than herself? She had no clan. No kin.

It had a way of making a kid feel utterly unmoored, when everyone else seemed to have touchpoints to define their place in the world. Daisy was only Daisy, and that was about it.

"Daisy? Did I say something wrong?" he asked.

"No, not at all." She powered on, though, before Luca could wonder why his question was so hard for her to answer. "I suppose at first I just wanted to be exotic. When I was seven, that meant Native American princesses and women in saris."

Luca nodded and laughed, clearly having met a seven-year-old girl or two in his day.

Daisy tried to explain. "You have to understand, I lived in Brooklyn. The most exotic things I ever saw were my Pocahontas movie and the Hindu grandma who lived downstairs from us."

"That's cute," he said.

"Anyway, after that I definitely had the requisite pony phase and my veterinarian phase, too—but only because I'd convinced myself that I could talk to animals."

"That is a skill I think I could use," Luca laughed.

"Right? I mean—it would probably work on half the humans walking around, too."

"Agreed."

Daisy went on, "Later, I broadened my scope to forest ranger. I figured that would cover both the animal thing and my newfound love of nature. I had no idea what was involved, of course—I've been a city girl my entire life," she grinned.

Luca chuckled. "I can not picture you in one of those big hats or the shorts with all the pockets. Like that cartoon bear, *sì?*"

"Smokey Bear. Right," she said, impressed that he'd heard of him. "I was very mystical in my teens. I was pretty sure I could be a witch or a druid out in the woods somewhere, if only I could figure out how to get the magic part down."

Luca looked both amused and perplexed. He was still smiling, but his brows twitched together in an adorable little frown, as well. He looked down at his phone and tapped something out, then muttered, "*Druido,*" to himself with a broader smile and a nod.

"I can believe that," he told Daisy, searching her face. "Your eyes are very wise. Sometimes they see too much, maybe."

God, that was the truth. Side effect of her kind of upbringing, Daisy supposed. "It wasn't just animals. I thought I could tell what people were thinking, too," she admitted. "I probably should've taken up poker instead of cameras, right? I might've made a killing."

"Why did you? Study photography, I mean."

For the ten-thousandth time in her adult life, Daisy cast out some good vibes for Mrs. Barousse, wherever she was. "I had the best teacher in the world in middle school," she told Luca. "She took a special interest in me and helped me figure out what made me happy, and how to connect that to what I did best."

"That's wonderful. Not everyone is so lucky. I'm pleased for you."

It was one of the only ways that Daisy *had* been lucky. "I'm grateful to her," she said. "She probably changed the whole direction of my life."

Luca stared off into space. "It only takes one person, sometimes," he mused solemnly, like he knew exactly what she meant.

Daisy didn't want to be nosy, but she had noticed how depressed the rest of his family had seemed that day. Carefully, she said, "Anyway, I wouldn't feel too bad about your week—you're obviously not the only one who had a bad one."

Luca's mouth turned down as he tilted his head. "You did, too?"

"No, actually I meant your family. Everyone seemed really glum today when they came by."

"Ah." He sat back and polished off the remains of his gelato, then told her, "We're pretty tight-knit, as families go. Bad moods tend to have a ripple effect, I'm afraid."

"Oh. Well…at least that's all it was. I was afraid something bad had happened."

Judging by Luca's face, Daisy had hit the nail right on the head, but he didn't admit it to her. Why should he? They barely knew each other. Maybe whatever had his family down was personal, and none of her business.

Lying smoothly, Luca told her, "No, nothing bad. You're sweet to be worried, though. Thank you."

Daisy shrugged. "It's nothing." She was far more sour than sweet, but he didn't have to know that.

Luca changed the subject. "You were right—this lemon flavor is terrific. I wish I'd gotten the larger one, like you."

"There's still time—go back in and you can eat another small one on the way back to your grandmother's."

"Not a bad plan, but have you tried any of their other flavors? Maybe I need to spread my wings and go a bit wild. Try strawberry, or pistachio."

"Honestly? I've tried all of them. You really can't go wrong."

As he sat there debating, Luca slipped off his glasses and polished them on his sweater. He hummed under his breath and Daisy drowned in his hotness.

Would she have looked twice at a guy like him back in Manhattan, or even in Brooklyn? Hard to say, now that she'd met him—but probably not. She would've made assumptions about what kind of guy he was based on how he looked, and passed him over.

In fact, back home Daisy hadn't really spent a lot of time thinking about who *she* was interested in. Guys occasionally approached her around the NYU campus, or when she went out with friends, and then Daisy tried to determine if they were total tools or not.

Reactions, rather than actions.

Some of the guys took longer than others to show their true colors. If they were good at hiding it, she might not learn they were knuckleheads for weeks. Her ex Jason had lasted far longer than that—clearly operating at a pro level of assholery that most others hadn't achieved yet.

The problem with being a woman of indeterminate race, as it turned out, was that it became this *thing* that some men fetishized. Was it as bad as what the girls with large breasts went through? Daisy couldn't say. She only knew that it was there, and it was weird.

Daisy somehow ended up being the top draft pick for the white dudes who dug "ethnic" girls, and also for the brothers who liked women with lighter skin. Given that *Daisy* didn't even know what her racial makeup was, it was a definite point of contention.

She found it difficult to identify fully with either group. It was as if her inability to classify herself on the basis of culture, or racial identity, made it impossible to connect with the guys on all the other levels.

Daisy wasn't in New York now, though—she was in Florence. Despite Italy being just as color-conscious as America in some ways, so far she'd yet to experience that.

In case she never got to come back to Italy—or go anywhere else, for that matter—Daisy was determined not to miss a thing here, and she felt more unguarded, perhaps, when it came to the possibilities.

When it came to a man like Luca.

He was smart. Gorgeous. Curious and sophisticated. He looked impossibly sexy eating gelato, playing hooky from a family dinner. Luca hadn't seemed to register Daisy's race as anything more meaningful than the color of her teeth—and it was nice not to have the burden of that between them.

When she peeked at him, he was glancing at his phone again.

"Do you have to go?"

"*Sì.* I think I'll have to pass up that second gelato, after all," he said. "I should get moving before I'm in real trouble with my grandmother."

"That's all right," Daisy assured him. "I can tell you with complete confidence that this place will be open again by lunchtime tomorrow. You can try another flavor then."

Luca chuckled. "Miss Daisy, more than anything, I'd like to see *you* again. Can I please take you to dinner sometime soon?"

Was she really going to do this? Were they?

"You sure can," she said, batting her eyes and flirting like she never had before.

It appeared they *were* going to do this. At least Daisy hadn't tacked on the phrase, *you big stud*—even if Luca was one.

It was going to be fine, though. Daisy had standards and she had willpower. She could totally hang out with Dr. Luca a few times and not do something dumb.

Like…catch feelings for him.

Thirty-Eight

DAISY HIKED UP her strapless dress one last time before she took her seat at the big round table next to Red and Piper. Her navy-blue gown had a way of riding precipitously low on her cleavage when she sat down—a fact she'd only discovered on the car ride over here.

In the store where she'd also bought her gallery show dress, Daisy had been too flummoxed by the owner delightedly calling her their "best customer" to do much more than pick something that fit.

She hadn't been sure whether to be sad for the shop that two dresses made her a high roller, or freak out at how strange it was that she even needed that much formalwear.

If history was any indicator, Daisy probably wouldn't spend this much time in heels for the next five years.

Nevertheless, the dress she'd ended up with fit in perfectly with the benefit dinner crowd, so Daisy pulled her water glass closer and relaxed a fraction as she scanned the room.

She hadn't spotted Luca at the cocktail hour beforehand. With every table filled and the caterers swarming around her in the ballroom, he could be anywhere, but Daisy would never know it.

She knew he wasn't sitting with them, so at least her biggest worry was taken care of.

Red and Piper were already in conversation with the couple on their right, and for the moment the man on Daisy's other side was chatting with friends.

Daisy was content to be left alone with her swirling thoughts. To keep herself busy, she fussed with the wilted salad a server plunked in front of her, picking out all the cucumbers and cherry tomatoes, and eating them one by one.

While she ate, she listened with half an ear to the man on stage, who was enthusing about the full turn-out and all the extra money they'd raised to round out PKM's donation.

Daisy looked over at her boss, but Red was too busy whispering in Piper's ear to react to the emcee's words. If he felt smug at all about his role, he wasn't showing it.

Up on stage, the announcer introduced Dr. Harlan Green, and Daisy perked up. That was the man from Red and Piper's engagement party—the one who'd been so eager to lure Luca to New York so he could hire him.

Since then, Luca had spoken fondly of the guy, and Daisy could see why. Green was high-energy but likable, and he obviously cared deeply about his patients and his research.

Then, Dr. Green said something that really caught Daisy's attention. Like everyone else in the hotel ballroom, she abandoned her prime rib and focused immediately on the stage.

"The treatment of gastric cancer is always an intimate process," he said. "And this is the case for all of the physicians and researchers at Weill Cornell. However, for none of us is it quite so personal as it is for our newest colleague, for whose brother our new department will be named."

Green paused a long moment, and Daisy held her breath. Then he bowed slightly and announced, "May I present Dr. Gianluca Delledonna."

All eyes in the room were glued to him, as Luca rose from his table near the stage, climbed the stairs, and went to the podium. He pushed his glasses higher on his nose, adjusted the microphone up to his level, and cleared his throat. Twice.

Daisy drank in the sight of him in a tuxedo, and thought he'd never looked more handsome. Luca spent a long time arranging his notes before he finally looked up into the crowd.

And then he began speaking.

OH, GOD. DAISY wanted to smack herself right upside the head. She'd *known* how important family was to Luca. She'd seen it for herself, over and over—how close he was with his grandmother, his mom and dad, and his siblings. As Luca explained about the brother who'd died, Daisy did the math in her head.

It sounded like Matteo had only been twenty-three years old, with a wife he'd been married to for a mere two years when he died. He'd had a new baby that he'd never gotten to know. He'd also had a little brother named Luca, who, all this time later, still clearly idolized him.

When Matteo died, Luca must have been no more than twelve. It was heart-breaking and tragic and the kind of thing that changed a kid's entire life.

It set him on a path that would shape the rest of his days and turned him into a man who healed others for a living—even when it had to hurt him over and over, deep in his soul.

Daisy sat there, frozen and numb that no one—*no one*—had ever told her that Luca had had another brother. Not only that, but a brother who had died horribly, when Luca was just a kid. Shouldn't that detail have come out at some point?

How had she not heard something in Florence? Some fond reminiscence from his grandmother, maybe, or an aside from his mother or other siblings during dinner?

Why hadn't Luca himself ever said a single word?

Daisy had been utterly ignorant to the big truth that underpinned all the others. It had never, not once, occurred to her to ask the simplest of all questions: *Why?*

Why had Luca chosen the medical specialty he had? Why were his work and his patients so deeply important to him? Why had he chosen to become a doctor at all?

Not because of some cat named Alma, that was for damn sure.

Daisy had gotten wrapped up in the fact that Luca had let her down, after he'd vowed so hotly to be at her show to support her. And maybe that had been easy to do, because she was still trying to soldier past his original lie of omission.

She'd only agreed to that first tentative truce, after all, because she knew she was guilty of the same kind of deception—not because she'd understood his.

Right now, those felt like weak excuses for a rash, knee-jerk reaction on her part.

Daisy hadn't wondered *at all* why Luca had acted so out of character on the night of her gallery show. He'd never given her any reason before that to believe that he was a callous, thoughtless man—and yet the notion that he'd ghosted her without a second thought, on one of the most terrifying nights of her life, had not seemed strange in the least.

That made Daisy one hell of a selfish brat, didn't it? She'd thought she had all the answers, but it seemed she was just as clueless about love as she was about every other thing in life.

Love. God, she was in *love* with that man up there on the dais. He was passionate and committed and loyal and honorable, and it was all wrapped up in the most devastatingly sexy package Daisy could ever have imagined. And, even though she was the worst kind of doofus, Luca still adored her.

At least, he had. Before she went mental on him.

Looking back on their argument in light of this new revelation, Daisy knew her fury must have hurt him deeply. She had no clue how to undo that damage, but she also knew that if she didn't try…

She'd never be able to live with herself, if she didn't at least try.

THE BENEFIT DINNER had continued on after Luca's speech as if nothing earth-shattering had happened. From the vantage of her table, Daisy had watched him exit the hotel ballroom through a side door immediately after leaving the stage, and then saw him return fifteen minutes later.

He'd looked better, then—less likely to break down if he had to talk to anyone else.

There'd been no good time to approach him since then without making a scene. Daisy could at least spare Luca that, since delivering his speech had clearly taken such a disconcertingly large bite out of him.

Finally, however, the dessert plates were cleared away. Some guests sat in groups socializing over coffee, others took to the small dance floor, and still others took their leave entirely.

Daisy checked on Luca's position obsessively, terrified that he'd somehow manage to slip by her and leave, without her getting a chance to tell him anything important.

Red leaned over his fiancée to poke Daisy in the arm, saying, "Told you. Didn't I?"

She nodded, "You did. I'm just glad I believed you enough to come along."

Piper snorted. "Don't worry. Even if you'd fought it, Red would've found a way to drag you here."

"I appreciate that."

"Anytime, Daisy. Seriously," her boss said. Then he nodded toward the front of the room.

Luca had broken away from the men he'd been speaking with near the stage, then turned and started walking down the narrow aisle formed by the tables. He spotted Red first, then Piper, and gave them a sheepish smile.

A moment later, however, his eyes lit on Daisy, paralyzed in her seat beside them.

She could tell the instant it happened, and she wasn't the only one. When Luca's step hitched and his face changed, Red and Piper quickly took their leave, heading toward the dance floor to waltz around with the other couples.

Luca came to a stop beside Daisy and gripped the abandoned seat next to her tightly.

"I didn't know you would be here," he said carefully. "But thank you for coming."

"If you have to blame someone, it was Red and Piper's idea," Daisy replied.

"Why am I not surprised?" He let out a long sigh and sat down. "You look beautiful, Daisy."

"Thank you." The last two people across the table gathered their things and left. Once they were alone, Daisy told Luca, "You should have told me."

"You never asked."

She rolled her eyes. "You never gave me the slightest sign that it was something I *should* ask. How could I have guessed that?" Did he expect her to practice telepathy like he practiced medicine?

"*Who, what, when. Where, why, how.* These are the questions we must always ask ourselves," Luca intoned forlornly. There was no heat in his words, though, only sadness.

"Spoken like the practical scientist you are. Except, I'm an artist, Luca. We aren't always quite that…thorough. Sometimes we get by on feeling things out. Sensing things."

"The facts still apply no matter who we are. It's only what we do with the information that changes." Luca looked depleted, somehow. Hollowed out. It was awful. "Besides, the reason I went into medicine doesn't matter anymore. I am a doctor now. I am committed to my patients and I always will be."

Daisy argued right back, "You're wrong. The reason you are the way you are *does* matter. It places your whole life into context. Luca—the reason is everything."

He lifted his eyes from the cast-off teaspoon he was toying with, and stared resolutely toward the corner of the room, where the four-piece band was launching into a moody jazz number.

At last, he sighed again. "Daisy…even if my reasons were as important as you say, it still doesn't change anything. I can't alter who I am. Not even for you, much as I'd like to. It wouldn't be fair to either of us."

"Luckily, I won't ask you to," she said. "Luca, I really wish you'd trusted me enough to tell me about Matteo sooner."

"I'm sorry I didn't. Please know that I would have, eventually—I could never have kept that from you for very long."

Daisy had assumed Luca was coldhearted, putting his job and his research ahead of all else. Family. Love. *Her.* She was mistaken.

His entire career was a larger-than-life expression of his love and commitment to his family. He was as big-hearted as a man could be.

Daisy could probably learn a thing or two from him.

When she used to think about the future, she'd never cared if the man she eventually spent her life with was artsy like her, or a graph-and-ruler kind of guy. She hadn't cared if he was rich or poor, tall or short, homely or handsome. The single most important quality to her had always been, simply, that her life's mate appreciate family.

It was the single biggest thing she'd never had, and the one thing she'd wanted more than anything else.

Daisy wanted someone to choose *her*, over and over. To choose her as a wife, to choose her as the mother of their children, to choose her to grow old with. She knew she could be that for someone. She *yearned* to be that for someone.

Not just someone—Luca. Daisy wanted to plant that seed of love and grow it with him, so that no child born of her blood would ever know the disconnect and loneliness that she had.

All this time, she'd thought Luca was just another guy who put work first. But as it turned out, she was wrong.

"I'm wrong a lot," she warned him. "I should tell you that right now. But I know for certain that I am not wrong about this."

For the first time, Luca looked at her with a little bit of hope. "About what?" he breathed.

"I love you. Forever and always, with all of my heart. If you want me, I'll be here right next to you, supporting you the same way you've done for me, as long as you'll have me."

"Daisy," Luca choked out, "I love you, too." And then he yanked her into his arms and cried.

Daisy held him, rubbing his back gently as he tried to stifle his sobs. Eventually, Red caught her eye from across the room, leaned down to murmur something to Piper, and led his fiancée back over.

"When I invited you here, I didn't think you'd use the opportunity to break the man for good," he teased Daisy.

Luca sat back abruptly, grabbed a napkin and wiped off his face. "*Cretino*," he muttered.

Piper told them, "We've got some champagne back at the house. Why don't we relocate there and toast Luca's new, fully-funded research project?" To Luca, she added, "You did an amazing job with your speech, by the way. Everyone was very impressed with you."

Luca stared into Daisy's eyes, took her face worshipfully in his hands, and planted a long kiss on her lips.

"Another time," he told his friends. "We have our own toasts to make tonight."

Thirty-Nine

LUCA MADE SURE everything was in position, arranging it over and over until it was perfect, before he went to the door and let Daisy in.

"Oh, good!" she said immediately. "The gallery told me they'd delivered your pieces, but I wanted to make sure everything arrived safely."

"Everything was in pristine condition," Luca assured her. "Even these."

He'd set up a new arrangement above a side table Piper had found him the week before. He'd given her very specific dimensions, and once again, his friend's future wife had come through like a champion.

Daisy wandered over and arched an eyebrow at him. "Very interesting. I wondered who bought those, but the gallery told me the collector wished to remain *anonymous.*"

"Well, you were still mad at me. I couldn't take the chance that you'd put me on some kind of no-entry list."

"So you went? You saw the show?"

"I did. Everything was really beautiful, *cara.* I was so proud of you."

"But did you see…all of the show?"

"Oh, yes. I saw what you did with my hideous face. You can probably unload those to a horror museum somewhere," he told her.

"No way. Those babies are coming home with me. Hanging them right next to my bed," she grinned, fluttering her eyelashes at him.

Daisy hadn't noticed what was on the table yet, and now she was getting inconveniently distracted. Luca reached over and straightened one of the figurines, and hoped she'd notice.

Right on cue, Daisy frowned and peered closer. "What are those?"

"Ah. Well, naturally, this is the Tower of Pisa, this is Big Ben, and this is the Eiffel Tower. I found a website that sells world monuments for fish aquariums. They assured me they were safe for turtles, too."

Daisy began blinking rapidly. "You bought new things for Jerome's habitat?"

"Not just any things. I got him sights from around the world. So, he can travel without having to leave the comfort of home."

"Luca, that's…oh my God, that's really, really cute."

Luca patted the table. "I set this up here, so it wouldn't be too bright for him."

"But why—"

"Daisy, do you think Jerome would mind very much if I asked him to come live with me?"

"You want me to give you my pet turtle?"

"Well, I was hoping you might consider coming along, too. You know, to keep us company. This apartment is really big and empty with only me rattling around in it."

"Luca, you've got to be crazy," Daisy protested. "I can't move in with you! I'll drive you *nuts*."

"Nonsense. Why do you say that?"

"Because I have quirks, that's why. I'm messy and I like loud music and I work in the middle of the night."

"*I* work in the middle of the night."

"It's not the same!"

"Of course, it is. This way, we'll get to spend more time together, even with our crazy schedules. Trust me. It will work perfectly. Give me a chance, Daisy."

"What makes you so sure, anyway?"

"Look at my parents. They've been married for more than forty years, and worked together for almost that long, too. And not only have they not killed each other, but they're also still crazy about each other."

Daisy frowned. "They work together, too?"

"Yes. My mother is his office manager. Just think how superb *that* would be. You could put your hair up and wear pointy glasses on the end of your nose. A tight little skirt and those shoes you wore to the opera."

"I borrowed those shoes from Piper."

"We'll get you your own pair."

"Luca, you dirty boy. Are you seriously telling me you have a secretary fantasy?"

"That's better than a nurse fantasy, isn't it?"

"I'm not sure it is."

"Here," he said, offering her a pencil from his counter. "Let me see you chew on this. Nice and slow."

Daisy narrowed her eyes. "You realize that if I accept that pencil from you, I will probably stab you in the eye with it."

Luca burst out laughing and tossed it aside, then pulled Daisy close so he could wrap his arms around her.

"Say yes, *cara*. I've missed your violent and unpredictable nature while we've been apart. I want to make love to you in the mornings in my excellent bed and then bring you coffee before work. I want to come home at horrible hours of the night and catch you stealing my pillow. I want to be grouchy because you ate all the cookies, and then let you try to make it up to me."

"That sounds…actually, it sounds pretty amazing," she admitted. "Which is slightly weird. You're weird, you realize that?"

"But we're the same weird, I think. And that makes it okay."

"Strangely, I think you might be right." Daisy looked so puppy-dog hopeful when she said that. It was like she couldn't stop what came out of her mouth next. "Oh, for the—*okay*. Fine. You win. We can shack up together. I'll be your on-site booty call, but you better cook me that freaking carbonara whenever I feel like it."

"Your wish is my command," Luca said smoothly, and then moved in for a kiss that would melt her spine and turn her legs to plasma. Once he had her good and breathless, he lifted his lips from hers just enough to murmur, "And you are so much more than a booty call, Daisy. You are everything to me."

She couldn't possibly argue with that. "I love you," Daisy admitted, and each time she said it, it felt better and better.

"And I love you. Listen, I have to ask you another question."

Something in his expression must have made her panic a bit. "Are you sure you don't like nurses, too?" she babbled quickly, "Because I dressed up as a nurse one time for Halloween and I could probably find the costume again."

Luca would bet good money that Daisy's costume had been more along the lines of a zombie healthcare worker than a sexy one, and that her little white dress had been splashed in gruesome red paint. Still, her diversion had the intended effect.

He paused and cocked his head, studying her intently. "Okay, yes. We can definitely talk about a possible nurse fantasy more. But later."

Daisy's eyes snagged on the clock in his kitchen and she burst into sudden action. "Much later!" she cried. "We've got to get to Trident. Come on, we're going to be late!"

THE PROBLEM, AS Luca saw it, began the moment Daisy had let Tabitha Lovell take her picture during a meeting at work one day. It had clearly given the author some crazy ideas.

It also meant that, when he and Daisy had run into the woman on the street a few weeks ago, she had stopped in her tracks, looked them over like they were a particularly decadent pair of truffles, and demanded to know, "Well, well, well—*who* do we have here?"

Poor Daisy hadn't seen the trouble before she'd walked right into it. She'd only smiled and introduced everyone. "Tabitha, this is my boyfriend, Luca. Luca, this is Tabitha Lovell, the author whose book covers I've been designing."

"Of course," he'd said. "It's a pleasure." He'd shaken her hand, but she wouldn't let go.

"Now, we're talking," Ms. Lovell had crowed, and then she'd fired right back at him with, "And what do you do for a living, kind sir?"

"I'm a doctor."

Daisy must not have liked the look in the author's eye, because she'd muttered, "Oh no."

"You're Italian, huh? I don't suppose you could try playing a 19th century Mexican. Could you?"

Luca had taken a couple of seconds to make sure he understood what was being asked of him, and then he'd stamped his foot, thrown an arm up in the air, and asked her, "Olé?"

Daisy and Tabitha had burst out laughing, and rightly so. Once they'd recovered, Ms. Lovell had said, "Okay. Okay, not bad. That was more matador than tequila seller, but I think we can work with it. Now—how do you feel about holding Daisy here in a passionate embrace, while enthusiastic professionals take your picture?"

"With or without clothing?" Luca had asked. Daisy had punched him hard on the arm for that, of course.

"I like the way you think," Tabitha had said. "But I think we have to go with clothed. At least partially, anyway."

He'd told her, "I'm generally open to the idea, but it's really up to Daisy."

"Luca, no!" Daisy had protested. "You don't know what she's doing. She's trying to get us to pose for her book cover!"

Maybe he shouldn't have grinned like he had, when he inquired, "Will I get to bend you over my arm and pull your sleeve off your shoulder?"

The author had clapped her hands and gleefully yelled, "Yes!"

Daisy had stamped her own foot in horror. "No," she'd groaned.

THAT FATEFUL RUN-IN, naturally, had led right to where they stood today—in a Trident photo studio, decked out in old-fashioned clothes while a collection of Daisy's coworkers poked and prodded them into various uncomfortable positions.

It was less romantic than Luca had imagined it would be, but it *was* funny. Tabitha was begging them to 'get into it,' Daisy was keeping up a running stream of creative invective, and her colleagues were good-naturedly ribbing them. He was having trouble staying serious.

When they were finally able to take a break, Luca kept Daisy close so he could keep peeking down her wonderful, corseted décolletage.

"Ms. Lovell," he inquired, "It occurs to me that you never mentioned the *names* of these two characters we're impersonating."

"Didn't I?" Tabitha looked mischievous. "They're called Desi and Luke. So fitting, right?"

Daisy groaned, loud and long. "You have got to be kidding me."

"What happens to them?" Luca prodded. "This isn't one of those stories with a family feud and a rash of impractical suicides, is it?"

The author laughed, "I don't write Shakespearean tragedy, you handsome devil—I write *romance*. Desi and Luke get married and have babies and live happily ever after."

It was like she'd handed him the perfect opening, even if Luca hadn't planned it to be quite so public.

"I like that story much better," he announced. "Daisy? I don't suppose *you'd* like to get married and have babies and live happily ever after with me?"

The entire room went completely silent.

Daisy gaped at him in shock. "What…you…"

"Hold that thought." Luca rushed over to the changing area in the corner, pulled his grandmother's ring from his pants pocket, and came back to get on one knee in front of her.

Camera shutters began clicking again. A certain author in the room emitted one ecstatic whimper.

"Where were we?" Luca asked Daisy.

She wailed, "I believe it was Crazytown."

"Don't think about the *what-ifs*," he told her. "Just think about the love. Take a chance, *cara*."

"Do it," Tabitha whispered, along with a few others in the room.

"Seriously?" Daisy cried.

"It's Nonna's ring," Luca explained. "She gave it to me, to give to you."

Daisy's lovely jade eyes got very watery. "She did?"

He nodded, hardly daring to hope. The woman he loved looked around the room, and encountered encouraging nods from everyone there.

She stared down at Luca. "Am I dreaming?"

"Not at all. Pinch me. I'm very real, trust me."

"I'll do it later. First…" she swallowed loudly and straightened her spine "I'll just say…*yes.*"

The room erupted in cheers, Luca leaped to his feet and slipped the ring on her finger, and then he shielded her from the others until she had a chance to get the tears out of her system and get her bearings.

Daisy had done the same for him at the benefit dinner, and his father had been oh, so wrong about how she'd react to his display of emotion. Now, it seemed fitting to return the favor.

Forget Romeo and Juliet.

Luca and Daisy had their own love story now—and he had a feeling it was going to be one for the ages.

Epilogue

LUCA AND DAISY met up that weekend with Red and Piper, to celebrate their engagement news at a sophisticated little gastropub Piper had found in Gramercy Park.

Piper brought along her friend Lyla, too, and introduced her as the writer spearheading Trident's fledgling *Red Devil* mystery imprint.

Looking around at the gathering, Luca could only think of one thing missing. He joked, "Not that I'm complaining, but we could really use Tate to round out this company."

"Oh, no," Piper argued. "You and Red sharing inside jokes all night is more than enough. The last thing we need is all of TDH here."

Luca chuckled. "I see Red has told you about our little fraternity."

His future bride looked distinctly unimpressed. *"Fraternity?* No way."

"It was very exclusive," he told her, "Only Red, Tate, and me—though the hazing was formidable."

"You should call him," Lyla said. "Don't you think he'd join us?"

"I'm sure he would. No one's friendlier to an unaccompanied woman that Tate Monroe. Unfortunately, it would probably take him four days to get here from whatever Middle Eastern desert he's currently fighting in," Red explained.

"He's a soldier?" Lyla gazed from Red to Luca, and back again. "Geez, you guys are like a bad joke, aren't you?"

Red frowned and asked, "How do you figure?"

Piper smiled, though, understanding Lyla instantly. "You know—a CEO, a doctor, and a soldier walk into a bar…"

Beside Luca, Daisy chuckled and held up a finger while she reached down and dug through her large handbag. Moments later, she produced a small sketchbook and a pencil. She flipped to a blank page and began drawing, and before long, the suggestion of a long bar emerged, along with three stools, and three men sitting on them.

Piper continued, "The CEO said, *I'll have a whiskey.*"

Daisy drew a highball glass near the first man's hand, then announced, "The doctor said, *I'll have a glass of Chianti.*" She proceeded to sketch out the second figure's drink, then, with a smirk, added several large lip prints to his cheek and collar.

Luca chuckled and planted a hearty, very real kiss on her cheek.

Daisy raised her eyebrows at the group, her pencil hovering over the paper.

Piper rubbed her chin, then continued, "The soldier said, *I'll have a beer with a bomb chaser.*"

Grinning from ear to ear, Daisy drew a beer stein in one of the last man's hands, and an old-fashioned round bomb in his other. She added a tiny flame to the fuse and shaded in camouflage on his clothes, while she waited for someone to deliver the punch line.

Luca was confused, though. "What's the bomb for?" He didn't kid himself that Tate's profession was easy or safe, but he also didn't like to think about his friend anywhere near such a devastating device.

On the paper, Daisy added a conversation bubble above the supposed doctor's head, and wrote in Luca's exact question.

"Ooh!" Lyla's hand shot up like she was the teacher's pet, and they all turned to look at her. Her eyes were dancing. "The soldier replied, *I like to end the week with a bang.*"

Piper barked out a loud, surprised chortle, and Daisy began giggling as she hastily sketched a growing horde of starry-eyed women beside the soldier.

"I don't get it," Luca complained. "Why is that funny?"

Red groaned, "It's *not.*"

His fiancée disagreed, however. "Oh yes, it is."

Luca tried again, irritated that everyone seemed to understand something he didn't. "Tate would never handle an explosive so carelessly." He pointed at the crowd of women at the side of the picture. "And who are these people supposed to be?"

Lyla looked like she was fighting to stay serious. "I'm sure your friend is very meticulous with his incendiary devices. But—and correct me if I'm wrong about this—didn't you just insinuate that he was a bit of a player?"

Luca looked at Red for clarification, but his friend just rolled his eyes. "Dog. Hound. *Bracco,*" his friend said.

Realization dawned. Daisy looked quickly around the table, then leaned in close to him. As he always did, Luca breathed in her sweet, citrusy scent until it filled his lungs and warmed him from the inside out.

"The bomb means three things," she murmured. "First, it's just a retro-looking bomb, which is a silly thing for a guy in a bar to be holding at all. Second, 'to go out with a bang' means to end something dramatically, with a flourish, you know?"

Luca nodded. She pressed her lips together but couldn't contain her mirth at the final part. "Last, but definitely not least, to 'bang' someone is to—"

"*Fottere*," Red interjected loudly.

Luca gaped and looked down at Daisy's cartoon once more. "Okay," he admitted. "That is pretty funny."

His cell phone began vibrating in his pocket, and with a quick apology to the group, he fished it out. Luca frowned when he saw who was calling. "Mrs. Monroe? Is that you?"

Luca had to press his fingers to his other ear to hear Tate's mother over the din of the happy hour crowd. Eventually, however, her words began to make sense. Luca shot to his feet, his chair tilting backward and nearly hitting the floor, and told her what she needed to know.

Across from him, Red got to his feet as well, his expression grim. "What? What is it?" he demanded.

"Tate's being flown to Landstuhl tomorrow. His company ran into an ambush—he's been injured." Luca looked down at Daisy, searching her face.

She knew what he was asking without him having to say a word—and she didn't even hesitate before she nodded, eyes wide and worried.

Luca looked back to Red. "I'm going to meet his parents there. There's probably not much I can do, but—"

"I'll go too," Red said. "When he's ready, we can bring him home on the PKM jet." He stood with his hands on his hips for a minute, and then shook his head. "Fuck. He's going to hate this."

Around the table, everyone began gathering their jackets and bags and discussing arrangements. Lyla slid the forgotten drawing toward her for a moment, staring down at it morosely. "Suddenly, this is not very funny anymore," she sighed.

Daisy ripped it from her sketchbook and handed it to her. "Keep that," she said, "Until it's funny again."

"It will be," Luca told her. "We'll make sure of it."

Review

Did you enjoy **The Doctor Was Dark**? If so, please consider leaving a review at the retailer where you purchased this title.

Book reviews can be as simple or as detailed as you wish, but all of them help authors sell more books, and assist other readers in finding the stories they want to read.

Almost any book can be reviewed by simply logging into the website where you purchased the title, then scrolling to the bottom of the title's product page to find an area called "Leave a Review."

Up Next

The Hero Was Handsome

Triple Threat, Book Three

Lead the way...

Yeah, right. All "leading the way" had gotten Tate was a seat too close to a roadside bomb and a psych eval gone sideways. He was benched from the Army for months while he healed, but he wasn't going to mope around about one unlucky roll of the dice. He was going to get better and return to active duty, in just a few more weeks.

In the meantime, he needed to keep busy so he wouldn't go climbing-the-walls crazy. So, Tate agreed to pick up a couple extra bucks, hit the road, and rub noses with some minor celebrities—all by working security for a hot little author his buddy wanted protected. What could go wrong with a cake job like that? After all, Lyla was a writer, not a terrorist.

However, Tate's temp job quickly turns all kinds of complicated when he begins to suspect that he's not the only one who's fallen for Lyla's charms. And, when a mysterious fan starts getting too close for comfort on her book tour, it looks like some of the pretty bookworm's gritty research has followed her into the real world—and is none too happy to find Tate barring the door.

Can he find the person scaring Lyla out of her wits before something truly bad happens? Or will his impractical crush keep him from completing the one mission more important than any other?

This job's about more than guarding some asset.

Tate's protecting the woman who holds his heart in her hands.

The Hero Was Handsome

One

TATE AWOKE, AS he often did these days, with the white-hot bang that came at the end of his dream. Sadly, it wasn't the sort of bang that had him balls-deep in a good-hearted woman. Instead, it was the kind that knocked him flat on his can if he was lucky—and sent him straight to his maker if he wasn't.

He sat up and blinked away the lingering fog of the recurrent nightmare and did a quick assessment. By all accounts, he was luckier than most. Tate was alive and whole, for one thing, and back home in the States, for another.

He'd been born to a nice, solid set of parents who'd been coddling him for months and, courtesy of his kick-ass best friends, he'd spent the night on a posh hotel mattress instead of on the rocky ground of the Middle East.

On the other hand, Tate's career would soon be swirling down the toilet like a college kid's bar-binge piss if he couldn't get his shit together today, and his current condition didn't make that look terribly promising.

It wasn't like he had a ton to do—no mountains to scale, no insurgents to neutralize, no wounded teammates to hump out of the desert on his back. No, by his count, Tate only needed to accomplish three small, non-life-threatening tasks in the immediate future.

One, move through his day as calmly as possible, so his dumb-ass brain would keep healing. Two, nail the job interview his buddy Red had set up for him this morning—and three, act like an upstanding civilian convincingly enough for the next few months that the Army finally let him go back to being a soldier.

Where life made sense.

True, it was a peculiar sort of sense, but it was what Tate knew and what he was good at. Fuck if he was any good at being normal anymore—these last few months he'd discovered the hard way that he was too far gone for that.

Tate groaned and scrubbed his hands over his face. In the Army, he didn't have to confront the fact that his two best friends were both killing it in their careers and personal lives while Tate was just killing.

He didn't have to face that Red and Luca would soon be settling down with the loves of their lives, while he was stuck in a bizarre pseudo-adult stasis—responsible enough to carry firearms capable of grisly destruction, but completely oblivious when it came to, say, shopping for groceries.

It shouldn't be okay that a 99-cent cheeseburger from the drive-through had taken on all the ambrosia-like qualities of a once-in-a-lifetime five-star meal. It definitely wasn't okay that Tate had ended up at said drive-through last week because sitting at his mom's table for a holiday meal had made him want to claw his way out of his own skin.

He pushed to his feet and shuffled over to the hotel room desk, where he'd left his list the night before. It was crumpled and messy, and he'd scrawled it on the hotel stationery before he'd crawled into bed, but it still seemed to be accurate.

A while back, Tate's doctors had suggested he make lists to help himself stay on top of the things he needed to do while his memory remained unreliable. Lately, it felt like Tate's whole life revolved around these goddamned lists.

Wake up. Shave and shower. Take a cab to Red's office for the interview.

Tate's eyes hitched on what he'd written in parentheses after that: "*Uber?!?*" His old friend had suggested he take one of those, and while Tate knew very well *what* an Uber was, he didn't have the faintest idea *how* a dude went about securing one.

But maybe that was more of a city-versus-country thing, instead of a soldier-versus-civilian thing. He decided a taxi would get the job done old-school this morning, and later—if he remembered—Tate could google the whole Uber issue to death for next time.

On the nightstand, his phone dinged out a reminder, and he went over to check it. *Ten a.m. appointment. Don't be late, Fucktard.*

Tate huffed out a laugh. His prior-day self had clearly left nothing to chance. Yesterday's Tate had probably also asked Red to text this morning—not that he'd needed to.

Ever since Red and Luca had shown up at Landstuhl with a company jet and world-revolves-around-them demeanors, they'd been all over Tate like white on rice. If they had their way, they weren't going to let him forget his own name, much less today's interview.

The idiots had always had his six, right from day one of freshman year at college. You couldn't pay for that kind of loyalty with blood, and that was another reason why Tate couldn't screw up today. He absolutely refused to let Red and Luca down.

One more glance at his list, a hasty line drawn through the words *Wake up*, and Tate headed for the fancy marble bathroom attached to his suite. When he showed up at Red's office later this morning, there'd be no trace of the sweating, blood-stained, barely human thing that had played the starring role in his dream this morning.

Tate was going in spit-shined and tight, and there'd be no way on earth anyone could refuse him.

NO TWO WAYS about it, the chick was an absolute babe. And sure, Tate knew you couldn't say that kind of thing about a woman you were trying to work for. He knew he had no business whatsoever noticing the looks of a stranger on the street right now, much less one of Red's most important employees.

But facts were facts, and Ms. Lyla Lawson's shiny brown hair and hot secretary glasses were totally doing it for him. She had a sweet ass and pretty hazel eyes and a soft, husky voice that was so sexy it ought to be criminal.

His buddy appeared to be utterly immune to her charms, but then again, Red had always had a ferocious poker face. Tate listened to his former roommate define terms and kept his eyes on Ms. Lawson's back while he surreptitiously readjusted himself in his pants.

No use having her bust him rearranging his junk. Nothing in the world said *Not Qualified* quite like sporting untimely wood in your dress slacks.

While he sat there trying to rein shit in, Tate attempted to convince himself that Lyla had breath like festering sewage or a nasally, cackling laugh. He hadn't gotten close enough to determine either of those things for certain, however.

Since Tate had retreated to the chair Red offered him once he'd shaken Lyla's hand, and she had immediately paced over to the big windows overlooking downtown Manhattan, his dick still knew there was doubt.

She was keeping her distance and keeping quiet, while Tate attempted mightily to ignore her charms and Red talked.

He talked a hell of a lot. Once Tate was sure his ill-advised condition had gotten a little less obvious, he checked his buddy's face to see what was up—and met Red's narrow-eyed glare of death. *Shit.*

Red gave him a tiny shake of his head, delivering the most subtle and dangerous *Back Off* in history. Tate widened his eyes and shrugged, one-hundred-percent the innocent boy scout.

The glare got darker and more threatening. Clearly, his old roommate had seen him on the prowl one too many times to buy the whole *Who me?* charade. Tate would have to remember that. He wasn't with his unit anymore.

People knew him better here—knew his habits and his history. Plus, they were peers instead of subordinates. They didn't have to accept his bullshit just because he told them to.

Tate wanted to believe that he might have one or two new tricks up his sleeve that his friends hadn't seen yet, but that might be wishful thinking. Like so many other things were, these days.

"Here's the thing," Lyla said suddenly, spinning around and placing her back to those precarious-looking windows.

Tate took a moment to admire the way she'd cut off Red's big-man bluster so handily. It diverted him from obsessing about how any fuckface with a decent scope out there could so easily get a bead on them.

"I'm supposed to be going on a book tour next week to drum up buzz for Red Devil and my new series with them. I've been telling Red that we ought to just cancel it, but he's..."

"An over-bearing ass who doesn't want you to be in danger," Red supplied. He pulled out his chair and sat down heavily.

Tate snapped to attention. While he'd been dwelling on shades of hotness and degrees of unsafe exposure, the real reason he'd been summoned here had somehow dropped into the room without him noticing.

When Red had broached this idea to him last week—indeed, while his buddy had been expounding on it for the last ten minutes—the job had not, in fact, been about some cake security guard position, as Tate had assumed.

All this time, he'd been envisioning a geeky gray uniform with a stupid patch on the breast pocket. Tate had been thinking he would fritter away his days sitting at some desk in an office lobby, with Lyla working upstairs getting Red Devil, the new publishing imprint, up and running.

He'd been entertaining fantasies of telling her, *"Morning, Ms. Lawson,"* and *"Evening, Ms. Lawson,"* when she walked by his station. Five seconds ago, Tate had every intention of flirting with her for the next few months like his pants were on fire.

But that kind of job involved no *danger* whatsoever.

Tate cleared his throat, and inquired, "What kind of danger are we talking here?"

"It's no big deal," Lyla scoffed, at the same time Red explained, "Unfortunately, Lyla's acquired a stalker."

Holy *crap*. This woman didn't need a security guard—she needed a *body*guard. For her very female and attractive *body*.

"I see," Tate said, so he wouldn't blurt out his thoughts on *that* subject.

Lyla looked troubled. She pivoted around again and returned to her post near the windows.

He asked, "Could you, uh…"

She peered over her shoulder at him and bit one of those full, peach-glossed lips of hers.

Tate swallowed and looked to Red, instead. "Can we close the blinds, maybe? There's an awful lot of open space…there."

Red blinked and sat back, studying him. In an undertone, he murmured, "Light hurting your eyes?"

Tate sat back, too. Injuries sucked, but they were better than letting people know how freaking paranoid he'd apparently become. "Yeah. Little bit," he said.

Red hit a button near his desk phone, and a thin, tinted screen began its slow descent from the hidden niche near the ceiling. As Tate had hoped, Lyla came and sat safely beside him once she was deprived of her view.

She smelled like a meadow of wildflowers, damn it. Not even a hint of sewage wafted his way.

Once she was settled, he continued, "Are the police involved?"

Red muttered pissily, "Those guys."

Lyla sighed, "I didn't want to call them. And when the letters stopped coming to Trident, I thought whoever it was had moved on. But then…" She stopped. Paused and took a big breath. "Then one came to my house."

Tate looked at Red. The man stared back at him, six-and-a-half feet of bristling fury. Lyla might be trying to downplay the situation, but whatever was going on had his friend plenty worked up.

"You insisted she go to the cops?" Tate confirmed.

"You bet I did."

"And they said?"

"Without any fingerprints or overt threats, they can't do anything," Lyla told him.

Tate couldn't read her expression. Was she scared—or embarrassed? Hard to say.

He zeroed in on the most obvious issue. "Guys, what makes you think I can help here? I have no experience whatsoever with this kind of thing. I don't do investigative stuff in the Army. I just shoot things."

"Tate's right," Lyla told her boss. "The last thing this mess needs is a gun."

"I disagree," Red countered. "I think the last thing it needs is for some deranged punk to show up at one of your signings *with* a gun, and all anyone has to protect you are a stack of paperbacks and some permanent markers."

"We should just let the police handle it," she tried again.

"Lyla, we've been over this," Red said. "NYPD does not have the manpower to assign someone to you day and night, and they're not going to send a cop on the road with you, either. I am, however. I think it should be Tate."

Tate's gaze pinged back to Lyla to see her return salvo.

"This is overkill," she countered.

"I wish you'd chosen any word but that one," Red retorted.

Tate held up his hands. "Okay, kids, let's back things up a step." He pointed at Lyla. "How long have you been getting freaky letters from this person?"

"About six months, as far as we know," Red replied.

"Not talking to you," Tate fired back. This time, he emphasized the author's name, "*Lyla*, what do they usually say?"

"They're angry and they get personal. They talk about my books and they always tell me I 'got it wrong,' whatever that means."

"How angry are we talking?"

Lyla opened her mouth to reply, then shut it again when Red drummed his fingers loudly on his desk. She ran an unsteady hand through her silky-looking hair and tucked it behind one ear.

"Okay, fine—they *are* pretty creepy. And the person seems like they're getting madder. Or more frustrated, maybe? I don't know. But the last few letters have come to my apartment, and now, once or twice they even…"

"…mentioned what she was wearing," Red finished for her, unable to keep silent any longer.

Suddenly, Tate had a good idea why his buddy was taking the steps he was. The thought of some crackpot watching Lyla had Tate steamed, too, and he'd only met the woman a little while ago. He couldn't imagine how much worse he'd feel if the fucker managed to lay hands on her.

"What makes you think the person is going to up their game for the book tour? Maybe they can't follow Lyla out of town. Maybe they're just some house-bound looney-tune with too much time on their hands and not enough meds."

Red stared Tate down. "Lyla is not some chess piece we're moving around on a game board, dipshit. She's a very prominent mystery author that I lured to Red Devil using highly refined and specialized business world techniques."

"He pays really well," Lyla interjected.

"Lyla is also my future wife's friend," Red barked back, "And, therefore, *my* friend. Ergo…"

Tate had never much cared for mathematics—he was more of a history buff, himself. But even he could follow the simple A+B=C equation being presented to him now.

"Ergo, you are now *my* friend," Tate informed Lyla. "And no friend of mine is going to be out swinging in the wind for a sociopath on her upcoming book tour."

Lyla groaned and slumped back in her plush armchair. "Oh, for the love of—the fix is in, isn't it? You two really aren't going to let this go?"

Tate scoffed, "Do we look like the kind of guys who would let a threat to our friends go?"

"*Jesus,*" Lyla muttered.

In her slim black jeans and slinky polka-dotted blouse, she looked like a model straight out of the pages of *Hot for Teacher*

Weekly. And Tate had to commend his friend Red on his taste in office furniture—the dark leather of the chair Lyla was perched on highlighted her looks perfectly. It made Tate want to grab a scotch and then *her*.

Probably not in that order, though.

"So, am I hired?" he wondered.

He might not have experience, but Tate could ask around and probably look up the rest of what he needed to know. He had heart and he had drive, and he had quite a few weeks of involuntary leave left that he wanted to spend productively.

Red set his big hands carefully on the sides of his pristine desk blotter. "I'll call you later and let you know."

"I'm sorry, what?" After all that bickering with Lyla, his buddy was pulling back *now*? "What's that supposed to mean?"

"It *means*, I am now going to get Ms. Lawson's thoughts on the subject before she and I make a final decision on whether you are a good fit for the position." There was no wiggle room in that statement—only the sky-high brick wall of Red MacLellan's indomitable will.

Fuck if Tate hadn't found himself *here* a time or two before. And he'd learned that if he couldn't scale the wall, he had to find a way around it. His gaze swung to Lyla's, but she was focused on her hands, knitted together in her lap. He couldn't read a thing there.

What was more, her profile was a smooth, impossibly-pretty mask and gave him absolutely nothing to go on.

Tate forced himself not to chew out Red in front in Lyla. He simply said, "I look forward to hearing from you," and got to his feet.

Then, because he couldn't quite help himself—this was *Red*, for crying out loud—he clicked his heels together and snapped off the world's most sarcastic salute before he stalked out of that posh office door.

Behind him, Tate heard Lyla giggle, and he grinned. Score one for the good guys.

To read more, please purchase The Hero Was Handsome from your favorite bookseller!

FREE BOOK

Get a glimpse of Morgan, Meg, Molly and Mina—*before* their happily ever afters take place!

Sign up for the author's Reader's List and get a free copy of the Lost & Found prequel novella "Girls Night Out."

Visit Here to Get Started:

http://eepurl.com/ctGk1j

Also by Kristen Casey

The Lost & Found Series

Girls Night Out
Finding Home
Finding Love
Lost in Love
Lucky in Love
Christmas in Cambridge
The Flynn Sisters Box Set
Finding a Husband
Heroes & Husbands
Finding Forever
Forever and a Day
Forever Starts Now
The O'Connell Sisters Box Set

The Black Watch Security Series

False Flag
Heat Seeking Missile
Brothers in Arms
Fight or Flight
Search and Destroy
Squared Away

Acknowledgments

The Doctor was Dark was an absolute blast to write, and not just because I got to research Italian swear words every other day (though that helped!). Reading about all the beautiful sights in and around Florence was pretty fun, too, as was remembering the quirks of my own Italian grandparents. But more goes into a book than what I can come up with.

As ever, no acknowledgments would be complete without thanking the wonderful Deborah Bradseth at Tugboat Design, whose lovely covers always bring my characters to vivid life. She's delightful and perfect at turning my ideas into things of beauty. I'm so lucky I got to work with her again.

Next, comes my editor and beta reader Helen Snay. Her eye for typos and errors is definitely sharper than mine, but her insight into story holes and weaknesses is especially invaluable. And, she does all that before we even get to our therapeutic breakfast dates masquerading as "book meetings."

As ever, my husband and children get my eternal thanks for their unwavering support. They always pitch in to keep the trains running, so I can keep writing. They named the turtle in the story, and their pride in what I do makes it easy for me to keep going.

Last, but never least, thank you to my readers: The excitement you have for each new book makes this the best job in the world—and if your comments on social media are any indication, we definitely have the same taste in book boyfriends!

About the Author

Kristen Casey writes the kind of heartfelt, steamy books she loves to read—full of relatable characters and snarky dialogue. She lives in Maryland with her husband, two kids, and assorted cats, and in her free time enjoys all things crafty—especially projects she finds on Pinterest.

Sign up for her newsletter to receive exclusive content, sales, and new releases emailed right to your inbox.

Follow her on social media, for even more fun stuff!

Goodreads: Kristen_Casey
Facebook: AuthorKCasey
Twitter: AuthorKCasey
Pinterest: KristenCase0461
Instagram: Kristen.Casey.Books
BookBub: Kristen Casey
TikTok: KristenWritesRomance

Reading Order of Kristen's Books

The Lost & Found Series

Girls Night Out (Prequel exclusive to subscribers)

Finding Home (Book 1)

Finding Love (Book 2)

Lost in Love (Book 2.5 – Includes *Lucky in Love*)

The Flynn Sisters Box Set (Includes *Christmas in Cambridge*)

Finding a Husband (Book 3)

Finding Forever (Book 4)

Forever and a Day (Book 4.5 – Includes *Forever Starts Now*)

The O'Connell Sisters Box Set (Includes *Heroes & Husbands*)

The Triple Threat Series

The Titan was Tall (Book 1)

The Doctor was Dark (Book 2)

The Hero was Handsome (Book 3)

The Triple Threat Box Set (Includes *The Masquerade was Magic* and *The Hero's Brother*)

The Black Watch Security Series

False Flag (Book 1)

Heat Seeking Missile (Book 2)

Brothers in Arms (Book 3)

Fight or Flight (Book 4)

Search and Destroy (Book 5)

Squared Away (Book 6)

9 781949 529104